As a writer, Donald Jahor of the bestselling nov*ire*. He is also a successful composer, having recently completed work on *Russia's War*, IBP's ten-part documentary for American public television. Finally, he is the author of essential reference works on modern history, including *The Penguin Dictionary of the Third Reich*.

Donald James was born in London where he lives with his French wife.

MONSTRUM

Donald James

ARROW

Published by Arrow Books in 1998

5 7 9 10 8 6 4

First published in the United Kingdom in 1997
by Century Books
20 Vauxhall Bridge Road, London SW1V 2SA

Random House Australia (Pty) Limited
20 Alfred Street, Milsons Point, Sydney
New South Wales 2061, Australia

Random House New Zealand Limited
18 Poland Road, Glenfield
Auckland 10, New Zealand

Random House South Africa (Pty) Limited
Endulini, 5a Jubilee Road
Parktown 2193, South Africa

Random House UK Limited Reg. No. 954009

A CIP catalogue record for this book is available from the British Library

Papers used by Random House UK Limited are natural, recyclable products made
from wood grown in sustainable forests. The manufacturing processes conform
to the environmental regulations of the country of origin.

ISBN 0 09 922632 4

Typeset by Palimpset Book Production Limited,
Polmont, Stirlingshire
Printed and bound in Great Britain by
Cox & Wyman Ltd, Reading, Berkshire

There is no such thing as a favourable wind for a man who has no idea where he is going.

Seneca (4BC-65AD)

Monstrum. *By the time of the third murder, it was a word evoked by every shout of alarm, by every blast on a militia whistle, by every woman's scream in a district of Moscow where shouts and screams had never been uncommon. Within a week of the third murder there were the beginnings of a cult: the word appeared as elaborately worked graffiti on concrete walls; young men swaggered the streets with the word emblazoned across the back of their jackets; in the cellar discos, reckless girls wore T-shirts with the Monstrum's swollen hands engulfing their breasts.*

But on the streets all women are equal. At night they hurry home no longer thinking of footpads and snatched purses. A new word – Monstrum – has entered their vocabulary of terror. Like a rising tide of infected river water, the word washes against the shanty houses of Red Presnya, swilling through the lives of the inhabitants of the dark alleys and ruined tower blocks, leaving a scum of fear.

All this was happening in Moscow in the year 2015, the year Russians had begun to think of as the New Dawn.

I

We have already begun our descent on Moscow Airport. If I look out of the window of Police Flight 120, I see, through a gap in the clouds, the Moskva River snaking south towards the city. Even from this height I can see the destruction. Where the Anarchist forces fought to the last, shelling has destroyed whole districts. Elsewhere, everything seems normal.

We are losing height rapidly now. I see a big road and parallel rail lines and, as we bank, I see the long lake and the suburb which surely must be Chimki-Chovrino. I have my map open on my knees. My eyes move restlessly from it to the patchwork below and back again, trying and failing to identify landmarks.

If I behave like a provincial, my excuse is that I *am* a provincial. From where? From the town of Murmansk. You will have heard of it surely? On the far north Gulf of Kola. This will be my first time in Moscow.

When the cloud thickens, I am no longer staring down at the city. In the glass I see the image of my face thrown back at me and I examine it with the surprised head-cocking intensity of a bird before a mirror. I turn this way and that. When the stewardess passes I pretend to fiddle with my seat belt.

Believe me, brothers, I didn't always look like this. You see me here today, with my new straight nose, my upper lip fuller by a fraction and laugh lines prematurely wrinkling the corner of my eyes . . . And you ask, perhaps, like Julia Petrovna who knows my vanity as only an ex-wife can, you ask why I should possibly want to add a few years to my thirtysomething God given? My answer, feeble for a man who aspires to be the hero of this account, is that I was never really in a position to choose.

My compensation, in the meantime, is that in Julia's view the new leaner jawline makes me look distinctly more sympathetic. She said that. And I'd like to think that it's a remark that's meant to be taken at face value, so to speak. With Julia, of course, I can never be quite sure.

So for the moment, we are banking over the lake at Chimki. We shall be landing at Moscow-Tushino in ten minutes. To the other police officers travelling to the capital I am exactly as introduced: the prominent Homicide Inspector Constantin Vadim (I who have never investigated a homicide) newly promoted to Moscow District 13. A homicide inspector of skill and subtlety, so my fellow police officers will conclude from the simple fact of promotion. I, of course, know better.

So, very soon, will you.

But for the full chronology of my decline and fall I must begin my story earlier and take you back almost three months, to my sparsely furnished studio apartment in Murmansk, early on the historic evening of September 1st, 2015.

In response to an insistent tapping at my door, I came out of my shower, winding a towel round me. This year we have heating. September in Murmansk you need heating. I opened the door, already anticipating the waft of cold air from the landing. They say, in September, only Norilsk is colder.

'This one is on me,' the black-marketeer wheezed. He was bending over a carton of champagne, catching his breath at the top of the long flight of stone steps that leads up to my apartment. I couldn't see his face but I knew it was Vassikin from the fringe of black hair round his yellowing, dented skull. A small boy of perhaps six or seven years stood in an over-large blue parka beside him.

Vassikin lifted his head. 'All good things come to an end,' he said. He pushed the carton towards me with his foot.

I opened the door wider. 'What's all this about, Vassikin? What's come to an end?'

'Ah.' He smiled spectrally. 'You've not heard the news, Inspector? They've just announced that Moscow fell to the Nationalist Army an hour ago. The Anarchists have surrendered on all remaining fronts. We've won the war, Inspector.'

'Moscow's fallen? The Popular Front has capitulated?'

'The good people have won,' the boy said.

Vassikin rubbed at the back of his dented head. He allowed himself another ghost of a smile. 'And I bring you champagne to celebrate the peace. May peace prove as profitable as war!' he added piously.

They stood there as I picked up the champagne and swung it onto the hall table. Vassikin is tall, pear-shaped and ungainly. His clothes seem to have been carefully selected from some rich Westerner's cast-offs. He wears a worn blue pinstripe suit and a yellow tie decorated with horses' heads. With his sad eyes, you can only think of him as a kind of shabby dandy.

'What will you do with the peace, Vassikin? Go back home to Petersburg?'

'My son prefers we stay in Murmansk.'

The boy had his father's dark brown eyes. He nodded confirmation.

'Your son decides for the family?'

'There are only the two of us now.'

'Why do you think the good people won?' I asked the boy.

'Because we have love in our hearts for our country,' he said unhesitatingly. 'And for justice.'

I looked at Vassikin. He shrugged.

'You think the Popular Front don't have love in their hearts?'

3

At that age there's no doubt to contend with. 'The Anarchists and Marxists have love only for themselves,' the boy stated authoritatively.

I didn't ask Vassikin in for a drink. That would have broken the delicate balance between us. All the senior inspectors in Murmansk Station 7 recognised that. You accepted gifts from Vassikin in return for a blind eye cast over his bulging warehouse. But you never invited him to your table.

I closed the door on Vassikin and his son and stood looking down at the champagne. The end was not unexpected, of course. The Marxist-Anarchist alliance, which fought under the name of the Popular Front, had been reeling back on all the major battlefields. And now the long Civil War was over. Our armies, the Nationalist armies (more accurately the armies of National Democracy) under the white flag with its black double-headed eagle, had won. Professor Peter-Paul Romanov and General Leonid Koba had finally brought us to victory.

Like all victories it was a victory of sorts. It seemed that half the Russian land surface had moved back a millennium. Where the Popular Front armies had been defeated a vacuum had been left which would take our own White armies a long time to fill. Warlords ruled the marshes and forests and would have to be dug out before the reconstruction could begin. But at least Moscow had fallen. It was only a matter of time now before the American president would recognise the new government of the Russian National Democratic Party.

A good Murmansker would celebrate his fortune. The people of Murmansk had been supporters of the party of National Democracy from the beginning, five years ago. Unlike so many others across Russia, we had suffered little. Today we had won. But for me there was a deep shadow over this victory.

I carried the champagne into the kitchen, took out two bottles, opened the window and stood them on the ledge to chill. For a moment I looked out over the low-rise 1980s rooftops to where the pale sun was setting over the Gulf of Kola. The cold air brushed my chest. In a month the sun would have disappeared for the winter. Four months of Arctic night. Temperatures so low that braziers had to be lit beside the bus stops to keep workers from freezing to death while they waited in lines. But *peace*.

I had entered this war with a woman I loved, though our causes differed. Today, five years later, my cause had triumphed. But it was Julia who had attained renown. As a decisive general, a gifted leader of a division comprised entirely of women, how could she not become famous? During the war the Western media had followed her exploits. There had been articles in the *New York Times*; I had heard profiles describing the beautiful Russian Anarchist woman general on the BBC East European service.

But where was Julia now? In hiding somewhere in the birch woods outside Petersburg? Or one among a restless drift of prisoners behind coils of barbed wire? Or dead. Lying, God forbid, beneath a wind-brushed mound of snow at any one of a dozen Anarchist battle sites between Petersburg and Murmansk?

2

Murmansk *en fête*. Julia would have smiled at the idea. But she would certainly have stopped, as I did, to watch the jitterbugging in Koba Square. Mid-twentieth-century American jazz was the rage. Some very young girls wore home-made ballerina shoes and bouffant petticoats. I watched a tall, strong girl dance wilfully with her partner. A miniskirt for her, and heels. She fought him every inch of the way, with terrific rhythm and style, forcing him to follow her lead.

Thirty-eight years old, I should be too young for nostalgia. But I'm beginning to believe that for Russians nostalgia begins in the cradle. We're like the Irish, you know, obsessed with our past. Like the Irish in one or two other ways too, perhaps. No matter, for me, as I stood on the side of the square and watched the students dancing, it was all very touching and reminiscent of a youth which had seemed to me to pass in hours rather than years.

From time to time the blast of whistles stilled the band, and the rattle of kettledrums would announce the approach of another victorious Nationalist column. Then the dancers would fall back and begin a slow hand-clap which would build up to a tremendous cheer as a regiment of infantry marched through the square, in tattered uniforms, the huge white flags with the black double-headed eagles of Old Russia unfurling at the head of each column.

And the jazz band would play 'Rodina', our national song, and the crowd would sing and weep that the war was at last over and Russia was emerging from her long agony.

Why shouldn't I confess that I wept too? I had enough to weep about. But if a city can be, Murmansk was beside itself with joy. The curfew had been suspended. The streets were awash with revellers and soldiers. Horses were being stabled everywhere – in cinemas, meeting halls and even the ground-floor hallways of some apartment houses. A twenty-first-century war it may have been, but when gasoline ran out it became a war fought and won on horseback. A very Russian war.

I crossed the square and headed for the building now known as No. 1, Pushkin Street. The Okhrana, our Nationalist secret police, are housed here. Those of you who recognise the name Okhrana as a revival from Tsarist days will see this as just another example of the way Russians are so reluctant to lose touch with their history. But that's only half the story. The Nationalists having revived the name of the old Tsarist police service, popular usage now insists the Okhrana is called the *Cheka* – the first *Soviet* service.

Thus we Russians try to swallow our history in one vast indigestible bite. One day soon we will have to learn to be selective about what we want to take from the past. In the meantime the Okhrana, which we prefer to call the Cheka, hold the best parties and I am invited by Katya.

I have never actually fucked Katya Rolkin but on many of these celebratory occasions the distinction has been so fine as to be pornographic in the recounting. The problem is usually the ubiquity of her husband, Roy. Roy is also a major of the Cheka, which accounts for a degree of caution in this matter with which I would not normally shackle myself. We attended grade school together, Roy and Katya, myself and Julia. In the last years of the old Soviet Union we were all Pioneers together. Into our middle teens even, we were inseparable.

Across the large upper room in Pushkin Street I could see Katya talking to a pair of middle-aged strangers. Glass

7

in one hand, her back resting against a carving of the Virgin and Child (did I mention that at one time this building was a convent?), Katya's eyes slid desperately about the room. I've no doubt that I was only one of half a dozen of her eligible *invités* and perhaps she'd already passed the time of day with one or two of the others. But she did react well to seeing me, abandoning her guests within moments and weaving shoulder first through the crowd to arrive by my side. When she reached a small clearing in the guests right in front of me she sashayed forward, rolling her hips.

'What do you think?'

'Of the dress?'

She stuck out her tongue. 'Constantin—' she came up close, one hand outstretched holding her champagne glass – 'it's months since I've seen you!'

I kissed her perilously close to the mouth and felt her tongue brush at my cheek.

'Have you been so busy with your footpads and cat burglars that you've not an hour to spend with honest people? And good friends at that? But what a night! Have you seen the crowds out there? They're ecstatic.' She stopped. 'If only Julia had been here to see it!'

'If Julia had been here to see it, she would not be up here drinking champagne with us,' I said. 'She'd be downstairs locked up in a basement cell.'

She screeched with laughter and stopped suddenly. 'That's not funny,' she said. 'That's not something to joke about, Costya.'

'I wasn't joking.'

'Here, give me another glass. You know what I mean,' Katya went on as I reached out and took a glass from the loaded table beside me. 'If only Julia had seen things the way we did. The way we *do*.' She paused, eyeing me, already quite drunk. 'Do you understand it?'

'No.'

'Why did she see things differently, Costya? What is

it in her make-up that made her an Anarchist and us Nationalists?'

How many times I'd wondered. But it wasn't something I wanted to debate with Katya. Nor something she was very interested in debating with me. 'The gossip is—' she had a mind which switched subjects with the speed of a camera shutter – 'that Leonid Koba is having an affair . . .' she eased her pelvis back and forth . . . 'with President Romanov's daughter. The married one.'

'Her husband is not likely to raise objections,' I said. Her father may have been nominal president of the new republic but Leonid Koba was, after all, head of the Cheka.

'Naughty of you,' she said. 'Is that why you've never taken up the chances I've shamelessly offered. Because Roy is a major in the Cheka?'

'And because he's an old, old friend,' I said with a smile she knew I didn't mean. 'Where is he tonight, incidentally?' I said, looking over heads of guests for the portly figure, inevitably in uniform.

'He'll be along later,' Katya said. 'I was rather hoping you might have got here earlier.'

'Why is that?'

'I have something to show you. Something I'd like your opinion on.'

'Shall I bring my drink?'

She stood on tiptoe and cast a quick glance round the room, a last-minute check in the direction of the door.

'He isn't here,' I said. 'I've already looked.'

She rolled her eyes. 'Bring a bottle.'

Moments later we were glued together in an upstairs storeroom, our tongues twisting and thrashing like the mythical mating of serpents. Our breath sighed and whistled, glasses crashed to the floor, pieces of silky underwear became detached. 'My God, Constantin . . . Costya . . . You drive all other thoughts from a woman's mind!'

Except thoughts of her husband. We both heard Roy

Rolkin's voice calling up the stairwell. Katya and I were clearly never destined to be real lovers, never even destined to slake our lust fully.

She was not unaccustomed to moving swiftly in these circumstances and was out of the darkened storeroom within seconds. I waited five minutes, smoked a cigarette and looked out at the comings and goings in the floodlit courtyard below, before making my way downstairs and slipping inconspicuously, I thought, into the press of Cheka guests.

Roy Rolkin's plump hand took me by the elbow. 'Let me get you a drink, Constantin,' he said. 'I want to talk to you.'

He was in uniform of course.

I watched him collect a second glass of champagne and return to where I was standing. We were the same age, but the plumpness of his face and body seemed to give him the gloss of extreme youth, his cheeks smooth as cheeks that have never known a razor. His small eyes were almond shaped, the lids tightly stretched towards his ears like some Orientals'. Or a lizard's perhaps. But his eyes were blue.

'So many people . . . We must find somewhere private,' he said, beckoning me.

I followed him to the stairwell and thought for a moment I might end up with Roy in the room where I had been forced to abandon my lovemaking with his wife, but he turned left at the landing and we descended a flight of stairs. I knew where we were. I had never been down into the convent basement before, but like everybody in Murmansk I knew it by reputation.

We passed along a stone passage where two startled guards got to their feet on rubber legs and saluted. An empty bottle of vodka rolled across the table top and was deftly caught and stood upright by a smiling Roy Rolkin. 'To the relief of Moscow,' he said, tossing the bottle to the guard.

The young man lifted the bottle. 'To the relief of Moscow, Major,' he slurred.

We walked on, holding our champagne glasses before us, past silent cells. It was impossible to see if they were occupied, but the deeper into the bowels of the convent we penetrated the more fetid and heavy became the air, like the dank warmth of a stable.

'Have you heard from Julia?' Roy said over his shoulder as he led me into a small room at the end of the passage.

'Of course not.' The room smelt bad. Of blood and urine under the sharp smell of carbolic. Some smears had not been completely washed from the walls. Other marks would never wash off, the scratches gouged by prisoners' fingernails in the plaster. He had brought me to the torture room.

There were two chairs. He gestured to one and I sat. He sat opposite me. There was no desk in between us and we both leaned forward, forearms on our knees, champagne glasses in our hands.

'How long is it?' he asked.

'Since I heard from Julia?'

He nodded. There was a niche behind his head that had once, I suppose, held the statue of a saint.

'Three years. Three years or more since I got the message from her that Mischa had been killed. I reported the fact I'd received it.'

'Mischa,' he said. 'He was a lovely boy. What would he be now? Eleven? Twelve?'

I had no wish to talk about my son in this place.

'Sorry,' Roy said. 'So you've not heard from Julia for three years or more. And you've no idea what's happened to her?'

'She fought on the Petersburg front. I know what everybody else knows, that she's become a Popular Front hero. I think it was you who told me she had become a senior commander . . .'

11

'Commander of a women's combat division. She occupied a very senior position in the Third Anarchist Army.'

'You knew her for as long as I did. And as well, almost. She was a leader even at school.'

We sat opposite each other in this ghastly room, in this absurd position, champagne glasses lolling in our fingers, our foreheads no more than two feet apart. He sat back, his eyes on me, making small musing noises. 'Your loyalty to the cause of Russia has not gone unnoticed. Unappreciated,' he said.

'It's a cause I believe in, Roy. I don't think we're always right . . .'

He shrugged.

'But I believe that President Romanov and Leonid Koba are leading Russia in the right direction.'

'And that is, in your opinion?'

'Back to where we Russians come from. The country's ancestral roots. In the village. Isn't that where we should look for Russian models?'

He smiled at me. 'You've never been at all attracted by the Anarchist ideal?'

'You know I haven't, Roy. For God's sake, I broke my marriage on its back. Anarchism is anarchy. There is no freedom without law. Camus said that.'

'And Communism?'

'I don't see how Anarchism and Communism ever managed to get into bed together. Unless you see them as two different ways of approaching the totalitarian ideal.'

He nodded. His strange eyes never leaving me. For a few moments we sat in silence. I could hear noises which were somehow both muffled and echoing. A man coughing . . .

'You didn't bring me down to this awful place to discuss politics,' I said.

'Not entirely.' He paused. 'I brought you here to say . . .' He was speaking very slowly, his heavy lip jutting. 'I brought you here to say that if ever Julia did contact you, and you omitted to inform me, I should be very sad.'

12

'Sad!'

He nodded.

My mouth was dry. 'Sad. That's an odd word to use in this connection.'

He shook his head. 'Not an odd word to use in this place.'

I took a deep breath. 'If she were captured, what would happen to her?'

'She would be honourably treated, you could rely on that, Costya,' he said, suddenly the cheery old friend again. 'A prisoner of war. She's committed no crime beyond opposition to our cause. God knows, enough good Russians have been against us. We could hardly shoot all of them.'

'Much as you'd like to.'

He laughed heartily.

I sipped my champagne. With the burn of carbolic in my throat the taste disgusted me. I flicked my wrist and the contents of the glass sloshed against the scarred wall.

'You're an idealist, Constantin,' Roy Rolkin said. 'I won't even mention promotion if you play your cards right.'

'Don't.'

He stood up. 'Remember, Costya. We are not looking for vengeance.'

I stood next to him. Even in this terrible place my heart lifted. I had to hold down my feelings of hope. 'That's really the case, is it, Roy?'

'Shake off the old habits of thought.' He nudged me in the ribs as he had done in the schoolground a thousand times before. 'It's the new Russia, Costya,' he said. 'It's what we've been fighting for, people like you and me. It's just going to take a little time to get used to, for all of us.'

3

Drunk I was. Russian drunk. Blind drunk with hope. By two o'clock Roy Rolkin's guests were out on the streets waving bottles of vodka and kissing passing girls and falling down in doorways and scrambling up to stand in circles, holding hands to sing the Scottish song 'Auld Lang Syne' and cry our eyes out as we went on to the 'Rodina', our voices rising across the flat concrete rooftops of our unlovely but treasured city.

So drunk I have no memory of arriving home. Perhaps I slept an hour in a chair, I have no way of knowing. But at some time towards dawn (we still call it dawn although no streaks of light touch the September sky until approaching midday), some time an hour or two after I returned home, there was a knock on my door.

I was, I found, sprawled on the sofa. The television set was on. Majorettes in white hot-pants were marching with double-eagle flags back and forth in front of a rickety cardboard model of the Kremlin. The sound was off.

Another knock, louder this time, reminded me what had wakened me. I got to my feet, not thinking very clearly, and opened the door.

I found a woman standing there, a straight imposing figure but with cropped, spiky hair and a thin-lipped, hard face. For a moment her eyes studied me. 'Are you alone?' she said, and her head moved so that she could see past me into the apartment.

I worked my tongue around my dry mouth. 'Who are you? What is it you want?'

Her voice dropped. 'I have a message for you from

Julia Petrovna,' she said, and waited expressionless for my reaction.

By now, after my short spell of sleep, I was sozzled rather than drunk. I could still hear gunfire in other parts of the city. I knew there were old scores being settled. My hand stole towards the shoulder holster that hung on the back of the door.

There was still no change in her expression. I found myself disturbed by her blank, watchful look.

'Julia Petrovna means nothing to me,' I said.

She hissed impatiently. 'Ask me in at least.'

I stood aside. As I closed the door I took the shoulder holster from the hook.

'You're a very cautious man,' my visitor said. If there was the trace of a smile on her face, and about this I was far from certain, it was a smile of contempt. 'Julia said you would be content to hear she's alive.'

I tried hard to control the muscles in my face.

The woman walked past me, quickly inspected the bedroom and bathroom and came back to stand in the middle of the living room, her hands deep in the pockets of her seaman's jacket, watching my struggle. 'You are more than content to hear that she's alive.' Her eyes crinkled with amusement.

'Julia and I are divorced,' I said slowly. 'I haven't seen or heard of her for three years. Why should she send me a message by you?' I raised the flap of the holster so that I was holding the butt of the Tango 762 police issue.

The woman lifted her hands from her pockets, palm upwards, then clasped them together in front of her. 'We fought together at Starya Russia, at Pinsk and at other places. I was her deputy for over a year.' Pride rang in her words. 'She trusts me.'

Roy Rolkin had said Julia was alive. I believed him. But to hear it from this strange woman was something quite different. 'Is she really alive?' I asked her.

'Alive and unharmed.'

15

'When did you last see her?'

She hesitated. 'I was with her a matter of hours ago.'

'She's here in Murmansk?'

'No more questions,' she snapped.

'Why didn't she come herself?'

'You don't need me to tell you the answer to that. She's too well known to your Nationalist Cheka. As a divisional commander she's not far from the top of the death list.'

'Professor Romanov has promised there will be no death lists. Trials when appropriate but no death lists.'

She pursed her lips. 'There'll be death lists, whatever you or people like you say ... Whatever the old fool Romanov says. Leonid Koba will want his pound of flesh.'

'I don't believe it.'

'Believe what you choose. You hear that gunfire coming from Memorial Street?'

I shrugged.

'You believe it's just drunks shooting into the air?'

I shook my head. 'A few vendettas being settled – but that's all.' I hesitated. 'Is she well? I mean unharmed?'

The woman nodded. 'Julia bears a charmed life. She has taken risks enough to kill a dozen women. There's a sense,' she said, 'in which Julia is indestructible.'

Could I believe her? 'A message, then, you said.'

'Do you still have the portrait?'

Now something soared inside me. Who else but Julia and I knew about the portrait? This could only be information freely given to this woman. I dropped the shoulder holster on the table.

'You have vodka?' she said.

I crossed to the kitchen and came back with a new bottle and an extra glass. She was standing where she had been in the middle of the room, upright, if anything her head thrown backwards a fraction, smoking a long Black Russian cigarette. She took the vodka and stood

16

with the glass in her hand. 'Julia Petrovna says you are not a Nationalist at heart.'

'I'm a Russian,' I said. 'What was her message?'

'She says you're a soft unthinking bourgeois but that there is no real harm in you.'

'From Julia that's praise indeed.'

The woman looked at me, her head oddly angled. 'Julia says ideas are anathema to you.'

'Her Anarchist ideas certainly are. How can people live without government?'

'They must be forced to be free.'

'Easy. You simply quote Julia.'

She smiled a brief smile. 'No. Jean-Jacques Rousseau.'

'I'm tired of bloodshed, strange lady,' I said. 'What was the message from Julia?'

The woman shrugged as if my unwillingness to engage in argument were only what she had been led to expect.

'Julia asks you to sell the portrait. She has an arrangement to get a ship to the West. But she needs money.'

'I can give her money,' I said. 'The portrait will take time to sell. It's not the sort of picture you dispose of on a street corner in the snow.'

'The ship she has arranged doesn't sail until November.'

'Even so, it's better if I give her money. She can take the portrait with her. In the West it'll fetch five to ten times more.'

'She needs money now. For other comrades too.'

'For other comrades?'

She nodded.

'You?'

'One among several. Julia Petrovna will not abandon the comrades who fought with her.'

'Tell me about her. She's survived unhurt?'

'So far. She led her division under the black flag on the Petersburg front for two years. Twice the division was almost totally destroyed. We were down to half a dozen staff officers, no more than a hundred effectives. The Women's Division wrote a bloody page in history.'

I closed my eyes. 'Where is she?' I asked her.

'She's with her divisional staff in one of the abandoned diamond mines on the peninsula.'

'I want to see her.'

'There'll be no visits.'

I swallowed half a glass of vodka. 'I won't do it. I'm not prepared to risk my life for Julia's *divisional staff*. I'll give you money for Julia. The rest of you will have to make your own way in the world.'

'And you think Julia would do that – accept money for her own passage and leave her comrades to the scaffold? You must sell the portrait. You've no choice.'

I knew the woman was right. How often I'd found myself in this position with Julia. Trapped. If I wanted to help Julia, I had no choice.

'How would I get the money to her. Through you?'

'Ten in the evening: November 1st. That will give you nearly eight weeks from today. Go on foot to Constitution Square. Walk round it once or twice. Walk slowly. You've got long legs.'

'Someone will make contact?'

'And take you to the port.'

'To Julia herself?'

She nodded.

'I will deal with no one else,' I said. 'No intermediary.'

'She will come herself. Eight weeks. Will that give you time to sell the portrait?'

'Perhaps.'

'Do you have a message for Julia Petrovna?'

A million messages. All hopeless. I shook my head.

'Surely . . .'

The emotion of the last hours was too much for me. I was willing her to go before I broke down. 'No message,' I said.

She swallowed her vodka and walked out into the hall. I held open the front door. As she passed me I heard the gun in her pocket bang heavily against the door jamb.

4

I sat down with the bottle in my lap. I was to see
her. In a few weeks' time I was to see her. Would she
look imposing and soldierly like her nameless friend?
Would her wide mouth no longer smile? Would her eyes
be sunken with the long responsibility of command? I
drank from the bottle in elation and sorrow about equally
mixed. Julia . . . ! Why is nothing ever simple with you?

I closed my eyes and saw Julia's amused smile against
my lips. Even a cry for help is not just for help. I, a police
official of the new Nationalist government to be installed
within days throughout the whole of Russia, am being
asked to arrange finance for the flight of an unknown
number of its erstwhile enemies.

Yet there was Roy Rolkin's word that she would not
be victimised, his belief that the new order would bring
us a different Russia.

Do I believe him? He's a friend. Julia's friend. But also
a Chekist. And a Chekist is not something you become.
Even as a boy there had been something sneaky about
him. Skipping in the playground, Julia used to recite, as
one of her schoolgirl tongue-twisters: *A secret is not a
secret secret unless it's secret from Roy.*

She would not believe his promises, that was certain.

I put aside the vodka bottle and went into the bedroom.
Behind the huge, Alexandrine cupboard, I reached my
arm. The angle was excruciatingly painful. My fingertips
brushed the hessian wrapping until finally I got a thumb
and finger to the frayed edge and pulled gently. The
portrait came out in a rising dust cloud. I carried it
into the living room and stripped off the hessian. It

was painted in the early 1990s, just before his death, by a British painter named Francis Bacon. This was the Yeltsin era when Russians were free to travel Europe. I should mention of course that Julia's mother was the poet Abrakova, you've heard of her brothers, beautiful as well as talented. In the West, everybody wanted Abrakova at their parties and somewhere in Spain she met the debauched genius Bacon.

Now this is not a drawing-room study, not a portrait that even touches upon the beauty of the woman's features. But it does show things about Abrakova that, in the few years I knew her before she died of cancer, I knew well were part of her. Great pride, great courage. Great confidence in herself and in her beliefs. And the decay behind the smile.

I slumped in my chair, looking and drinking, drinking and looking, at this cruel yet beautiful portrait of the mother of my much loved Julia. All those qualities were there, like a television ghost, for Julia too. The qualities that had made her mother famous, the qualities that had driven her daughter to support the Anarchists, that had driven Julia away from me. And the decay behind the smile? Was that Julia's smile, too?

I blame it all on Vassikin. Vassikin the black-marketeer. Where else would I lay the blame? With a history like ours, we Russians have learned not to blame ourselves. Vassikin was officially known to District 7, of course. That's to say, from time to time he was picked up, shaken for a few pieces of useful information about somebody more important, and put down again. Every police district has people like Vassikin. If you arrested all of them you'd have seriously depopulated Murmansk.

But on the morning after my visitor from Julia, when the whole of Murmansk was nursing its collective head, I ordered Vassikin picked up. He was so relaxed about it that he brought with him a hundred grams of real

Colombian coffee, not as a bribe, but just so that he and the interrogating officer could drink good coffee while they went through the motions. He knew he would be released by lunchtime.

In the interview room I drank Vassikin's coffee and posed him questions. A picture, I told him, by a minor Russian master, Lyubkhin, *The Snipe Shooters*, 1912, had been stolen on its way back to the Hermitage, after having been stored here in Murmansk during the recent troubles. If a man had such a picture, who in Murmansk would he go to – for safety and for a good price?

'In Murmansk, Inspector,' he told me, 'only a truly desperate man would try to sell a good picture. I can give you five or six names but you'll be offered no more than two or three per cent of the Russian market value. A fraction of one per cent of the true, London art market value. Or they'll steal it from you.' He paused. 'Well, perhaps not from you.'

Our eyes met over the coffee cups. 'You talk as if I'm selling the picture,' I said.

'Probably no more than a slip of the tongue,' he said. 'Lyubkhin has never been hung in the Hermitage. It is highly unlikely we are talking about Lyubkhin.'

'Francis Bacon,' I said. 'A British painter.'

He raised his eyebrows.

'You've heard of him?'

'Oh, yes.'

'I am selling it for the legal owner.'

'Then you must go to Petersburg. You're police. You can travel. You can write your own permit.'

'And how much shall I ask?'

'If it's truly a Francis Bacon, good provenance, not stolen or fake, you might be offered up to 50,000 dollars at this address on the Nevsky Prospekt. In the West it would be worth a fortune.'

Of course, by the time I got there I've no doubt Vassikin had already phoned them in advance and arranged his

22

own cut. When I arrived in Petersburg they knew to the last dollar what to offer. But I had good reason to be grateful to Vassikin. On my own I would have come away with a few thousand, maybe even a few hundred dollars.

I left the shop and walked onto the bridge over the Neva and stood at the parapet where the hypnotist Rasputin had been bundled over into the icy river that night in 1916. In the inside pocket of my leather jacket I could feel the envelope with five hundred, 100-dollar bills. Fifty thousand American dollars. Enough for fifty Anarchists to escape for ever to the West. And Julia with them.

I returned to Murmansk next day and walked into the station at No. 7 District. The desk sergeant had what he called good news. 'That Batov robbery and assault won't be on your back any longer, Inspector,' he said. 'The Prosecutor's Office decided it was time the case was wrapped up.'

I frowned. Mikhail Batov was mayor of Murmansk. His wife had been attacked as she let herself into her apartment last week. The robber had bound her up comfortably, with a minor sexual assault on the way, and gone through the apartment taking his not very well educated pick. Since it happened, Batov and the public prosecutor had been onto me twice a day for an arrest.

And now the Public Prosecutor's Office had decided to act itself.

'They want a quick trial,' the desk sergeant said. 'Apparently the PP's Office have guaranteed that Vassikin will be sentenced within a week and will receive the death penalty for rape.'

'Vassikin? Rape? Vassikin's on the black market. At worst he's a fence,' I snarled at him. 'Vassikin never broke into an apartment in his life. Vassikin never assaulted and bound a woman. Let alone touched her up. In any case

23

he knows too much to steal the sort of cheap junk that's missing from the Batovs' place.'

'Sorry, Chief,' the sergeant shrugged. 'The PP's Office were here demanding a name. You know how it is. Who were you working on? Who was your prime suspect?'

'How did they get onto Vassikin?'

'He was in the book,' the sergeant said. 'You had him picked up last Friday, remember? No specific inquiry involved, according to your entry in the book. Release without charge.'

'But that was good enough for the PP's Office?'

'They decided it meant you must have had a lead. I told them it was nothing. That you were probably trying to liberate some fancy set of underwear for a new lady from Vassikin's warehouse. But you know them, Chief. When the bit's between their teeth . . .'

'There's not a scrap of evidence.'

'Now there is. Batov's wife was here to identify him by photograph yesterday, while you were in Petersburg.'

I felt my shoulders slump. 'Where's Vassikin now?'

The sergeant jerked a thumb over his shoulder to the cells.

I didn't have the courage to go in and see Vassikin. I trailed off home instead and watched Murmansk's first soccer game against Petersburg Dynamo for four years. A friendly. We lost 16–1.

I called in sick the next day and went out for a long walk round the city. It was the only way to keep off the bottle. I returned some time in the dark afternoon and was taking my keys from my pocket when I saw him.

Vassikin's boy. He stood by the entrance to my apartment block in his over-large blue parka and looked at me with his over-large eyes. He said nothing as I unlocked the front door and let myself into the hall, but I caught his eyes again through the reinforced glass window panel of the door as I turned for the stairs.

The weekend passed in a haze. I went out twice and

the boy was there each time. Why didn't I speak to him? I didn't trust myself to speak to him. The good people had won, you see. Those that have love in their hearts for Russia and for justice. I phoned in again Monday and stayed in the flat, afraid to go out. Afraid of those big brown eyes. On Tuesday, the day of the Vassikin trial, I was due in court giving evidence against a pickpocket.

Perhaps he was there as I left. I was too drunk to see. I didn't look. At my office I called for the file against Vassikin and took a bottle of vodka from my desk drawer to help make the lies more digestible. The evidence against him was provided by old Sergeant Belevsky who couldn't really be called a liar since he no longer recognised anything as truth. His evidence claimed that he saw Vassikin leaving the apartment block shortly after the time of the assault. He was carrying, according to Belevsky, a large number of assorted objects, among which Belevsky particularly noticed a pair of candlesticks which he later found to be among the goods stolen from the Batov apartment.

Then there was Madame's identification.

I thought we weren't going to do things this way any more. It's what General Romanov and Leonid Koba promise us is not a necessary part of the Russian way. And I know they mean it. The good people really have won. But meantime, on the level of District 7, Murmansk, barely a week after the black flags came down in Moscow . . .

I drank through the morning. I sent my deputy out for another half-litre at about two. By the time I was due in court I was blind drunk. Russian drunk. I never made anything you could call a decision. I finished my glass. I went through to the outer office and picked up the station record book. I entered in the relevant details and I tucked it under my arm and marched across the street to the Hall of Justice. I mounted the steps quite steadily and passed between the big square columns that still showed scarring where the hammers and sickles had been hacked off. Through the entrance hall, past the large empty pedestal which had once held a bronze Lenin pointing giddily towards the future, or a mildly smiling Stalin, already knowing what that future was to be, and entered Courtroom No. 1. The tattered green baize door swung closed against my back, propelling me further forward than I intended. It was the Judge-General of Murmansk *oblast* himself, who looked up over dark bushy eyebrows. Poor Vassikin was within an inch of the executioner's axe when I identified myself and asked the Judge-General permission to speak. I know no sane police officer would have behaved like this, brothers, but I was far from sane. I held up my record book and intoned: 'May it please the court to receive this book in evidence?'

A Finnish or Baltic journalist lurking at the back of the court wasn't out of the question. I think I was given permission to describe the nature of the evidence. I'm pretty sure I was. In any event I did. I called attention to a serious oversight in my department's preparation of the case. I called attention to the page in the record book showing that on the afternoon and throughout the day of the alleged major theft, Feodor Vassikin was securely locked up in cell 15b of Murmansk District 7 station, having been arrested by me on suspicion of involvement in a black-market offence.

I stood in the well of the court feebly waving the evidence that would save Vassikin from the axe. But I knew, at that moment, that the over-cautious Constantin Vadim had stepped forward into a deep black hole.

5

I never spoke to Vassikin again, although I did see him once, a few days later, loping towards Murmansk Dynamo soccer stadium, striding his long ungainly stride, the dark-eyed boy skipping along beside him.

My own problem was to fill the days. I had been suspended the afternoon of Vassikin's acquittal and I was hanging around all day watching television or going for long walks to keep myself sane. Roy Rolkin came round to invite me to a football match and we even managed to recover something of our old comradeship after our crippled Murmansk Dynamo pulled off an almost creditable 3–0 defeat at the hands of Norilsk. Norilsk! In the old days they would never have managed to get the ball into our half.

It was one of those rare occasions when he wasn't wearing uniform and we dropped into a bar on the way back from the stadium for a glass. It was a forlorn-looking place which somewhere at the end of the last century had been decorated as a Paris existentialist hangout. There were large grainy portraits of Jean-Paul Sartre and that woman who hung around him, and a lot of 1950s Gauloises and black Citroën advertisements and bottles of coloured water that read *Suze* and *Dubonnet* on the labels. When Julia was educating me we had 'done' existentialism. The only one of them I had any real sympathy for was Camus. He was a man prepared to take a few risks.

Is that what I admire? A man prepared to take a few risks? And if so why can't I be proud of what I did for Vassikin?

Because it wasn't a carefully organised, soberly taken decision. If I'd really thought about it I wouldn't have done it. Perhaps that's it. Although I know that half the heroes in most wars are drunk when they run at the hail of bullets. But I'm not proud. I didn't do what I did for the right reason. As an act it was more Simone de Beauvoir (that was her name) than Camus. The right act for the wrong reason.

I didn't do it because it was an expression of my nature, because it was the right, the just thing to do. The reason I did it was because I could not sleep with that memory of the boy's eyes. Dark eyes while Mischa's were blue. But in the same, serious boy's face.

'I'd like to do something to help,' Roy said as we leaned against the zinc and sipped our beers. 'But what can a friend do? You really messed that one. What I don't understand is why you didn't just tear out the page when you found you'd arrested him on the day in question. Why go and wave the book in front of the Judge-General? Costya, there are times when I think you're crazy.'

I grunted. There were a few people in the bar and I had an idea that Roy was making sure they heard. It amused him. His parka was on a spare stool. He wore jeans and trainers and a yellow and black hoop-striped rugby football shirt. He looked like a fat wasp.

'No news of Julia?' he said, dropping his voice now.

Leaning on the bar I shook my head. Those wrap-around eyes looked up at me.

'You're sure she's alive?' I said.

'Sure,' he said. 'Certain. In the very last days, all that remained of her division was three tanks, a few motorised vehicles and maybe fifty or sixty horses. They abandoned the tanks and convoyed north. Our patrols have found a few of the vehicles abandoned, the remains of some of the horses eaten. They were last definitely sighted on the shore of Lake Top, say two hundred miles south of here. Julia was leading a group of maybe twenty or thirty. By then they were down to a couple of dozen horses.'

'You're sure it was Julia?'

'A fisherman at the lake gave us a description,' he smiled affectionately. 'You'd recognise it immediately.'

'If she reached Top coming from the old Petersburg front, she's probably heading for Finland,' I said. 'I think I heard that a lot of the old Anarchist Third Army made their escape across the Karelian border.'

'You should take another look at the map, Constantin. If she was at Lake Top, and she was, she'd already passed along two hundred and fifty miles of border without choosing to make the crossing into Finland.' The odd eyes didn't leave me. 'Why would she do that?'

I knew I had to be very careful. 'No reason,' I said, 'unless she was heading for Murmansk.' I had to say it.

He nodded, satisfied. 'That's what I think. But why?'

I shrugged.

'Let's work on this,' he said, tapping the zinc bar with an urgent index finger. 'So why is she heading for Murmansk? OK, it's an area she knows. The Laplanders up here don't take sides in this war, fuck your mother, so they'll give Julia reindeer meat. But no one would choose the peninsula to hide up this time of year. It's like choosing Norilsk for a warm winter break. So what was she thinking of?'

'Roy, how would I know what Julia was thinking? Jesus, I never knew that when we were living together.'

He laughed. 'That's true enough. But there was one thing you could be sure of, uh? However difficult Julia was, she was crazy about you. I mean she never ran around after loose cannon like Katya.'

'Well, I don't know about Katya . . .'

He smirked. 'But Julia looked no further than you. Am I right?'

I was not unhappy with the idea of Julia's faithfulness.

29

Far from it. But in some superstitious way I was afraid to confirm it. 'Maybe,' I said.

'I mean you broke up because of politics.'

'That's what it seemed like at the time. As the years pass I realise it must have been more.'

He leaned forward. 'You don't think she's coming back to Murmansk to see you?'

'You're a romantic, Roy. And worse than that if you think Julia has marched four hundred miles to introduce her divisional staff to her ex-husband.'

I knew immediately I'd made a mistake.

He bared his teeth until his top lip got stuck to his top gum and let his mouth pop into shape again. It was one of his tricks. 'Divisional staff . . .' he frowned. 'What made you say that?'

'I don't know. You said she was with a small group of twenty or so. I assumed they were staff officers. Anything wrong with that?'

'On the contrary,' he said. 'Very accurate. Our intelligence was able to recognise some of them from the fisherman's descriptions. Sophia Denisova, for instance. A tall rod of iron creature. Her deputy. Yes. Julia's hiding up with her staff somewhere on the peninsula. Somewhere not too far from Murmansk.'

I frowned. 'Waiting for what, you think?'

He finished his beer. 'You'd tell me,' he said casually, 'if she contacted you . . .'

'You know I would.'

He rubbed the palms of his hands down the front of his black and yellow sweater. 'It'd be important for you, Costya.' He leered. 'To tell me straight away, I mean.'

I remembered why. If I didn't, it'd make him sad.

The inquiry into my professional conduct was brief. It took place in the office of the police commander, Murmansk. He was a hard-faced man who had twice already intimated that he didn't find my attitude to work sufficiently devoted.

I knew things were not shaping well when he decided to resurrect my earlier misdemeanours. 'Inspector Vadim, I could consider your present case alone. But you have received two reprimands in the past three years for dereliction of duty alarmingly similar to the present incident. In the first—' he tapped his keyboard. 'In the first you assaulted an officer of the Nationalist Army and offered no defence for your act . . .'

What defence could I offer? That the captain had insulted in the crudest sexual terms a woman divisional commander of the Anarchist Army? Could I defend myself by insisting I was defending my wife's honour?

'The second incident for which you were remanded was less than a year ago. You were assigned to act as bodyguard to the wife of a senior party leader from St Petersburg. When the husband returned early from a meeting with an asthma attack, he found you having improper relations with his wife.'

It had done terrible things to his asthma.

'You seem to approach your work with a fundamental lack of seriousness, Vadim.'

'If I may say so, sir, that is not the case. It is true that I have a weakness for alcohol and women that I realise needs very careful attention on my part.'

He nodded gravely. There was never any harm in a Russian court in confessing simple failings like alcoholism and satyriasis. But would he fall for it?

Perhaps. 'I accept your failings in those directions, Vadim. And God knows, you're not alone . . . But I also detect a certain irreverence in your attitude to your work.'

Now this *was* serious.

Murmanskers are more inclined to be irreverent than Muscovites and he was a Moscow man. There you have it. Except now I'd made a complete fool of his department before the mayor, or more importantly the mayor's wife.

His face hardened. 'Inspector Constantin Sergeivich Vadim . . .'

I straightened my shoulders. Did this mean Norilsk?

'You have risked bringing the judicial system into disrepute.' His fingers slowly scrabbled as if he were trying to crawl across the desk at me. 'You will receive a severe reprimand for failure to check your record book against the charge sheets . . .'

Demotion?

'You will retain your rank of inspector but will be reduced to the first year's pay scale.'

I was beginning to sigh with relief.

'But you will be placed on the postings list for a new appointment.'

The unkindest cut. Posting list appointments were for awkward customers, as I was now clearly perceived to be. Nobody anywhere decent wanted to make an appointment off the postings list. It was only a matter now of which part of Siberia *my* new posting would take me to – Norilsk or Norilsk.

I was desperate. I still had over a month to wait before my meeting with Julia. If my posting came through beforehand she would assume I'd had second thoughts about helping her. That night I dreamed of her in flak jacket with red silk scarf knotted at her throat, sitting over her camp fire in the mouth of her abandoned diamond mine on the Kola peninsula. She scribbles orders and rips them off her pad and hands them to waiting messengers. Then, picking up an earlier conversation, she turns to the ramrod-stiff creature who is her deputy. 'Didn't I warn you that Constantin's nerve might not be able to stay the course?' she says with her beautiful but gallingly superior smile.

But the day after the inquiry fate intervened. In the

portly shape of Roy Rolkin, as raconteurs with a narrative bent like to put it. He phoned and told me to get over to his office in the convent right away. Wear a suit and tie and put my head under the tap if I'd been drinking.

I arrived at the Nunnery but instead of being taken to Roy's office, I was shown into a small waiting room where five other men were sitting. They all nodded amiably and I settled down to wait. One or two of the men were reading *Polar Pravda*, our local Murmansker paper, one was staring at his fingernails, another smoothing creases from his trousers. But whatever they were doing I found a curious similarity in their movements. I had nothing else to do, so as an exercise I tried to work out why all these movements were so curiously related.

And it was only after about ten minutes, by which time one man had been called for and another two men had arrived, that I hit on the answer to my minor riddle. All the men in the room looked, not passingly, but really remarkably alike. They were all a little over six feet tall, fairly slender and aged between mid-thirties and early forties. Each man had dark, slightly curly hair. Each man had rather long features and a quite small, straight nose. I suppose it was while I was running these physical characteristics through my mind that I slid from detached outside observer to the realisation that I was also describing myself.

I was called a few minutes later and followed a Chekist sergeant along a corridor to a room I knew was not Roy's. Inside, sitting behind the desk, was a rather attractive woman of about forty-five. She continued entering something into a notebook computer and I had time to look round the room. There was the obligatory loyal portrait of either Professor Romanov or Leonid Kóba; in this case, since it was a Cheka headquarters, it was the Cheka commander, Leonid Kóba, who occupied the largest wall space. There was an

33

arrangement of three free-standing mirrors in the corner. And a chair.

The woman looked up, smiled agreeably and silently motioned to the chair.

'I was expecting to see Major Rolkin,' I said.

'No matter.' She continued smiling while subjecting me to the most intense and frankly unnerving examination I've ever experienced from a woman.

Her hand again motioned me to the chair. I sat down. 'Will the major be coming?' I asked her. And when she didn't appear to have heard, I tried again. 'Would you like me to wait outside perhaps until he turns up? I mean if you're busy . . .'

She gave a quick shake of her head and refixed me with the stare. During it I once tried to move my position and she said, peremptorily, but still smiling, 'Sit still, please.'

The problem was there was no way of knowing her rank. But my antennae were suggesting it was something pretty senior. I couldn't be sure whether what I heard in my ears was tinnitus or the tinkling of tubular alarm bells.

So I continued to sit. And she continued to stare. It seemed like minutes although it was probably not more than twenty or thirty seconds. At the end of that time she stood up and took one of the latest American instant cameras from a bag I hadn't seen behind the desk and began to take my picture. Not one picture: five, and then ten. And asking me to stand and move about, sit on the desk, lean forward, smile, raise my eyebrows, look serious, she continued to take first another cartridge of ten, and then ten more.

I was at a loss, brothers. Had I been anywhere else I would most certainly have walked out, but nobody just walks out of Cheka headquarters. I tried several times to pose my lady a question but she smiled, ordered changes in the angle of my head and continued clicking in so confident a fashion that I at first hesitated then began to comply. This lady, in the short-skirted blue suit, was at least a major, I decided, if not a Chekist colonel.

When she had finished photographing me she sat me down again, produced a pair of chromium callipers and began to measure my head, my nose, the distance between my eyes. Details were spoken onto her computer and from time to time she stood and silently, thoughtfully, surveyed the screen.

Then a second pair of callipers was produced, smaller this time, and she inserted them into my mouth and began measuring my teeth from eye tooth to eye tooth, and my mouth from various angles at full stretch.

'Major Rolkin says you are in some sort of departmental difficulty at the moment,' she said conversationally.

'I am to be reposted,' I said. 'Somewhere between Norilsk and Ambarchik.'

She smiled.

'May I ask if what you're doing has any relevance to my departmental difficulty.'

'It could have,' she said, again smiling. 'It could mean a Siberian city might be deprived of your services.'

'I could stay in Murmansk?'

'Probably not. But a posting to Petersburg or Moscow might well be the outcome.'

Petersburg or Moscow? Nobody but the seriously influential ever achieved postings to Moscow or Petersburg. *Blat*, we Russians call it. Heavy duty influence. And you don't obtain blat by being the son of a Murmansk fishing boat captain.

'From your expression, am I to imagine that such a posting would not be disagreeable?'

'It would not be disagreeable, but I'm a Murmansker. If I had a choice, I would rather stay here in Murmansk.'

'You won't have a choice,' she said briskly. She was already packing away her instruments. She paused, looked up, one eyebrow raised. Her question seemed to be: did I want to go the next step? Whatever it was.

I lifted my hands and let them drop.

'Excellent,' she said, with one more glance at her screen. 'Surgery, in your case, should be minimal.'

6

I returned from the clinic in Petersburg in the first week in October and was required to keep to my apartment for at least two weeks. Food and newspapers were delivered to me daily by one of Roy's Chekists and I sat about with a large plaster taped to my nose and so many separate plasters covering different parts of my face that every time I passed a mirror I felt I was playing a part in an old American movie called *The Invisible Man*. My body had been left alone, except, curiously, a long cut from my right thumbnail to my wrist. This had been badly sewn, so badly that I had complained about it at the clinic, but I had got no satisfaction. The scar had healed but as a rather ragged line, one that was going to be with me for a long time to come.

At the end of the second week I had visitors. Roy Rolkin, I wasn't too surprised to see. The lady surgeon I didn't expect. She had a nurse with her whom she instructed to remove my plasters. After my face was rubbed down with some sort of stinging alcohol, the surgeon took out her American camera and photographed me again as though I were the last of the species.

When she left, Roy remained. I went immediately into the bathroom and examined my face in the mirror. I don't deny, brothers, that it was a shock. I had expected some dramatic changes but if I ignored the redness and the fine line scars I found I looked more or less as I had. A little older if anything. Certainly leaner around the jaw ... That plump roundness of youth had gone. I came back into the living room and poured us both a drink. Roy was smiling, clearly pleased with himself. 'Now, perhaps I can know,' I said, 'what in God's name is going on?'

He toasted me with his vodka. 'What's the hurry?' he asked. 'So far I saved you from Norilsk, didn't I?'

'So far?'

'We have to wait for the colonel-doctor's report. It could take a few days.'

'And then?'

'And then we'll know.'

'Know what?'

'Know whether I really did save you from Norilsk.'

I knew I wasn't going to get any more out of him. He sat there with his almost permanent smile and sipped his vodka contentedly. 'No word from Julia?' he said, looking up. He managed to ask the question as if Julia had gone away for a few days, to look after an ageing aunt who had had a bad fall.

I took my cue from him, shaking my head. 'Nothing,' I said.

He nodded. 'I only mention it because they're coming in every day now . . .'

'Giving themselves up?'

'They're farm boys and girls, conscripted by the Anarchists as cannon fodder. They just want to get back home.'

'You can understand that Julia would feel differently. I mean she wouldn't feel she could just walk back into Murmansk or Petersburg or wherever she is and pick up where she left off.'

'No,' he said reasonably. 'No, I suppose not.' He rose to go. 'But if she does get in touch . . .'

I slapped him on the shoulder. 'Of course . . .'

Of course. Betray Julia to you? If she gets in touch . . . Of course.

I sat down and turned on the television set. Somewhere there'd be a game of football. I flipped channels. Kola One was showing *Gone with the Wind*. There was news on Two and a cartoon on Three. Five other satellite channels were dark. I switched back to the news. Mostly the news these days was reconstruction stories. Pretty tedious propaganda accounts of the cleaning up of rubble in Orel, or the restarting of the railroad to Pinsk. Old Professor Romanov, the Democratic half of the winning team and now our President, was too feeble to move around the country, but Leonid Koba was everywhere, encouraging, exhorting, praising, criticising . . . In this one news broadcast covering a single weekend I think I saw him in half a dozen places, sometimes fifty, a hundred, two hundred miles apart. I admired the man. There was no doubt that his political grip on the Nationalist cause had been a massive factor in our victory. Of course Professor Romanov was important. He had prestige and foreign contacts. His poetry was highly thought of in the West. The Anarchists and Communists had had no one to match the 'Poet-President', as the *New York Times* had dubbed him. But Koba was the energising force in war and was proving his worth in peace.

Here he was now, at a small village in the Urals. The gas pipeline had been cut there and a huge ramp to support the new structure was being built by the direct toil of hundreds of men and women with shovels. There were no bulldozers, precious little fuel for the old tractors hauling rock, but Koba was out there in the bitter cold, taking a shovel from one of the workers, laughingly demonstrating its use. Grasped just so. The right hand tight round the handle; the left more loosely round the shaft. 'This is an instrument,' our vice-president said, 'designed for the human body.' The weight of the thigh behind the forward push. The man knew how to use a shovel. A close-up showed his grip.

I sat back from the television screen in shock. His hand, his right hand holding the handle of the shovel, showed a long scar from thumb to wrist.

A scar like mine.

November the 1st was a cold night and skeins of sea mist hung around the yellow street lamps. I won't deny I was nervous. But I was so many other things as well. I had left my apartment early and I called into the Planetarium bar as I often did. I had been supplied with plain-lens spectacles for my first few times out in the neighbourhood. The colonel-doctor had assured me that even people who had seen me daily would ascribe any change to the effect of the new horn-rimmed glasses. Failing that, people would impose their own interpretation. Nobody would ask: why have you had plastic surgery to make yourself look marginally different but certainly no better than before?

She was right. The fat woman downstairs concluded I was not eating enough and twice offered a nourishing soup. Katya, Roy Rolkin's wife, looked me up and down. 'You've found a new woman,' she hissed in my ear. 'You're on her all night, every night.'

But for most people, for casual acquaintances, the horn-rimmed glasses were enough.

I came off the Leonid Koba Prospekt onto Constitution Square and began to walk round it at an easy pace. Some of the girls recognised me and would nudge up to me with outrageous offers and I'd shake my head and push them away and tell them I was on plainclothes duty. And they'd wink and renew their offers until I moved on.

But there were a surprising number of new girls in from the outskirts, girls I'd never come across before. To them I was just another potential customer, one of several hundred men, mostly soldiers and sailors strolling round the square in a similar fashion. On every corner there were bands of girls in heavy white parkas but very short skirts who would sidle and whisper or call out after him if the man shook his head. It wouldn't be long before the government began the massive task of cleaning the streets of Russia's big cities, but for the moment, I remember, that autumn in Murmansk there were more girls than customers along the Prospekt and the prime locations around the square.

This was, of course, still in the early days of our victory over the Popular Front. The world had not yet recognised us. But the West was definitely inclined our way. After all the Popular Front was just Communism with a little Anarchism thrown in to catch the intellectuals. And the Communists, first under the Soviet Union and then in their recent period of power, have twice led Russia down that frightening dark alley short-cut which history so often seems to tempt Russia to take.

Rome, they say, wasn't built in a day. But as National Democrats we know we've got some way to go. We've just come out of a civil war, for God's sake. We won it because we're a Russian party, openly Russia first. And, as President Romanov has promised, elections will follow just as soon as we can pull the different pieces of the country together.

For that we need immediate Western aid. The rumours are that Leonid Koba is on his way to Washington to persuade America that the new government is capable of providing Russia with both order and justice.

As a policeman, I think the sooner the better. I don't like vigilantes. I don't like to see these Public Service Units, as they call themselves, usually half a dozen armed ruffians in a white van, the double-headed eagle stencilled on the side, cruising the streets to maintain public order, looking for anybody on the wanted list.

Looking for someone like Julia, I had no need to remind myself.

I had nearly completed my tour and had talked to and refused a good number of girls already when one very young Siberian with a dark blue parka, trainers, ankle socks and a pelmet skirt, skipped across the pavement towards me. I lifted a hand to wave her away when she grasped my arm and leaned her head tight against my shoulder. 'Julia's waiting for you,' she

41

spoke into the thickness of my coat collar. 'Just stay with me.'

We walked together into the streets behind the square. There are no lanes or backstreets here in Murmansk, everything is post-World War II at least, so the girls mostly take their customers for a walk down to the freight yards. When we headed in that direction, nobody on the square was surprised. One or two of the girls who knew who I was yelped in derision, but nobody was surprised.

The Siberian's eyes, I noticed, were everywhere. She clung to me convincingly enough, but her head was squirming against my sleeve as she checked we were not being followed. I knew from Roy Rolkin that the Cheka were still going through the motions of making a drive against Anarchist agents, but it was being stopped by a mobile Public Service Unit that worried me most. The Siberian girl too.

So close to the sea, the mist was thicker here, rolling forward and falling back as it mimicked the motion of the waves which bore it to land. This end of the freight yards is surrounded by streets of blank factory walls. We hurried across the halogen-lit open spaces, past fires of smouldering rubbish, and plunged once more into another of the long faceless streets.

It was dark here and my heels struck and echoed off the walls. We were about halfway down when I saw a white van turn into the end and begin to cruise slowly towards us, sidelights only, its windscreen wipers working slowly to clear the droplets of sea mist. In my jacket pocket I carried 50,000 American dollars.

The Siberian girl stopped and pressed her back to the wall. It was unlikely that anybody in the van had yet seen us. Hitching her skirt round her waist, she slipped strong arms round me to pull me to her. 'You've paid for this, you turnip,' she hissed at me. 'Look as though you're enjoying it.'

I reached out and held the top of her naked thighs.

While she pushed and ground against me, her eyes were on my face. 'Don't turn your head,' she said.

I looked down on black, shining hair, high cheekbones and a tense unsmiling mouth. Below that, her thin, bare legs were parted and braced against the wall. As she thumped against me the van lights flicked on. The girl tightened her arms around me, forcing my body to conform to the wild exaggeration of her own movement and the van passed in a blast of cold air and a trail of jeering voices.

We stood in darkness. Her rhythm slowed. Tight as she was against me, she seemed almost unaware of my presence. I could smell the sea and the sharp tang of her nervous sweat. After a few moments she stopped moving and took her arms from round my waist.

We continued another fifty metres, the girl constantly turning her head to watch the end of the street where the white van had disappeared. Then she pointed ahead. I had not realised we were so close to the quaysides. I could make out now that what I'd thought was a white building closing the end of the street, was the deck of a large cargo ship at berth. Then the figure of a woman stepped out under a street light. For a second she lifted a marionette hand in a signal before she fell back into the shadow.

The Siberian girl had gone, running on soft shoes towards the freight yard end of the street. I walked on towards Julia.

It is five years since I've seen her, Five years since the divorce. Five years since she took the train south to Petersburg with our six-year-old son to join the Anarchists there. As I reached the end of the street she stepped forward into my life again.

Even in the November cold, she was bare-headed, her light hair cut short as if she had emerged from some Paris salon an hour ago. She wore a long pale trench coat and leather boots to the knee. Her face was thinner and her eyes undersmudged with shadow as I had feared. She had changed, of course she had changed. But not as I feared she might have. Above all, the mouth that smiled was the same mouth.

I suppose I had stopped, a pace or two from her perhaps. I knew I was waiting for her to speak. Perhaps that would make it real.

'Constantin,' she said. 'Costya.' She stepped in close to me and I reached out and put my arms round her waist. I held her for seconds until I thought I might be able to speak. I could feel the tears in my eyes and see the tears in hers.

'I pray I haven't put you at risk,' she whispered.

I shook my head. 'I got a lead,' I said. 'Got a lift over to Petersburg on the excuse of business. Sold the portrait for 50,000 dollars.'

She lifted her head back and laughed. 'I *knew* I was right to ask you. I *knew* it. You may be a fundamentally unserious man' – an old jibe from one of our many arguments before she left – 'but who else could have got 50,000 dollars in times like these?'

Then she stopped as if to focus more accurately and turned me round under the street light. She was studying me intently.

'You think I've changed? The straighter nose, the fractionally fuller lip . . .'

'Constantin, idiot.' She looked again. 'But you *have* changed.'

'Yes.'

'A leaner look, these last years have given you.' She laughed. 'Perhaps understanding goes with it.' She reached up and touched my cheek. 'You really have changed.' She shrugged. 'I suppose we all have. Anyway, I like your new face.'

'I had it made over for you.'

She smiled. Sadly, I think.

We stood in silence, not because there was nothing to say. Because there was far, far too much. 'I must know about Mischa,' I said.

'There's no more to tell.' Her tone was suddenly brusque. She looked down and then quickly up again. 'Don't ask me, Constantin.'

'But just a note, a six-line note, is not enough to signal the end of a child's life.'

'It's all I dared send, Costya.'

'Tell me now.'

She looked round her, then ground the toe of her boot in the snow. 'Here? In this bleak place?'

'Where else?'

She nodded. 'We were mounting an attack towards Pavlovsk,' she said slowly. 'I had left Mischa well behind the line with friends, an old couple, committed Anarchists, good people.'

'But strangers to him.'

She looked at me and squeezed my arm. 'It was only to be for two days. We knew we could easily take Pavlovsk. The Nats were weak and badly dug in. Ready to run before a determined assault.'

'Mischa,' I said.

'I left him playing with a new German toy one of my staff had liberated. A bright yellow crane.'

I saw my son's face, his dark curly hair, the blue eyes that could have been hers . . . 'A yellow crane,' I repeated. I seemed to have little control over my lips.

'The rest you know,' she said.

'For God's sake . . . Tell me.'

'You hurt yourself unnecessarily.'

'Tell me, Julia.'

She stared at me, catching the corner of her lip in her teeth. When she released it she said: 'We pressed our attack on Pavlovsk. We were successful, better than I'd hoped. Four low-flying Nationalist aircraft tried to dislodge us. We fought them off and they circled looking for a target. Any target. All I knew was that they dropped their bombs and flew away.' She looked up at me. 'It wasn't until I went back for him that I discovered where the bombs had fallen.'

I fought the turmoil in me. 'You found him yourself?'

She shook her head. 'He was already at the field hospital. I spoke to the doctor. He said Mischa would have known nothing.'

'Where is he buried?'

'In Pavlovsk,' she said.

'For God's sake tell me more.' I heard my voice rise. 'Where is it? Where's Pavlovsk?'

She gripped my arm. 'A small village thirty, forty kilometres from Petersburg. A few houses only and a church. He's buried in a small cemetery there.'

I was fighting for breath. 'In a small cemetery,' I said.

'There's a yew tree in the corner of the stone wall. A wooden cross which says: "Mischa, beloved son of Julia and Constantin".'

'It says that?'

'I did not dare say more.'

I had never mourned him. Before this day I'd had no picture of his death. I was shaking.

'Are you all right?' Julia asked.

'Yes.'

Again she looked round. Ships' sirens sounded out in the mist.

'I'd like to kiss you, once,' I said, 'before you go.'

She thought for a moment, then nodded. Putting her arms around my neck, she lifted her face to mine. I touched her cold-warm lips with mine. We kissed with the open-mouthed passion of our first meetings. A hundred memories flung themselves around within my head. Then our lips rested softly together and for seconds we both surrendered to the past.

Both of us. I swear it was both. From this bitter night

in a shabby concrete Arctic port, she would sail for a new life. And I would stay. If only I had been able to tell Julia what it was I loved about Russia! I knew that was my failing.

I put my hand into my inside jacket pocket and brought out the envelope. Even at this late hour I was willing her to say: 'Come too.' She had said it so often in the past and I had shaken my head.

I'm still not sure what I would have done if she had said it again tonight. But she turned and walked away and I was left with the image of a child's grave beneath a yew tree. And the taste of her mouth on mine.

7

For the new National Democratic Russia, events moved fast. Recognition of the new Nationalist government under Peter-Paul Romanov was in the air. The United States had invited Russian representatives to discuss the question of aid. Britain, France, Germany, Italy, Japan and Canada swiftly followed. Chargés d'affaires were appointed.

President Romanov himself being too infirm to travel, Vice-President Leonid Koba was invited to Washington. Photographs of handshakes and smiling faces on the White House lawn filled the world's television screens.

On the streets of Murmansk things changed too. The white vans of the Public Service Units disappeared overnight. Where the thugs went who had operated the vans I had no idea. It was enough to know that they were gone. And that the militia, inadequate as it was, was regaining its traditional role.

For me these were strange days. My surgery was completely healed. I had abandoned the horn-rimmed glasses and still nobody seemed to notice anything much. Katya continued for a week or so to grimace and leer but after that she became, like everybody else, comfortable with my new look. As I did myself. My only question was, what was it all about? This question I addressed constantly to Roy Rolkin.

In the week before I was due to leave Murmansk for God knows what destination, Roy called me to his office in the Old Nunnery. There was no sign of the lady colonel-doctor. Roy poured vodka and we reminisced about legendary feats of ice-jumping, a sport all Murmansk boys play (unknown to their parents) as the ice begins to break up on the lake in late spring. Reminisced and toasted the recognised champions of the sport. In between we toasted a few of the girls, Katya at my insistence, and Julia at his.

This took us on to probably the happiest days of our youth when we were seventeen, eighteen, in the mid-1990s, Yeltsin years, and the early autumn fishing trips along the River Umba. There, in the wilderness of birch and fir forest with abundant mushrooms and wild cranberries, we would pitch our camp on the riverbank and fish salmon all day and make love to the girls half the night. Was Russia on the edge of tumbling into the desperation and greedy exploitation that would provoke that great split in our society which led to civil war?

Young people on the threshold of our lives, we thought salmon fishing and lovemaking could go on for ever.

By now Roy and I weren't drunk exactly, but were moving comfortably in that direction. It's times like this when my wariness about him dissolves. I never forget of course that he's an officer of the Cheka, but I feel again in that sort of mood when I can ask him anything. 'Tell me about the surgery,' I said.

He downed a half-full glass of vodka. 'I thought you'd have guessed.'

I shook my head. A sudden Russian caution persuaded me not to mention the scar which corresponded so closely with that on Leonid Koba's hand.

He looked up at me, not as he used to in the playground with a touch of hero worship, but now with a distinct edge of superiority. 'Have you ever thought about the problem of governing Russia?' he said. 'Television will never be enough to pull us together. Every peasant woman wants that lucky touch of the Tsar's hand. In the villages you'll find they especially want to kiss your scar.'

I looked down at the long scar on my hand.

'You'll have training,' Roy said. 'You'll watch hundreds of hours of him just walking, talking, drinking from a glass or cup. We all do these simple things in our own distinctive ways.'

'Leonid Koba? Is that what I'm to be – his double?'

'Don't flatter yourself, Costya,' he said. 'You'll be joining a team. He already has six or seven.'

'But I shall be one of them. A double?'

He nodded, grinning. 'What do you think?'

Brothers, what was I to think? The truth is I got an enormous lift out of the idea. I sat there and thought about it with Roy grinning inanely at me and I could feel myself swelling with, what – pride, anticipation? What did I think about it? I felt *great*. Perhaps I would even get to stay in Murmansk.

I shot out a finger and prodded Roy. 'And you'll have to watch your step with me from now onwards, fuck your mother,' I said in as close an approximation to Koba's accent as I could make, and we both fell backwards laughing like teenagers.

'So where will I be based?' I said, recovering myself. 'Where's the school for doubles?'

'You're to be posted to Moscow,' he said. 'Same rank: senior inspector. A quiet, backwater job. It could have been worse.'

'It could have been Norilsk,' I said, and we both laughed.

In America, Leonid Koba achieved a stunning impact on public opinion. He had flown from Washington up to New York and in a sombre but deeply moving speech to the United Nations he had recounted the horrors of Russia's last few years. He had emphasised the suffering of Russian men and women in the recently concluded civil war. By linking it to Russia's agony in the mid-twentieth century he had engaged the attention of the world audience.

His face on the television screen was grey with strain. Everybody knew that the weight of Russia's world was on Leonid Koba's shoulders. Our ancient president, Romanov, was not really a political figure. Russia's leading poet and literary critic, but not Russia's leading political figure. Except in name. But the West liked and trusted him and I'm sure that's why Koba had asked him to stay on as president.

One day when we could stop worrying what the West thought about us we would be able to have the president we wanted – but for the moment I was pretty sure Koba was right. To the Westerners old Romanov spelled out a safe Russia. A Russia as much like a Western democracy as you could get.

Yes we would have all that, I had no doubt. But we would also have what made Russia, Russia: a belief in ourselves as Russians, a belief in our unique history and our Church and a belief that we must act as a national community to recover from the past.

In his speech Koba had declared that Communism was dead. Its weird twentieth-century attraction for the Russian people was over at last. And its strange bed-fellow, Anarchism, he said, would follow it into oblivion when Russians understood the strong fascist thread that connected it to Communist theory.

We needed Western aid. We needed Western expertise to dismantle these dangerously clapped out nuclear missiles that festered in sites across the country. We needed aid to replace the rusting power stations with oil or gas-fired utilities. We needed Western aid just to remind ourselves we really were part of the civilised world – and not a monster of resentment and cruelty baring our teeth at anyone who approached.

Leonid Koba's sincerity was unmissable when he talked about the past. Now, when he turned to the future, he spoke with a restrained passion. There would inevitably be more bloodshed while the government suppressed the warlord figures who had seized power in so many remote regions of the country. He promised that this would be an operation conducted with as much regard for the safety of the citizens of these regions as possible. Then, at the end of the speech, he said: *Our wish is to live in peace, Russian with Russian. For our country, the years of bloodshed must end. As a first practical step President Romanov has authorised me to announce that the Nationalist government which he leads will proceed against nobody who has fought against us, except for a few, very few, notorious war criminals. We will name these persons: we will bring them to trial.*

Every other Popular Front soldier or sympathiser, Anarchist or Communist, is free to report to his local militia station where he will register his acceptance of the victory of National Democracy. There will be no arrests. Those who take up the amnesty are free to pursue their own lives. To you who have fled abroad, who are eking out a life as an émigré, I say return to your motherland. We need your talents and your skills. There is a vast work of reconstruction to undertake. Every Russian has the right to join us in the tasks that lie ahead.

I was sitting in the bar opposite my Murmansk apartment watching the speech on television. I suppose tears must have been running down my cheeks. *Something* was dripping into my beer. Julia was free to return. The government, my government, had committed itself before world opinion. She was free to come home.

8

We land in Mother Moscow. Among all the official cars waiting at Moscow-Tushino, I find a taxi with difficulty. Tushino appears to be an airport used principally by military and political people and the waiting cars gleam in the weak sunlight. The taxis most noticeably don't. At some time in the recent past someone has decreed that all Moscow taxis should be painted yellow. House paint must have been all that was available, leaving streaks of the original colour visible on the bodywork. This is along with bad dents and scratches and side windows that are often shards of glass held in place with brown adhesive paper. Things will get better.

I carry my cases across a mud patch. There the taxis are corralled, resentfully, at a distance from the sleek official cars. A driver, bald, with a pre-revolution cavalry moustache, chews a matchstick and watches me load my cases into his boot. I get into the front seat and ask does he know District 13 police station in the borough of Red Presnya? He does.

I inspect the taxi's tattered dashboard in silence. Brothers, this last two weeks or so since leaving Murmansk has shown me a lifestyle of a very different quality from what I have been used to. I have taken, it has to be said, quite quickly to the idea of being driven around in springy limousines. This part of my new double life has not been at all distasteful. In the last weeks I have been in Petersburg, Orel, Minsk and Kharkov. At each airport there was a guard of honour to inspect and a comfortable limousine to carry me off. But I have also listened to speeches in the rain in Vitebsk, I have inspected a sewage plant in Bryansk. I have smiled benignly on columns of marching schoolchildren, warbling 'Rodina, Rodina, we'll die for you,' in the main square of Prem or was that Tula or does it matter? Chekhov himself said you could never tell the difference.

It's exhausting work. Faces and places begin to merge after only a few days. Phrases ring in the head: *We welcome Leonid Koba and appreciate his visit to the Uniform Weaving Cooperative of Polotsk* ... Why should those words haunt my waking dreams? There have been so many others.

But I have been a success. My minders make sure nobody comes too close, of course. And I'm not yet expert enough in the Koba gestures, the Koba voice – he has a slight accent of the south – not yet expert enough, or trusted enough I suppose, to do more than smile at schoolchildren. But I have been promised a few words on my next tour of duty.

Most of my minders agree I look the part: a thick black moustache attached to my upper lip, a sprinkling of grey dust at the temples. For work I wear a very well cut suit, and adopt a slight limp.

To all intents and appearances, I am Leonid Koba if you please, deputy president of the Russian state, general commanding the Cheka secret police. While the real Leonid Koba devotes himself to the serious matters of state, I stand in the rain in Prem or Tula and listen to the songs of schoolchildren. Like a medieval progress it's something that has to be done. I know that now. Russia is so big and so uncertain; we are still, as Roy says, a people with a need to see our leaders in the flesh.

So there you have it, brothers. Appearances are never more deceptive than in Russia (everybody knows the story of the Potemkin villages). Even my normally grim minders shook my hand at the end of my first tour. No date for my second tour has yet been fixed, but they are quietly confident that I'll be called on. Until then life will continue in my new Moscow sinecure at Homicide 13.

I look forward to it. Pretty girls naturally radiate towards the capital. There are some badly damaged districts, I've heard, but most of the city is its old bustling self. In the countryside, at least, they swear that the Moscow ration is twice that of any of the provinces and they say the markets in this city are bulging with second-hand goods. I have serious hope of finding something new and exciting, like that pirated second-day recording of 'Penny Lane' that sells for over £25,000 on the London market, or a cure for tinnitus.

Did I mention that I suffer from tinnitus? No. Perhaps it was Dostoevsky who called it a kind of high-pitched buzzing in the soul. Not always unpleasant. In fact, on certain levels, there's an almost companionable comfort in its presence. At other times, most times, it acts as an internal alarm, a reminder that, as a man, I don't always sit easily in myself. But mostly it comes and goes, part of me, but a part, too, with a mind of its own. At its best and worst I think I'm close to distinguishing a voice within its uninterrupted flow of sound. A woman's voice, mostly. I won't offer you a bent kopeck for guessing that it's Julia's.

Enough of that. I'm a healthy sort of fellow for the most part. I've had my nights of unstable dreams, especially after Julia and Mischa went away: that I won't try to deny. But these days I look forward.

'Mother Moscow,' the cab driver says. 'It's not one city – it's a whole bag of cities. There are parts of it, most of it, where you wouldn't know we'd had a civil war . . . clubs, restaurants, smart shops, new housing developments . . . And not just for foreigners. These are places for the Russian rich – the people who've never let go of the money they made back in the days when Yeltsin was the *vozhd* . . . Then there are the other parts of the city – those where the last month of fighting took place. Ruins, beggars, crime . . .'

'It's not the picture I've been painted,' I said.

He hooted as if I'd told a good Russian joke. 'You take a place like Red Presnya, where you're going . . . There things are so bad the street criminals are in trouble. They're running out of honest folk to rob.'

I grunt and wonder out loud how many he's tried that one on. With so much practice, I tell him, his timing should be better. But this banter covers a chill note. This is the first indication I have that perhaps Red Presnya isn't one of those smart inner city Moscow districts that escaped the fighting. I decide to wait and see.

We bump and rattle along St Petersburg Prospekt. A thought preoccupies me. A remark of Julia's. Spoken at the time she left me. My weakness, she said, was that I lacked the ability to achieve life's necessary deceptions. I, Constantin Vadim, who is now employed as a professional double! Ironic, uh?

I didn't tell her that my real weakness was that I was afraid that to practise these deceptions would reshape me. That still gives me sleepless nights. I worry about what is the real me. What I *think* is the real me is an important part of it. Like all men, I'm constructed from my own reflection. Now that my reflection has changed, however subtly . . . will the man change?

Perhaps it might have been different if I'd had a choice. But Roy Rolkin put it clearly enough to me. 'There are worse places than Norilsk,' he told me. 'But not much worse, fuck your mother.' He'd slapped me hard on the chest with the back of his hand. 'Hey, think about it Costya,' he said. 'There are some parts of Norilsk *oblast* where it's even too cold to grow *girls*.'

I know what he meant. The monastic life of a northern camp guard. A life entirely without women. A posting as guard in one of the all-male criminal camps up there was barely more tolerable than being one of the prisoners themselves.

I had agreed to surgery. Promised to become capable of life's necessary deceptions. I didn't tell Julia on that brief meeting by the dockside. I preferred to let her think the last five years had aged me ten. But I was nevertheless pleased that she liked my new leaner jawline.

The battered taxi carries me towards central Moscow. 'Three murders,' the man fighting the wheel in the front seat is saying. 'Three nice Russian girls. They call him the Monstrum.'

I nod. But I am more interested in looking out of the broken window of the cab. My first impression is that press reports have exaggerated the damage to the city. The fierce rear action fought by the Anarchists has left very few signs here. Huge white flags with the black, double-headed Russian eagle drape the front of the occasional wrecked building. I sit back in my seat. I close my eyes. Loudspeakers play Russian songs. Perhaps I shall become a real Muscovite and really learn to enjoy Moscow. One of my secret ambitions, secret from Julia even, is to acquaint myself with ballet and opera.

I open my eyes.

Everything has changed with shocking rapidity. A kilometre back we were travelling down a broad avenue with just the occasional battered building every hundred yards. Now it looks like God has sent the Angel Gabriel in a giant bulldozer to wreck the district. Buildings still stand but they are pocked with huge burn marks of exploded shells. Debris is scattered across the roads. Rubble is piled high. The people are different, trudging, carrying back-packs and bedding rolls, gathered round cooking fires on street corners.

A real sense of alarm rises in me. Murmansk, by contrast, might be Paris or Rome. I am not at home in this landscape. How can I possibly be happy here?

'What d'you think?' The cab driver starts me out

of my dark reverie. 'My sister-in-law was told by her boyfriend in the militia that he eats them,' he says as we cruise through one of the few red lights that seem to be working.

'He does what!'

'The Monstrum, when he cuts these girls up, it's for food. True as I'm driving this cab. He eats the bits he takes away.'

I grunt. Even in Murmansk we know the reputation of Moscow taxi drivers.

'The police suspect an ex-soldier, an Anarchist on the run. Doctors say once you've tasted it, some men can only live on human flesh.'

Rumour and Russia dance hand in hand. 'The Monstrum?' I ask. 'Where does that name come from?'

'Nobody knows.' The driver slowly expels the words from his mouth. He takes his hand from the wheel and makes an expansive, forward-rolling movement. 'It arrived out of the mist of the Moscow River, fuck your mother.'

'The victims, what are they? Tarts, hotel girls?'

He's shocked. 'No, no, no. Don't say that. Everyday Russian working women, little brother,' the cabbie pronounces with emphasis.

'And where in Moscow do these murders take place?'

'Where you asked me to drop you, of course,' he says. 'Right here in Red Presnya.'

'Of course.' I cover my eyes. 'Sail on, O Ship of Fate, sail on . . .' I murmur.

'I'll sail on as far as the next corner,' the cab driver says. 'That way I don't inflict Severensky Street on my suspension.'

9

District Office 13 was what shellfire had left of an imposing building. Broad steps led up to a cracked stone porch ill-supported by four dangerously tilted Doric columns. On either side of the columns were two wings with fine long windows, now mostly boarded up. The right-hand wing was missing its roof; blackened flashing around the eyeless upper windows suggested that that part of the building had been gutted by fire.

I carried my bag up the steps and entered through the tall double doors. The reception room retained some of its original grandeur, a large circular space around which a dozen ten-foot-high columns supported a modest dome. In front of me a broad uncarpeted staircase led to another floor beyond the cupola. Painted in gold leaf on blue, above the half-circle of columns on either side of the staircase, were the legends: MURDER, ASSAULT, ROBBERY, PETTY OFFENCES, FRAUD – a pantheon of Moscow crime.

When the eye dropped to ground-floor level this elegance ended. Twenty or thirty tables had been set up in the large circular space, the uniformed militia girls seated behind each table surrounded by a gaggle of Moscow citizens. I had no need to eavesdrop. It was the aftermath of civil war: people enquiring after missing relatives, enquiring after dead relatives, enquiring after imprisoned relatives.

Exhausted, distraught families sat in little clutches around the base of the columns and from one desk a long line of people, mostly men, snaked back towards the door. Next to the desk stood an easel with a rough cut piece of brown cardboard on which someone had scrawled in red wax crayon: *Amnesty Applicants*.

Assistant Inspector Ilya Dronsky met me halfway across reception and led me through a swing door under the gilded legend MURDER. He was a stocky man in a khaki suit and blue boating shoes. My age perhaps, but with his hair short cropped and deep creases bracketing his mouth. He looked like a soft man who'd been forced to harden with the years. But maybe in Russia a lot of us look that way.

My new deputy insisted on taking my bags. In Dronsky's tone, and his soft Moscow accent, I immediately saw a disconcerting deference. What was alarming about it was that I was almost certain that it wasn't genuine. I didn't like it. I'd been in the police hierarchy long enough to know that a subordinate who takes against you is almost as dangerous as a senior officer out to get you.

As we crossed the busy Murder Room I felt the eyes of the detectives rise from their paperwork. Nobody nodded. Nobody smiled hallo. In Murmansk a newcomer would have been surrounded by officers trying to shake his hand. But this was Moscow.

The homicide inspector's office was a good-sized square room well lit by a large window looking out onto a railway line. A door with a cracked, clouded glass panel was inscribed (in reverse as I sat at my desk) with the name of my predecessor. Or perhaps even the name of *his* predecessor. There was a high ceiling with moulded plaster, badly cut into in order to fit a neon light track, and walls that were panelled wood to hip height, painted a scratched French grey.

'Good,' I said, when I finished my examination of the room. 'Good enough.' I swung round in the old swivel chair. For a moment I had forgotten Dronsky. I stared out of the handsome window across a wasteland of concrete debris and thought that from this place I was going to have to pull all the loose strands of my life together, succeed at my new work, find a woman I could live with in comfort if not in love . . . and see Russia grow and flower again.

Again?

I turned to Dronsky. 'Between you and me, Dronsky . . . when, in your opinion, did Russia last grow and flower?'

Impossible to interpret the expression that flickered across Dronsky's face. 'About that I'm not entirely sure, Inspector,' he said.

'Think about it, Dronsky. It's one for the history books.'

Official life in Russia begins with a courtesy call on your superiors. District Commander Brusilov was a small, round man with a well-developed sense of his own importance. The open file on his desk was from Murmansk. I wondered how much it contained.

'Your record, Vadim . . .' Brusilov mused. He had small red hands and fat wrists around which he could barely button his cuffs. He was clearly proud of the hands. He displayed them on the table, pressing flat the palms, lifting them, splaying the fingers to examine the fingernails. He picked up his thought: '. . . is second to none. It so happens that we are desperately short at this moment of a man of your extensive homicide experience . . .'

I nodded gravely. Creative additions were no stranger to Roy Rolkin's pen; usually for less good causes.

'Of course, your reputation would have reached Moscow before this, had it not been for the war. I constantly keep an eye open for new talent. But no use crying over spilt milk. We've got you now. Exactly when we most need someone of your calibre and experience. I'm putting you on the Monstrum case.'

Of course.

'Two additional matters . . .' He allowed his eyebrows to move up, held them there until they ached, and

61

lowered them again. 'I have been informed that from time to time I must release you for work of the highest national importance.'

'Indeed.'

'No questions asked. No explanations given.'

I gave him an apologetic smile. 'And the second matter?'

He stood up. 'I've arranged for the photographer to be here in fifteen minutes.'

'The photographer?'

'Major Rolkin's instructions were that you should appear in tomorrow's edition of the Red Presnya *Pravda*,' he said stiffly.

'Major Rolkin . . . He's in Moscow?'

He nodded briskly. 'He called me personally this morning.' He stood up and offered me one of his small red hands. I shook it and he withdrew it quickly, before it might be damaged. 'Meantime,' he said, as I paused at the door, 'I remain your direct superior officer and shall expect quick results on the Monstrum investigation, Inspector. An arrest before the reputation of the beast spreads.'

Downstairs again in my office, I told Dronsky the news and watched the smile spreading on his face. 'You look as if I've just won the New York State Lottery.'

'I knew you'd be assigned, Inspector. Your reputation guaranteed it . . .' Again the way he said it made me wonder. 'Now, before I ask the lads in,' he said. 'I'd just like to bring you up to date . . .'

At floor level a movement caught my eye. Something had disappeared behind a filing cabinet. 'What's *that*?' I turned to Dronsky.

'He's shy,' he said. 'That's all.'

'*Who's* shy?'

'V.I. Lenin.'

'Vladimir Ilyich Lenin?'

'The office cat.'

'Dronsky,' I said patiently. 'I *hate* cats.'

'Not this one you won't, Inspector. Maybe you're used to dogs . . .'

'I hate dogs too.'

'Ah.' He paused. 'Well, I suppose that at least gives V.I. Lenin an equal chance.'

'Get rid of it,' I said. I was watching the filing cabinet as a cat's head edged into view. The face was long for a cat and with a ridiculous touch of darker fur on the chin that I suppose might have passed for a Lenin goatee. As it emerged sinuously into the middle of the room I saw it was what you might call a dark marmalade in colour. Insolently it sat on the carpet before my desk.

'Dronsky,' I said. 'Let me forewarn you. Not only do I not like animals, I'm not all that happy about animal lovers. Very often, they seem to me to have a screw loose somewhere. A part missing. You understand me.'

He nodded cautiously.

'What about the *people* in dire straits all around the world, Dronsky? And don't tell me caring for domestic animals teaches respect for human beings. Hitler was inseparable from his dog. The only good thing I can think to say about Joseph Stalin is that he *didn't* keep a cat.'

'Perhaps when you've had time to think it over, Chief.'

'I mean it, Dronsky. Get rid of it.'

I looked down at the animal. The cat raised its right paw. In greeting? For silence?

'What is this?' I said.

'He's introducing himself. V.I. Lenin. That's what he does. Lifts a paw. Friendly.'

'I'll choose my own friends,' I said. 'Put him outside. We'll deal with this later.'

Dronsky picked up the cat and bundled it outside.

'Better,' I said when he came back. 'So now we have the office to ourselves, do we?'

'Chief?'

I craned my neck theatrically, peering about. 'I mean

no hibernating hedgehogs I don't know about? No gerbils fast-breeding in the filing cabinets?'

'Not with V.I. Lenin about, Chief.'

Maybe I'd overstated my case a fraction, but I really never have been keen on cats. For the pursuit of self-interest you can't equal the species. My feeling is that if there was ever an animal on the take, it's the cat. Or man, I suppose. But there's no room in an office for us both.

The photographic session was over in a matter of minutes. A young woman directed the work of the equally young photographer. I sat at my desk and looked thoughtful, quizzical and determined by turns. Dronsky stood in the corner watching, his face blank. The only time he came close to a smile was when the girl suggested a picture with V.I. Lenin in my lap. Human interest, she said.

I refused and had the cat ejected for the second time. When the photographers had left, I signalled to Dronsky to begin his run-down of the case. I sat at my desk with pen and notepad but my mind was not on what Dronsky was telling me. Why was Roy in Moscow? Why was he insisting I be photographed for the local paper? Unease about this whole appointment began to spread over me.

'The latest murder,' Dronsky was saying, 'was Tania Chekova, address, occupation so far unknown. Found just off Severensky Street in a rubble lane there—'

'When was she killed?'

His eyebrows rose involuntarily. 'Like I said. Last night, Chief.'

'Last night.' Suddenly I realised what I hadn't even begun to understand in Brusilov's office: that I was going to be precipitated into a murder inquiry before I had time to blink.

'So we have three murders so far, Chief . . .' Dronsky said. 'The body of the first one, Anastasia Modina. September the 14th. Less than a week after the Moscow Anarchist army corps surrendered. Found partly naked, savaged as if she had been attacked by a wild animal . . . corner of the Bullfrog and Severensky Street.'

'How long after that was the second murder?'

'Three weeks. Nina Golikova was found sexually assaulted and badly hacked about. There were various pieces of the body missing when Dr Karlova, the district pathologist, examined the body. She thinks we can't exclude cannibalism from the frame . . . And then the murder last night. So, what I need to know from you, Chief, is how you intend to conduct the investigation. What working systems you favour, where we put our main effort, which areas you want to reserve for your own special attention, that sort of thing.'

I stopped him with a hand in the air. A familiar panic was rising in me. Girls with pieces of them hacked off. Cannibalism. The trail so hot that the last murder only took place last night. This didn't sound much of a sinecure to me. This definitely did not point in the direction of a quiet life.

I was experienced enough in Street Offences but I had no idea how a senior inspector of homicide takes even the first steps in a murder inquiry. Or assesses the evidence when he decides on an arrest. Obviously I was going to be called upon to examine bodies. Mangled bodies. The thought made my stomach turn over.

Dronsky, I could see, was eyeing me cautiously. That at least was as it should be. I stopped pacing. 'Monstrum,' I said. 'How did the name come about?'

'It's old Latin, Inspector.'

'I know it's old Latin, Dronsky. What I want to know is who gave the killer this name? How it came about. What it really means.'

Dronsky pulled at his ear. 'The name just grew up naturally. It had the right ring. People began to use it . . .'

'Consider the Jack the Ripper murders for a moment. London. Autumn of Terror. 1888.'

'Who is this Jack the Ripper, Chief?'

'The father of all serial murderers, Dronsky . . .' I had read this recently in a book by a Scotland Yard detective and, as my single piece of information about the homicide business, I was determined to show it off. 'In the murder of five women in London well over a hundred years ago, Jack the Ripper exhibited every known characteristic of the serial murderer. Worth studying.'

'I'll try and look that up. Jack the Ripper, you call him?'

'Jack the Ripper, *he called himself*. You get the point now.'

'I think so, Chief,' he said uncertainly.

'The point is that serial killers are often exhibitionists. Even in the case of Jack the Ripper as far as choosing his own name. We should be on the lookout for exhibitionism here.'

'Got you.'

'Who's been in charge of the investigation to date?'

'Major Brusilov assigned me, Inspector, on a purely temporary basis. I can give you a full report of the investigative steps taken so far.'

'But you can't yet answer the primary question: *what is the significance of the word Monstrum?*'

'Is that where we start, Chief?'

'It's where I start.' I stood up. 'I'll leave you for the moment in charge of running the formal investigation, Dronsky. The nuts and bolts of the operation. Find out why Tania Chekova was where she was when she was killed. That sort of thing.'

Dronsky's mouth dropped open.

'As for myself, I've certain things to attend to that can't wait.'

The quarter is Presnya, more accurately Red Presnya, a district west of the Kremlin between the Garden Ring road and the Vagankov cemetery. By recent redefinition it no longer includes the parliament building and the riverbank or any of Moscow's undamaged streets. It is now a district entirely delineated by the damage caused by the recent fighting.

At the beginning of the century, the twentieth century, that is, Presnya was a slum area of scowling factories and unspeakable workers' housing. In the 1905 uprising against Tsar Nicholas, the workers of Presnya distinguished themselves by erecting barricades and fighting the Cossacks to a standstill. *Red* Presnya entered the language of Muscovites twelve years before the Bolshevik uprising and has been there ever since. A local Metro station is named after the Barricades, the battered main avenue is still 1905 Street.

The modest cachet the district acquired in the Brezhnev and Yeltsin eras has been blown away. The recent fighting was more savage here than anywhere else in Moscow. Red Presnya was the site of the Anarchists' last stand. Today it is a wasteground of burnt-out, shell-shattered concrete, a land of refugees, of temporary shanties and unsafe tower blocks. It is a district landscaped by shellfire.

But it wasn't an irrepressible urge to see Red Presnya that took me along the alleys among the shouts of whores, the smell of food cooking on open fires and the brick dust billowing in every gust of wind. No, the truth is I had to get out of the office. And not just to escape a visit to the morgue. My dreams of a quiet undemanding job while I cultivated my role of Leonid Koba's double had been shattered by the last hour. I had to find a phone and I had to speak to Roy Rolkin.

I found a phone by bribing the owner of a vodka house up a narrow whores' alley called the Bullfrog. But it took almost an hour to track down the newly arrived Major Rolkin at his Cheka offices.

'Costya, what're you doing? How you settling into the sweet life?'

'Sweet life be damned,' I said. 'I've been pitched into a hornets' nest!'

'A hornets' nest, how's that?' he said in something that passed for genuine surprise.

'I'm expected to investigate a murder. Three murders.'

'Well, you're a senior homicide detective. What the fuck did you expect?'

'Roy,' I said carefully, 'I thought I was destined for bigger things than investigating murders. You know what I mean?'

'I know what you mean.'

'So I'm here up to my neck in bodies, with a new boss who wants a quick result and I'm panicking, Roy. I don't know a damn thing about the murder business.'

'Play it by ear, Costya. A big suave jock like you should be able to handle it.'

'I don't like dead bodies.'

'They grow on you,' he said softly.

I never took to Roy's jokes. Even when he was a schoolboy they tended towards the more than usually nasty. I thought it best not to ask him what he meant. 'There's another thing,' I said. 'This picture for the papers. What's that all about?'

'A little boost for your career, Costya. I thought you'd be grateful.'

'Listen Roy, for Christ's sake. I'm not grateful. Get

me transferred to somewhere really quiet. Some small town just outside Moscow so I can be on call when I'm needed. And let me go back to Street Offences, for Christ's sake.'

I heard him grunt irritably. 'There's going to be no transfer, Costya. Get that into your head. You're senior homicide inspector at Red Presnya. And you're staying there. Come and see me tomorrow, fuck your mother,' he said. 'I'm going to have to tell you about the birds and the bees.'

Vodka houses or rooms, where a man or woman can quietly drink the day away, had sprung up all over Moscow in the months since victory. This was exactly what I felt I needed to do now. I moved along the Bullfrog from one decrepit shanty to another. Most of the clientele were already too drunk to remember their names. At one place I sat with the owner of the bar morosely listening to a radio report of an attempt to assassinate two senior government ministers. A bomb had been hurled at their cars as they swept in convoy down the Romanov Chaussée. Hitting the leading automobile, the bomb had bounced back and exploded against a wall, killing several women and children watching.

I didn't view the report with the sort of detachment I might have a month or so back, before I became a double for a very senior government minister. 'A lot of crime in Moscow these days,' I ventured to the proprietor who sat on a high stool across a makeshift bar.

He raised his eyebrows and lowered them so heavily his eyes almost closed. 'All kinds,' he agreed sleepily.

'Three girls dismembered in this very district.'

He nodded gloomily. A customer gave a strangled shout and waved his arms. The owner got up and stumbled over to him with a quarter-litre.

'Three girls . . .' I began again when he returned to the stool on his side of the counter.

'Dismembered . . .' the bar owner confirmed with a

deep sigh. He leaned forward on the bar. His chin was getting closer and closer to his crossed arms.

'Is anywhere safe?' I asked.

The owner grunted. My question was an intellectual challenge too far. His head subsided onto his crossed arms. He was asleep.

The vodka room that I found further down the Bullfrog was better. Half a dozen stools, a few old armchairs and a sofa that was serviceable despite looking as if it had been strafed by machine-gun fire. Customers sat around, their bottles beside them on numbered tin trays on the floor, staring into the centre of the room like an encounter therapy group waiting for the first touch. A woman of about fifty was sitting on a low stool, hunched forward, tears slowly dribbling down her cheeks. I sat next to her and held up two fingers to the owner. Moments later a glass and a half-litre on a blue flowered number six tray were placed on the floor between my feet.

The man opposite spoke into the centre of the room. 'I fought against the Anarchists for four winters,' he said. 'Koba's own Guards Cavalry Division on the Smolensk front. We had a few tanks but, believe it, we were mostly down to horses when we took the city. Still, we really did a number on Smolensk.' Thick stubble erupted patchily from the cavalryman's wind-raw face. 'We chased those Anarchist girls from cellar to attic,' he said. 'We really did a number on Smolensk.'

Pouring from the half-litre I wondered if Julia Petrovna had ever fought on the Smolensk front. If she had, she hadn't told me.

In the long silence someone began to hum into the mouth of his bottle, a tuneless hooting. There was a wet coughing from the corner which turned into a guffaw, a deep throaty laugh that made me think that the long greasy hair belonged to a man. But it was a woman's voice that issued from behind the candle flame. 'Smolensk,' she said, 'was where I was married.' She was quiet for a moment, sniffling. 'If anybody comes across a tall baker named Kalemnev . . .' The voice trailed away.

The woman with the tears on her cheek turned to me. 'I was raised on a farm in the Sverdlovsk *oblast* in Khrushchev's days. You remember Khrushchev?' She looked at me more closely. 'Before you were born,' she said.

'I've heard of Khrushchev.'

'The only real peasant we've had to rule over us.'

'Surely you're forgetting Rasputin,' an educated male voice said. 'Virtual ruler of Russia from the Tsarina's bed. You've heard the story of Rasputin in the restaurant? Introduced one evening to a pretty young bourgeoise, he was plagued by her to arrange a meeting for her with the Tsarina. Exasperated, the monk finally roared: "You insist on meeting the ruler of Russia, madame? Here is the ruler of Russia!" And from under his robe he thumped his reputedly enormous member on the table in front of him.'

In the room the story was greeted by coughing laughter and the stamp of feet. In the silence that followed all that could be heard was the shuffle of the owner's horsehair slippers. He came like a shadow in response to raised fingers, his bulk guttering the candle flame.

'I'll tell you this, though,' the woman continued, wiping tears from her cheeks. 'I tell you this, brothers . . . wanted or not, the peasant Monstrum's doing us a service, all us city dwellers.'

'Eh? A service?' a voice croaked.

'These killings are going to call attention to the conditions we live in here in Presnya. The new government aren't going to be able to shut their eyes to it for long.'

There was an interval while roubles for new half-litre orders were handed over and counted by candlelight to the last kopeck. 'These three girls that have been killed,' I asked; 'are they all local?'

'These three girls . . . ?' A young woman with blackened front teeth mocked my northern accent. Turning to me, she waved her bottle to make her point. 'These *twenty*-three girls. These *thirty*-three girls, more like.'

I felt a surge of real shock. I looked around me at the heads nodding agreement. 'Anybody who's lived in Presnya through the war,' the girl said, 'knows the bastard's had twenty or more.'

'Don't the police know that?'

She scowled. 'Half the police have changed,' she said. 'When the Anarchists were in control, we had Anarchist police,' another woman said. 'Now we've got Nationalists who don't know what it was like here before.'

'During the fighting,' an old man's voice said, 'you didn't report bodies to the police. There were too many of them and, in any case, people were too busy looking after themselves. If the Monstrum wanted a girl, he could have his choice. Alive or dead.'

I felt sick to my stomach. 'These things always get exaggerated,' I said. 'People like telling stories, it makes them feel important. Three girls killed is enough for anyone, surely?'

They were all shaking their heads. 'Listen, I can tell you're a newcomer to the city.' It was the educated voice speaking now. 'What she says is true. We all know of someone who stumbled across a young girl at that time. With the peace it's become more difficult for him, thank God. But the devil was already out there during the shelling, you can count on it, stranger.'

I spat on the floor, refilled my glass and drank, puffing my cheeks to take the heat out of the spirit. When the tearful woman next to me rose to go, I went with her.

This end of the Bullfrog is narrow and on a dark afternoon, lit only by the candlelight shining from the windows of the ruined mid-century buildings and the makeshift wooden cabins on either side. The noise and action take place down at the other end. It was snowing

72

big wet flakes as we left the vodka house. She wiped tears from her eyes. 'Frostbite,' she said. 'It damages the tear ducts.'

I had seen it enough in Murmansk. 'Do you believe the police have got it wrong? About the number of girls killed.'

'I don't think we'll ever know how many,' she said. 'In wars, bodies get buried. Nobody examines them very closely when they're dying at the rate of hundreds a day. But the girl my sister found in Crossways Lane hadn't been hit by a shell. There was no shelling that day, to begin with.'

'Your sister found a woman's body that had been cut up? Is that what you're saying?'

'Not a stranger, not a story someone told me. My sister.'

'Do you know where this girl was buried?'

She gave me a sideways look. 'You're police, aren't you?'

I nodded.

'Just been posted to Moscow? Well, I'm not against them like most of the people round here.' She slipped and slid along beside me, making heavy use of my arm. 'The girl was buried in the rubble on the north-west corner of Crossways. You understand me?'

'I understand.'

She indicated a doorway just ahead of us. 'I'm only a few yards down,' she said. 'You want to come in?'

'Too much to do,' I said. 'But thanks.'

She grimaced.

'Why did you say the Monstrum is a peasant?' I asked her as we stopped at her door.

She looked at me blankly. 'Is that what I said, a peasant? Moscow's so mixed up these days he could be anything.'

'*The peasant Monstrum*, you said.'

She shrugged. 'I suppose they must have had them in

cities, too. The midwives couldn't have strangled them all at birth.' She bent to fiddle with the padlock on her front door.

I was looking down at her bent back. 'The midwives couldn't have strangled all of *who* at birth?' I said.

'The mindless ones,' she said, over her shoulder.

'Mindless? Brain damaged, you mean? And the midwives . . . ?'

'Made sure of them.' She stood up, nodding vigorously. 'In the old days, your country midwife knew what to do,' she said. 'Unless some interfering doctor was present, and that was rare.'

'And if a doctor *was* present?'

'Then the midwife knew to keep her hands to herself, of course. The doctor would look at the damage, take up his pen and enter on the birth certificate the word *monstrum*. In the good old days Mother Russia regularly gave birth to a monstrum in every village in the land.'

I returned to a District Office in chaos. As I entered the circular reception hall I could see the waiting public had been pushed aside and that every uniformed militiaman and half the detectives from Fraud, Petty Offences, Assault, Robbery and Murder had emerged from their respective rooms to fight their way through the desks for a last glimpse of the disappearing figures of a group of people who were being led up the broad central staircase to the district commander's office.

Pushing the swing door, I entered a silent Murder Room. Dronsky was standing among the deserted desks with a young blonde woman in a white coat. He looked immensely relieved to see me. 'Thank God you're back, Chief. You're wanted on the second floor,' he said, his eyebrows working in agitation. 'The commandant.'

'I'm Dr Karlova,' the girl with Dronsky said, offering her hand. 'I'm medical officer on your case. I'll leave my notes on your desk.' There was a wry smile on her face. 'Perhaps we can get together later. When everybody's blood pressure has returned to normal.'

I shook hands with her quickly and turned to Dronsky as she left us. 'What's all this about?' I gestured through the wire glass of the swing doors to the reception hall. The knots of detectives, calming now, were beginning to drift back towards their offices.

'The Amnesty Commission,' Dronsky said. 'One of them's a woman. An *American* woman.'

There is a difference. I had seen American women in old movies of course, but it was nothing like the real thing. She was an artefact. Perfectly beautiful. As I slipped into Brusilov's office and took my place discreetly among the other departmental inspectors standing in an awkward line against the wall, I was only really aware of the woman in the packed room. Sitting in the deepest armchair, her legs crossed, she glistened. A sheen came off everything she wore – her stockinged legs, her shoes, the bright lipstick on her lips.

The commandant was introducing the late arrival. Brusilov spoke in Russian; she replied in perfect, colloquial Russian.

I inclined my head to her and she smiled, her teeth even, her short sleek dark hair glistening as she put her head on one side. Did I even detect a tiny accent of the north?

'Inspector Vadim is our star homicide officer. He has just taken over the Monstrum case. He's no doubt profiling the killer now.'

Her crossed leg swung slightly. Her eyebrows lifted. Her eyes were focused on me.

'Profiling the Monstrum? I wouldn't know where to start,' I said.

'But in the right hands, I'm sure you agree profiling can be a useful investigative tool,' the American woman said.

'Indeed. I'm exceptionally keen on profiling.' I changed tack hurriedly. 'I meant I haven't yet assembled the material to begin a profile.'

'You know the work of my colleague Professor Benson of New York?'

I rocked onto my heels and back. 'Recently published?'

'Quite recently.'

'Then I'm afraid it hasn't yet reached Moscow. Sadly.'

'Do you speak English, Inspector?'

'The language of Shakespeare,' I said in English. 'And of Beavis and Butt-Head.'

She laughed. 'Good. I shall arrange for you to see a copy of Professor Benson's book.'

'Dr Shepherd,' Brusilov said, bringing our exchange to an end, 'is head of the Amnesty Commission in three Moscow boroughs, including our own, Red Presnya. She is supported by English journalist Richard Mottram and French prison governor Jules Laventier.' I nodded towards the two middle-aged Westerners standing on either side of the American woman.

Brusilov turned towards Dr Shepherd, bowing fatly in her direction. 'Perhaps I could ask you to say a few words, Doctor?'

The American woman stood up. She was tall and shapely rather than very slender. In her beautiful Russian (her accent was definitely northern), Imogen Shepherd hoped that the Commission would not disturb any of the normal processes of police work in Presnya and hoped that the departmental inspectors would contact her directly, should they in any way feel this was happening. She made her telephone number available to the team and I scribbled it on an envelope.

'There are something like a hundred of us working in the whole Moscow district,' she concluded. 'All foreigners, of course. But I hope you don't think of us simply as interfering busybodies. We are here at the behest of your government to see the amnesty at work.'

And a bad school report will immediately turn off the tap of US aid, I was thinking to myself, when I became aware that her eyes were on me again. 'Any questions, Inspector Vadim?' she asked.

It was as if she had read my thoughts. I shook my head hurriedly. She smiled again and turned her eyes back to Brusilov before sitting down. I saw then that she exerted an extraordinary natural authority. That brief glance at Brusilov authorised him to get to his feet to speak. Just as the question, sweetly addressed to me earlier, was a rebuke for allowing my mind to wander from her address. It was an imperial performance.

Brusilov gestured towards her, accepting her permission to speak in his own office. 'The Commission has undertaken,' he said, 'to see that we register people applying for amnesty status in a proper manner according to the Amnesty Law just passed. The commissioners have rights under that law to ask any questions and examine any documents they require.' Brusilov glanced down at the paper on his desk. 'Finally, Dr Shepherd and her fellow commissioners have done us the honour of accepting my offer of offices here in Presnya and they will therefore be exercising their responsibilities throughout the three boroughs from this very building.'

The departmental inspectors were dismissed. We all trooped together silently down the broad staircase. I glanced at the others. There wasn't a man there not thinking thoughts about the new amnesty commissioner.

I crossed reception and tried to walk straight through the busy Murder Room with a deeply preoccupied air but Dronsky was folding out his cigarette and up on his feet before the outer door swung shut behind me. Two sergeants from plainclothes militia followed him, carrying files.

I held my office door open. 'I can give you two minutes each,' I said to the sergeants. 'But Deputy Dronsky first.'

I rounded my desk and threw myself into my swivel chair. The woman was *extraordinary*. I could feel the heat rising under my clothing as if it were a damp summer day on a Murmansk autobus.

Dronsky stood waiting, hands in the pockets of his khaki trousers. I didn't tell him but his crew cut made him look as if he had just graduated from labour camp. Yet there was a slow smile there and an untidy look that might just make women want to mother him.

'Constantin Sergeivich,' Dronsky began.

I held up my hand like a traffic officer, then waved him to the chair in front of my desk. 'To you, Dronsky, I'm Inspector Vadim. Or as comrades, Constantin. When we're drunk together – Costya. This is what National Democracy is about.'

'Inspector . . .'

'Constantin, if you prefer . . .'

'If you don't mind, Chief, I'm happier with Inspector,' Dronsky said. 'The post-mortem on Tania Chekova takes place this afternoon, sir. I asked Doctor Karlova to delay it until you could be present.'

'Thoughtful of you, Dronsky,' I said, tapping my fingers on the desk. I imagined white tiled rooms, the stench of pale cadavers on steel tables; green-gowned figures haunting them with saws and cleavers. My stomach pitched and rolled. There was no possibility of my being present at a post-mortem. I don't share the juvenile taste for the abattoir. 'Let's hear what the sergeants have got to say for themselves,' I said.

Dronsky went to the door to call them in. I left my chair and sat on the corner of my desk. I remembered their names with difficulty. My small select team, Sergeant Yakunin and Sergeant Bitov. They were not unalike. Both of about thirty, of middle height, dressed in old *démodé*, imitation Armani suits with sleeves that covered their knuckles. Bitov's tie had views of New York printed sideways and his Armani was blue. Yakunin favoured a brown suit and a tie depicting a high-kicking chorus line. *Chacun à son goût*.

On examination I saw that their faces differed importantly – Yakunin long headed and horsy, Bitov with an eager pug face composed into seriousness for the moment. Both men opened brown plastic files as they entered the room. I nodded to Yakunin to begin.

'Further to the investigation of the culpable homicide of Anastasia Modina, the first victim, on the wasteground of the former zoo park in the Moscow district of Presnya, sometimes called Red Presnya—'

I waved him down. 'In your own words, Sergeant, for pity's sake.'

Yakunin turned a page or two and cleared his throat. 'In the matter of the first murder, Chief, following Deputy Dronsky's instructions, Sergeant Bitov and me interviewed all known visual and aural witnesses to the murder and circumstances surrounding the murder.'

'Let me have a summary of what was said. I'll read your reports later.'

Again the sergeant consulted his notes. 'Every single witness claimed to see or hear things that point to something out of the ordinary, Inspector.'

'What sort of thing?'

'Reports of howling in the street immediately after the murder was committed, sir,' Bitov said.

'Do we have anybody who actually saw anything?'

'A shadowy figure running away from the scene of the crime,' Yakunin offered.

'Did anybody see this figure? Or did they just report a shadow?'

'A shadowy figure, sir,' Yakunin said uncertainly.

'A shadow.'

'Definitely a man, Chief.'

'Anything else?'

'Strange footsteps in the alleys. Not at all like your normal running,' Bitov said.

'What about the other murder?'

'In the case of the victim Golikova, same reports: shadowy figure, howling sounds . . . After the discovery of the victim Tania Chekova, the same.'

'So we have no usable description whatsoever? Tall, short, fat, thin, Russian, Uzbek, Yakut . . . Nothing except that, not too astonishingly, he appears to be a man? Our Monstrum does not yet have a face.'

The sergeants were silent.

I let my gaze settle on Bitov. 'Let's review the essentials,' I said. 'How many bodies?'

'Three,' Bitov said.

'Within an area . . . ?'

'Of less than a kilometre.'

'Injuries?'

'Severe injuries caused by a knife, possibly even the same knife,' said Bitov. 'And the removal of organs as detailed in the notes.'

'Sexual assaults in all cases?'

'Probably in all cases,' Dronsky contributed for the first time.

'Probably?'

'We're not going to be sure either way with last night's murder,' Dronsky said. 'Tania Chekova was found after exposure to two hours of heavy rain. Any signs of sexual assault were washed away. But everything else indicated our man. Violent assault followed by the removal of certain organs.'

I looked at Bitov. 'Making three murders altogether?'

'Yes, Chief.'

I turned my eyes slowly to Dronsky and he nodded.

'So what do you make of the reports of similarly ravaged bodies found during the siege?'

'We have to work with what we have, Chief.' Bitov shrugged away the possibility of other victims.

'We've all heard that sort of thing, Chief,' Dronsky said. 'We've never had any supporting evidence.'

'Have you looked for it?'

'Chief, after the shelling, there were hundreds of bodies.' Dronsky pointed out through the window. 'Some of them were taken to cemeteries. Some went into communal graves. Some were buried on the spot. There was no time for a forensic examination.'

'But you'd heard the rumours?'

'Russians love telling stories. Especially to the police. For myself, I think this devil started work when the war ended.'

I turned to the sergeants. 'Do you know Crossways Lane?'

'Of course, Chief.'

'I want you to take a team with picks and shovels. North-west corner, under the rubble. The remains of a young woman. See if that blonde pathologist can confirm the *modus operandi* is the same as our man. I've a feeling it will be.'

The sergeants, I could see, were impressed. Dronsky's face was blank.

'Before you leave,' I said to the sergeants. 'Tell me . . . The witnesses you interviewed, did they all use the word Monstrum?'

'Every single one, Inspector. The whole district's bursting with it.'

'And what does it mean?'

They both stared at the floor.

'Dronsky?'

He looked up and shook his head.

I dismissed the sergeants.

That left Dronsky. Dronsky with his khaki summer suit and blue boat shoes, leaning against the door jamb, waiting for my next move. That mixture of deference and incipient insolence was typically Russian. I needed a rabbit to pull from the hat if I were to impress this one. Did I have it by the ears?

I slid off the desk. 'In the real Russia . . .'

I had Dronksy's full attention. He stood, cigarette between the fingers of one hand, lighter in the other, his head slightly to one side.

I ran my hand slowly along the top of the French grey panelling that lined the wall and blew away the dust that collected on my fingers. 'In the real Russia of the village community,' I repeated, 'I seem to remember it was the ancient practice to endorse the birth certificate at certain damaged births, brain-damaged births, with the Latin word *monstrum*.'

'Very interesting, Chief,' Dronsky said matter-of-factly. 'Can I confirm with the medical examiner that you can make it at the Marisilov morgue at 6.30?' Dronsky's hand was on the phone.

I felt my blood run cold. 'You can take care of the post-mortem,' I said airily. 'Highlight any significant details in your report.'

'I'm sure Dr Karlova would be prepared to delay the PM if you asked her, Chief.' He looked at me challengingly.

It's well known that some homicide officers can't take post-mortems. I knew that's what Dronsky was thinking. 'Take the post-mortem,' I said, more sharply than I intended. 'I have plenty of other work to do.'

When Dronsky left I picked up the sergeants' files and the bulky green-covered *Report of Murders 1, 2 and 3* with its white window written in Dronsky's hand. This wasn't how I was going to spend my first night in Moscow. Dropping the files into the stringed suede Louis-Marc Perrier carry-sack Vassikin had sent me when I left Murmansk, I pushed the lot into a desk drawer and locked it.

I left my office and crossed the suddenly silent Murder Room, the eyes of the two or three late-duty detectives lifting towards me. I could see reflected in the smudged, cracked glazing of the Murder Room door that their heads had turned to follow me. Distorted by the glass, their faces all seemed to carry a quizzical, slightly disbelieving look.

I picked up a taxi and told the driver to take me somewhere the women were well dressed and the vodka was served in something less than half-litres. He took me through a brightly lit area of Moscow to the Royal American Hotel.

It was the sort of place I'd never really seen before. We

had big hotels in Murmansk, but not *fabulous* places like this. Expensive cars swept in and out of the forecourt. Liveried doormen in tall, cockaded hats guarded the revolving doors that spilled out perfumed warmth on every revolution.

'In such a night ... Troilus methinks mounted the Trojan walls and sighed his soul toward the Graecian tents, where Cressid lay that night,' I declaimed in English as I mounted the steps and converted the nearest doorman's suspicious glare into an eager smile. English is, of course, the language of the dollar holders. I walked past him, through the lobby gilded and painted like a designer's tomb of Nefertiti and through into a bar crowded with well-dressed girls. Before I'd finished my first vodka I'd discovered the price of any of these glamorously turned-out creatures was far, far above my head. Come to that, the drinks were too.

But I decided to spend the best part of a week's income on a few more and I sat for an hour or two in a haze of bright light and perfume and watched the *va et vient* of Moscow life. Perhaps because this sort of thing was my real trade as a policeman, I soon realised that almost everybody in the bar was dealing in something. The girls and boys were obvious. The drug dealers were pretty obvious. Less easy to pin down were all these young men in smart suits worn without a tie who were talking so earnestly, exchanging scribbled slips of paper and buttoning their mobiles. One of the girls (who bought *me* a drink) said today you could buy or sell anything in Moscow. Anything.

She didn't have time to stay and talk and I soon found that being drunk and alone in a big city is as miserable and humiliating as being drunk and alone anywhere else. I watched her sashay across the bar to where a group of young Germans were sitting, and signalled the barman to set me up one more. I drank while the lights dimmed to a misty reddish glow and a presenter in frock coat and fishnet tights introduced a floor show on the theme, she claimed, of 'The Rape of the Sabine Women'.

When I finally decided the last roubles had to go on a taxi, I was too drunk to go back to pick up my bags from the District office. Too drunk to remember where it was. But I had a key in my pocket and a tag on it gave an address in Fili, which the taxi driver seemed to know.

I stumbled into my apartment building. A lot of pushing at doors that wouldn't open, and button pressing in elevators that didn't work, got me to the fourth floor and to a door which seemed to correspond to the numbers on the key. And when it turned in the lock and I saw that someone from District had delivered my bags into the small hall in front of me, I registered one of those brief, laughing, moments of triumph that only drunks can savour. Drunks who know that walls, furniture and circumstances are naturally constructed to rise and strike them down, that upside-down maps and wrong turnings are in the nature of things, but who have nevertheless succeeded in outwitting the pitiless laws of the universe.

Smiling tenderly at my reflection in the hall mirror, on my first night in Moscow, I collapsed onto my small collection of worldly possessions and slept.

I 2

I found my way back to District 13 early enough to chase out the cat, sit at my desk and start reading the file on Tania Chekova before anybody else arrived. There was a photograph that had been found in her bag of a passingly pretty dark-haired girl of twentysomething, her nose slightly too long but with a well-shaped, smiling mouth. She was wearing a green one-piece swimsuit and seemed to be sitting in a public bathhouse of some sort.

I looked at her for a good few moments. I suppose it was the first time that the whole thing really meant something to me. She looked a very ordinary, *nice* girl. What did she do for a living? What did we know about her? I turned to the file. The top sheet was a standard Murder Victim form.

A name. But no address. No occupation. A physical description: height 1 metre 62, weight 50 kilos. No scars or distinguishing marks. Clothes: not particularly expensive, local Moscow Marks and Spencer department store labels. Hands: clean, well-kept. Contents of bag: the photograph of herself. A key. Five roubles and twelve kopecks. A small ebony cross with a real ivory Christ. A packet of mint cachous.

The mints made me sit up. Mints were often used by streetwalkers who liked a drink. Often used by perfectly ordinary girls too. And Tania Chekova seemed like an ordinary girl.

I sat at my desk feeling sick from last night's excesses. Or sick at the thought of this monster prowling my small patch of the city? It wasn't a sensation I was familiar with. I could feel myself on the edge of involvement. I looked at Tania's picture. At the way her mouth shaped into a smile. I wanted to get this man who had savaged her. I wanted to do the job well. To find him, and quickly. I *wanted* to be involved.

I had reached for the files on the other two girls when I saw the shape of my deputy hazed by the glass window as he crossed the Murder Room towards my office door. Quickly I reversed the action and shoved the drawer closed. Tania Chekova's file I left on my desk.

Dronsky knocked and put his head round the door. 'Morning, Chief.' He was tugging his tie into position as he spoke. 'Can I get you coffee?'

I thanked him and he disappeared again leaving the door wide enough open for the cat to come in. I ignored it and grabbed quickly for the other files. I had no time to pick up more than a few quick facts. Anastasia Modina had been a shop assistant on Koba Prospekt. I quickly flipped over the death photographs. Time of death around 1 a.m. The other girl worked in the flea market. Body found by patrolling militiaman, 2 a.m. I saw Dronsky's blurred shape and put the files away.

'First things first,' he said, and put my coffee on the desk in front of me. He had his own cup of coffee in his right hand and was withdrawing papers from a folder he was holding under his right arm. 'Car and gun indent, Inspector. I need your signature.'

I signed papers while I drank my coffee. He replaced the papers in the folder and with a flourish produced some more. 'PM report,' he said, 'on Tania Chekova.'

I was forced to pretend I was reading it but the detail was too much. The devil had removed Tania's womb, kidneys and part of her liver. I pushed the report aside. 'So we know nothing about her,' I said.

'Not so far,' Dronsky shook his head. 'She probably had a room locally and worked from there.'

'On the game, you mean?'

'None of the Bullfrog regulars know her.'

'She had a crucifix in her bag,' I said. I was trying to defend her from the charge of being a whore.

'Dr Karlova estimates the time of death at between three and four in the morning. Unless she was hooking I don't see what else she was doing out that time of night.'

'Can we establish any common link between the three girls?'

'We haven't been able to so far, Chief. The first two girls had jobs. This last one we don't know yet.'

I stuck my feet up on the desk. 'How would you like to walk from say the Barricadnaya Metro to, say, the District station here, by yourself at midnight, one o'clock?'

Dronsky said slowly, 'You're asking what the girls were doing out alone in the middle of the night in a place like Presnya?'

I nodded.

He lit a cigarette. 'One lived at home. Anastasia. She'd taken to going out. Not often, once a week or so. Back late and very secretive. Her family suspected a new boyfriend. Perhaps a married man. But we had no luck tracing him.'

'The second girl?'

'Lived alone in one of the condemned tower blocks.' He was looking down at the floor as he spoke. 'Neighbours were no real help but a woman upstairs said she'd warned her about coming home late. So it wasn't the first time.' His head was following something back and forth across the floor.

I took my feet off the desk and the chair thumped upright.

'It's V.I. Lenin,' Dronsky said. 'It's time for his breakfast.'

I looked down and saw the animal pacing back and forth in front of my desk like a caged lion.

'He enjoys a fishburger about this time of day,' Dronsky said.

My stomach turned over.

'And I have to admit, so do I.'

While Dronsky went off in search of breakfast for two, I closed my eyes and wondered if my head was lurching harder than my stomach. When the phone rang it was a woman's voice announcing she was phoning on behalf of Colonel Roy Rolkin. Colonel?

Colonel, she repeated firmly, and instructed me to be at Alexander Square in an hour. No greeting from an old friend newly arrived in Moscow. Simply be there in an hour.

I scribbled a note for Dronsky that left him in charge of the investigation until my return or until further notice. Passing through reception I caught sight of him on the far side of the huge room carrying a brown paper bag and followed by a frisky marmalade cat.

I looked away from Dronsky and the cat to see Dr Karlova hurrying across my path. She was wearing a drab olive green overall with alarming dark marks on it. Just behind the temples her pulled-back blonde hair was flecked with caked blood. 'Forgive me,' she said, indicating the green overall with a sweep of her hand. 'I don't usually emerge from my lair like this, but the rumour is the station shop has chicken.'

I fell into rapid step beside her. 'Is that good?'

Her amber eyes opened wide. 'It's wonderful,' she said. 'Where have you been living that chicken isn't an event?'

'I've just come from Murmansk,' I said.

'The frozen north. Poor you.'

'Murmansk is not Norilsk,' I said stiffly.

'Ah, I spoke too quickly. I'm sure Murmansk has its attractions.'

'I was born there,' I said. 'I grew up there.'

'I spoke without thinking, Inspector. My mind is on the chicken. Some time I will make a proper apology.' She was already beginning to peel away. 'I mean it,' she said, but she was biting back a smile.

'No need.'

'A formal apology,' she said. 'We must meet in less hurried circumstances.'

Muscovites have this reputation for mindless superiority, I told myself as I descended the broad, cracked steps. To them all other Russians are country cousins.

Less than an hour later I was waiting in a tiny anteroom overlooking Tsar Alexander (formerly Uprising) Square. There was a blonde secretary in the office with me as I waited. No longer young, and with a visible life attachment to the style of Marilyn Monroe, she was still something to look at. And since she seemed to have no other duties but to sit with me, we exchanged views on the world in a desultory manner when she wasn't nodding off in the fierce central heating.

After almost an hour had passed, she took lunch of bread and sausage and was good enough to offer me some while I returned the kindness with extravagant compliments. In this way, time passed. Some time in the early afternoon I was called for and the secretary led me along a corridor which smelled of cabbage soup to another small office where Roy Rolkin sat smiling behind a desk. His shoulder boards, I noticed, confirmed his promotion to colonel and I made a big thing of congratulating him. If he'd been in any other organisation than the Cheka I would have meant it.

I was genuinely pleased to see him. I think I would have been pleased to see anyone from Murmansk. His wife, Katya, most certainly. Even the black-marketeer Vassikin. The truth was I was already feeling lonely in Moscow.

As he poured vodka, Roy told me he had been posted to the metropolis. Katya, he said, was furious that he'd decided to leave her in Murmansk. 'Especially,' Roy said, with an unfriendly wink, 'when I told her you were now living here, stuffing a new Moscow girl every night.'

I tossed back my glass and made a performance out of puffing my cheeks in appreciation of the vodka. I never knew how much he guessed about my unconsummated wrestling bouts with his wife. 'I'm not stuffing anyone,' I said. 'I've just arrived here, for God's sake. Get me out of this, Roy. I'm out of my depth.'

He smiled. 'Stay with it, Costya. You're doing well.' My minder's report on my tour as stand-in for Leonid Koba was favourable, he told me. There would be other tours, and eventually, when I had mastered more of the subtleties of Koba's gestures, the possibility of a visit to New York or Tokyo.

'New York?' I said. 'I've always wanted to see New York.'

'The field's wide open,' Roy said. 'Vice-President Koba considers many of the obligatory activities on foreign trips to be nothing but a waste of time.'

'On a foreign trip it can't be easy to substitute a stand-in.'

Roy laughed. 'It's true you'll never get to touch up the First Lady under the table at a White House dinner, Costya. But you might be slipped in to attend some dreary opera or a game of American football while the chief takes the opportunity to put his feet up for an hour or two.'

'And how does he put his feet up, the chief?' Standing in for the man, I had become intrigued to learn almost anything about him. 'He's not married. I'd say he's quite fond of the ladies . . .'

'Him and you have that in common, yes.'

I let it go. 'Drink? Does he drink?'

'What are you saying? Does he get gutter drunk?'

'No . . . no,' I said hurriedly. 'Just asking if he likes to drink. Like a Russian, that's all.'

'Like a Russian?' Roy said shortly. 'Believe it or not, mostly he likes to work. He believes it's his work that has stopped Russia bleeding to death. And only just in time.

Think yourself lucky you're only a double. His workload would break your back.'

There was something cold and harsh about the way Roy said that. Perhaps he was saying you may have been carved about so you look like him – but don't try to compare yourself with him.

'Have you ever met him in person?'

He nodded slowly. 'It was the vice-president who summoned me to Moscow. He has given me a special task.'

'A special task?'

Roy had no intention of explaining further. For a few moments we talked about living in Moscow. I told him about my solitary night out at the Royal American Hotel. After a while the distance between us receded and he was offering me another drink. He poured two glasses, picked one up and peered into the clear liquid. 'Vodochka,' he murmured. 'Queen of my heart.'

He lifted his glass in a toast and we drank. To vodka or the queen of his heart, I wasn't sure. Perhaps it was the same thing.

'No word from Julia before you left?' he said casually. 'No word from abroad?'

'If that's where she is.' I knew Roy well enough. I could *feel* this was the real purpose of calling me here.

He rummaged in his desk drawer. 'That's where she *was*. She's been seen in London. Photographed in New York.' He flipped a picture onto the desk top.

I picked it up slowly. He was watching me with a half-smile.

The photograph showed Julia getting into a smart-looking Rapallo sports car. A well-groomed man in leather and cashmere was holding the door for her. I could think of nothing to say. 'She's changed,' I said finally.

'Since when?'

I hesitated. 'Over the years.' I breathed out. 'So she's in New York.'

'She was. She moves about. Three weeks ago she was located in Paris.'

I struggled to phrase the right question. 'What's she doing in Paris?'

An inane question to a political policeman. Roy's lips twisted. 'Mostly speech-making against our government leaders. But,' he added, suddenly genial, 'rest assured the amnesty would apply equally to her.' He got up and poured more vodka. 'I tell you what, Costya,' he said. 'Moscow Dynamo is not a bad team. We should get to see them play. Buy scarves, beanie hats, become fans.'

'Is that why I was instructed to be here today?' I stood and moved towards the door. 'To become a Moscow Dynamo fan? I have a murder investigation going on.'

He got up from behind his desk. 'OK, I won't keep you. I know where to find you. And you can always reach me through the old blonde, Miss Lovely Legs of Leningrad 1989. Either way, we'll keep in touch,' he said. 'Old Murmanskers should. Drop round for a chat if you have a moment.'

'Not if I have to wait six hours to be invited to become a Moscow Dynamo fan.'

Roy grinned, standing at the door. 'Becoming a fan is not such a bad idea, fuck your mother,' he said. 'You should try it.' His eyes narrowed. 'Believe me, little brother, it's something that's always been lacking in your life.'

He was laughing again as he pushed the door at my face.

There was a case of wine on my desk when I got back to District 13. Hungarian? Romanian? No. French, would you believe? Château Margaux 1999. Was this possible?

'The American woman had it dropped off for you,' Dronsky said, lifting his eyebrows in his unconscious Groucho imitation. I hadn't been aware that he'd followed me in, silent in his blue rubber-soled boating

93

shoes. 'Sent it round with her driver,' he added. 'With this!' He handed me a book. 'In English. Can you read English, Chief?'

I took the book from him. Harvard University Press. *Case Studies in Criminal Profiling*. By Paul Benson, the Professor Benson she had mentioned in Brusilov's room. I flipped open the book. On the title page there was a dedication in the author's hand. *To Imogen Shepherd without whose encouragement this book would never have been completed*. It was signed: *In love and admiration, Paul Benson, July 2011*.

'You can read all that?' Dronsky said.

'It's a medical book,' I said. I translated from the introduction. ' "In this book, Professor Benson recounts the history of profiling from the first attempts to create a psychological description of Jack the Ripper in 1888 to his own studies of some of the late twentieth century's most publicised serial murderers." '

Perhaps some time I would read it.

Dronsky pointed to the wine. 'Some of the senior inspectors get vodka,' he said, with a turn-down of the mouth which suggested I'd come off a definite second best.

I stood the wine on the floor and the cat jumped on top of it and sat, upright, like one of those Egyptian god-cats. I scowled at him and faced back to Dronsky. 'What about Crossways Lane?' I said. 'Did Bitov and Yakunin find anything?'

He took a long draw on his cigarette. 'The remains of a young woman.'

'Don't make me drag it out of you, Dronsky.'

'Dr Karlova says the corpse was too far gone to say much.' He paused. 'But you were right, Chief,' he said, not too reluctantly. 'It's one of his. Almost certainly.'

'The Monstrum's? So we're not talking three victims.'

'No more we aren't, Chief. From today we're talking from four to forty. We just don't know.'

As soon as Dronsky had gone, I took Dr Shepherd's phone number from my inside pocket and tapped out the number. I was already dry-mouthed when she picked up the phone. 'Dr Imogen Shepherd,' her voice said.

'Dr Shepherd, this is Constantin Vadim. From District 13. I'm calling to thank you for the Château Margaux.'

'It's not vodka.' There was a laugh in her voice.

'It's not ordinary wine either. I have never drunk anything of this class. More than that, I understand that 1999 was an extraordinary year in Bordeaux.'

'Ah,' her voice showed her pleasure. 'I was right. I sent a small gift to all the department inspectors . . . I amused myself trying to get it right from the records Commandant Brusilov gave me. And from the evidence of my own eyes. Vodka for Kerelsky, Tukhin and Borisov . . . a liqueur whisky for Grigoriev. And Château Margaux for Constantin Vadim.'

'I think I'm flattered.'

'Yes,' she said. And then with an abrupt change of tone: 'Thank you for calling, Inspector. I do hope you enjoy the claret. No doubt we'll meet at the station in the next few days.'

'And the book,' I said. 'Thank you for the book.'

'Let me have it back when you've read it.'

'Of course . . .' I wanted to say something about the dedication but she had already rung off. Dammit, I could have handled that better. '*Thank you for the book. I'm most impressed, Dr Shepherd . . .*'

'*You must call me Imogen. Will you promise to read it?*'

'*It's on my desk now . . .*'

I caught the cat's eye and it yawned ostentatiously.

Carrying my case of wine, but leaving the book, I took the damp, echoing, concrete back stairs down to the garage. I felt strangely light-headed at the thought of receiving a gift from so spectacular a woman. I had mishandled the phone call of course but that was partly her abruptness. Yet there had been something conspiratorial in her voice. A curious balance of flattery and dismissal. Was that the American way? Was the flattery just something that Americans do? Meaning nothing?

I loaded my case of wine into my newly issued blue and white police Renault Economy and felt the euphoria of a moment ago drain away. Anybody I could think of to drink with would have felt short-changed it wasn't vodka. Anybody I could think of to drink with was living in Murmansk. Except Roy, and I had seen enough of him for one day.

As I closed the car boot, I was swamped with misery. A sense of aloneness is something I have sometimes used, especially in the last few years, as a shield against the world, something perversely to reinforce the outline of the man. But here, in this bleak Moscow garage, as I watched the movements of my hand unlocking the driver's door, it was as if I could feel everything I thought of as *me* dissolving into the space around me. It was as if that hard outline of myself which I counted on to present my face to the world, was ballooning and reshaping itself.

Don't misunderstand me. My eyes saw in detail the dials and clocks on the dashboard in front of me. My ears heard the echoing shouts of police mechanics at work. What I was suffering there in the garage, suffered it more acutely than ever before in fact, was something different, an assault, if you like, on all my *essential* senses. Most of all on the sense of being myself.

Now this, I'm prepared to swear to you, does not leave a man comfortable in his skin. Especially as it wasn't any longer entirely *my* skin. It had been fashioned in the likeness of someone else. And worse, here I was at the head of a Moscow district murder team, with not the slightest real claim to the job. What I was feeling was almost as if my identity were sliding away from me. My *self*. I stood beside the car and tried to compose sentences beginning with the first person nominative singular. This was not a success.

I got in the car and started the engine. Waiting for it to warm up, I watched the gunmetal smoke of the exhaust fumes drift under the orange overhead lights. An underground police garage with visible carbon monoxide floating past the car window is no place to review your life, brothers. I put the car in gear and drove for the twisting ramp. A militiaman checked me out and I headed the Renault in the direction of my apartment, down through Red Presnya and across the river.

At just six o'clock, it was already dark. Big soft November snowflakes slid through the darkness and exploded wetly on my windscreen. There were a good number of street lights once you got away from the area of the worst shelling, and some of the traffic lights were working again. But across the river from Presnya, it was like being in a different city. Murmansk was not Moscow, but even so I had never seen anything like the traffic on Koba Prospekt, buses, trolley buses, and army trucks of all sizes converted for use as buses or delivery vans. A few Economys were the only Russian-made cars I saw. Between the trucks, Audis and Rovers, Nissans and Chevrolets from the last burst of black-market buying before the war, weaved back and forth across the four-lane avenue seeking overtaking positions. They were, I supposed, the property of government departments or had been assigned to senior army officers, though there were still, Dronsky told me, plenty of big black-marketeers and political mafiamen about. Some of them I guessed I had seen last night at the Royal American Hotel.

Darkness lent glamour to these foreign automobiles, their powerful headlights gleaming on the paintwork of the cars in front, the extravagant rearlights throwing sudden banks of glistening red as the driver touched the brakes. Meanwhile the people of Moscow, released at last from the long hours in factories or searching for food, were thick on the pavements or crammed steaming into the backs of army-truck buses.

On the road we're supposed to keep the police frequency open but if I switch on I always tune to the news. The bungled attempt on the lives of President Romanov and Vice-President Koba was the lead item. Both men were unhurt, though several bystanders were badly injured. It gave me a curious feeling to listen to the details. I'd never thought before of a risk attached to being Koba's double but, of course, there was. I could see Roy enjoying my alarm.

This was not an isolated case. Last week, it appears, the senior Cheka officer for Moscow city was gunned down outside his office. But slowly we're getting control of our own Russia. The United States embassy is opening up on its old site, although it's only occupied by a small staff and a chargé d'affaires. Full recognition will come. The British, French and Germans are sharing one of the old trade union palaces. The Japanese are somewhere. The rumour in the vodka houses is that we're going to be able to coax McDonald's back.

My apartment is across the river at Fili. During the war this area saw a short period of bitter fighting in the last days of the struggle. The buildings are mostly a mix of Stalin and Yeltsin concrete but one or two pieces of old Moscow survive. The shelling has shaken great patches of plaster from some of the yellow stucco house fronts, exposing the old red underbrick, but compared with Red Presnya itself the area seems untouched by war. Officials of my rank get assigned small flats in the Stalinist apartment buildings in the less agreeable parts of the borough. More senior figures get sizeable apartments in the Arbat. Those below me in rank are in danger of being consigned to the unkempt, concrete wastelands of the New Districts.

'Today,' said my fourth-floor neighbour, a water stand-ards inspector named Dimitry, 'the lift is working, Inspector. If you have supplies of wood, or coal even, this is the time to bring them up.' He spoke as if my case of wine was not a serious burden.

'You mean the lift is not to be relied upon?'

'I mean our caretaker is not an elevator engineer of note.' We rattled upwards at what I now thought of as breakneck speed. Dimitry sighed. 'There are compensations, however,' he said. 'We, on the superior floors, all develop fine, shapely calf muscles.' He paused to make the main point. 'Especially the ladies. Have you had the opportunity to observe Madame Raisa?'

'Madame Raisa? No.'

'She has an apartment on the floor above us. God knows how she came by it. She's not employed by the administration as you and I are, Inspector. She's not young. In her early fifties, but a taxi picks her up twice a week, Tuesday and Friday evenings as regular as . . .'

'Clockwork,' I said.

He stared at me as the lift came to a stop and the door slid open. 'Perhaps you think I'm merely an old gossip,' he said, petulant. 'But I thought information was the all-important tool of your profession.'

I accepted the rebuke. 'You're right, of course,' I said. 'A long day tires a man.'

He appeared to hesitate. 'You can come in for a drink, if you choose,' he said sulkily.

In Moscow today, as in Moscow yesterday, one does not make casual enemies. I accepted.

Two hours later when I let myself into my apartment, my head spinning from vengeful gossip and speculation, I saw the white paper on the mat as I closed the door behind me. I picked up the envelope without real curiosity. There was no one in particular I wished (or rather, expected) to hear from, and I was ready to fling aside the note as a reminder of water restrictions rules or the use of electricity in peak hours.

But as I held up the letter and saw *Constantin Vadim* in that strong, clear script, as mercilessly haunting as her blue-grey eyes, my heart began to thud. I tore open the envelope.

The letter read: *When you arrive home, look out of the window – but for God's sake take care.* It was in Julia's hand.

The apartment was a bedroom/living room, a small kitchen and a bathroom. The kitchen and bathroom face back onto another row of buildings; the main room looks down into the street and a derelict site opposite. Stuffing the letter into my pocket, I barged my way into the living room. Should I turn on the light? I threw the case of wine onto the sofa bed and crossed to the window. One weak street lamp shone at the end of Semyon Lane. Most of the light came from passing cars or the fires the beggars light under their corrugated iron shelters on the rubble of the bomb site opposite.

If I strained my eyes, I could make out the dark shapes of the beggars, even see that some of them were women. Fili was a stopover on their journey to the safe haven of the ruins of Red Presnya. I knew, I had seen them on my way home, that there would be some maimed, some very young, holding out their tin cups in what seemed like a hopeless attempt to attract into them the rattle of a few kopecks. But a surge of desperation rose in me as I realised that from four floors up I could never see, never make out the shapes of faces, not even the shape of that face.

I turned away from the window. I switched on the light so that she would know at least that I had her letter. My brain was racing. No, not racing, scurrying like a frightened mouse, back and forth, in a vain effort to understand.

Julia was in Moscow – that was point one. Julia was

afraid, despite the announcement of the amnesty – that was point two. My mind scurried back and forth over possibilities and rejected them: perhaps she had not yet heard of the amnesty. *Impossible.*

She had heard of it, but was not convinced of Leonid Koba's sincerity. *Very much more likely.*

She had heard of the amnesty but believed it did not apply to herself because of her high profile as the leader of the only all-women division in the Anarchist army. *Most likely of all.*

But I knew that, whatever the answer, I had to respect her fears. Unless I did, I could not be expected to be allowed to help her.

From the cupboard I took an old naval greatcoat, the only thing of my father's I had kept. When I put it on it altered my shape; when I turned up the collar I could have been any of a million Muscovite beggars.

I ignored the lift and took the staircase down. On the ground floor I could hear a football commentary coming from the caretaker's apartment. I threw a quick glance over my shoulder. For centuries in Russia the caretaker has doubled as police spy. He had no need to be a lift engineer of note.

On the basement level I knew there was a backdoor exit into overgrown gardens. Early this morning I had carried my empty cases down here to have them chained together with all the other empty cases in a basement piled with unwanted furniture and rustling with rats. I passed the caretaker's door and took the last flight of steps. Letting myself out into the snow, I stood close to the wall. Above me the caretaker moved about his kitchen, throwing a shadow on the brambles outside. Keeping close to the houses, I moved from garden to garden across crumbling dividing walls until I came to a narrow footpath leading into Semyon Lane.

Turning my collar up, I shuffled along the wet pavements. Not even beggars accosted me. Opposite my own building I stopped and leaned back into the shadows. The caretaker's living-room light was on, as were several others up to the third floor. That floor was entirely dark. The floor above showed my living-room light, Dimitry's drawn curtains and two more eyeless windows. On the fifth floor a woman flitted back and forth behind lace curtains. Madame Raisa, perhaps. And on the same floor two other lights shone through curtain cracks. The top floor was entirely dark.

Then a thought struck, so simple and so frightening I almost gagged: while Dimitry whined on about our neighbours, Julia had been waiting on the street below.

She had seen me enter the apartment house. She had imagined I had taken up her note a few minutes later, read it, and decided not to help. Decided that I had done enough. The idea that she might this moment be thinking that of me caused me the purest anguish.

My pulse raced as I scanned faces that passed me and I lost my breath any time my imagination told my eyes I was seeing Julia. That night she appeared in a dozen forms. I saw her in real women passing. I saw her as a shadow in the beggars' flickering firelight; I saw her in the collusion of car headlights. I saw her everywhere I looked. And nowhere.

In my light-headed state I asked myself could she really be in Moscow? Was there any chance that her letter was a device dreamed up by Roy? A new panic flared in me. I dragged out the note and examined the writing in a beggar's firelight. Roy knew her writing of course. And he had access to experts in forgery. I was shaking as I stared at the letter.

Very slowly my certainty returned. Surely to God this was her hand, although it was undoubtedly different. Weaker somehow, tighter, whereas before her Russian script had always reminded me of cranes flying across the snowy whiteness of the paper. But it was Julia. All doubt flowed from me. And if it was Julia, then what was she doing in Moscow? Had I not myself taken the risks of a young lover to help my ex-wife escape to the West?

It was far into the night before I returned home, to hear the phone ringing long before I reached my apartment.

13

Sirens wailed over Red Presnya. Squad cars raced in from Barracadya Metro and Tertevaya Street. Blue lights flashed from every corner. When I arrived, small clusters of people, mostly women, were pointing to the rooftop of a long factory building about eighty metres away across wasteland and ruin. Dronsky had already set up a tripod searchlight and a militiaman was moving its beam along the level of the coping of the flat-roofed factory.

A figure was caught in the light. The thickening crowd murmured and gasped as they used to when a lone Anarchist bomber plane was trapped by searchlights over Murmansk. Then the figure turned towards us, feet apart like a rock star, his arms waving, slicing back and forth in front of his face.

'Where are our nearest men?'

Dronsky was by my side as soon as I spoke. 'I've sent two cars to the back of the building, Inspector. Sergeant Yakunin and Sergeant Bitov are breaking into the side door.'

I looked back quickly across twenty metres to the concrete block on which the girl was splayed, her bloodied legs wide. It was a statueless plinth. On the side, in bronze letters of running blood I read the name: JOSEPH STALIN.

'Move these people away,' I said to Dronsky. 'Put a ring of men round her and cover her with a blanket or something. Then follow me over to the factory.'

'A blanket?' Dronsky's face glistened above the gleam of his Moscow 13 blue and yellow police slicker. 'Not a blanket, Chief.'

'Anything,' I scowled at him. 'A coat. A sheet of plastic. Anything.'

'Inspector, the doctor hasn't examined her yet.'

'So?' The rock star danced on in the searchlight, scissoring his arms.

'Any covering will slow the rate of body cooling,' Dronsky said. 'Time of death will be more difficult to establish.'

I told him to forget the covering and clear the area, then follow me as soon as he could.

I jumped into the Economy, switched on the sidelight blue police flashers and drove along the outline of a road between rubble, turned left and ran straight towards one end of the factory building. Glancing up I could see the spotlight searching the rooftop. The figure had gone.

I pulled up among some charred wooden sheds. Getting out of the car, I tore my ankle on a nail sticking from a burnt length of timber. Somewhere behind me other cars drew up, blue lights flashing. A rusted iron fire-escape ladder led down from the roof, held on some balance mechanism about six feet above my head. I looked around for an instrument and my eye settled on the charred timber with the nail which had torn at my ankle. About two metres long, a rafter probably, it might just reach the ladder. I hauled it out of the rubbish it was embedded in, lifted it in the air and hooked the nail over the bottom rung of the ladder.

The mechanism creaked as I pulled, but the nail held and the lower section of ladder slid down to hand height. Grasping it, I began to climb.

Most man-hunts are a deadly comedy of errors. I have never seen a murder victim before, but I've chased pimps and pickpockets over half the rooftops of Murmansk. Danger comes from your own men's guns, and I was acutely aware as I came up to roof level that I was not wearing a slicker and that Yakunin and Bitov didn't know I was joining the hunt.

The searchlight probed the far end of the roof as I climbed the coping and ducked down behind it. What I had thought was a flat roof was in fact made up of glass and tar-paper panels, sloping so that rain and snow-water would run into a gully just below the coping. There was little or no place to hide up here. For me or him.

At this point caution and cowardice converge. That's to say you come to your senses. Up here I was probably alone with a homicidal maniac. Perhaps I should just slow down, wait a minute or two until help arrived. His knife could still be dripping blood. The thought sent ice-water thrilling through my veins.

I had risen to draw my gun from my holster when a blinding flash of God knows how many hundred thousand candlepower exploded in my eyes as I was picked up by the searchlight. For a moment I stood gasping in shock before I turned my back and bent away from the light. With my eyes tight closed I dropped into the darkness below the level of the coping and crouched there on hands and knees as the searchlight beam wavered just above my head. When my eyes readjusted I could see, through the glass roof, the flashlights of Yakunin and Bitov as they moved through plywood-compartmented rooms below.

I crawled for a dozen yards along the old zinc gully, my exposed back tingling at the thought that he had somehow worked his way behind me. But in the darkness ahead there was a sound different from all the other sounds of sirens and shouts that floated up to me.

Closer, I could see that the farthest point on the roof was a flat, concrete section with a wooden shed that probably housed lifting machinery for the plant below. I crawled further forward. The door was partly open. A low howling, or moaning perhaps, was coming from inside. What to do? Wait for help, or take him by myself? Senior Homicide Inspector Constantin Vadim gets his man within days of arrival in Moscow. I liked it. But the noise he was making had an inhuman edge. I slipped the safety on my gun and moved across the flat roof beyond the range of the searchlight beam.

For a moment I stood in that half-dark of reflected light. I was suddenly aware that I was shaking like a lunatic. Where were the others? Did they expect me to take this monster myself?

I'm on the edge of one of those life-threatening decisions. I take the deepest of breaths and step forward so that I'm standing beside the door, listening.

It isn't howling, or even moaning. It's singing. Drunken, tuneless singing. I can hear the words clearly:

> 'Forsooth, forsooth
> Cold to crack a bear's tooth.'

A nursery rhyme. Tension left me like strength draining. I stepped into the hut. I could see, by the light of the searchlight beam, a man crumpled in the corner. He was nursing a vodka bottle and gurgling out his song.

I took him by the collar of his jacket and pulled him out onto the flat roof.

He came willingly enough. Even in the part-light I could see he was not a man who had just left the scene of a bloody crime. His hands, the long fingers round the vodka bottle, were innocent of blood.

'Who are you?' I said, refusing his offer of the bottle.

He was tall, unshaven, wearing a jacket made for a smaller but fatter man. 'Mikhail Mikhailovich Gromek,' he announced, rawboned wrists leaping from his sleeves as he drew himself up. 'Night-watchman, caretaker and maintenance engineer.'

'Of this plant?' I pointed through the glass roof to the shadowed outlines of the machines below us.

'The very one. You'll do me the honour of allowing me to offer you a conducted tour.'

Glass smashed and clattered close to my feet and

Bitov's face appeared through a hole in the roof. 'Ah, you've got him, Chief,' he said, disappointed. His voice came from what seemed a severed head.

More militia had arrived by the time I got down from the roof. I sent Bitov back to District 13 with the night-watchman and told him to have Gromek checked for blood, his record, if he had one, pulled, his finger-prints taken.

But I didn't believe anything would come of it.

I got out of the Economy and walked slowly back through the ruins. This complete block of houses and small factories had been demolished by shelling. Broken walls stood ten, sometimes fifteen feet high, forming courtyards linked by rubble-strewn paths that had once been alleyways. Charred timber poked in all directions. The Stalin plinth stood before a flattened area of build-ings that were no longer recognisable.

Small knots of people had gathered outside a circle of militiamen. Inside the ring of grey fur shapkas and long brown greatcoats I could see that a huge and ramshackle plastic tent had been erected over the cement block on which the girl's body had been found. Hazy figures moved in the green light within the incident tent, five or six people in a rough circle. Every few seconds the walls of the tent whitened with a camera flash.

As I came closer I could see the outline of the block, the plinth. In this shell-torn wasteland of Red Presnya it seemed as if an operation were being performed on the spot.

The militiaman on the door failed to recognise me and I stood for a moment searching my pockets for my ID. It was time I needed. As I am about to look, close up, on violent death, I feel all those fears and uncertainties that most people feel. Will I tremble? Will I vomit?

I took a deep breath and pushed aside the wet plas-tic flap.

It was unbearably hot inside. Two photographers were packing away equipment. Dronsky was smoking a cigarette. A green lamp with a huge silvered bowl had been rigged up in the corner and the light was shining on the tied-back blonde hair of a young woman in green overalls and red rubber gloves who stood over the cement block. The feet of the corpse, one bare, one shod with a broken high heel, overhung the rough edge of the concrete. The rest of the body was mercifully hidden from sight.

For the moment.

Dr Natalya Karlova turned towards me as she heard my voice. A halo of green light sparkled round the hair that was escaping from her green cap. There was a smear of blood on her cheek. She smiled grimly.

'Dr Karlova,' I said.

She held a bloodstained wooden probe in each hand. 'Natalya,' she corrected me. We might have been in the marquee of a smart garden party.

My ears were buzzing. My eyes blurred and cleared, blurred and cleared again.

'Constantin,' she said, 'Deputy Dronsky says you caught a man up on the plant roof.'

'I caught a night-watchman.'

'You don't think he was responsible for this?' She turned and gestured, stepping to one side a little.

I stared in open-mouthed horror at the cement butcher's block in front of me. Blood showed black in the green light and ran down the sides, over the bronze letters of Stalin's name. At the apex of the girl's exposed legs was a mass of stabbed and battered flesh. Above that her stomach had been torn open. I looked at her face, small, green hued, her mouth open showing rabbit teeth.

'Constantin,' Karlova touched my arm with her elbow.

I had no idea how long I had been looking down at the corpse but I had the impression that my eyes were unnaturally wide, staring.

'Savage,' she said.

I blinked. Then turned to her. 'Yes.'

'Have you ever seen anything like it?'

Had I ever seen anything like it? Was the woman serious! I shook my head and concentrated on her efforts to take a cigarette and light from Dronsky without using her red-rubber-gloved hands. I hadn't smoked since the last century but when Dronsky offered his packet I took one.

Karlova inhaled and curled her tongue expertly round the cigarette to deposit it in the very corner of her mouth. 'I'll talk you through the injuries,' she said. She walked towards the Stalin plinth. Smoke plumed from the corner of her mouth and curled through the green light. My eyes were beginning to water, my throat seemed to be coated in slime. I put my head down and drew deeply on the cigarette. I was a practised smoker. I drew the smoke deep into my lungs. My head span and stilled. I felt better.

'Provisionally,' Karlova said, 'cause of death was blood loss and massive trauma caused by the removal of the womb.'

I reached for the plinth and steadied myself. 'Removal of the womb was the *cause* of death?'

'Yes,' she looked at me from under her eyebrows.

'You don't mean she was conscious?' My voice was little more than a croak. 'When it happened.'

'More or less, I'd say. What we're dealing with here, Constantin,' she said calmly, 'is, in the full sense of the word, a vivisection.'

'The girl was alive?' I forced out the question. 'Alive and conscious when *that* happened . . . ?'

'As in the earlier deaths.'

Dronsky was watching me. Did he know I still hadn't even properly read the murder reports? Did I care any longer?

'Again, we have the same pattern of marking on the windpipe,' Natalya Karlova's unhurried voice said.

110

I looked at the pale face of the corpse. She looked eight years old. Beneath her chin were two half-circles of deep black marks. Teeth marks.

'As in the last three crimes, I believe this points to the murderer silencing and partially suffocating his victim by biting hard on her windpipe as he carried her.'

'Carried her. Where from?'

'I'll leave you to tell me that,' Karlova said coolly. 'Presumably from wherever he first attacked her.'

I stayed silent while Karlova gave a detailed, technical description of the corpse. *Lining membrane above the uterus severed* . . . But my thoughts raced. What mind could conceive an attack like this on another human being? A shooting, a stabbing, yes. The object is simple death. Murder. But not here. The object of this butchery was not simple murder. *Patterns in blood just below the crease of her left thigh indicate that the knife was cleaned by stropping motions* . . . What manner of lust, of hatred for humanity, for women, underlay it, I could not even begin to guess.

'We have what is certainly semen on the inner right thigh,' Karlova was saying. 'Given the injuries sustained we're not going to be able to establish whether or not there was penetration.'

Did it matter? Certainly not to this poor child.

'I have removed a good number of fibres from the back and sides of the girl's coat,' Natalya Karlova continued. 'Also from the skirt. Carpet fibres I would guess, at this stage. These may prove interesting when we have the opportunity to examine them further. One other point . . .'

I looked down at the corpse. I was surprised that I now could, without that feeling in the throat. 'What's that?'

Karlova was bending forward. 'Look there,' she said. She was pointing to an area just below the poor creature's knee. I crouched.

'Closer. What can you see?'

On the side of her left calf, about halfway between knee and ankle, there was a reddish mark about three inches deep. I straightened up.

'The same as on the other two victims,' Karlova said. 'This confirms it. He is no longer a total mystery man to us. We have opened the box. We know one single thing about him.'

I looked expectantly.

'He's left-handed. This is a blow delivered with some sort of instrument, probably wood. A baton or a piece of timber held as a left-handed person would hold it. So . . .' She demonstrated.

'From behind?'

'Exactly. On the other bodies you will recall there were bruises to the left leg at just this point.' She was excited, waving her red-gloved hands in the air, puffing on her cigarette and expelling jets of tobacco smoke into the green light of the incident tent. 'My contention is that he approaches his victims silently from behind. Crouching as he runs forward, he delivers a scythe-like blow to the girl's legs. She is literally swept from her feet. He drops the baton. He catches her in his arms. As her scream forms in her throat he sinks his teeth into her windpipe.'

Nerves screamed in my head. When I came to Homicide I thought I would sit in a comfortable Moscow office signing forms and pushing papers from department to department. Or at the most be called upon to deal with the occasional drink-maddened husband or wife at the end of their tether. Blows delivered cleanly with fists or pokers, even the occasional shooting. I never for a moment expected something like this.

Karlova was looking at me.

'Yes, I see,' I said. 'Teeth in her windpipe.' I was fighting for something to say. 'And for all this, for all the rest,' I asked her, waving a hand towards the dead girl, 'would he need medical knowledge?'

'Only of the most rudimentary nature.'

'He's not a doctor?'

She smiled, her lips pressed together. 'Most doctors have only a rudimentary knowledge of surgery. He's probably not a surgeon, is all I can say.'

I made an effort to ask the questions I felt I must ask. 'The knife, do we know anything about that?'

'Long and sharp.'

'That's all?' I mused for a moment, my head turned away from the girl's body. 'He must surely have been up to his armpits in blood.'

'Hence these.' Karlova held up a large plastic bag. The contents looked like fish swimming in blood. With a pair of medical tweezers she drew one out. It was itself a plastic bag, covered with wet blood, an elastic band hanging from part of it.

'As in the earlier cases,' she said, 'the murderer wore, as he worked, two narrow plastic bags over the hands and forearms, secured by an elastic band.'

'Might he have had an apron too?'

'Possible.'

I turned to Dronsky. 'Who found her?'

'We don't know. A woman. A call to the station. A brief description and she hung up.'

'Do we have any identification for the girl?'

'No name. A weekly metro ticket from Barricadnaya into Red Square found in her coat pocket. I'd guess she's a local girl.'

'No money, no handbag?'

Dronsky shook his head.

'Somewhere there's a handbag,' I said. 'When Doctor Karlova has the body moved, leave a permanent guard on this tent and use the rest of the men to search the area for that bag. We'll find it within a few feet of where the initial attack took place.'

I turned back to the body on the plinth. I no longer seemed to see the ripped flesh. I saw the small white face, the rabbit teeth. The trace of lipstick still adhering to the thin lips, the discreet eyeshadow. Not a *putana*, this one. So what was she doing, like Tania Chekova, crossing the wasteland of Red Presnya in the middle of the night?

When Dr Karlova was finished I signed the order for the corpse to be wrapped in plastic and taken over to the morgue. I watched while Karlova stripped off her gloves and packed her grisly bag. She saw my eye on the bottle of vodka it contained and lifted it towards me. I unscrewed the cap and offered it back to her and she took it and drank. Dronsky next and then myself. The spirit burnt as it should. My throat cleared of slime just as Karlova's assistants rolled the body in plastic and carried it away on a bloodstained stretcher.

14

It was approaching dawn as I drove home through Presnya's dark, rubble-piled streets, through a district handed to the poor, the beggars, the drifting bands of street children, the horse-drawn carts laden with furniture or hay. The homeless sit around wasteland fires and drink vodka. Women and young boys ply their trade on street corners. In these shameful circumstances, I was forced to wonder whether the tearful lady in the vodka house had been right, forced to wonder if what I had seen tonight carried its own message: whether the Monstrum who had committed this appalling act was by the very freedom with which he moved, in a world of endless rubble and moral decay, mocking our desperate Russian condition.

And more than that: the thought that tonight Julia was in Moscow, alone perhaps, walking the streets perhaps, even the streets of Red Presnya, made my blood run cold.

Beyond the limits of Presnya it was different. On one corner of Leonid Koba Prospekt a number of gleaming cars had pulled up in front of the sidewalk canopy of something called the Club Ironique. Well-dressed girls were being escorted from the club by men waving cigars as they talked. Further on, the entrances to big hotels glittered with lights, their forecourts filled with the limousines.

I put my car into the small garage I had been allocated in an alley near the apartment and walked slowly down Semyon Lane. A family passed me, even the youngest children carrying bundles of possessions. An old man supported by a girl of about eighteen was almost too exhausted to put one foot in front of another. Two of the youngest children walked, their eyes closing in fatigue.

These people are the reason my district is not favoured by the rich. Too many refugees stream through it daily (and nightly) on their way to Red Presnya. There, people tell them, among the unsafe tower blocks they will be able to find shelter without being moved on by the police.

I stopped the young man who was carrying a small child in his arms and an old Soviet army mountain pack on his back and gave him a few roubles. It didn't do much to assuage the sense of guilt I carried from tonight's scenes, but it's better than staring desperation in the eye and passing by.

The lift was not working. After the ground floor there were no lights. I took the stairs to my apartment, scuffing the soles of my shoes wearily against the dusty, concrete steps. It was just after six o'clock, still dark on the streets but with a steely greyness in the eastern sky just visible as I paused at my landing window.

My door was to my left. The door to the apartment of Dimitry, the inspector of water standards, was in front of me. The sound I heard, the soft sighing of clothing against wood or stone, came from the staircase above me.

I moved from the window and stood in the deep shadow of an alcove. I slipped my hand inside my jacket and loosened the Tango in the holster. But what filled my anticipation was the thought that it might be Julia standing in the darkness of the stair.

A match flared, died as it touched a candle wick and a yellow light slowly invaded the darkness. A woman stood on the half-landing above me in long nightdress and flowered robe, her dark red hair long and luxuriant. Lipstick and some rouge accentuated the maturity of the face. She was perhaps in her very early fifties.

'Madame Raisa?' I said softly. She touched a finger to her lips and beckoned to me to follow her. She had reached her own floor before I turned at the landing. Her door was open. She paused, holding the candle high above her head, and beckoned me on.

I'm cautious by inclination, nervous even. The operatic nature of our meeting, emphasised by flowing robes and thick dark hair, by the generous proportions of the woman disappearing in candlelight into her apartment, failed to dislodge my fingers from the butt of my gun. I stepped through the doorway and she stood facing me in the narrow passage. 'Close the door, Inspector,' she whispered.

I closed the door and she reached out and switched on the light. Somehow she looked less operatic, even under the low-wattage bulb.

She beckoned again and I followed her into the sitting room of her small apartment. 'Be careful about the noise,' she said. 'Dimitry lives directly below. He spreads gossip about me. Sit down and I'll bring coffee and something stronger.'

Am I mad? I was sitting at six in the morning in the apartment of a middle-aged opera singer who had beckoned me on with flirtatious candlelight gestures. About to drink coffee and something stronger.

When Madame Raisa returned she carried a tray with coffeepot and cups, a bottle of Armagnac and two small glasses. She put it down on the low table and I expected her to put on the music.

She did. An old-fashioned disc player. But not really soft music. Hits from the great operas. She stood in front of me, still rather a magnificent figure of a woman. I could see she had once been beautiful. Some would say she still was.

'You will appreciate the coffee,' she said. 'I have it flown in from the West every month.' She smiled. 'My brother Nicolai is a senior pilot with Air Russia. He is fortunate enough to fly to New York several times a month. Do you know New York, Inspector?'

'Madame Raisa,' I said, accepting coffee but declining the Armagnac, 'you're very kind. But it's six o'clock in the morning. Almost seven. I've just returned from work. A most hideous murder of a young girl in Presnya.'

'The Monstrum,' she said.

'We don't like to use that term,' I told her, although every man in District 13 used nothing else.

'The Monstrum, Inspector, is a visitation upon all of us.'

I rubbed my eyes. 'You could be right,' I mumbled.

'Please have some Armagnac. Do you like the music? This is myself singing some of the great arias. Fragments from another world, Constantin. Do you mind if I call you Constantin? Constantin,' she came and sat next to me on the sofa, 'we must be discreet.'

I agreed, uncertainly.

She pointed downwards. 'You realise that below is a man who takes every possible opportunity to look up my skirt on the stairs.'

'The inspector of water standards?'

'Dimitry is a false Dimitry.'

I stared.

'You know the story of the false Dimitry?'

'The substitute Prince Dimitry . . .'

'. . . who was once made to look like the real Prince Dimitry and placed on the throne of the tsars,' she said vigorously. 'Dimitry below is a false Dimitry. He works not at the Office of Water Standards. He works at Lubyanka Square.'

'At the Lubyanka prison? You mean he's an officer of the Cheka?'

'I'm sure of it.' She came closer. 'He must not know you are visiting me. Have more coffee. Have Armagnac. Have biscuits.'

'Won't the music at this hour suggest visitors?'

'I play music at all hours. My own music. I also sing. Now you must listen to me, Constantin. I have a story

118

to tell you. I was once an opera singer of some note. I sang in London and New York. Now I have no means to sustain life but my two old gentlemen. From the university. Without them I would have starved. You understand what I'm saying, Constantin.'

I nodded.

'I ask myself – am I morally justified to do this to keep body and soul together in these hard times?'

'We all do what we can.'

'Apart from my brother, I have no family, no friends to be shocked.' She laid her plump hand on my thigh. 'I would do anything to have friends. I am loyal. Honest. Why do I have no friends?'

Fatigue was pressing my eyelids. She poured me more coffee. This time I accepted a glass of Armagnac.

'I have no friends,' she took up the refrain, 'because I am foolish. Loyal, honest, yes – but indiscreet and foolish. I talk too freely. I talk to people in cafés, in the tram queue. Huddled on the back of an army bus, I talk, talk, talk.'

I didn't doubt her. I finished my Armagnac in one gulp and half rose to go.

'No.' She pressed heavily on my thigh. 'You see why I have no friends. I have suffered beatings from both sides in this last war. Under torture – no, I exaggerate, beatings only – under beatings, I remain silent. In a café, I babble. As I did to that young woman in the park.'

I accepted a generous tip of Armagnac. I was lost. 'Which young woman?'

'Sonya,' she said. 'She believes she knows you.'

I sat upright. *Sonya*. When Julia and I were young, barely more than children, we had fooled about calling each other by the names of those comic book cretins, the perfect Soviet teenagers, *Sonya and Vassily*. I was suddenly wide awake. 'This young woman, Sonya, what did she look like?'

'Tired, very tired.'

My stomach turned over. 'But tall, short? And her features . . . ?'

'Tall,' she said. 'As tall as me. Slim. Blonde, striking features, exhausted.'

'You met her in the park?'

'I've seen her twice. Yesterday, this morning just past, I left the house to buy fish,' Madame Raisa recounted. 'I was determined to buy fish. One of my university friends had given me extra money. What for, you won't ask, a gentleman like you. No. Fish I was determined to find.'

'Where did you go?'

'You know the food mart they hold in Koba Park now?'

'Is that Koba Park, along the big boulevard?'

'A month or two ago it was Kropotkin Park, named for the Anarchist saint, but we don't complain. There I found fish. A daunting queue, but I joined it, stayed with it even when the baggage serving us claimed it was all gone. And ended the morning with a fine piece of smoked cod.'

'The young woman you mentioned?'

'I carried my fish off to the Park Café and treated myself to a fine warming pepper vodka. A moment or two later a young woman in a pale trench coat entered. She had presence, we would say in the theatre. The café was quite full. Her eyes calmly passed from table to table. She observed that I was sitting alone. She moved towards the table and stopped. With the merest smile, she enquired whether she might sit at my table. Such manners are rare nowadays, Constantin.'

'You talked.'

'Non-stop, I fear. I told her how I kept body and soul together. She was not shocked. I told her where I lived. I told her about the false Dimitry below me. I told her about the young handsome inspector of police who had just moved into the building. I babbled.'

'And the young woman, Sonya?'

'She listened. She told me that she had once known

a young man named Vadim when she was a student in Murmansk. On the merest off-chance that it was you, she gave me the note.'

'The note that you posted through my letterbox?'

'Yes.' When she poured Armagnac again, I made no attempt to refuse.

'There's no chance Dimitry saw you?' I asked her.

'He was out.'

'You spoke of meeting this young woman twice.'

'Within a few hundred metres of the front door here. I was coming home this evening. Late. I had been to see one of my professors. No, no. No wicked thoughts, Constantin. This time I sang for him. I swear that's all. Sonya approached me in Semyon Lane. Greeted me gaily with a kiss on both cheeks.' Raisa got to her feet and crossed to a small table. From round her neck she took a key and unlocked a nineteenth-century walnut writing box. From one of the compartments she took a letter, the same in size and shape as the one I had found on my doormat. 'She gave me this. It was midnight but she said nevertheless that it would be the act of a dear friend to deliver it to you personally. With all possible speed.'

I slid the letter into my jacket pocket. 'I've much to thank you for, madame,' I said. I took her hand and kissed it.

'You'll come and take coffee with me again?'

'Soon,' I said.

'We must exercise the utmost discretion.' She pressed a packet of French coffee into my hand.

'We shall.'

I left her apartment and stole down the stairs to my own floor. Letting myself in, I pulled Julia's letter from my pocket and immediately tore open the envelope.

It read: *Please Vassily. Please, please take me to the all-night show at the President Romanov Cinema on Washington Prospekt tonight. Midnight to 4 a.m. Sonya.*

I leaned back against the closed door. While the late

show played in the President Romanov Cinema, while Julia waited alone, while Julia needed me, I had been huddled in an eerily-lit green plastic tent with Dronsky, Karlova and the mangled body of a nameless girl on a dripping plinth inscribed JOSEPH STALIN – DEFENDER OF THE CITY OF MOSCOW.

15

I slept a few hours and woke in my clothes on the sofa at about nine. Outside I could see that the heavy cloud had cleared, showing blue sky flecked with small bright clouds. In the streets the treacherous November snow had melted and people walked with their heavy coats open. We were to have, last night's radio had said, a few days of clear, almost mild weather. But my head was thick and the taste in my throat reminded me nauseously of the odours of the stifling tent last night. I made some of Madame Raisa's French coffee, stripped off my clothes and showered and shaved. I dressed in clean clothes and threw this lot into the basket. Then I stood at the window, sipping coffee and looking down into Semyon Lane.

The clean bitter taste of the coffee cleared my throat, even partially cleared my head. I tried to think. Why had Julia decided it was safe to make contact with Madame Raisa, but not directly with me? Was it possible that she knew that I was already being watched by the Cheka? Was Madame Raisa not quite as scatty as she seemed? Was she right that my neighbour was a false Dimitry, working for the Cheka?

The thought brought on confused emotions. The Cheka are no more than the secret police of my own side. Our vice-president, Leonid Koba himself, is Minister for State Security, their chief. But people like Roy Rolkin revelled in the old fear-laden name from the days of the Soviets, and they still worked out of the Lubyanka, once the mild-sounding All Russian Insurance Company, but since early Stalin days a place of cells and torture chambers and execution yards. The Cheka and their Lubyanka had history enough to strike terror into any Russian heart.

My eyes roamed up and down the length of the street. Below me passed the sad caravan of refugees on their way to Presnya. I stood sipping coffee, trying to suppress the fear I felt, trying to pretend that it was fear only for Julia.

I had to assume I was being watched. I had to assume Julia felt it was too dangerous to contact me. I had, therefore, somehow to make it easier for her.

I left the flat and ran down the stairs and through the hall. I would be better off without my car. On Filovskaya Avenue I picked up a trolleybus for four or five stops, got off and entered the great church on the corner. For a few moments the warmth and glowing colour imparted a comforting sense of security as I stood at the back watching the service. People filed past and out through a number of doors and by following one line I found myself on a small outside gallery on the far side of the church. From here I walked with care, not obviously trying to avoid a follower, yet making sure I took every opportunity to check. I had chosen a route through faceless streets towards Leonid Koba Prospekt. It was a route that would take me past the Park Café.

The terrace was crowded. In the park the grass was miraculously green again, though patched with white. The cool sunlight was a luxury Muscovites would indulge, even though the morning temperature demanded heavy coats and in some cases winter fur hats. Yesterday it had been snowing.

I entered the café and took a place at the bar, where I ordered a small black coffee and drank it slowly. Out on the terrace people vacated tables to new arrivals. A black dog came up and sniffed at my shoes, stopped in intense interest and began to lick. I moved my foot but the mutt snarled and came for more. I pushed him away in disgust. It was the smell of last night's blood the hound had picked up.

I finished my coffee. I had not really expected Julia to be here, but I felt I knew the way her mind works. Or rather I felt that I knew what she would see as the way *my* mind works. If for some good reason I had been unable to get to the Romanov Cinema, the Park Café was the place she had selected for her meeting with Madame Raisa. It was therefore the place I would come to. The place she would return to.

Some time. I looked round again. Not today.

I left the café, caught a lorry bus and walked through Presnya's shattered streets to District Station 13. Reception was as crowded as yesterday but perhaps a little less chaotic. The amnesty line had divided into two and was now serviced by four desks with the detectives recording names on new-looking computer equipment. The arrival of Dr Shepherd and her decision to base herself at District 13 was already showing results.

I went to the head of one of the queues and flipped my ID at the detective at the desk. He turned away from the man he was questioning.

'What happens here?' I asked him.

'Easy enough, Inspector,' he said. 'We take the name, date of birth and military service details of each applicant for amnesty. If they've no adequate identification we send them over for fingerprinting – then we try to match names or prints with people on our list of wanted for war crimes.' He brought up the list on the screen.

'Scroll it,' I said. There were no more than a few hundred names. None of them Julia's. 'What happens if the applicant's clean?'

'Couple of days later he gets issued with a citizen's identity card and he's free to walk.'

'As simple as that.'

'As simple as that.'

I thanked him and turned away. Then why, in God's

name, was Julia behaving as if she was in fear of her life?

I was stopped by a cloud of scent. Before I could turn towards the entrance I heard the click of Dr Shepherd's heels and her voice: 'Inspector Vadim,' she said.

She was crossing reception, flanked by her two Western colleagues. She wore a black business suit under a sable coat. We shook hands. 'I have to thank you for lending me the book,' I began, but she cut me off with a brief movement of her head. It was not just the heady scent. I swayed slightly before her extraordinarily perfect features.

'My subject,' she said, 'is psychology. My specialty, children. The science of bringing up children and the reason I first came to Russia. There are so many damaged children in your country. They were the reason I first opened my clinic. The *bezprisorny*, the millions of orphans who are in danger of becoming damaged adults if they're not treated in time.'

'And where is your clinic?'

'My clinic was destroyed during the shelling. I am working to get it reopened. There's desperate need in Moscow, Inspector.'

'And what's your interest in criminal profiling, Doctor? I see from Dr Benson's dedication to you that it's considerable.' There, I'd hit the nail beautifully that time. I could see the pleasure in the minute relaxation of her lips.

'Damaged children become damaged adults,' she said simply.

'Indeed. But do you believe they can be identified as the sort of children who will become criminal adults?'

'I do.'

'And you believe that science can intervene in the progression from damaged child to damaged adult?'

Her eyes sparkled with an extraordinary vivacity. 'Exactly that,' she said. 'Your Monstrum interests me as one such damaged adult. What would fascinate me, while the man is still unknown, is to profile him back to childhood, so to speak.' Her face was transformed as only a committed interest can transform a face. 'I would welcome the chance to discuss the subject with you.'

'My pleasure, Doctor,' I said.

She lifted a long index finger, the nail brightly enamelled. 'Then we shall arrange it.'

With a brief smile to me and a nod to her colleagues she swept on. Every man in reception, detective and applicant, turned to watch her progress.

I barged open the swing doors to the Murder Room. There were about ten detectives busily at work on their phones. As usual they barely raised their eyes as I passed. I was closing my office door as I saw Dronsky coming towards me, the marmalade cat following him.

I reversed actions and opened the door wider. Dronsky was wearing the same clothes he had been wearing at the murder site. Do homicide detectives work all night?

'Good morning, Chief.'

V.I. Lenin raised a paw. I find this sort of thing difficult to handle. Especially embarrassing when I realised I'd raised a hand to return his salutation. If that's what it was.

'We have to discuss this animal,' I said to Dronsky.

'We do, Chief. Coffee?'

'If you've got some going.'

'Sweetcake or bread and smoked fish?'

'You have a sad sense of humour,' I said. 'Just coffee.' I paused. 'Dronsky,' I said. 'There are upwards of twenty detectives out there working the phones and I'm lucky if they as much as nod. Now, I'm not pushing rank. But as senior homicide inspector, I think I ought to know what they're doing. Do *you* know?'

'Don't ask, Chief. They don't work for you.'

'They're in the Murder Room.'

'That's true,' he conceded.

'But they don't work for me?'

'No, Inspector.'

'So who do they work for?'

He took a deep breath. He was looking acutely uncomfortable. 'Commander Brusilov's brother-in-law, Chief.'

'And who's Commander Brusilov's brother-in-law?'

Dronsky looked down at the floor and rubbed at the linoleum with the toe of his blue boating shoe. 'Igor Sergeivich?' he said, looking up. 'He's one of the biggest restaurant suppliers in Moscow. Vegetable and fruit. It takes a lot of man hours to keep track of new supplies coming in from Georgia by air, put in a bid, allocate them to selected restaurants . . .'

'What! These detectives are running a market in vegetables in our Murder Room. *My* Murder Room?'

'Don't complain, Chief. They're not really detectives. Just on the Presnya police payroll.'

I turned away. Things will get better, I repeated as a silent mantra. But I really wanted to ask when. I sat down and swung the chair. The décor had changed since yesterday. There were three maps in wooden frames up on the walls, large maps of maybe a metre by a metre square. They were labelled *Murder 1*, *Murder 2*, *Murder 3*, *Murder 4*. In each case, a red dot marked the murder site. The site of the wartime murder in Crossways Lane was marked separately, with a large question mark. Sites one to three were in streets of Red Presnya unknown to me but none of them too far from the Bullfrog. Number four, of course, was the Stalin plinth where the girl had been killed last night.

I wanted to ask more about the first two girls. Things I should already have known, but the earlier murder reports were still in my carry-sack, unread. When Dronsky came in with the coffee he seemed pleased to see I was studying the maps. 'Your work, Dronsky?' I asked him. 'Very helpful.'

He smiled his pleasure. I took the coffee from him and

stirred in the sugar he'd left lying in the spoon. This was a man who thought of everything. 'So, did the search of the area around the plinth turn up anything last night? Sit down.'

He sat in front of the desk and ran his hand across his closely razored head. 'First we have fingerprints. All the fingerprints we'll ever need from the plastic bags he wore over his hands and arms.'

'That's promising. But no matches?'

'Nothing from Moscow.'

'Further afield?'

He grimaced. 'The violent crimes record division of the Moscow Fingerprint Bureau survived the fighting more or less intact. But some of the provincial records have been badly damaged. If he originally committed crimes in, say, Novosibirsk we haven't much chance of a match. Who knows, we may strike lucky.'

'There were definite traces of semen on her thigh, Dr Karlova said.'

'We've troubles there too. The Forensic Medicine Centre was evacuated from Moscow during the war. We've only just got it back. Dr Karlova will be sending semen slides and fibre samples to them this morning.'

'What happened to the earlier cases?'

'The doctor had some private arrangement. Everything was a bit rough and ready then, Chief. We had to manage as best we could.'

'So . . . the search around the area of the plinth?'

'Very fruitful. In fact, we have victim identification. And we have the location of the initial attack.'

'You found the handbag?'

'On the edge of the wasteground. Wedged where it had fallen in the rubble. Say twenty to twenty-five metres from the plinth. Within less than a metre of where you predicted it would be.'

I grunted. It wasn't my remembrance that I'd been so prescient. 'What was in it?'

'Contents of bag: make-up, cigarettes, twenty-five roubles. Lydia Primalova, aged seventeen, born Moscow Presnya. Employed as a cleaner at the Stakovsky Flag Company.'

'That's the factory next to where she was killed?'

He nodded. 'We're checking her shift times. Maybe she was working late. Probably walking home to the tower block on the corner of Pavlova Street where she lived. I've sent Bitov and Yakunin to the parents or neighbours.'

'Let's see the bag.'

'I'll check if it's back from Forensics.'

While Dronsky was away I contemplated taking up smoking again, decided I took enough risks as it was, and instead counted off thirty seconds' closed eye rest as I had been taught to do in the navy. I'd reached twenty-five, muscles relaxing, tension oozing away, when a weight from on high thudded into my lap.

I yelled out loud and leapt to my feet, scraping my knees against the underside of the desk. Only the sinister hiss of the beast, by now skulking behind the filing cabinet, told me what had happened.

The door swung open and Dronsky came back with a black plastic sack. He stopped in the doorway and looked at me anxiously. 'You all right, Chief? You look as though you've just seen a ghost.'

'Old navy technique,' I said, sitting down. 'Thirty seconds' closed eye rest. Drains the blood from the head. Leaves you pale but refreshed.'

'Catnap?' he said. 'Good idea if you can do it.' He fished out the girl's purse and placed it on the table. A simple brown cloth bag with a black stitched design.

'Any fingerprints on the bag?'

'None other than her own. Various smudges from the past.' From square brown envelopes he took objects which he laid on the table in two lines. A slim imitation tortoiseshell face powder compact. A lipstick. A packet of

American Camel cigarettes, open, three smoked. Twenty-five roubles in three fives and a ten. And a packet of monthly pills.

'Contraception pills?' I picked up the plastic envelope and studied the days marked on the shiny metallised surface. In the plastic circles for the first week the pills were unused. 'Lydia Primalova seems to have started on the pills, or at least on these pills, just ten days ago. And took the last one like a good girl yesterday morning.' I looked up at Dronsky. 'German make. They're expensive, aren't they?'

He smiled spectrally. 'Depends on your priorities, Chief.'

'This girl works as a cleaner in a factory. Unless German contraceptive pills in Moscow are one tenth of what they are in Murmansk, Lydia couldn't afford them herself.'

Dronsky pursed his lips. 'You're thinking about a protector. An older man?'

'Something like that.' I got up. 'Have you got transport?' I asked.

'A pool car.'

'Good. Mine's kaput. Let's go and find out some more about this girl.'

We walked out into the Murder Room together 'What about Gromek, the night-watchman?' I said to Dronsky. 'Did they test his clothing for blood?'

'He was clean.'

'I thought he would be. Have you released him?'

Dronsky nodded. Was he embarrassed? 'What is it Dronsky? Did you question him yourself?'

'Yes, Chief.' The words were drawn out slowly.

'You mean he saw something?'

'He *claims* he saw the killer.'

'Why the hell didn't you tell me? *Did* he see anything?'

'I got him working with an artist on an identikit.'

The adrenalin pumped. 'He saw the man? Why didn't he tell me that?'

'Drunk or sober, Chief, Gromek's crazy. You'd better see what he gave us. It's not a picture we're going to want to release to the general public.'

We had just passed through the swing doors into reception. From the entrance to one of the rooms that led off the hall came shouts and the wailing of women. About twenty or thirty civilians were crowded at the door of the identikit room, pushing and shoving to get a look at something inside.

'Oh my God, no!' Dronsky ran forward, yelling at the crowd. 'Back away . . . Back away from there!'

I followed him as he elbowed his way through. It wasn't difficult to understand the agitation of the crowd. The night-watchman's version of the killer was propped up on a desk, facing the open door. Indulging his own weird sense of humour, Gromek had outlined the Monstrum of everybody's nightmare.

From today Gromek's vision would be fixed in the imaginings of the people of Red Presnya. From today the Monstrum would have a physical presence – a bald, stunted, broad-shouldered, shambling figure. A knowing, evil smile. A huge face. A great dome of a forehead and the tiny deep-set eyes of a milk-fattened child.

16

'Are you a lunatic? Are you a drunk? Or are you just an anarchistic rumour-monger with no conscience whatsoever?'

Gromek raised an apologetic eyebrow. 'Under pressure, I would confess to a little of each, Inspector.'

We stood in the wooden hut with the factory lift housing smelling strongly of hot oil and Gromek handed me his bottle.

I took it and drank it until I saw the alarm spread on his face. There was still some left in the bottom. I walked out onto the flat section of roof, swung my arm and released the bottle to let it describe a slowly tumbling arc against the blue sky.

The groan behind me was deeply felt. The bottle shattered on the wasteground below and I turned back to Gromek. 'You've got another in reserve in there.'

'No.'

'You're lying, Night-watchman Gromek. Lying to a police officer.'

'Not *really* lying,' he said desperately.

'You have another bottle in the hut.'

'Yes.' He lowered his voice. 'Yes, I have.'

'You want me to look?'

'Please, Inspector, no . . .'

He turned. 'There's more than one perhaps,' I said. 'I'm prepared to have a search made.'

He sighed then disappeared into the hut. Through the glass roof panels I could see the lines of girls working at their benches, heads bent over their sewing machines. I had walked through there to the roof staircase a few moments ago, among the bales of rolled white flags. The manager who conducted me from the foot of the staircase to the roof where Gromek was to be found told me that, with a further factory planned across in the zoo administrative building, Red Presnya would become the biggest single centre of flag manufacture in the Moscow *oblast*. His voice had dropped as he confided: 'Next year we plan to solicit foreign orders from all over the world.'

'For Russian flags?'

He looked at me as if I were an unbeliever.

On the roof, Gromek returned from his hut, disconsolate, with two bottles. I took them from him and stood them on the parapet. 'Can we talk about what you saw last night?'

'About anything you like, Inspector. You've found my weak spot.' He grinned tentatively. I found I liked the lunatic Gromek but it was too early to let him guess. I took a backhanded swipe at one of the bottles and toppled it over the coping.

The grin faded and he winced at the faint sound of the bottle smashing below. 'I described what the artist was expecting me to describe. I could feel him drawing it out of me. Sometimes I'm just mad, Inspector. Irresponsible. I didn't think anything of it. I certainly didn't think anybody would see it except a few militiamen.' He paused. 'But I did think it might bring you yourself round to see me.'

'You wanted to speak to me?'

'At the station it was bedlam. A madhouse. What I have to say is for you alone.'

'All right,' I said, resting my weight on the parapet, my hand next to the last bottle. 'Start from the beginning. Did you see the girl leaving the factory?'

He frowned.

'You didn't know the victim worked here? Lydia Primalova. A cleaner.'

'Oh no.' His face took on a tortured look. 'Oh no . . .'

I waited while he sucked in deep breaths. Then he glanced at the remaining bottle and when I nodded, reached for it quickly, unscrewed the cap and drank. After a moment's hesitation he offered the bottle to me. I shook my head.

'I didn't know her that well, Inspector,' he said slowly. 'Does her . . . family know?'

'I sent someone round as soon as we discovered her address.' I paused. 'So you didn't see her leave?'

He puffed out his cheeks in anguish. 'Lydia wouldn't have been working late, if that's what you're thinking, Inspector. Cleaners finish at eight or nine o'clock.'

'So what would she have been doing here?'

'It's possible,' he said carefully, 'that she might have been meeting her sister.'

'At past one o'clock in the morning?'

He shrugged.

'Listen, Gromek,' I said. 'I get the marked feeling that you're heading for trouble.'

'I get that feeling too, Inspector.'

'So let's have some straight answers. Did you see Lydia last night?'

'No. That I swear. I heard her heels. I leaned over the coping here to look down, but for whatever reason, my balance was not too good. I pulled back. It was just a girl passing.'

'You must hear a thousand women pass here on an average evening . . .'

'The alluring click of high heels,' he said desperately.

'Gromek, I'm asking you. Why did you choose to hang over the parapet to look at this particular girl?'

'Chance. Drunken libidinousness.'

I glared at him. 'You're holding something back, Gromek. You're saying you saw nothing.'

'Except the Monstrum himself perhaps.'

'Listen, Gromek,' I said, reaching threateningly for the vodka.

'No, Inspector.' He hugged the bottle to him, 'No huge *monstrum* face, no evil tiny eyes. Just a man. Down there.'

'Where exactly were you standing?'

'Here.' He pointed and I moved along the gully a little to be in the same spot. 'I first saw him about ten minutes before I heard the girl's footsteps. He was standing on the corner there, waiting.'

My heart was thumping. 'You got a good look at him.'

'It was dark, there's just one factory light that works down there. And I was drunk.'

'What did you see, Gromek?' I said slowly.

He drank again from the bottle. 'A man of middle height.'

'One metre seventy . . . say?'

He nodded. 'He wore a long overcoat. Perhaps even of good quality.'

'Why do you say that?

'An impression. It seemed to hang well. The skirts swung as he walked back and forth. Like an officer's greatcoat.'

Was this the man who could afford to give his girl-friend contraceptive pills? 'Like an officer's greatcoat. Why do you say that, Gromek? Were you once an officer, yourself?'

'A lifetime ago, Inspector.'

'What else about him?'

'He carried a bag, a small case. Not slim. Square. More like a lunchbox. Unusual.'

Big enough for a set of knives, I was thinking.

'Big enough for a set of knives,' Gromek said. 'Military surgeons carry such boxes.'

'You were a military surgeon?'

'I was a specialist officer, medical branch. But I promise you my connection with surgery was minimal,' he said hurriedly.

'The man on the corner . . . you saw his face?'

'He was wearing a fur hat. There was little I could see for certain. No glasses. No beard or moustache. The best I can do, Inspector.'

'All right. The man walks up and down as if waiting. Then what?'

'I went back to get another bottle. It wasn't a night to bring a chair out and sit up here on my terrace as I do sometimes.'

'Lydia . . . ?'

'I heard a girl's footsteps a few minutes later.'

'And came out onto the roof?'

'The man, I noticed, was still there. But he had stopped pacing. He was looking towards the girl, or at least towards where the footsteps were coming from.'

'Did he make a gesture? Raise a hand? Anything to suggest they had arranged to meet?'

'By then I was no longer looking at him. I was hanging over the parapet as I described. And nearly toppled over.'

'You went back into the hut?'

'Yes.' He paused. 'I did think I heard a cry a moment or two later. Or was that earlier? Inspector, I don't know.'

'Think.'

Gromek's face contorted. 'I heard the scream first, Inspector.'

'*Before* you heard the girl's footsteps.'

'Yes. Some few minutes before, as it seems to me.' He shook his head. 'Too much vodka. How could I have heard the girl scream before I heard her footsteps?'

'She wasn't running away? What you heard weren't running footsteps?'

'No.'

'Did you leave the hut again in the next few minutes?'

'You mean did I see him carrying her towards the Stalin plinth? No.'

'What brought you out of the hut again?'

'Nellie Christiakova's scream. That's a scream I remember for certain. But that was perhaps twenty minutes later.'

'Nellie Christiakova was the young woman who found the body.'

'She's also,' he said slowly, 'Lydia Primalova's sister.'

'My God.'

Our eyes met. 'Yes,' he said.

'What was she doing here at that time of night?'

Gromek looked down at his feet.

'I'm not the vice squad,' I said. I watched him. 'Or any other petty crime squad. I'm investigating a murder, Gromek. That's all. You understand.'

He nodded.

'You have my word.'

'You must talk to Nellie. Let her tell you.'

'I will.'

'Nellie had just loaded up her van . . .'

'You mean she has something going here at the plant.'

'A few bales of cloth only. Doesn't everybody have something going somewhere?'

'I'm investigating a murder. Four murders . . .'

'Exactly. So you'll have no interest in Nellie's business activities.'

'Probably not.' I reached into my pocket for a five-rouble note and slid it between the big knuckles clasping the bottle. 'For the vodka,' I said.

He sketched a bow but his face was drawn and tense. 'Poor Lydia,' he said. 'Who could imagine it. So anxious to better herself . . .'

'Materially?' I was thinking of a rich lover.

'Materially? No, she was not at all like Nellie. I meant spiritually. She wasn't an educated girl by any means . . .' He paused. 'Yes, she always hoped to find herself spiritually. To find what she called the truth.'

*

138

The wasteland looked better by daylight. A little better. Most important was that I was able to get my bearings properly for the first time. The area was a rough square. To the north there was the flag factory wall and the cracked and broken road running alongside it that Lydia walked along. At the far end of the factory wall was the street corner where Gromek's waiting man had been positioned. Low-rise apartments with their facing walls missing made up the other sides of the square. And here, the Stalin plinth which had once stood on a street corner before the shelling had levelled the buildings around it. From plinth to factory wall across the rubble was no distance. Even at night, if Gromek had looked out a few moments after he heard the girl passing he would have had a grandstand view of the whole gory vivisection.

I followed Dronsky to a point about twenty metres from the plinth. 'The bag was found there, Chief—' he pointed down into a large crack in the rubble. 'If Gromek the night-watchman is telling the truth . . .'

'He is.'

'If he's telling the truth, the girl walked along the side of the factory wall, and was caught by the Monstrum here, just twenty metres or so from the plinth.'

I looked back at the base of the Stalin monument. A militiaman stood beside it. In other days he wouldn't have had his shapka pushed back from his glistening brow, nor would he have been smoking a cigarette.

I tried to imagine the terror of the girl as she was engulfed in plastic-covered arms, dragged or carried that twenty metres, gasping for breath, the maniac's teeth sunk deep in her windpipe. What manner of creature were we talking about? Could I, Constantin Vadim, even in my maddest dreams, conceive of doing this, of pleasuring myself in this way? I shook my head. We Russians are, of course, known to be preoccupied with madness. With reason. God, how I longed for Murmansk and petty thieves and fences like Vassikin!

I was looking down at the rubble at my feet. There was a brown stain on a broken slab of concrete not a yard from where the girl's bag had been found. I didn't need to be an experienced homicide investigator to realise that it was blood. I should, of course, have ordered the area surrounded by yellow tape as they do in the West. I should have had a scene of crime squad here, sifting the dust for any clue to the monster's identity. I shrugged. We probably didn't have enough yellow tape anyway. And Sergeant Bitov was my scene of crime expert.

Dronsky had picked up a piece of timber, a broken rafter perhaps, almost a metre long and was hefting it in his hands. I knelt down and looked more closely at the concrete slab. The sunlight showed tiny black ribbons or threads of what might have been flesh within the matt brown stain. 'We need to take this to Karlova,' I said.

He pointed.

I looked up and saw a small white van running towards us. It stopped between the plinth and where we were standing and Natalya Karlova got out. What first struck me was how young she was, not more than twenty-five or twenty-six. And the way the almost summery breeze lifted her shoulder-length dark blonde hair. And the short white coat over a dark linen skirt to just above the knee. She smiled in greeting and came towards us. 'You weren't at the PM this morning,' she said, that disturbing glint of challenge in her eyes.

'Did anything new come out of it?' I asked.

'There was a single heavy blow across the back which I hadn't spotted last night among all the other excesses.'

'Delivered by something like that?'

She glanced at the length of timber in Dronsky's hand. 'Could be,' she said. 'We can check the measurements. I have a pretty clear outline of the weapon.'

'The blow to her leg and her back are from the same instrument?'

'No doubt. The outline fits perfectly. So he came up

behind, struck the first blow to her leg, failed to bring her down, struck her again across the back.'

I pointed down to the slab of stone. 'Brought her down to her knees?'

She examined the slab. 'I need to look at that in the laboratory. Perhaps you could put it in the back of my van,' she said to Dronsky. 'It's open.'

Dronsky tucked the timber baton under his arm. Lifting the slab, he began to waddle the short distance to the van. Her head was turned to watch him. There was a moment of silence broken only by Dronsky's wheezing and the scrape and slide of his blue boating shoes over the rubble.

'What did you think of our American amnesty commissioner?' Karlova said, her eyes still on Dronsky.

'I've never met an American woman before. Are they all like that, I wonder?'

She turned to me. 'I shouldn't think so. Imogen is unique.'

'Imogen? You know her?'

'I used to work in her children's clinic when I first came to Moscow. We treated injured and war-traumatised orphans. She ran the psychiatric department, I was responsible for surgery.'

There was something in her tone. Something hard. 'Are you still friends?'

'She dismissed me for incompetence.'

'Ah . . .'

She lifted her head. 'And you, Constantin. Am I to assume you don't like post-mortems?'

The subject of Dr Imogen was closed.

'I don't like morgues or casualty wards or operating theatres,' I said. 'It's nothing personal.'

'Good. Because I've an apology to make to you.'

'Forget it,' I said.

'Oh no,' she said. 'I used two ration points on a half-chicken at the station shop with my apology in mind.'

Was she laughing at me again? She stood there, her legs braced slightly apart, hands deep in her white coat, amber-coloured eyes fixed upon me. 'I thought maybe you'd like to share it with me this evening,' she said.

Not when Julia might call, or make contact somehow. 'Evenings are tight at the moment,' I said carefully.

'The apology stands anyway,' she said nonchalantly. 'Are you going back to the station?'

'I came in Dronsky's car.'

'Let me give you a lift back. Things I want to speak to you about.'

'OK.'

As we turned for the white van I saw the tall loping figure of Gromek the night-watchman crossing the rubble towards us.

'Inspector.' He was breathing heavily. 'Something I forgot. Something Nellie Christiakova wouldn't be able to tell you.'

We waited while he recovered his breath. 'She had recently joined the Church. She told me about it a week or so ago. Meetings were held on Wednesday nights, she said. So it's possible she might have just come back from a church meeting.'

'Past midnight?' the doctor said. She pursed her lips. 'It's possible, I suppose.'

'Why wouldn't Lydia's sister be able to tell me this?' I asked him.

Gromek searched in his pocket and pulled out a clay pipe. 'Lydia didn't want to tell Nellie about the church. She thought she'd disapprove.'

'Why would that be?'

'I couldn't make it out,' Gromek said. 'I wouldn't call Nellie a Christian, but I wouldn't call her an atheist bigot either.'

While I stood thinking about that, Gromek turned to Dronsky who was glaring at him. 'I'm sorry about the identikit, Deputy Dronsky,' he said. 'It wasn't much

142

of a joke. Too much alcohol makes a man see things differently.'

Dronsky pointed to the pipe. 'Too much alcohol or too much *stoke*,' he growled.

Gromek pulled his face into a grimace. '*Stoke* I could never afford, Deputy Inspector. Vodka is my mistress.'

I looked from Gromek to Dronsky. '*Stoke*?' I said, 'what is *stoke*?'

Karlova plucked me by the sleeve. 'I'll explain,' she said.

'Look after him, Doctor,' Gromek said. 'A Moscow homicide inspector who doesn't know what *stoke* is has an innocence that's worth preserving.'

'*Stoke*, to *stoke*, to get *stoked* up ...' Karlova was intoning as if she were reading from an addicts' dictionary as we bounced along in the white van. '*Stoke* is today's drug of choice for Moscow's young. It has a cocaine base and an LSD graft and can hit you harder than the Monstrum's timber baton. Recreationally, directed sexual fantasies are the name of the game.'

'So if they can play it out on *stoke* why are they still raping on the streets?'

She shrugged.

'Have you ever tried it?' I asked.

'Experimentally.' She smiled. 'I am a doctor, after all.'

'And ... ?'

She glanced at me bleakly. 'I'd sooner fondle a flesh and blood man,' she said.

'What did you want to speak to me about?'

She glanced at me and then looked back to the road ahead. 'I want to know who you are,' she said, as if it were the simplest question in the world.

It was the way I decided to play it: simple, direct. I spread my hands. 'Who I am? Constantin Vadim, Homicide Inspector, Moscow 13.'

'And the rest?'

'The rest is not that much. Born Murmansk, 1977. Son of a fishing boat captain drowned at sea, 1992. Mother, English teacher, nurse in the National army, decorated by General Romanov himself, killed in action Pinsk front . . . How am I doing?'

'It's you I want to know about.'

'Me? What are you looking for – an in-depth appraisal?'

'Just go ahead,' she said.

'How can I do myself justice? Conscientious, energetic, loyal . . . that sort of thing?'

'I'm serious.'

I glanced at her face. She was.

'OK. Department of English Studies, University of Murmansk. Navy service, submarines. Joined militia . . .'

'Joined what?'

She had heard me. 'Joined the militia,' I said.

'Or was it the Cheka you joined?' she said with quiet deliberation.

My head jerked up. 'Good God, no. Is that what you think?'

'That you're an officer of the Cheka? Yes,' she said coolly. 'It's what a lot of people think around District 13. Especially your assistant, Dronsky.'

'Dronsky . . . ?' Ah, some things at least were explained. 'Is that what he thinks?'

'Why not? Why shouldn't he think you're Cheka? Why shouldn't we all think that? You arrive from the far north, pretending to be a trained inspector. But you're not a homicide man.'

'What's it to you what I am?'

'I'll just have to be careful.'

'Careful?'

'I wouldn't want to fall madly in love with a man who's a Cheka officer, that's all. Surely you can understand that, whatever you really are?'

My mouth fell open. *Fall in love*. What was this, Mother Moscow big city talk?

144

'Don't be flattered unduly, Constantin,' she flashed a quick smile. 'You may think there's not much to commend you. And you may well be right. But at least you're a man. Not at all bad looking. And presumably with all important items functioning . . .'

I shrugged agreement.

'All I'm saying, Constantin,' she said, smiling broadly, 'is that should, by any chance, my lustful glance wander in your direction, I'd just like to know the decks are clear, that's all.'

'Well, pretty clear,' I said uncertainly. 'In that I'm *not* a Cheka officer and all important items *are* functioning. I'm prepared to offer assurances on those two scores at least.'

'Good,' she said briskly, swinging the van to a stop outside District 13 station. 'Then we can take it from there, can't we?'

17

I got a lorry bus to the Park Café. People who were buying, people who could afford to buy, were inside, beyond the steamed glass windows. The tables out on the terrace were occupied by small groups of refugee vagrants, families, young men legless or armless, begging on their injuries from the war. I walked between the tables quickly, my eyes trying to penetrate the steamy glass of the café's elegant, bowed Alexandrine windows. So much was I concentrating that my toe caught a step and I tripped, reeling to regain my balance among the cheers and clapping of the vagrants.

As I steadied myself against a leafless plane tree, I caught sight of her, sitting alone at one of the furthest tables on the terrace: the Siberian girl who had acted as go-between for Julia in Murmansk.

I stood for a moment, my back to the tree. She sat with her chin on her fist, watching a group of children playing in front of her. Stay calm, Costya, I told myself. Her head turned; the dark eyes above the high-cheekboned Siberian face wandered across the terrace before returning to the antics of the children. She wore an old blue anorak, jeans, trainers, a girl utterly unremarkable in the drab world of Moscow. And yet I had to be careful. There were, as Madame Raisa said, so many false Dimitrys. Was it possible that my little Siberian girl had just been arrested, turned by the Cheka, delivered here to the Park Café to trap me . . . ?

I shrugged irritably. This indecision, Constantin, does not become you. The note was from Julia – I had no doubt about that. She had played the Vassily/Sonya game for the very purpose of assuring me that it was genuine. That it was really Julia, Julia in desperate need. And this Siberian was the girl who had led me to her once before. I pushed away from the plane tree and walked across the terrace.

Almost immediately, a heavy hand seized my arm. Alarm paralysed me. I turned and found myself staring into the bearded face of a beggar. 'A few roubles,' he said. 'I once had a wife, a family, a house to live in. Now I beg you for a few roubles.'

I dug into my pockets and gave him ten roubles. His grip was still tight on my arm. 'Let me tell you my story,' he said. 'You seem to be a man with a heart. Rare today in Moscow . . .'

I shook my head.

'Why do you give then?' he asked. 'If you have no interest in my story?'

I unclasped his hand. 'I give from fear, brother,' I said. 'Forgive me.'

His eyes on mine, he turned away. The Siberian girl had been watching us. When I reached the table, she was smiling grimly. 'If you could have seen your face,' she said. She stood up and stretched to whisper in my ear. 'Inspector Constantin Vadim thought his hour had come.'

'There's nothing so shameful in that,' I said. But there was a strident note in my voice. I recognised the fear that runs in Russian blood. In the old days my father had spent six years in a camp *for no reason he ever discovered*. When he returned he had about him a nervousness that infected the whole family, infected me throughout my childhood. No, not nervousness, something more frightening. A sense of *guilt*.

I turned and walked with the girl away from the table on the terrace. 'Where is she?' I said. 'Where is Julia?'

'Patience.' Her eyes were everywhere. With hardly a movement of her head, she was checking the pathway in front of us, the overgrown lake with its ruined summer-house, the open spaces before the trees and bushes began.

'What is she doing in Moscow? I thought she was safe somewhere in the West?'

'It's a long story,' the girl said.

'Then take me to her. She can tell me herself.'

She shook her head.

'Listen,' I said, 'there's an amnesty, for God's sake.'

'Not for Julia.'

'I have specifically checked. With a friend who's a senior figure in the Okhrana.'

She smiled at me in the maddeningly superior way that Julia's bright young friends at university used to smile at me.

'All right,' I said. 'Of course you know better. You know the government's intentions better than the Cheka. You've a message for me. Money?' It was all I could think of. 'Does she need more money?'

A pair of ducks cut through the air and touched down on the surface of the lake. The girl seemed to be absorbed by the pattern of overlapping chevrons of rippling water as the birds came to a stop.

'Is it money?' I repeated.

'It isn't that simple. It's not money Julia needs.'

'What then?'

She walked beside me for a few paces without answering.

'What?' I said desperately.

'A doctor.'

My stomach turned over. I took the girl by the arm, shaking her. 'What's wrong with her, for God's sake?'

'All I can tell you is that she needs a doctor. Someone with some surgical knowledge. Someone who can be trusted.'

'Trusted to treat a known Anarchist officer in secret? How in God's name can I find someone to do that? If Julia presents herself as an amnesty applicant . . .'

'She's in no condition to move.'

I took a breath. 'Then I'll register her at my station . . .
No. Better than that, I'll let my friend in the Cheka know
where she is. Tell him she needs medical assistance.'

'Julia said she could trust you to tell nobody.'

My head was spinning. 'She said that?'

'Yes. She said you would find a doctor. Somehow.'

I felt suddenly, unbearably, hot.

'You'll do it?'

'I must know what's wrong.'

The girl twisted away from me. 'I know no more than
I've told you,' she said. 'Meet me outside the old zoo
gates with your doctor.'

'I have no doctor,' I said, anxiety flooding me. 'I've
just arrived in Moscow. I know no one, for God's
sake!'

'Julia trusts you.' The Siberian's eyes narrowed as if to
doubt her chief's wisdom. 'She relies on you implicitly,'
she said.

'How serious is it? Tell me that at least.'

The girl looked at me with hard, pursed lips. With
contempt too. 'Serious,' she said. 'A car accident.'

I changed tack. 'I'm not asking for myself,' I lied. 'Any
doctor is going to need more than that. When did it
happen? Is she in danger? A doctor is going to need
more facts.'

'The zoo gates,' the girl said. 'Tonight, at midnight.
I'll be waiting.'

She ran. She ran like an animal in flight, the long coat
billowing behind her, running round the gravel path that
edged the lake. Causing a flurry of wing and water among
the ducks. In seconds she had reached the cover of the
shrubs and bushes and was gone.

I took the lorry bus back to Red Presnya. I sat down on
the tailgate and dangled my legs as we trundled across
Moscow. I could perhaps invent a car accident of my

149

own . . . could perhaps pass Julia off as the victim . . . but before she could be accepted in hospital, she would need papers. Did she have false papers with her? If not, how many days would it take me to get some made? In Murmansk I could have done it in an afternoon. Here in Moscow it would take a week – and probably land me in gaol.

There was another factor. Julia's face was well known. More in the Petersburg area where her division had operated than here in Moscow, certainly. But she would still have been shown on Moscow Television when it was in Anarchist hands for two years of the war. She was one of their heroes, after all.

I was sweating in my coat. False papers, staged accidents – I didn't believe any of my schemes. I knew well enough the fact I was avoiding. I had one single hope. I knew no doctors in Moscow but Natalya Karlova.

It had to be her.

I dropped off the lorry bus before the 13th District and walked the last few hundred yards to the station.

Dronsky was already back, hovering at the door of my office. I looked at his pale worried eyes, the stubbled cheeks, his boating shoes and khakis with, today, a cheap sports jacket, too brightly crosshatched. I wished I could tell him I was no danger to him, tell him I was not an officer of the Cheka. But the life I was living argued against it. It was safer to let the poor man worry. I lifted my head.

He made no mention of my absence for two hours. 'I was wondering, Inspector, whether you wanted me to conduct the interview with Nellie Christiakova.'

'No. We'll do it together now,' I said. 'Anything else?'

'Yukunin and Bitov have prepared a list of men with previous sexual offences living in the Presnya area.'

'I'll see it. One phone call, then send them in.'

When he left I picked up the phone and dialled the medical examiner's office at the far end of the building.

Karlova answered. For the first time I registered that she had a slight southern accent. 'This is Vadim,' I said.

'Not another one? Another body.'

'No.' I hesitated. 'I was wondering if I could come over to your office.'

'Do,' she said. 'Come right away. You have, in any case, something to sort out here.'

'What's that?'

'I'd prefer you saw for yourself.'

I got directions from Dronsky and made my way across reception to the corridor leading to the pathology labs. I was following the signs when I heard raised voices and looked up to see Natalya and Dr Shepherd confronting each other.

'I'm asking you to extend me a professional courtesy, nothing more,' Dr Shepherd was saying.

They were two remarkable-looking women. Both formidably angry, but there was a difference. Dr Shepherd's features were composed and coolly furious; Natalya's face was black as thunder. She turned towards me. 'Technically, the senior homicide inspector is responsible for the body. It's his decision.'

The American doctor turned more slowly, with a smile. 'I was simply asking for permission to view the body of the Monstrum's latest victim.'

'Why would you want to do that?' I said in genuine bewilderment.

'It helps to profile a murderer if one is able to examine his work.'

'Is that necessary?'

'Not absolutely necessary, but it might help.'

'I see absolutely no reason for you to be examining the body,' Natalya said fiercely.

'A professional interest. "The child is father to the man." I've quoted it to you enough in the past, Natalya.'

151

She turned to me. 'We were discussing, Inspector, the bridge between the traumas of severely disturbed children and the adult consequences – theft, rape, murder ... Your Monstrum is obviously at the extreme range of anti-social behaviour. I thought, as one scientist to another, Dr Karlova might allow me to view the worst-case result of failure on the part of people like myself.'

It seemed reasonable enough to me. If you like that sort of thing.

'I'm refusing the request,' Natalya said bluntly. She turned to me. 'I hope you will support my refusal.'

'Natalya,' Dr Shepherd said quietly. 'If that's your decision, then OK. But it's time we put the past behind us.'

Natalya faced me. 'Will you support my decision? Yes or no?'

I looked from one to the other. 'I'm sorry,' I said to the American, after a moment.

She looked at me with a wry smile. 'I understand.' She paused. 'At least I think I do.' With a slow and defiantly hostile nod to Natalya she walked slowly down the corridor.

I watched her go. 'What the hell is all this about?' I said as she disappeared.

'It's about Dr Shepherd trying to involve herself in everything I do. When I started in Moscow, I was her protégée ... Dr Shepherd doesn't find it easy that I have a department of my own. A professional interest, she calls it! She wants to supervise, to criticise ... !' She stamped her foot in a conscious effort to calm down, then smiled up at me. 'Sorry,' she said, exhaling a breath that shuddered her shoulders. 'Imogen has that sort of effect on me. She shouldn't, but she does.' She turned to go, then stopped. 'You called me earlier. Was there something you wanted?'

'I was wondering how you'd go for a change of mind. For tonight.'

She raised her eyebrows. 'The schedule not so tight as you thought?'

'Something like that.'

'I'm not proud, Vadim,' she said. 'You couldn't resist my chicken. Let's leave it at that.'

I took her address.

She moved towards the swinging door to the lab, pushed it part way open and stopped. 'I'm glad you're coming,' she said.

'I'm glad too.'

She puffed air, or maybe even a kiss, at me and let the door swing to.

I was hardly back in my office when I saw, through the glass panel, Dronsky approaching. I closed my eyes. I needed thinking time. Julia was injured. I saw her image against my closed lids. Her face pale, her lips speaking some final words to me. Fool . . .

Dronsky rapped on the door and came in. Yakunin and Bitov, looking like apprentice undertakers in their Armani suits and today's black ribbon ties, followed him. There were chairs only for two, leaving Bitov to stand resting his back against the wall. Each man, I saw, carried a file. I glanced guiltily at the carry-sack hanging on the elaborate bentwood clothes stand. Three days into a serial murder case and I still hadn't read all the murder reports on the other victims.

I put it out of my mind and turned to Dronsky. 'I have to warn you,' I said, 'that I could be called away to other duties at any minute. This case would then fall entirely on your shoulders. You should be prepared for that.'

Dronsky took the announcement the way he was meant to. He nodded vigorously. 'I understand, Chief.'

Could I really be so evil? I had no reason to expect I would be called away on my stand-in duties, but the statement had the required effect on Dronsky and the two sergeants. It reinforced their view that I was a Cheka officer primarily engaged in things other than a simple serial murder in Red Presnya. It could serve to cover any time I might need for Julia.

'So what do you have for me?' I asked my deputy.

Dronsky got to his feet. We were on November heating and the day was unusually mild. His round face glistened. His jacket looked more awful than ever. The over-long sleeves fell past his knuckles and made it look like a reach-me-down from a taller brother.

He bustled about with the help of Bitov and pinned a long list to my noticeboard. The last government had tried to impose Roman script on us and Dronsky's word processor came from those days. Some schoolchildren could only read Roman when we changed back to Cyrillic; old people schooled in Cyrillic stared uncomprehendingly at City Hall notices written on Roman typewriters. This was Russia in the opening years of the new millennium.

'Do you read Roman, Inspector?' he asked me anxiously.

'With great reluctance,' I said. 'Unless I'm reading English, of course. Now what's all this about?'

'The Moscow lists for sex offenders with extreme violence were partly destroyed in the shelling, Inspector. But fortunately the Red Presnya section's more or less complete.'

I got up from my desk and stood in front of Dronsky's lists. There were three gradations of violent sex offenders. The biggest category and the mildest, Category 3, covered flashers, voyeurs and stalkers.

'Stalkers. Why are we interested in stalkers?'

'Generally harmless, I agree, Chief. Except for the woman who becomes aware she's being stalked. From then, the shadow stalking her can have a terrifying effect on her life.'

I looked at Dronsky. He suddenly sounded human. 'How often do the flashers, voyeurs and stalkers move on a stage? To physical violence.'

'More often than most people think. It's now known that they're not all the harmless old wankers they were thought to be. In fact most of them are young. And as they get older they can become more ambitious. As often as not they move up into Category 2.'

I looked at the board.

'Criminal assault or rape,' Dronsky said. 'Rape achieved by menace: blackmail, work-rape, even by threat of physical harm, a knife to the throat for example, without actual direct violence. Men who stop short of direct violence because maybe they don't hate women quite enough to take them over the edge. We're talking about two hundred or so.'

I turned to Yakunin. 'Do you think men rape women because they hate them?'

'Feminist bollocks,' Yakunin said.

'Because they fear them, perhaps?' I asked his colleague.

'Feminist bollocks,' Bitov said.

'This is not the first time you two have discussed the subject,' I said. 'What do you think, Dronsky?'

'I think Category 2 men rape the way many men steal. You got it, I want it. But there's another category, and they do hate or maybe even fear women.' He pointed to the board. 'Category 1. Rape with violence. Often with mutilation. Sometimes with murder.'

We stood staring at the board in silence. 'But the fact that we have the names means that none of these would be at liberty,' I said.

Dronsky shook his head. 'When the Anarchists controlled Moscow they emptied the jails and drafted prisoners into the army. Penal battalions. We've no idea how many of those men were killed, left Moscow or are even back here in Presnya.'

I groaned. 'How many are we talking about?'

'We only have fifty-one names here currently at liberty. Fourteen are back in jail. Bitov, who was born in Presnya, tells me three names he knows for certain are dead, although unrecorded.'

'Fifty-one minus seventeen.' I looked at Dronsky's list. 'Thirty-four Category 1 men who might or might not be in Moscow.' I looked up at Bitov. 'You were born here?'

'Yes, sir.'

'And Yakunin?'

'I grew up east of the Urals, Inspector. But I came to District 13 before the war. Between us Bitov and me have worked over most of the villains in Presnya.'

'But maybe not this one.'

'With respect, Chief,' Bitov said, 'he's on that list somewhere. Or he's a completely new arrival. If he's a new arrival we've got different problems. But if he's an old hand he'll be on the deputy inspector's list.'

'Maybe.' I looked at the two detectives. 'All right, we'll go the obvious route first. Get out on the street this afternoon. Start on the list of thirty-four. See if you can establish that any of them have been seen in Presnya in the last weeks.'

They clicked their heels respectfully and left the room. V.I. Lenin slid in before they closed the door. He stopped a foot or two inside the office and scratched at his goatee. I sat for a moment looking down at my desk. When I lifted my head I was staring into Dronsky's pale eyes.

'The inspector's not convinced by the category approach?'

I twisted my mouth. 'I can see the logic part of the way,' I said slowly. 'The slow burn, the movement through petty sex crime to beating women . . . to violent rape. Until . . .'

Dronsky was nodding.

'Until some time during the war he makes his first all-out attack.' I paused. 'Cutting up a girl, removing half her innards.' I sat for a moment. 'That's where I come to a full stop.'

'Why?'

'Because common sense tells me that there are two *different* rapists. Your Category 2, minimum violence rapist, rapes because he wants to screw that woman. Because he's excluded by his physical appearance, race or economic circumstances from screwing a woman like that. With our Monstrum, I can't help believing that the rape is incidental. I can't help feeling we have someone with a burning contempt for human life. Particularly female human life. And it's a new discovery for him. I don't think we're looking for past offenders. I don't think a man *grows* into being the Monstrum, Dronsky.'

'He might.' A touch of stubbornness.

'Let's hope the sergeants turn up something from the top of the list,' I said. 'We'll leave the rest on the wall in case any name hits us in the eye. But you and I, Dronsky, I think we're looking for someone totally different. In the meantime let's go and see Nellie Christiakova.' I looked down at the cat. 'And, Dronsky—' I said.

'Yes, Chief.'

'I've finally decided. Get rid of the cat.'

'I thought so,' Dronsky said.

'Thought what?'

'You wouldn't get on with him. Your predecessor never liked him either. V.I. Lenin had a bad time with him. If things weren't going well . . .'

'He'd take it out on the cat.'

'Something like that. Shame, because I could see he was settling down again.'

I looked from Dronsky to V.I. Lenin. 'OK,' I said. 'For the moment, keep the cat.'

18

Nellie Christiakova was a red-faced woman of about forty with a Moscow accent that stung the eyes. She sat in her small apartment surrounded with stolen goods and offered stolen vodka to two inspectors from District 13. We both accepted.

'This room alone would send me down for two years,' she said. I looked around and she shrugged. 'What difference does it make now?' She took a deep breath. 'The fiendish bastard,' she said. Tears started in her eyes. She put her hand to her head. 'For Christ's sake, I saw her there on that plinth and didn't recognise my own sister.'

We waited a few moments while she blew her nose and took another pull at her vodka. She was plump, pretty in an open-air, peasant sort of way, though I doubt if she'd seen a green field since she was born. 'Tell it to us in your own words,' Dronsky said. 'What sort of girl was she?'

'Well, not like me, you could say that without even thinking about it. Never got down to life . . .' She glanced at the rolls of flag cloth stacked round the room. 'If you see what I mean. Spent her spare time mooning about, reading books.' She got up and passed me a handful of cheap pamphlets, the sort of things I'd seen on sale in the airport or at the bus kiosks – *Find Your Way in Life*, *Find Truth with Jesus*, *Find Hope with New Theosophy* . . .

'Most nights she'd sooner stay at home and read.'

'What about boyfriends?' Dronsky asked.

'She talked a lot about finding a boyfriend but she talked a lot about finding everything else. She was very, very young, Inspector. Not to look at . . .' Nellie handed us down a framed picture of a smiling girl looking up from a book. She wore glasses and her hair was pulled lightly back behind her head. There was no sign of the rabbit-teeth look I'd seen as she lay on the plinth.

'Her favourite picture of herself,' Nellie said. 'She wanted to be a student, really – but there was no money for that.'

'Did you know she was on the pill?' I said.

'Never! Lydia on the pill? Is that really true?'

'Yes,' I said. 'I think there were probably some things about Lydia even you weren't aware of. You don't know where she went last night?'

'Just out. With a friend from the factory, I think she said. I didn't ask. She didn't like me asking. She'd go to meetings and lectures sometimes. I wasn't interested in all that rubbish.'

'You know nothing about her attending a church?'

'A church? Why should she do that? And where's the churches open at one o'clock in the morning, tell me?'

'Tell us about last night.'

She looked from one of us to the other. 'I've got the use of an old van,' she said cautiously. 'Gromek's told you what I use it for.'

'Yes,' I said.

'Registration,' Dronsky said. 'For elimination purposes.'

'Just tell us the make and colour, Nellie,' I said.

'It's an old Ford Kiev. Blue.'

'OK.'

'First of all I should tell you that I'd arranged to meet Lydia at about one o'clock by the factory gates. She said she'd be on her way back about one so I said I'd pick her up.'

'About one at the factory gate?'

'Yes. I picked up the van and by about a quarter after midnight I'm driving down past the Planetarium to the factory.'

159

I leaned forward. 'At that time of night,' I said, 'is the area around the factory empty?'

She shook her head. 'How can you empty the streets of the beggars and the homeless? People on night work, early morning traders? And the tarts, of course. Although they mostly stay over where the trade is, along the Bullfrog.'

Dronsky grunted and she poured him another vodka.

'By the time I drove into the factory yard it was probably half-past twelve. Close to. The street, I noticed, was clear. The back fire exit was open by arrangement. The rolls I was to load were stacked in the corridor.'

'Rolls?'

'Of flag material. I sell on the rolls to a dressmaker sweatshop. You know, three dozen Uzbek women working eighteen hours a day and pleased of the chance. Of course, since we've adopted the white flag it's been a great boon to business,' she said. 'When the Anarchists held Presnya, it was terrible. Can you imagine? There's only a certain amount of black cloth the market will take, even when the shelling's at its heaviest.'

'So business has picked up under the white flag.'

She took another slurp of her vodka. 'Without a shadow of a doubt. In any case we've always been Nats in Presnya. Russia for the Russians is our motto.'

'You and Gromek loaded the rolls of material. That took how long?'

'Under half an hour. Before one o'clock we were finished.'

'And you drove off?'

'I would have, but Gromek proposed I take five hundred metres of undyed flag cord.'

'Flag cord?'

'Best-quality single-twist nylon rope. In fifty-metre lengths. We haggled, agreed a price and I said I'd take it. But he didn't have the length cut ready yet. He said it'd take a few minutes so I walked outside to see if Lydia had arrived early.'

'Outside the factory gate? So the plinth would have been less than fifty metres away.'

'That's right.' She struggled to control herself. 'It hadn't happened. There was nothing on the plinth, I'm sure of it. I had a van behind me with a stack of stolen goods in it. I was keeping my eyes peeled for the militia. No, I would have seen her. She wasn't lying there then.'

Dronsky's pen was scratching away in his notebook. He stopped and looked up. 'But there were people about?'

'Not a lot. And with the ruins all round you you can't be sure who's there and who isn't. People sleep any old hours these days. Most nights the Bullfrog district's busier than during the day. Life's like that now. Girls, young boys selling their asses. People dealing in jewellery and dollars. People selling cemetery lists . . .'

'Cemetery lists?' I said.

'How else are you going to trace a missing husband? Visit every cemetery yourself?'

The drink was making her ramble. I touched her arm. 'Go on with your story, Nellie.'

She closed her eyes, taking herself back to last night. 'I turned to go back into the factory and it was then I looked and really did get a fright.'

'What did you see?'

'On the far corner of the factory road, at the intersection there, I saw a car, no headlights, edge forward and stop. I thought – this is it. Militia. I crouched down behind an old water tank and watched.'

'Could you say what sort of a car?' Dronsky asked her, pen raised.

'A big car, limousine size. Official looking. I didn't dare move. Then with its lights still out, the car backed away from the street corner.'

'Disappeared?'

'From my sight, anyway. But a moment or two later, a man appeared on the corner, more or less under the factory light.'

'You're not certain he came from the car.'

She lifted her shoulders. 'Not certain – certain maybe. But he appeared there within seconds of the car being backed out of sight.'

'What did you do, Nellie?'

'I was still thinking militia, but then I began to think the man didn't look militia. And if he'd been militia, he wouldn't have been alone.'

'Give us whatever description you can manage, Nellie.'

She thought. 'Medium height. He was wearing a fur hat and a long overcoat, collar turned up against the wind. In his right hand he was carrying a light-coloured case.' She used her hands to indicate a small attaché case. 'Squarish. And the light was reflecting off it. The street light. It was metal. Some sort of metal case. Squarish, not very deep. Like a little dog kennel in shape, maybe.'

I looked at Dronsky. His lips were pursed.

'He walked back and forth,' she said. 'Waiting for something. But he's very impatient. Keeps looking at his watch.' She paused. 'By this time I've decided he's no problem . . .' Her eyebrows shot up at the foolishness of her assessment. 'I get out from behind the rubble and walk back across to the factory.'

'Did the man on the corner take any particular notice?'

'Men do, don't they, when they see a woman walking alone at night.'

'What did he do?'

'Stopped pacing and just looked.'

'And you walked on.'

'Yes.'

'Was anybody else about?'

She screwed her face up with effort. 'No, nobody else.'

162

'All right, you went back to the factory yard.'

'The cord was all ready for loading, so I got to work.'

'But before you did that,' I said, 'you still thought it was worthwhile mentioning the waiting man to Gromek.'

She stopped. 'Just in case. He went up to take a look. That's when he heard her walking along. Heard Lydia, I mean. It must have been her.'

'You hadn't told Gromek you were meeting Lydia?'

She shook her head silently. 'He came down to the yard and said we'd better wait a while. Until the man had gone.'

'What did you do?'

'We sat around drinking for another ten minutes or so. I was nervous and maybe had more than I should have. So nervous I completely forgot about meeting Lydia.'

'Did you hear a scream, Nellie?'

She shivered. 'A shout more than a scream. But you'd be up and down all night in Presnya if you went out looking every time you heard something like that.'

'So eventually you drove out of the yard to get back on the road to the Planetarium,' I said.

'After Gromek had taken another look and seen the man had gone, yes. I went out of the gates, along the road to the corner where the man had been waiting. I looked specially. There was no man, no car. But I was really hyped up. Meeting Lydia went right out of my mind. I just wanted to get away from there as fast as I could. I turned left, came round by the plinth and that's when my headlights caught something. Somebody lying on the plinth.'

'You were sure straight away that's what it was? A woman.'

'Oh yes . . .' The rosy cheeks seemed to go pale. 'Oh yes, I was sure of that. What I couldn't see until I stopped the van was the state the poor creature was in.'

'That's when you screamed.'

'Did I? Of course I did. I reversed the van, pulling the wheel like a maniac and raced straight back to the factory.' She took up the vodka bottle, ignored Dronsky's proffered glass and poured five centimetres for herself. 'Gromek wasn't so drunk he didn't know what to do,' she said. 'He told me to drive off and get rid of the gear straight away while he called the police.' Tears began to stream down her cheeks. 'And all the time, Inspector, I never gave a thought to my own sister.'

'Until when . . . ?'

'Until I got back here.' She sat there, her mouth hanging open. 'And then the most awful, terrible thought struck me . . .'

We all three sat in silence.

'I waited an hour. Two hours. I phoned the District station but the militiaman there told me they didn't know who the girl was. I sat here, in this chair. I felt I couldn't move from it. Just sat on and on. Until it got light and the bell rang and I knew what it was going to be.' Her voice dropped almost to a whisper. 'The police to say that Lydia had been found.' She looked bleakly at us and lifted her hands in a hopeless gesture. 'The butcher! I'd seen her there on the plinth and I hadn't even recognised my own sister.'

We drove away in silence. Somewhere in the back of my mind the limousine, the pacing man, touched an image.

'What do you think, Chief?' Dronsky said.

I grunted unhelpfully.

'She hadn't heard of Lydia attending a church,' Dronsky said, 'because my guess is that there never was a church. That was just a story to tell Gromek. I see a man, like you said, Chief, an older man. He's the one who gave her the German contraceptive pills. The man waiting by the limousine.'

I didn't answer. The image was still there somewhere. The girl walking alone in the darkened streets. The limousine following. Where did that picture come from? I took one of Dronsky's cigarettes without thinking. Sat with it in my mouth while we stopped for a government bigwig at the Planetarium turning. And suddenly I had it. Or maybe I had it.

'Listen Dronsky,' I said, 'do you remember Beria? Lavrenti Beria.'

'Wasn't he one of Stalin's men? In charge of labour camps and that sort of thing?'

How short the Russian memory is! 'Mass murderer on a grand scale,' I said. 'Head of Stalin's secret police.'

It was Dronsky's turn to grunt. There had been so many mass murderers in Russian history.

'What do you know about his personal habits, Dronsky?'

He glanced at me quickly and looked back at the road. 'Beria's personal habits? Not a lot, Chief. It was before I was born.'

'We're talking about a man who could have had half the women in Moscow at the time and nobody would have dared to say a word.'

'Lucky fellow.'

'Dronsky,' I said patiently, 'Beria even had the wife of the Soviet Foreign Minister under arrest – and Molotov didn't dare to protest. What did Molotov do? Just continued seeing ambassadors, going to conferences as if his wife were at home in the kitchen cooking *blini*.'

'Those were the days.'

'Dronsky, concentrate on what I'm saying!'

'I'm trying, Chief.'

'All right, then. Lavrenti Beria, chief of the NKVD, KGB, whatever they were calling them in those days. The Cheka to us. Could have had his choice of any woman – *any* damn woman he wanted. Literally.'

'I'm with you, Chief.'

'Any woman. But it wasn't just good enough to call up

a leading ballerina, or the six o'clock news presenter or the attractive young wife of some junior minister . . .'

'No?'

'No. What turned on Lavrenti Beria, what really got those eyes glistening behind the steel-rimmed pince-nez was something else. It was the fear. That's what got Beria going. Do you know what he used to do?'

'No, Chief.'

'Night after night, he'd leave the Kremlin, Dronsky. In his limousine.'

'Limousine?'

At last.

'Exactly. With his chauffeur at the wheel, Beria would prowl around the area at the back of Red Square. When he spotted a girl that appealed, he'd stalk her, the limousine moving slowly forward until the girl was trapped against a wall or a shop window.'

'And what then? Drag her into the car?'

'The chauffeur would. And no one, Dronsky, no one on the old Marx Prospekt or Uprising Square, no one in the middle of Moscow would dare to intervene.'

I had his attention. 'The chauffeur would drive to a quiet spot under the Kremlin wall, park the car and get out.' I paused. 'He'd pace about on a corner somewhere, maybe even light a cigarette, whistle a tune . . . And in the back of the limousine Lavrenti Beria would be doing exactly what he wanted to with the terrified woman.'

'You mean he killed them?'

'As it happened, that wasn't what he got off on. But it could have been . . .'

We stopped in the parking lot behind District 13. I could see Dronsky was uneasy. 'What made you think of this story, Chief?' he asked me, offering a cigarette when he saw I didn't plan to get out of the car.

'Something Gromek said about the scream. Somehow the sequence didn't seem right. He seemed to think he heard a scream while the man was still waiting on the corner. Could that have been the scream when the chauffeur was pulling the girl into the car?'

Dronsky lit the cigarettes. As the lighter flared I could see there was alarm in his eyes.

'Or think in terms of the waiting man being a chauffeur, Dronsky. Think in terms of the real action taking place inside the limousine parked somewhere out of sight a few yards away.'

He plumed smoke through the steering wheel.

'What about it, Dronsky?'

There was a painful pallor about his complexion. 'I don't know, Chief,' he muttered. 'A senior government minister . . . I wouldn't like to think something like that about any member of our government.'

I understood. The poor wretch thought I, the secret Cheka officer, was setting him up, drawing him into treasonous allegations. 'Dronsky,' I laid a hand on his arm. 'I'm not even suggesting it's a member of the government. It could be one of our big-time businessmen, a war profiteer, anybody with a chauffeur who's willing to go along with the game.'

He gave me a sickly look. 'A war profiteer's better – but I still don't think it's much of an idea, Chief.'

Nor did I on reflection. But there was a grain of something somewhere. The man waiting around was not necessarily the man who committed the murder. Two different men? Partners in this disgusting act? Why? I shook my head. No, this was a private act of sadism, surely. Which seemed to rule out chauffeurs pacing while the murderer savaged the girl.

Or had I simply misled myself? Was the waiting man just nothing to do with the horrific vivisection on the Stalin plinth?

In the District 13 building a young woman was sitting outside Dronsky's office. I left him to deal with her and walked across the Murder Room to my own office. My desk chair is ancient, spewing stuffing, but it swings. I sat down and put my feet on the radiator. My back was to the door, to the list of Moscow offenders, the bustle of the outer office. Tonight I had to persuade Natalya Karlova to visit an Anarchist in hiding, even a well-known Anarchist in hiding. How in God's name was I going to be able to do that?

There was a knock on the door behind me and Dronsky brought in the girl who'd been sitting outside his office. She wore a short leather skirt, black high heels, no stockings and a warm brown felt coat. The make-up was heavy and meant to be. She was a tart. I completed my swing round to face her.

Tarts are a policeman's best friend. There are dumb tarts and smart tarts. Kindly and vicious tarts. Whatever . . . But I've always been persuaded that in observation they are a notch or two above your normal witness, man or woman. Why? Perhaps because their lives sometimes depend on it. But whatever the reason, if a business girl decides to offer help, she's often as not worth listening to.

'My name's Valentina,' she said. 'Deputy Inspector Dronsky says you're the boss.'

I shook hands with her and she took a seat in front of the desk. 'I love your cat,' she said. 'What's its name?'

I looked round for the cat. I slid my eyes over the chairs and filing cabinets, glanced along the shelves beside the window. 'Where is he?'

She pointed. When I leaned forward I could see he was using the big brown filing cabinet to remove himself from my line of sight. He was running through some cat stretching exercises. I could have shown him a few more.

'He's got a name, hasn't he?' Valentina said.

I looked at Dronsky but his face was blank.

'He's known as V.I. Lenin,' I said with difficulty.

The damn cat raised a paw.

'Oh, he's really something,' Valentina said.

'You want him?'

'I've already got three.'

Dronsky gently expelled cigarette smoke in silent relief. 'So what do you have to tell me, Valentina?'

The girl took out a cigarette, a Belomors King Size, and lit up. 'I was attacked in Presnya last night,' she said matter-of-factly. 'On the corner of the factory where they make government flags.'

I sat back in my chair. 'Jesus . . .'

'Less than a hundred metres from where that girl got killed,' Valentina said.

I flicked my eyes towards Dronsky. You can't call an attack on a girl a piece of luck – but for us it could be. I could feel the excitement rising in me.

I waited until Dronsky had his notebook ready. 'Let's start with the time,' I said.

'I'm not good on times, perhaps it was around half-past midnight, one o'clock . . . I was working that area up around the flag factory . . .'

She paused to be quite sure I knew what she meant, then went on. 'A busy night because we ran across a squad of young soldiers who'd been in the vodka houses on the Bullfrog.'

'Who's *we*, Valentina?'

'I don't know her name. Very big girl. She's called Dark Maria. Or Big Maria sometimes. She usually works the stations. The Belorussian or the Kievski. I don't know what she was doing round this way but I wasn't going to tell her to kiss off. There was plenty of business with the young soldiers and I was glad of the company of a big one like that if anyone turned nasty.'

'You want some coffee, Valentina?'

She looked surprised.

Dronsky jumped up and opened the office door. Valentina and I could hear a few muttered words.

'Milk and sugar?' I asked her.

She smiled at me.

I called out to Dronsky and he transferred the order to Bitov in the Murder Room.

Valentina smiled again. A nice smile.

'Where were you both when you finished with the soldiers, Valentina?'

'We were in a courtyard at the back of some apartments along about two hundred metres from the factory.'

'Are the apartments occupied?'

'Yes. There's usually enough light to see what you're doing. Not too much for the dirty old men to see much more than a flash of leg.'

'The dirty old men?'

'There are usually three or four of them at their windows watching us at work.'

'And you and this other girl, Maria, you were both in the courtyard?'

'Right.'

'So what happened when you'd finished with the soldiers?'

'We sat around on a bench there, relaxing, having a smoke and winding up the dirty old men.'

'Winding them up?'

'Flashing our legs about a bit. We were trying to get one old bugger caught by his wife. We could see her getting ready for bed in the next room.' She shrugged. 'Just a bit of fun.'

'And then . . . ?'

'We split. I walked off towards the Planetarium. The direction of the flag factory corner.'

'And Maria?'

'She was going to see her kid. Home, maybe. She didn't say where that was.'

'Were there people about?'

'The whole area's pretty deserted at that time of night,' Valentina said. 'You get people moving about, refugees.

You might see a few girls looking for business. A man prowling around looking for a girl. Sometimes a militia car. Not often. But there's a lot of old ruined buildings there. You can never really tell if there's a family taking shelter there, a girl taking a customer . . . You see a few beggars round a fire sometimes, but not last night.'

'You're up there a lot.'

'Most nights when the Bullfrog gets too crowded. Some nights on the Bullfrog you've got thirty girls lined up and not much doing. If that happens I wander up towards the flag factory. Like last night.'

'All right, Valentina, you left Maria and wandered up towards the factory. Did you see anything or anybody on the factory corner up ahead?'

'It's much darker up there. But there is one street light on the flag factory corner. I could see there was a man there. Well dressed, fur hat, long coat. It crossed my mind he might be the young soldiers' officer out looking for a bit for himself. Well, it's only human,' she said with a laugh.

'So you're walking towards him and he's what – about sixty metres ahead? So you had a good look at him.'

'Yes. Except he's got his collar up against the cold and he's pacing back and forth, so that he'd appear and disappear from my sight round the corner every ten seconds or so. I'm about twenty yards away when I heard a sound behind me. My first thought was that it was one of the young soldiers back for a free one, but I was concentrating on the well-dressed man ahead, so I didn't turn. Then it happened.'

'What happened?'

'I heard a footstep close up and suddenly I felt this tremendous blow, like a sledgehammer across my back. I went down.'

I stared at her. My stomach twisted at the thought.

'Did you scream?' Dronsky said.

'God knows. I don't even know how much time passed.

Only seconds maybe, then something exploded next to me. A vodka bottle. Like a Molotov cocktail except it didn't set alight.' She saw I was baffled. 'It was Maria. Bless her, she was taking a piss in the rubble back there, saw what happened, and threw her bottle at him.'

'What did he do, the man?'

'Disappeared. Into the ruins. Like a ghost.'

I looked at Dronsky. We both knew we were on the edge. Somebody had seen the Monstrum. It's that sense of the hunt that distinguishes a policeman from any other citizen. Maybe I'd never done homicide before but I could see when a case was about to crack. Or so I thought. 'What did he look like?'

'I never saw more than him crouched, running through the shadows.'

'And Maria?'

'She helped me up. My back was hurting. I decided to go the other way. She came with me as far as the top end of the Bullfrog. She's all right, Maria. A bit rough and ready. She was worried he'd done me some real damage. She swore what he hit me with was this thick.' Valentina made a ring of both hands. 'You can see the mark it left.'

She stood up, stub of the Belomors in her mouth, and took off her coat. Underneath she wore a black sweater. She tossed the coat aside, stubbed out her cigarette and peeled off the sweater. She stood there without a bra, hands up. I was entranced by the fall of her breasts. When she danced around to show her back, I saw a heavy bruise running diagonally from left shoulder to right hip.

'A left-handed blow,' Dronsky said.

'Seen enough?' She turned round, making her breasts bounce.

'Put 'em away, Valentina,' I said reluctantly. 'You had a very lucky escape last night.'

'Don't I know it? I didn't think of it straight away, but

it was the Monstrum, wasn't it?' she said, putting on her sweater.

'Maybe. The girl who was with you, Maria, she must have got a really good view of him.'

'She was near enough to throw a bottle.'

'Thirty paces?'

'Maybe.'

I had held back on the question, savoured it. 'How did she describe him?'

'Describe him? She didn't.'

I looked at her, open-mouthed. 'I don't believe that. She didn't describe him?'

She gave a short laugh. 'That's the way the police thinks things happen, is it? "Oh my good God! Do you realise, Valentina, that the man who just tried to brain you was 1 metre 90 with dark hair and a scar down his left cheek . . . ?"' She burst out laughing.

I lifted up a hand in surrender. 'So what *did* she say? Exactly.'

'At that time the penny hadn't dropped. Neither of us were thinking about the Monstrum. It was just a mugger. Any mugger. Who wants to know what he looked like?'

'As close as you can remember, Valentina,' I said slowly, 'what did Maria say?'

The girl shrugged. 'Something like: "What about that bastard! He must have seen us taking the money off that line of soldiers. If I see him again, fuck your mother, I won't miss him with the next bottle!"'

It sounded more likely. 'Where do we find Maria?'

'I told you, she works the train stations, is all I know. She lives out in the New Districts somewhere. I know she's got a kid. Comes into town to turn a rouble, I suppose . . .'

Dronsky was shaking his head grimly.

'The well-dressed man on the corner,' I said. 'Did you see what happened to him?'

'When I looked up afterwards, he was gone.'

'It couldn't have been him who came up behind you with the stave of wood?'

'I don't know. I'd stopped, I remember. And turned my back to him.'

'Why had you stopped?'

'You don't just march up to a client. Don't want to be too brazen about it.'

Dronsky lifted his eyebrows, raising runnels of skin across his shaven skull, like packed sand on a beach.

'But you saw no one else about?'

'No. And when I'd recovered my wits he'd gone.'

In an investigation, any investigation, if you want to know what really happened you have to be ruthless with your favourite theories. Maybe the well-dressed man had nothing whatsoever to do with the killing that took place at the plinth fifteen or twenty minutes later. Maybe we'll never know what he was waiting for. Maybe Valentina's scream scared him off. So much for my long number on Lavrenti Beria and the girls in the limousine. Except that Gromek, the night-watchman, had heard Valentina's scream. And ten minutes later the pacing man in the long overcoat was back again. Checking his watch again. Could it be that Valentina had not been attacked by someone who was after her money from the soldiers she had serviced that night? Could it be that Valentina was mistaken for someone else?

When we had signed Valentina off I went up to see my chief, Commander Brusilov, and explained my need for more men to trawl the rail stations and find Big Maria.

Seated behind his over-large desk he rubbed his hands together in a washing action and examined the results. Satisfied, he lifted his head to me. 'Constantin Sergeivich,' he said, 'can you imagine for a moment the responsibility of running a district station?'

Not to mention a fruit and vegetable business for his brother.

'And *this* district station? Where the tri-borough amnesty group has decided to make its headquarters? That takes men, Vadim,' he said. 'Ten detectives for the commissioners' security alone.'

'I'm asking for half a dozen more men . . .'

He lifted a small red hand to silence me, stared at it entranced and brought his attention back to me. 'District 1 has just this morning called on me to draft six of my best men to work on the assassination attempt on Leonid Koba . . . You see my problems. They're on matters of national concern. I'm not trying to diminish the importance of your work . . .'

'You gave me a month.'

'I see that might have to be extended.'

'Under the circumstances . . .'

'I can give you three extra men to trawl the main-line stations for this witness, this Dark Maria woman.'

'Three!'

'The very best I can do.'

I turned to go.

'One more thing,' he said. 'The amnesty commissioner would like to see you in her office as soon as possible.'

She had taken off the suit jacket she was wearing downstairs and was working at her desk in a blue candy-striped shirt and black skirt, contriving to look professional and efficient and infinitely desirable at the same time. She came from behind the desk and greeted me, with a wide and welcoming smile. 'I am sorry about the contretemps downstairs,' she said. 'Two women in a laboratory is like two women in a kitchen. Natalya was quite right to refuse me.'

'Is that what you wanted to see me about?'

She laughed. 'Not at all.' Her eyes became suddenly serious. She gestured me to a seat and walked slowly back to her desk, drawing waves of perfume with her across the large room. 'Everything in confidence, of course,' she said, standing behind the desk.

I nodded cautiously.

'As amnesty commissioner, I've been examining the files. Of senior Anarchist figures. Among them a certain Julia Petrovna. Highly charismatic commander. Formerly married to a man named Vadim.' She paused. 'A not uncommon name, of course.' Her eyes were on me. Almond shaped and dark. 'But there's the additional fact that Julia Petrovna comes originally from Murmansk. Would I be right in thinking . . . ?'

'It's no secret,' I said. 'Nor is it something I make a point of advertising.'

'I can understand that. You have no need to be concerned, Constantin, I shall be discretion itself. But let me explain my interest.' She walked out from the desk, slow deliberate strides, then turned. 'I'm anxious, very anxious, that this amnesty succeeds, Constantin. In my opinion it will be good for Russia, good for the world. I'm also anxious to play what part I can. I know, of course, that there's a certain reluctance on the part of senior Anarchists to believe in the amnesty. In this sense the voluntary surrender of a leading figure like your former wife would be important in persuading others. I'll be frank with you, Constantin. I should be very happy indeed if Julia Petrovna chose to surrender to me personally.'

'If you're hoping that I might influence events,' I said, 'I haven't seen Julia for over five years.'

She looked at me quizzically.

'It's the truth, Doctor.'

'Call me Imogen. All right, I accept that. But it's not impossible that she might choose to surrender through you?'

'Highly unlikely. She's a much bigger fish than I am these days.'

'All the more reason to use you to test the water.' She lifted both hands as I began to protest. 'Let's just say this, Constantin. In the event that Julia Petrovna should contact you I would be prepared to take her into my personal protection as amnesty commissioner at any time of the day or night.'

I stood up. 'In the event . . . I promise to tell her.'

She smiled and walked slowly, hips swinging, towards the door. 'We have another common interest, of course. Despite Natalya, I continue to take an interest in the Monstrum.'

I waited.

'Two killings this week. What have your investigations produced so far?'

'In the way of leads? Not a lot. But for me, it's early days on the case.'

'Which is why I'd like to talk to you. You're more intelligent than the average run of homicide detectives . . .'

I smiled.

'More receptive to new ideas. American ideas.' She was standing close, enclosing me in warmth and scent.

'Maybe.'

She reached for the door handle. 'Profiling,' she said, bringing her lips close to mine as if she were going to kiss me. 'Psychological profiling will track the beast down.' She opened the door. 'I've enjoyed talking to you, Constantin.'

I stood outside for a moment, suddenly exhausted. Imogen Shepherd seemed to suck strength from me. I started down the corridor and slowly descended the stairs. An idea was running back and forth through my mind. Imogen would offer Julia, she had said, her personal protection. In addition to which she was a doctor. Could I bring these two elements together? Would she then treat Julia in secret? I stood on the staircase. The din and turmoil of the crowd in reception was enough to bring me back to reality. Nothing like that was going to happen. Julia was not about to surrender, however sick. And Imogen, who was a paediatric psychiatrist, would not have the experience to give even emergency treatment for whatever injuries Julia had. I started on down the staircase. Conspicuous in her white coat, Natalya Karlova was walking across reception. She glanced up and waved to me as she passed below.

She was, I knew, my only hope.

Natalya Karlova's flat was in a once prosperous area of Moscow off President Romanov Bulvar. I found a touch of that insignificant irony that pleases me so much in the fact that, according to the Art Nouveau date in stone over the entrance, the building was built in 1905, the year the oppressed of Presnya in their satanic mills exploded in revolution.

Who lived here, in those days, in this building whose façade might have been found in any of the *grands boulevards* of Haussmann's Paris? Members of Moscow's increasingly prosperous middle classes, I suppose, in six- or seven-room apartments with servants' quarters on the top floor. They would have been lawyers and small manufacturers of boots and belts and cheap ribbons and brass candlesticks, the owners of those same satanic mills in Presnya. Many would have German or Jewish names. As so often, I found the morality of it all hopelessly confused. Before the Bolshevik revolution Russia had one of the fastest growing economies in Europe. The people who lived in these apartments were the owners of the mills of Presnya. But before the Bolshevik revolution they were also Russia's hope for a decent bourgeois future.

Today the apartments are divided. I can see that by the way front doors carry two or even three family names. I look for No. 25. Ground floor. I follow a corridor which half circles a courtyard in which an ancient automobile rusts and rots on flat tyres. The bold headlights are shattered.

There are three names for No. 25. I press the bell twice as the note instructs me. After a moment I can hear a woman's steps approaching. The confident ring of Natalya's heels on the old patterned tiles reminds me of what I have come to ask and my stomach sinks.

I could retreat back down the corridor, so outrageous does my mission suddenly seem. To ask a stranger to risk her career, even her liberty . . . Was I mad?

I can hear her turning the catch.

Am I mad?

Can I possibly go through with this?

She opened the door as I was in mid-flinch, about to flee even, with my American chocolates held aloft like a Bible to protect me from the approach of Jezebel.

The Jezebel wore a red woollen dress. Her eyes widened. 'You were about to change your mind.'

'No.'

'The chocolates were an over-generous gesture suddenly regretted?'

'No.'

'To me it's quite obvious. You had decided to hide them up there,' she pointed to a ridge above the door, 'and collect them again surreptitiously as you left later.'

'No. Absolutely not!' Could she be serious? 'No, I promise you. That is not the case.'

She stepped back, laughing. 'Come in, Constantin. You are my welcome guest.'

19

I stood in the middle of a large white-painted room, elegant with early twentieth-century cornices and polished chestnut flooring, a room softly lit and carefully under-furnished like a theatre set. While Natalya took my coat and carried it into the hall, I crossed to stand with my back to the wood fire. Thick red velvet curtains, discoloured at the edges by the summer sun, were drawn across tall, old Moscow windows. A worn black leather chesterfield with cushions from the southern republics faced me. And beyond that, a candlelit mahogany dining table stood against the far wall below a large oil painting of the Battle of Borodino, all gunsmoke and charging cavalry and with a large rent in one corner. On one side of the room was a curtained kitchen section, from which came the bubble of pots and the heavy cooking smells of roasting garlic.

It was an apartment that spoke to me in a way I didn't immediately understand. Most of my life had been lived with the detritus of Soviet style. Little as there was in this room, and battered as some pieces were, as I could see on closer examination, it still held out to me an unusual warmth and friendliness.

She came back carrying two fluted glasses of chilled wine. 'I hope you like the apartment,' she said. 'I was lucky enough to inherit it from the medical examiner I took over from. The furniture and the dreadful fake of Borodino I bought myself.'

'I like it as much as any room I've ever been in,' I said.

'And as little?'

I shook my head. 'No. I meant it, Natalya.'

I could feel my nearness to this woman. But my distance too. At table we sat opposite each other like actors on a stage. The man in jeans and an English sports jacket with dark hair that curled just too long onto the collar of his black polo shirt, the man who spoke about his life with what seemed to be a disarming candour but which concealed all its most important moments . . .

And the woman, younger by several years, in a red woollen dress and with good thick, harvest-gold hair drawn back in a chignon, the woman playing her part with a laughing insouciance as if the playwright's intentions for the devastating end of the act were still unknown to her.

For an hour, for two hours as we ate chilled beetroot soup and roast chicken with whole garlics and drank Moldavian wine, I held that other world, that real world, dominated by Julia and her desperate need, at bay.

I was surprised at the unfeigned ease with which Natalya spoke. Had I been able to relax it would have been relaxing. What she revealed was a girl born only twenty-five years ago, confident in the work she did, in the way she walked, in her clothes, comfortable in herself. She came, she told me, from Saratov on the Volga above Volgograd. Her parents, both former Soviet doctors, lived there still.

'Why did you come to Moscow?'

'I was invited by a man I admired a great deal.' She pointed to a framed photograph in a silver frame who I had imagined was her grandfather. 'Professor Kandinsky. He was born in Saratov himself but by the time I graduated he was already one of the leading figures in medicine in Moscow. He understood my need to get away from my parents. I lived with him and his family when I first came to Moscow.'

'Why did you need to get away from your parents?'

She laughed, spearing the garlics and offering them

to me on her fork. 'I had to get away because I could no longer bear to hear how perfect the Soviet life had been, how respected we Russians were throughout the world, how superior our morals, our sport, even our stereo systems were to the Western models.'

'Your Professor Kandinsky understood all this.'

'Somehow, although he had also come up under the Soviet system. When I graduated from Saratov medical school, he immediately invited me to come to Moscow. He understood I could not go on living in the shadow of a Golden Age.'

'The Golden Age had no appeal?'

'There was less truth in it than most Golden Ages,' she said sharply.

'But there *were* achievements.'

'In seventy years you would *expect* achievements. There was also a legacy. Our Russian society survived, but it emerged damaged. Its people too often became half-persons believing in half-truths, giving half-deference to half-idiots.'

'You're not a patriot, then?'

'On the contrary, I love Russia and I love the Russian people. Our sheer will to survive has dazzled the world. In science and the arts we have achieved miracles.'

'But . . . ?'

'But we have always fallen far short of creating a just society.'

'We're not alone in that.'

'Among all major Western societies, we *are* alone.' She paused, her eyes troubled. 'Don't play with words. Other Western societies are not perfect. Democracies have their problems and injustices. But Russia has never even approached a just society. Not even for a few years. Sometimes I even wonder if justice is really what Russians want.'

'You're saying we're different from other peoples?'

'One example, Constantin,' she said passionately. 'An

example from only yesterday. When the Soviet period ended, why was it that so few Russians, almost nobody in fact, dared to ask a simple question?'

'What question was that?'

'It's the question: how could we have had, throughout the Soviet period, twenty million crimes against humanity but only one criminal – Joseph Stalin? Where are all those other hundreds of thousands who committed the crimes for him, who shot and shackled and tortured and faked trials and drove men and women to their deaths? Where are they all?' She was flushed with anger. 'Like my grandfather, drawing pensions from the state? Or they were until the Civil War.'

'Your grandfather had been in Gulag service under the Soviets?'

'Twenty years as a guard at Magadan. How many hundreds, how many thousands, did he crush to camp dust in his twenty years? My God, he even boasted of the regime they imposed on innocent men! And don't tell me he was obeying the legitimate laws of a legitimate state. The Soviet Union had even less legitimacy than the Russia of the tsars. It was built on a *coup d'état*. On force and lies. And it continued on that course until the very end.' She thumped the table in her anger. 'And I swear to you, Constantin, that Russia will be nothing but the mentally sick man of Europe until we admit our guilt. I thought your National Democrats might do it. Will they? No! I thought the Anarchists might force their Marxist allies in the Popular Front to do it. Did they? No!'

What else could I do but sit and stare at her? Is it my destiny to be surrounded by women of powerful convictions?

She speared a garlic and smiled at me. Suddenly her voice softened. 'You see, of course, Constantin, that I am perfectly neutral. On the great issues of the day – Nationalist or Anarchist – I do not take sides.'

'But you've lived under both systems.'

'Yes.'

'You were here in Moscow during the last year of the war, during the siege, when the Anarchists were in control.'

Her mobile lips closed grimly. 'I was a butcher surgeon in a children's hospital under both regimes. I wonder how to God I kept my sanity,' she said. 'Maybe you will think I didn't.'

I was, myself, in a highly charged state. Listening to Natalya, I played out in another part of my mind the story I would present to her of Julia, Julia lying injured, Julia in need of her help, but I was unable to speak the words.

Helping her clear the table I filled in a few trivial details about life in Murmansk. But I had not yet revealed that I had once been married, certainly had not yet mentioned Julia. While Natalya made the coffee, I moved from the table and lowered myself onto the rug before the fire, resting my back on the chesterfield. Watching her as she crossed the room with two cups of coffee, I saw in Natalya an *ordinary* wholesomeness that left me contemptuous of the ambiguity of everything I touched.

'You're drunk, Constantin,' she said, sliding down on the rug beside me, somehow handing me a cup of coffee as she did so. 'What drunken thoughts are you entertaining?'

'I am,' I said, 'experiencing a minor political epiphany.'

'Political?' She laughed, sticking her tongue into the corner of her cheek in mock disappointment. 'But tell me all the same . . .'

'I see you as the model for our Russian statue of liberty, arm raised, torch held high, dress stretched tight across your breast . . .'

'And where would you erect me?' she asked.

'I should have a thousand of you cast and placed at all those crossroads of our history where Russia took the wrong turning.'

She was on the rug beside me, one elbow resting against the seat of the chesterfield. 'You don't mean a word of it.'

'You would make a good Liberty. I mean that.'

She took my chin in her hand and turned my face towards her. 'Are you really an officer of the Cheka, Constantin Sergeivich Vadim?' she said. 'If so you'll have noticed that this evening I have only criticised the past. I have been careful to make not one single comment on the present.' She had amber-coloured eyes of a warm intensity, quite unlike the unsettling blue of Julia's.

'I'm no Chekist,' I said.

'Can that be true?'

'Is it important to you?'

She hesitated, her eyes on me. 'Tell me about your women, Constantin.'

'You want a list of my conquests?'

She laughed. 'Your conquests? I suspect, most times, it's *you* who's been the conquest. You were once married.'

I sat back in surprise. 'How did you know that?'

'I checked your next of kin status. There was once a Julia in your life. Now scored through in red ink. Is she dead?'

'No, not dead.'

'Tell me,' she said quietly.

The opportunity stood there like open gates. Why in God's name did I not seize the moment? A lack of moral fibre, my father always said. I used to think that meant I was not as brutally blunt and blundering as he was. I should have guessed it meant more. 'Julia and I grew up in the same neighbourhood in Murmansk,' I said. 'Our families knew each other – both our fathers were captains of fishery ships, both our mothers were what we used to call intellectuals: my mother a teacher of English but a student of Russian history, a Nationalist to her fingertips – Julia's mother a poet. You've heard of Abrakova?'

'No.'

'An international reputation,' I said with raised eyebrows.

'I'm unrepentant.'

'Of course.' I picked up the story. 'At seventeen I left Murmansk. Julia was a gangly fifteen-year-old. I returned from my navy service two years later and found an extraordinary change. Not just those little things you might expect in two years, the change from child to young woman. Where she had been shy, withdrawn, she was now . . . outspoken, imperious even.'

'My poor Constantin!'

'Is it such an obvious story?'

'You would be fatally attracted to such a woman, I suspect.'

'Fatally attracted? What I felt for her was a passion that could never be requited. Even in marriage.'

'And did she love you?'

'I believe so. In those early days, at least.'

'Then why was your passion unrequited?'

'Because, whatever the circumstances, she never allowed me close. I was her companion, her lover, her husband. But never part of her. Never part of her essential being.'

'You wanted that?'

'Yes. I suppose I see that exchange between two people as part of the nature of love.'

We were silent for a few moments.

'We married,' I went on, 'while Julia was still at the university. She studied political philosophy, the History of Ideas, that sort of thing. I, by then, was at the police college. I think it amused her to tell her university friends her husband was a policeman.'

'And where did her history of ideas take her?'

'She was a Marxist – and increasingly attracted to Anarchism.'

She lifted her eyebrows. 'Then she is, as I have been thinking, *the* Julia Petrovna. The Anarchist general.'

'Yes. *The* Julia Petrovna. You never saw the attraction of Anarchism?'

Natalya's face became grim. 'I'll be blunt. I believe we are all too close to anarchy for any sane person to advocate it.' She got up, took the empty cups and returned a moment or two later with two glasses of plum brandy. She stood above me, looking down, the hem of her skirt at my eyeline. 'Was there never talk of children between you?' she asked.

'A son,' I said. I could hear the bleakness in my voice.

She knelt, one knee, two knees, the plum brandy unspilled. She handed me a glass and settled next to me on the rug.

'Our son was born in a new century, a new millennium,' I said. 'A little of us both in him, perhaps. Mischa was dark-haired, like me. But quick and full of life as Julia was then. Imperious too, though he was still a little boy when I last saw him.'

'What happened?'

'You won't remember much how it was immediately before the war. The turmoil, the futile strikes, the demonstrations and counter-demonstrations, the gang control of almost everything.'

'I remember. I was sixteen when the fighting first began breaking out. The small wars. Then the secessions, Siberia . . . then rival forces in Petersburg, Moscow itself. It took a year or two before the madness reached us at Saratov.'

'In Murmansk,' I said, 'there was not much fighting. Except in families like ours. Julia and her university friends were all Anarchists. They held meetings and made speeches under the waving black flags. I don't pretend I could argue with Julia. She has a mind a cut above my own. I couldn't argue but I still couldn't agree with her views.'

'Let's see now,' Karlova pursed her lips. 'Continuous

revolution as the only means by which we can be purged, freed to associate with each other in an Anarchist society. Is that it?'

'Something like that. But the way Julia put it was convincing, you have to understand that. I mean she is a believer. A true believer.'

'A separate ethnic community promised for each of Russia's one hundred different languages. And peace, perfect peace descending on us all – no border disputes, no squabbles over oil, gold, diamonds, nickel . . . no taxes for armies, or for water supplies or medical research . . .' Her face flushed, the derision heavy in her voice. 'Even in Saratov we had Anarchists,' she said.

'I see you weren't one of them.'

'And you, Constantin, you're not a revolutionary?' She had her hand on my shoulder, an index finger circling the hair on the back of my neck.

'No. I'm not an intellectual, I couldn't argue the case. I never believed what they said.'

'Never believed Julia?'

'I believed her,' I said. 'I knew she was sincere. But things seldom seem to me to work out the way the theorists think.'

'You saw no need for change in the way things were?'

'My God, yes, but what has revolution ever been but an excuse to murder your opponents?'

She smiled. Her finger in my collar had stopped moving. 'So against her Anarchism you, I assume, argued National Democracy. Russia for the Russians. A belief that our history has been something other than the murderous disgrace it seems to outsiders.'

'I see hope,' I said stiffly, 'in simple Russians like President Romanov. In Leonid Koba in particular. He has had the foresight to offer an amnesty to all who fought against us in the war. Reconciliation. It's what we need most.'

'To reinvent Russia? To make Russia great again?'

'We're great by virtue of our size,' I said. I felt she was needling me. 'There is no place in history for a prostrate Russia. Even our enemies know that the bear is more dangerous wounded than plucking berries from the trees.'

She pursed her lips. 'And this is how the marriage broke up – she an Anarchist, you a Nationalist.'

I sipped my brandy. It had a hot bite in the back of my throat. I took a breath. 'Political differences, arguments even,' I said slowly, 'had become part of our lives. But there came a moment in Murmansk when every man and woman had to choose. Julia chose to go with the Anarchist army which was forming outside the city.'

'She took Mischa with her?'

'Yes.' Bundled him in a blanket, kissed me on the nose. *Say goodbye to Papa*, I heard her cry out as she ran from the apartment and down the stairs to a waiting car. I had stood in the hallway of the small apartment watching the door still banging open in a fierce December wind. 'Yes,' I said. 'She took Mischa with her.'

'And . . .'

For a moment I was unable to speak.

'And . . . ?' she said again.

'He was killed a few months later in one of our own bombing raids. He was buried in the corner of a graveyard in a village just outside Petersburg. Pavlovsk. Six years old.'

'Ah . . .'

I drank the rest of the brandy in one gulp. If I was to ask her it would be now. She sat there beside me, vulnerable in the sympathy I had unintentionally generated for myself. But I could not bear to use Mischa's memory to manipulate her, even to save Julia. Quite deliberately, for the first time that evening quite deliberately, I broke the moment. 'And I swear, Natalya,' I said, 'on Mischa's memory, that although I may not be all I seem, I'm still no officer of the Cheka.'

'Nevertheless, you are something other than you seem.'

I hesitated. 'Perhaps,' I said, slowly. 'But it need not trouble you.'

'Some day you'll tell me?'

'Who knows? What you need to know now is that I am not a Chekist. As a policeman, as a citizen, I have no great love for the Cheka. My hope is that their powers will be quickly limited.'

'I believe you.'

'But not a word to Dronsky,' I said in a lighter tone. 'Better he believes the worst of me until he's come to love me for the man I am.'

She ran both hands through her hair, dislodging the clip that held it, letting it fall. 'So our handsome Constantin is not all he seems,' she mused.

'Who among us is?'

She leaned forward and her arm tightened round my neck. She pressed her lips to the side of my mouth. I reached over and touched her cheek. A reconnaissant hand was high on my leg. Her polished fingernails were drawn across the denim of my jeans where I lay tumescent beneath her touch.

I could have followed her lead. If I'd allowed her to continue a few moments longer, I knew I would have succumbed. Instead, I stilled the movement of her hand with my own.

She glanced down and smiled wryly. Unhurriedly, she sat back from me, withdrawing her hand from under mine. In almost the same movement she had picked up her plum brandy glass and had lifted it to her lips.

'Natalya,' I said. 'You see me here, a man of bad faith . . .'

She gestured dismissively, almost spilling her drink. 'Spare me that, at least, Constantin. I've no need of explanations. I present you with an open pair of legs and you choose not to respond. Your privilege,' she added

190

crisply, 'as it would be mine had the circumstances been reversed.'

'At any other time . . .'

'Of course.' She leaned over and put one finger on my lips. 'Quiet, Constantin. I made a mistake. But not a complete mistake. I want to rescue a friendship out of this mild sexual shambles. Can it be done?'

'Of course it can be done.'

'I can't promise you never to mention it again.'

'Never mention what again?'

'The way you shied off like a startled llama.' She laughed as she got up. 'Good, and now I must go to bed. Who knows – tonight I might try a tab of *stoke* after all. You too, must go. But we will continue meeting.'

'We work together,' I said.

'That's not what I meant. We'll continue meeting. And talking. And building a friendship. Yes?'

I got to my feet, nodding agreement.

'We didn't eat the American chocolates,' she said. 'You might have balanced them on the architrave after all.'

I tried to smile.

With the flat of her hand she slapped me on the seat of my jeans. 'Not so morose, Constantin. There have been triumphs this evening.'

'Have there?'

'For me, yes. Are you aware that we passed a whole evening together without once mentioning the Monstrum?'

'Is that significant?'

'I would think so,' she said slowly. 'Perhaps it means you have even more important matters on your mind.' She held open the door.

I tried to say yes, I have Julia on my mind. Her desperate need for a doctor. But something, cowardice, stopped the words forming. I pursed my dry lips to try again.

'You have already told me you are not entirely what you seem. An inspector of homicide who passes a whole evening without a word about the Monstrum confirms that.' She eased me into the narrow corridor. 'It gives me hope,' she said. 'If not for now – at least for the future.'

I lifted a hand to stop her, to tell her I was no cause for hope, but she had almost closed the door. Holding it no more than six or eight inches ajar, she said: 'Be warned ...' Her face was in half-light. 'My intention is to make you fall in love with me, Constantin. I have no plans to be just someone with whom you share office gossip.'

20

I took the vodka from Gromek, tipped it to my mouth and drank a neckful. The neck of the bottle, that is. The polite-size sup when sharing a half-litre. We were standing on the factory roof. From here we could see, across the ruined landscape, the fine sleety rain falling on the Stalin plinth. 'No further progress with the investigation, Inspector?' Gromek said, taking the bottle I handed him.

I looked at my watch. I still had twenty minutes before I was to meet the Siberian. I raised my head to see Gromek's eyes on me. 'You said you were once an officer, Gromek. A specialist officer.'

'A long time ago, I think I said.'

'How long?'

'A lifetime,' he said. He whistled a vaguely familiar anthem. 'It was during the Sovietschina. I was twenty-five, serving with the Red Army in East Germany.'

'Elite troops.'

'Oh yes. But I was in love with a beautiful German girl and when the order came to pack up and go home . . .'

'You stayed.'

'For a year. Until the German authorities caught up with me and sent me back.'

'What sort of specialist officer were you, Gromek? Medical, you said.'

'Chemical warfare.'

'But you were a doctor?' I felt a great surge of excitement. 'Something you said to me the other night made me think so.'

He waved the empty vodka bottle. It was a denial.

'But you know enough to give someone emergency treatment,' I pressed him.

'I took a one-month general medical course. I know a few terms, Inspector. I know a little basic anatomy. Why are you asking all this?'

'Someone I know. Someone I know needs medical attention.'

He looked at me, his upper lip twisted in puzzlement. 'A doctor,' he said. 'Why not call a doctor . . . ?' his voice trailed away in bewilderment. 'Because you can't,' he said after a moment. 'For some reason . . .'

'Just tell me this, Gromek. Could you deal with an emergency?'

He shook his head. 'My brain's sodden with vodka. I don't have to tell you that.'

'But if you had to.'

'No!' he shouted. He began to stride about the gully. 'You're a madman, Inspector. No!' He hurled the empty half-litre out over the wasteground.

I heard the bottle shatter in the darkness behind me. 'Come back here. If I found the drugs,' I said urgently. 'Any drugs you needed.'

He came towards me and grabbed me by the shoulders. 'Inspector, I am no doctor. Burns I've been trained to handle . . .'

'Burns,' I said.

'Burns,' he repeated. 'Burns are a chemical officer's speciality.'

'Don't go,' I said. 'I'll be back. And sober up for Christ's sake!' I yelled as I ran for the fire escape ladder. 'Or you'll go to gaol for a decade!'

The Siberian eyes had narrowed almost out of existence. 'No doctor?' she said. 'You've come without a doctor! How dare you come without a doctor!'

We stood on the corner like squabbling lovers. Rain sparkled in the single lamplight.

'I need to see her,' I said. 'I need to see Julia. How, in God's name, can I even begin to get a doctor until I can say what's wrong with her?'

'So you want to be taken to her.'

'Yes, I want to know what treatment she needs, what drugs. You tell me nothing except that she was in an accident.'

'That's all you need to know.'

'Was there a fire? Is she burnt?'

She looked at me through those near-closed eyes. She said, cautiously, 'Her problems are not burns.'

'My God you're a brutal woman. Tell me, for mercy's sake, does she have broken arms, legs? Is she conscious? Is she losing blood?'

The small dark face was taut with contempt. 'You want to make your own diagnosis first, is that it? *You* want to decide she's dying.'

'Dying?' I stood in my dark American trenchcoat, shaking. 'Julia's dying?'

'And you've lost precious hours. By God, I'd put a knife in you myself if you weren't Mischa's father.'

'Mischa, you knew Mischa?' The blows were too much for me to take.

'Get a doctor, you tearful oaf!' she spat at me. 'I'll be here waiting in half an hour. If you're not here—'

I swept her aside with my arm. As she fell to one knee the knife was out.

'Keep your threats,' I said. 'If there's a doctor to be had, I'll bring one.'

I drove back to Natalya's apartment with reckless speed. I ran in through the main entrance and took the corridor round the inner courtyard. At No. 25 I leaned on the bell. And then again.

No confident ring of heels this time. Soft, slippery sounds crossed the tiles towards the door. There was a good deal of drawing of bolts and the scrape and clatter of a key trying to find the keyhole. When the door opened a man stood there, bare chested but for the wide elasticated bands which held up his airforce uniform trousers.

I pulled my card before he could speak. 'Inspector Vadim,' I said. 'Division 13 Homicide.'

He stepped back uncertainly. Natalya, I saw, was standing at her own door. She was barefoot, wearing a long white robe.

'Another change of mind, Constantin?'

'No.' I shook my head. 'Can I come in?'

She held the door open. The airforce man stepped back into the shadows and, grumbling, closed his own door. I walked slowly forward into the big white room. It was in half-darkness now, lit only by the light shining through the open door to the bedroom alcove. She stood for a moment watching me, then she closed the front door and flicked on the centre light. I flinched and turned towards her.

'No change of mind?' She stood in the middle of the room.

I shook my head. I found myself incapable of speaking. My hands rose to rub at my face.

She came to me and put her arms around me. 'What is it, my poor Constantin?' she said. She changed position and led me to the chesterfield. 'You look so miserable, so helpless, so lost. Come and sit down, I'll make coffee.'

I sat down and she turned for the curtained kitchen. Just in those few moments I knew I could tell her. She might refuse but I could tell her. 'No coffee,' I said.

She stopped and came slowly back across the room. I sat for a moment quite still.

'Tell me.' She sat on the arm of the chesterfield, not touching me but close, looking down at me with concern, alarm even.

'Julia is dying,' I said.

I felt her hand on the back of my head, stroking me.

'Where is she?'

'Here in Moscow.'

'In prison?'

'No. In hiding.'

I felt her stiffen, then she resumed stroking the back of my hair.

'What happened to her, Constantin?'

'A road accident. I don't have any details. All I know is that it's serious, that she's dying.'

'Why was she not taken to hospital?'

'Her companions don't trust the amnesty.'

She had gone from the arm of the sofa before I really knew it. I turned and could see that the bedroom curtain was half pulled. Shadows of a woman dressing hurriedly were thrown onto the white wall. Within a minute she reappeared. She wore jeans, a dark plaid shirt and a blue pea-jacket. Her blonde hair was pulled through a black woollen stocking cap. In her hand she carried her medical bag.

I stood up. 'You're prepared to go?'

She lifted her free hand and put an extended index finger under my chin. 'You know where she is?'

'Someone is waiting in Presnya to take us to her.'

'Then let's go, Constantin, and see what can be done.'

In my car we ran along the back of Gorky Park, crossed the Moskva at Krimsky bridge and sped round the inner ring to the Planetarium. We travelled for the most part in silence. At some point she lit two cigarettes and gave me one. I smoked without thinking. Where my thoughts were at that moment I can no longer tell.

As we pulled up before the Planetarium the Siberian girl, light-footed, sped from the shadows to be beside the car almost immediately. She pushed her small dark face through the window and looked past me to Natalya. 'What is she? A nurse?'

'A qualified doctor,' I said. 'A surgeon.'

The Siberian girl got into the back. Natalya, I noticed, looked ahead, ignoring the passenger.

Under the girl's direction we drove, circling the zoo park, twisting back on ourselves, passed Barricadnaya metro twice, then crossed the railway and swung hard south to meet the rising bend of the river.

On the next instruction, Natalya turned in her seat. 'No more driving in circles, please,' she said coldly. 'If your colleague really is dying, it might be best I saw her before she goes.'

Perhaps it was said for my benefit as much as for the Siberian's. Whatever the case, it seemed to have its effect. At the next crossing, the girl warned me to slow. As I did so she leaned across from the back and pointed left into an alley.

'In there?'

'Yes. And stop almost immediately,' she warned. 'There's a guard.'

I turned into the dark lane. Rubble crunched under the tyres of the car as I braked. The headlights showed the back of a row of late twentieth-century buildings. The nearest had collapsed, from shelling or poor workmanship.

'Turn off your lights,' the Siberian said. We sat in darkness. 'Now flash them twice.'

I did as I was told and was answered by a hand torch flashing twice from among the ruins.

'Do we get out?'

'Not yet,' the Siberian said.

The torch flashed two or three times to indicate a track cleared through the rubble. I put the Economy into gear and edged forward, following the splash of light. We were under cover now, in a sort of strut-roofed shed. At the far wall I stopped the car.

'We can go,' the girl said.

We left the car and picked our way towards a figure standing with a torch. There was something familiar

198

about her outline. A tall slim woman with cropped hair. She shone the torch briefly in my face and then flicked the beam at Natalya. 'Is this the doctor?' I recognised the voice. It was the tall emissary Julia had sent to my apartment in Murmansk. 'Is this the doctor?' the woman's voice repeated.

'This is the doctor,' Natalya said briskly, 'and you'd do well to remember that I'm still free to walk out of this.'

The tall woman laughed.

'You'd find it counterproductive to put a pistol to the head of an operating surgeon, if that's what you were thinking,' Natalya said. 'Take me to her.'

The woman turned without speaking and led us through some factory corridors. I followed them with fear turning my knees to water. So strong were my images of Julia that I could only see her as she had been, her positive, commanding self – or dead. There was no room in my imagination for Julia on a sickbed.

We stopped at a door where there was a guard sitting on an old kitchen chair, a young tired-looking country girl, a Kalashnikov across her knees. Julia's deputy opened the door. I imagine I was looking into what had once been a factory office. A large room with old filing cabinets along one wall. Newspapers were pasted to the windows and the light over the single white iron-framed bed was dim.

I think I gasped when I saw Julia. She lay with her eyes closed, her features cut from gleaming yellow marble. I felt the tall woman's hand on my arm as Natalya went forward. At that moment, Julia's eyes opened. She looked directly at me. Her lips parted in a smile before Natalya's body interposed itself between us.

The woman drew me out of the room. 'You can see her later,' she said.

I looked at her. We were almost the same height. 'What's your name?' I said.

'You can call me Denisova.'

The anger was rising inside me. 'I'll call you Sonya,' I said. 'You must know Sonya. It was you who gave Madame Raisa the note in the Park Café. So you know Sonya, all right.'

Her face was taut. 'I know the *Sonya and Vassily* cartoon.'

'Good enough. So Sonya it is. All right, Sonya,' I said. 'What happened to the flight to the West that you and Julia were organising when I last saw you in Murmansk?'

'It's no concern of yours . . .'

'Sonya . . . I got the money, remember.' My anger was fuelled by my desperate worry about Julia.

'My name's Denisova,' the woman said.

'To me you're Sonya,' I repeated. I shoved my head forward, breathing roast garlic into her face. 'Did you ever intend to go to the West, Sonya? Was the money I delivered ever intended to pay your way out?'

The guard, the country girl, had got to her feet. The barrel of the Kalashnikov touched my back.

'Make sure he stays here until the doctor says he can go in,' the tall woman said. She had her hand on the door.

The country girl was puzzled. 'Is he one of us?'

'No.'

The girl nodded, happier with her role now. 'Sit down, over there, comrade,' she said. 'Don't even think about giving trouble.' I saw the deft movement of her finger as she took off the safety catch, and I sat down.

I was there, hunched forward on the narrow bench, for perhaps two hours. This building had once been the offices of an abattoir and I read every word of the peeling posters describing the butchery of a sheep or bullock. Normally I turn my head away from such things but tonight in this alien place, the long minutes punctuated by Julia's sharp cries of pain piercing the

200

door, I forced myself to read. Anything. Supplementary pensions for industrial injury? Public health instructions dating from the days of Yeltsin's presidency? I read through all thirty incomprehensible sections until at last the cries from the room opposite seemed to have ceased.

Some time later, I had lost track of how long it was, the door finally opened and Denisova stood in the doorway.

I glanced at the girl with the rifle and stood up. I didn't need to ask how Julia was. Denisova's face had relaxed into something close to a smile. 'Go in for a minute or two,' she said.

I could see past her into the room: the bed, the filing cabinets, the newspapers posted to the windows. There was no sign of Natalya.

'Natalya Karlova is in the next room,' the tall woman said. She held the door wide. 'Go in,' she said. 'Julia wants to speak to you.'

I walked past her and heard the door close behind me. Julia was sitting, slightly propped up with a huge white pillow. A makeshift rail had been set up and a drip was feeding into her wrist. Her face was still a waxy yellow, but her eyes were open, there was more than the ghost of a smile on her lips.

I crossed to the bed and sat in the chair beside it. The sheets were unironed but decently clean. My stomach turned at the roll of bloodstained bedding in the corner of the room.

'You never could stand the sight of blood.'

'No.' I locked my fingers together. 'Tell me what happened.'

She shook her head slowly from side to side. 'You mustn't ask, Constantin. Promise me you will not ask.' Two beads of sweat slid down her brow and ran along her eyebrows. I took the damp cloth on the table beside me and carefully wiped them away.

'Tell me, Julia. Tell me what happened. Why have you returned, if not for the amnesty?'

For a moment she looked up at me, her mouth, her eyes, perfectly still. Nobody I have ever met has this extraordinary marble beauty. No Renaissance Madonna has this perfection of feature. 'We are about to be sold out,' she said.

'I don't understand.'

She was breathing heavily. 'Your man Koba is trying to sign agreements with the West. Many thousands of our comrades have fled there. Koba wants the return to Russia of all Anarchists now claiming asylum.'

'What's wrong with that?' I said. 'The Act of Reconciliation and Amnesty has passed the Duma.'

Her voice was weak but there was resolve there too. 'We will never believe a Nationalist who offers amnesty.'

I was sweating myself. 'I don't want to talk politics, Julia,' I said. I took her hand. 'I want to talk about you.' Even the skin on the back of her hand glistered with sweat.

'It's true that I've missed you, Constantin.'

My heart beat faster.

'In New York, walking in Central Park, it seemed wrong not to be walking with you. You always talked so much about America . . .' Her voice was whispering away to nothing.

'We'll talk, Julia . . . not now . . .' although more than anything I wanted to continue talking like this. 'Not now. When you're stronger.'

'I went to a concert at the Lincoln Center,' she said weakly. 'I missed you, Costya. It was Jimmy Gabriel playing, "But not for you".'

It tore at me. After Mischa, American new jazz had been one of the key points where our life met.

'You can come and see me in a day or two,' she said. 'Natalya Karlova will give you antibiotics. Come after dark the day after tomorrow.'

People were walking across the room behind me. Julia's eyes closed. She smiled goodbye. I squeezed her hand. Without opening her eyes she said, hardly audibly, 'Thank you, Costya.'

I stood up. A hand took my arm and led me to the door. It was only when we were standing outside that I realised it was Natalya.

We drove without speaking back down 1905 Goda and took the boulevard to the Krimsky bridge. It was raining hard.

'I would like to stay with her tonight,' I said.

'There's no point,' she said, starting the windscreen wipers. 'She's going to sleep now for twenty-four hours.'

'She's in no danger?'

We were moving now. Natalya glanced at me. 'There's always danger with this sort of battlefield surgery. Any infection will not be apparent for a good many hours.'

'How can I thank you,' I said, as we ran past Gorky Park. 'How can I thank you for what you've done?'

I could *feel* her silent anger.

'Look,' I said, 'I know what a miserable wretch I am. Natalya, I've imposed on you more seriously than any man probably at any time in your life. Can you accept, at least, that I felt I had no choice.'

'I can accept that's what you felt,' she said, without inflection in her voice.

'Did you talk to her?'

'She rambled a bit under the Valium. A few words about your son, Mischa.'

'She spoke about Mischa?' For a moment I was silent. 'A mother would,' I said slowly, 'at times like this.'

I glanced at Natalya's set face. Two lines came straight from the cheekbones to the corners of her mouth. She looked as if she would never smile again. 'Did she talk about the accident?' I asked her.

She snorted angrily. 'The accident!'

'Yes. I never found out how it happened. She didn't want to talk to me about it.'

'You can't be surprised.'

'No. She was too weak to talk much.'

'That's not what I meant.' There was a dangerous snap in her voice.

We left Gorky Park behind us. The rain, too heavy for the worn windscreen wipers, began to stream in rivulets down the glass. My eyes were pricking like a witch's thumbs. I was drained by the evening, barely able to follow what she was saying. Certainly not able to follow her meaning. I glanced sideways at her.

'There were four of them,' she said. 'Your Julia and three others.'

'There were four involved in the accident?' I was thunderstruck. 'I had no idea there were others.' I turned the car and drove into her street. 'I told you I got no details from Julia.'

'I have some details for you,' Natalya said coolly. She reached into her pocket. There was a sudden hard rattle on the inside of the windscreen. Tiny pieces of metal rebounded all over me. 'Look at those for details, fuck your mother!' she yelled in my face.

I braked in shock. We skidded into the kerb, fifty yards or so from her apartment building.

I picked up one or two pieces of the metal that had fallen into my lap. 'What are they?' I asked her. 'Where did these come from?'

'Mostly from the renal area of your beloved Julia.'

'You removed them from her back?'

'And from two other comrades in the other room. The third was dead. A fragment had pierced the skull and lodged in the brain.' Every word was spoken with a deadly chill.

'What are they, for God's sake?'

'You've served in the forces. You don't recognise them? Pieces from a fragmentation grenade?'

'Holy Mother of God!' I said.

'Ah, the first glimmers of understanding begin to light his brow! Fragmentation grenade, Inspector Vadim. As in Monday's newspaper report: "The grenades, which bounced off Leonid Koba's limousine, exploded by the roadside, killing five bystanders and injuring one or more of the terrorists fleeing from the scene."'

She got out of the car and slammed the door. Putting her head into the open window, she said: 'You might like to know that three of the bystanders were children, placed in the front row to wave to their president.'

With a snarl of contempt she turned away. Running to the entrance of her apartment building, she disappeared inside. I was halfway out of the car. A scatter of rain chased back and forth across the empty pavement. I heard her door slam. I sat back heavily into the driving seat.

21

I passed the rest of the night in terror. You think I'm exaggerating but, I promise you, it was terror I was feeling. First an acute and present fear for Julia's life. Then, horror for what she had done. And anguish that I was now involved in an attempt on my own leader's life. All these things add up to terror.

My night, or the few hours remaining, passed miserably in a sort of tense half-sleep, from which I frequently awoke, cricking my neck in the direction of the doorway in anticipation of terrible news.

I was, therefore, awake, or very nearly awake to receive the call from K.

K is the designation given to the bureau responsible for my other life. In my dealings with it I had no real idea where it was located although I liked to think of it as a large double-room high in a Kremlin tower with oak sideboards and Turkish carpets and a portrait of Peter the Great above the desk.

Logic, of course, would insist that it was a drab green and cream painted room in the Lubyanka prison, the headquarters of the Cheka and Leonid Koba's own ministerial responsibility. It would be the more likely location of the office dealing with lowly doubles like myself, but I did not want to link my work with the Lubyanka. The truth is, brothers, that I receive, from the idea that I work directly for the thousand-year-old Kremlin, a powerful lift to my spirits.

Most Russians throughout most centuries have been held at a distance from what is really happening in their country. Even in the twentieth century when news spread so rapidly throughout the world, ordinary Russians were never allowed close to simple truths about our national existence. But to me, doubling for one of the leaders of our nation has brought me a closer sense of involvement than I could ever have imagined.

Early in the morning after Natalya's visit to Julia, I recognised the flat tones of one of my minders, though the voice on the other end of the line never identified itself beyond giving the designation of the bureau. I was being recalled to duty. Presumably some words would be passed to the district commandant, Major Brusilov. I never really gave it a thought.

Dronsky was already at his desk when I called him. 'I've important matters to deal with today, Dronsky.' I was standing naked from the shower, towelling myself down as I spoke. 'I won't be in the office.'

'I understand, Chief,' Dronsky said.

'Bring me up to date. Did you take the street girl, Valentina, on a tour of the rail stations last night?'

'We did a tour but no luck so far, Chief. No sign of her friend Maria.'

'Is Valentina prepared to try again?'

'I'm not sure, Chief. She gave me the slip after a couple of hours. She'd been complaining all night that we were costing her a fortune in lost business. Somewhere in the Finland station she slipped away. It's easily done, Inspector.'

'OK Dronsky, I'm not blaming you. But did you pick her up again?'

'I came back to the Bullfrog and asked around but there was no sign of her. I left it another hour and went to her room on the other side of the zoo. No sign of her there either. If she stayed somewhere overnight she won't be back home yet. I'll drive over and check again this afternoon, Chief.'

'I see finding her as a priority, Dronsky. Finding Valentina, and through her, the friend Maria. She is our only witness. The only living soul who's seen the Monstrum. I'll see you back in the office.'

When I replaced the phone I realised that Dronsky had not asked me a single question about how long I would be away.

An hour later a car picked me up on the corner of Semyon Lane and I was taken by a totally uncommunicative driver to a large dacha a dozen or so kilometres to the west of Moscow. It was approached by a road, perhaps I should call it a drive, about three kilometres long which ran arrow straight through a pine forest. Ahead, within a chainlink fence and steel security gates was a broad forecourt and the dacha itself, a vast ochre-painted wooden structure. The windows set in the clapboard walls were painted a rust red and the columned porch covered massive lime green doors. It was clear that it was a property that had once been well maintained and well guarded but it now gave out a desolate air. No smoke rose from its brick chimneys, the wooden jetty on its ornamental lake was listing badly and the gravel pathways sprouted grass and even small shrubs.

Inside, the dacha seemed to be a warren of dozens of rooms on several floors, served by landings, carpetless with plank flooring. The few pieces of furniture in the public areas were covered with grey dustcovers. Mice, or perhaps even rats, scuttled behind the wainscots.

In the hall two men took charge of me, neither of them the familiar, if unforthcoming, minder who had called me that morning. One short and stocky with grizzled grey hair and a Georgian accent, the other tall and professorial, they introduced themselves, without names, as professors of the Moscow Theatre Company. But from their air of careless authority I guessed they had not spent their lives directing Chekhov.

There was an almost total absence of all those trivialities that serve to ease human intercourse. I was not asked about my journey or offered coffee. I was plunged immediately into the work at hand. A maid showed me to a bedroom warmed by an electric heater. I had a moment to glance out of the window to see a long gravel drive which led the eye to some bronze Soviet family group before grey hills rose behind it. My thoughts were on Julia struggling to recover in that bare room. I could not be with her but I was deeply comforted to know that she was in Natalya's care. Whatever she thought of Julia's politics I sensed she was a doctor first and foremost. I knew she would not fail.

The make-up tray with which I had become familiar on tour sat on the dressing table under the window. Following the professors' instructions I applied the glue which would hold the moustache, shaded the under-eyes to add that indefinable southern translucence to the skin, rebrushed my hair and clipped in the jaw pads. When I was satisfied, I changed out of my leather jacket and jeans and into one of the quality suits I had worn during my visits as Koba throughout the early autumn.

I rang a bell when I was ready and the professors came and collected me and led me downstairs and along a broad corridor where the chandeliers still held stubs of dead candle. I felt, as I walked between them, a glow of excitement. I had adopted the slight limp as I left the bedroom. To be Koba again, I was aware, pleased me deeply. I was ready for whatever role was expected of me.

I was shown into what had once been a fine glassed-in terrace overlooking the lake. The furniture here was old rattan chairs and tables and there were a few southern rugs on the plain red-tiled floors. It reminded me of the set of a production of *A Month in the Country* which I had seen, as a student, played in a tsarist villa outside Murmansk. Then the tall professor spoke. 'You are wondering why you're here. It is because in certain areas your performance has not been judged up to standard, Inspector Vadim.'

It was a body blow. I found myself surprised at how deeply I felt my disappointment. I had felt so much *at home* in Koba's skin. Was I being dismissed? Could I not ask for another chance? 'But I don't understand,' I said. 'My minders, at the end of the tour, said how well I'd done . . .'

The tall man's face was unmoving. The Georgian smiled unpleasantly and rubbed his hair like a monkey. 'In addition, I've had so short a time to get it right,' I added desperately. It was a pathetic defence. But deeply felt.

The tall professor made a dismissive gesture. 'Amateurs. Your minders were unqualified to comment. My colleague and I are trained to take a much more rigorous view of your performance.'

'The television camera is an unforgiving eye, Inspector,' the shorter man said. 'If you are to appear on screen, there's work to do.'

Relief was as mysteriously intense as disappointment had been a few moments earlier. I was not being dismissed.

Lessons began with coffee and a croissant. Three television screens were wheeled forward and we watched Leonid Koba drink coffee over and over again. Each day, I was told, the vice-president took coffee and French croissants. It was his habit to break and crumble the croissant with his left hand as he listened to whomsoever he was with. Relaxed or concentrating hard (this was illustrated with twenty or thirty clips of Leonid Koba at small meetings of two or three or conferences of a half-hundred), the croissant was crumbled. Frequently up to half of it was left. Especially if the ends were over-crisp.

'So we begin,' the shorter of the two men said, placing a plate containing a croissant on the low table to my left.

'You want me to crumble it?' I said doubtfully.

'What else?' The professor's voice rose.

Twenty croissants fell to my fumbling fingers before the professors were satisfied. Perhaps in other circumstances I would have felt or even expressed a sense of ridiculousness with what I was doing. But the pain of criticism, the pang of disappointment was still acutely with me. Adjusting the movement of tired fingers to the professors' instructions I continued to crumble croissants.

Walking practice took up most of the rest of the morning. On film the professors had noticed errors in my adopted limp. A slightly shorter, less exaggerated movement of the left foot was counselled. The limp was slight after all, and the vice-president was anxious not to make too much of it, so the difference was small. But vital. The two professors crouched and watched, one wielding a Japanese camcorder, the other taking notes as I walked and rewalked the length of the terrace.

Minute adjustments were made: a slightly longer step, an out-turn of the foot, all checked and rechecked on the screens positioned at intervals to catch any error. For nearly three hours they worked, the two men in an intensity of commitment that left me dazed. Five steps from the door to a table were shot and reshot, and shot again. The professors argued and shouted at each other. Film of myself and of Leonid Koba flashed on the flickering TVs with a rapidity that left me confused about who we were watching, Koba or myself, about whether, in any given clip, I was actor or principal.

Lunch was served to me alone on the terrace by the maid, a middle-aged woman as uncommunicative as the chauffeur. Soup and fish, cheese and a decanter of water. I wondered what the professors were getting in some different part of this strange house. As I drank the soup I could hear their voices rising in argument from somewhere across the hall.

I was dying for a good pull of vodka. More than that I found my head swam and the instructions of the

211

professors, rapped out in tense, nervous tones, coursed through my mind, bullying any other thought from their path. Even thoughts of Julia, of her suffering, her recovery, were swept aside by the rat-tat voices of the professors.

When the two men entered the terrace room half an hour later I flinched.

Speech was to be the subject of the next session. From an aside, not offered to me, I learned that I was being prepared to step up a rung in the weird world of appearances and would be required in the next few weeks to speak a few lines of pleasantry – and that these lines might well be filmed, though not in close-up, for a regional news service.

We worked, again with the television camera and screens, repeating greetings and goodbyes, goodbyes and greetings, the professors screaming for a slower delivery, for more pitch, for less pitch, for more or less resonance in the last syllables.

My northern accent, a slightly harder Russian than Koba's, induced a particular fury in the professors. They now worked shift by shift, one man absent (and I suspect resting) at a time. By 8.30 that evening when darkness had brought a light snow across the ornamental lake I was finding it difficult to focus, difficult to hear the words or phrases I was speaking, impossible now to know who was on the screen, Koba or myself.

At just after nine the tall professor left and minutes later had still not been replaced by his colleague. I sat slumped in one of the rattan chairs. My left eye was twitching and words of greeting and goodbye spewed through my brain. From the direction of the hall, a door slammed. A moment or two later I heard a car engine fire and move away. Unbelievably weary I got to my feet and walked across to the television screens. One by one I turned them off.

I sat alone in the silence of the long terrace and felt

my facial muscles waver towards a sob. I fought it back and let the anger flow. I had been tortured. Those two fanatics had been aiming at my collapse. Aiming at breaking me down like an army recruit brainwashed into immediate reaction to orders. I was on my feet at a footstep in the corridor outside, anger exploding now in my chest as the door opened and the woman came in carrying a tray.

'Where are the professors? Have they left?'

She inclined her head.

'Will they be back?' I looked towards the tray, saw a bottle of vodka and a glass and was partly mollified.

'They will be back at 7:30 tomorrow morning,' the woman said.

'I need a car,' I said. With a car I could be back in Moscow within an hour. At Julia's bedside in very little longer.

'There are no cars,' she said. 'And even if there were, you'd never get past the guards. They patrol the woods at night. It's unsafe to even stand at the front door.'

'In that case,' I paused, gesturing with a hand I could barely control, 'get another glass.'

'Sir?'

'Get a glass for yourself. I can't stand drinking alone.'

Over the next three days my nightly drinking sessions with Olga Karmanova were the only things that kept madness at bay. Each session ended with a visit to her room during which she would insist that I kept my moustache and my expensive suit on as I mounted her and whispered crude endearments in the accents of the man she revered.

In the early evening of the third day there was a change of routine.

Again without explanation, the two professors left me alone. Within a minute or two Olga Karmanova appeared with a stranger, a young woman in a dull flowered dress. I was taken up to my room, where Olga left me alone with the stranger.

Acting as though I were not even in the room, the young woman began to inspect the dressing table. From time to time I tried to ask her what was going on but she blandly ignored me and continued sniffing base preparations, dipping a wetted finger in the eyeshadow or testing the softness of brushes against the palm of her hand.

For a few minutes I sat on the bed watching her and when she indicated with a movement of the hand that I should take the chair at the make-up table, I stayed where I was.

She stood for a moment, her strong short legs planted firmly in the middle of the room, appraising me with a look that fluctuated between disapproval and anxiety.

'Are you aware,' I said, braver by far with this single woman than I had ever been with the two professors, 'that you haven't spoken a word to me? Are these your orders, to allow no human contact? Is that what the professors demand – or the Cheka, or whoever is in charge of this operation – that you make not a single human sound for fear of establishing the most tenuous contact between us?'

I stopped. With her index finger the poor girl was pointing into her open mouth.

I was overcome with remorse. I jumped to my feet and took her hand. 'Are you able to understand?' I asked her humbly. 'Is it just speaking that's impossible?'

We stared at each other, standing a foot apart in the middle of the room. Then she stepped back and gestured again to the chair. This time I inclined my head, almost bowed, and took my seat.

Once she was satisfied I was properly positioned, the mirror lights blazing into every tiny cleft and dimple of my features, she began to move with extraordinary deftness.

I was made up as I had never been before. My Koba moustache was applied after several undercoats of gum, my hair greyed and brushed out, greyed and brushed out again to a precise level the woman clearly held in her memory.

When I had changed into the new dark blue pinstriped suit she had brought I stood before the long mirror perfectly converted. As I followed her down the stairs to where the professors were waiting in the hall, I walked naturally with the walk of Leonid Koba.

To my astonishment the professors who had bullied me through the last seventy-two hours now stood back respectfully.

The short one even opened the door for me.

Every seat in the stadium was taken. Schoolchildren, factory workers and peasants packed the tiered concrete seats. Below the glassed-in box in which I stood with the two familiar thugs who were my minders, yards of red cloth had been used to cover the hard seating for the distinguished guests.

From the corner of the room the young woman who had done my make-up now gave fluent directions to the cameraman who was recording my every movement. I had no time to reflect on her denial of speech. This was Russia – why look for a rational explanation? As the band below us struck up the 'Rodina' I stepped through thick curtains and began to descend the wooden staircase to the awards platform below.

The ceremony lasted almost two hours, although my own part in it was minimal. Under blazing lights, the mayors of a dozen Moscow districts read long citations of civic virtue.

The band would then strike up the 'Moscow March' and the searchlights would pick up a lone figure mounting the wide concrete steps towards the platform. I would leave my chair as he or she arrived before me and a minder would place a small bronze medal between the thumb and forefinger of my left hand.

I would step forward, shake the right hand of the person to be honoured, pin the medal on the lapel and receive a salute or bow or half-curtsy in return.

Like this I honoured a butcher who had hidden twenty sheep on a railway siding in order to feed a celebratory shish kebab to the Nationalist soldiers fighting their way up Kropotkin Prospekt, now renamed Lermontov Boulevard.

I honoured several women whose sons or husbands had been hanged by the Anarchists as Nationalist spies and I honoured a certain Father Alexander.

The good priest had, according to the citation, formed an underground community living in the old network of Moscow nuclear shelters and had guided advancing Nationalist units through the tunnels to allow the surprise attack which finally took the Kremlin from the inside.

It was not a bronze medal but a silver cross which was pressed into my hand as the bearded figure climbed the concrete steps towards me.

Father Alexander was young. No older than myself, that's to say. He wore a beard without a moustache, a very Russian Solzhenitsyn beard is the way I think of it. He had a metre width of shoulder and small round eyes, fixed on me as he mounted the steps. *Fath-er, Sash-a, Fath-er Sash-a*, dozens of young people were chanting beyond the glare of the searchlights which glittered on the priest's high gold shapka and gold-edged white robe.

To my surprise the priest fell on his knees some yards from where I stood and moved towards me awkwardly, one knee forward of the other.

In that second my Koba personality drained out of me. This was not *right*. This level of abasement was not right. But around me the stadium erupted. The roar was a physical wall of sound, of unimaginable sensuousness, intensely exciting. If it was Constantin Vadim who stepped forward and took the man's hand, it was Leonid Koba again who raised him grandly to his feet. I fought back the tears starting in my eyes. I lifted the silver cross above my head: 'Russia has need of you,' I cried. 'Of you and men like you.'

'Our Russia will rise again,' he boomed. 'Our Russia is rising from the dead.'

Again that exhilarating eruption of sound.

I placed the ribbon of the Order of Moscow 1st Class around his neck. As he raised his staff to bless me, the huge crowd spontaneously broke into the 'Rodina', the band hastening to catch up the early beats.

It was close to midnight when the silent chauffeur dropped me in my suburb of Fili. I headed for my street in a squall of snow, turned the first corner, ran down to the end and ducked into a doorway. For minutes I stood as the cold enclosed me. Moscow seemed utterly silent. I could hear no engine-start-up of a tram, no drunken voices arguing listlessly, no distant shunt of locomotives. Silence like this is rare in a city. If you listen hard, you can imagine you hear the snow falling through the air. When I was sure nobody was following I left the doorway, made my way to the garage and got into the car.

Haunted by the thought that I was being followed by someone from Roy's office, by the thought that I might lead them to Julia, I kept off the main boulevards. Instead I slid between the silent tower blocks, stopping sometimes for three or four minutes with the car lights off, killing the engine and walking back to the last corner to see if somewhere, waiting in the shadows, was a dark car without lights, its wipers slowly moving back and forth clearing the thickening snow from the windscreen, the glow of a cigarette tip just visible inside. But each time there was nothing.

Finally, more than an hour later, I made my way to the old factory building.

A threatening mixture of fear and anger seethed in the women's faces. The barrel of a Kalashnikov dug into my back, I stood in an absurdly stiff upright posture as I tried to relieve any accidental pressure of the trigger finger of the unseen angry woman behind me. Only when Denisova, Julia's deputy, arrived were some of the women cleared from the room and the Kalashnikov removed from the small of my back.

But Denisova's face, too, was stiff and white. 'So where have you been, Vadim?' she said, her voice barely under control. 'I demand to know where you have been.' I could see that she was within an ace of striking out at my face.

An altogether different alarm seized me. 'What's happened here?' I said. 'Why have you been looking for me? Has something happened to Julia?'

Some uncertainty was added to the anger in her face. 'We were trying to contact the doctor.'

'Natalya Karlova? Why? There was another emergency?'

She pursed her lips. 'Julia suffered a crisis the morning after the doctor treated her.'

'Jesus God! But she passed through it? She recovered?'

'Only just. At first we suspected it was induced deliberately.'

'By Natalya? Are you all quite mad?'

She thrust the idea aside with a movement of her hand. 'We tried to contact you. You were not to be found. Your doctor came in the evening when the crisis reached its peak. She was with Julia all night. She told us that to move her to some safer place would certainly cause her death.' Her voice pitched into a strange shriek. 'And all this time we had no way of knowing if, at that very moment, fuck your mother, you were busily betraying us to the Cheka.'

'You fleabag's daughter.' I raged at her, oblivious of the Kalashnikov. 'Would I ever dream of betraying Julia?' I reached out a hand to the wall to steady myself. Blood was pumping in my temples. 'Take me to her now,' I said. 'Now.'

'Not until you answer me. You've been away for three days. Where were you?'

I looked away from her small eyes. Had they had someone following me? I knew I was going to have to say something. 'I was with the Cheka, yes,' I said. 'They took me for questioning to a dacha about twenty miles outside the city. Two colonels questioned me without physical force.'

'They know that Julia's here in Moscow?'

'They suspect she is. They didn't tell me why. My impression was that it wasn't more than guesswork. Their last confirmed sighting was in Paris.'

'It took three days?'

'You know how the Cheka interrogate. Hours of waiting in between. They don't have to explain their actions.'

Denisova's face lost its shell-like hardness. 'And you told them nothing.'

'Use your common sense,' I snarled at her. 'If I had they'd have been here two days ago. Now let me see Julia. Where is she?'

'Wait here.' She left me with the guard and I heard her footsteps disappear down the corridor. 'You were lucky,' the guard, a girl of about eighteen, said with a grin. 'Yesterday she was going to shoot you on sight.'

I gently used my index finger to push the barrel of the Kalashnikov upward until it pointed at the ceiling. 'Yesterday she thought I'd be arriving with a unit of Chekists.'

In a few moments Denisova returned. 'You can't see her tonight,' she said casually.

'Did she say that? Did Julia say that?'

'She's sleeping.'

'Then I'll sit with her.'

Her small eyes opened in jeering surprise.

'Damn you,' I shouted. 'She was once my wife. She was the mother of my child.'

Denisova shrugged, her lip twisting. 'She's sedated. You'll have a long wait.'

She led me down the corridor and opened the door of the room. 'Make sure you keep the stove made up,' was all she said.

I approached the bed. Julia lay on her side, facing me, her hand half clenched on the pillow. I was made breathless by her, by memory perhaps of all those times I had awoken to find her beside me in the bed like this. The fold and tumble of the hair. The slight outward curve of the eyelids. My imagination fell back on the clichés of sculpting and marble. But she was much more than any sculptor's art could produce. She was a living, breathing woman, uniquely invested with the love I felt for her.

I drew a chair up and laid my hand on the pillow next to hers where I could feel the reassuring currents of her breath pass across my fingers. Like this I could believe we had never been apart. The truth, so harshly different, I had spent five years trying to understand. I thought now of the hours spent after Julia had left Murmansk, trying to remember, trying to recreate the exchanges between us.

Like a schoolgirl in love, I had laboriously committed the last arguments to a diary. And afterwards, when she had gone, I remember the horror I felt reading it as, entry by entry, I watched anger and emotions fanned by the words that passed between us, until each exchange grew to be something outside the will or wish of the participants, formless, pointless and lethal in its destructive power.

In those nights, sitting alone with a bottle of vodka,

I had asked myself a thousand times – was it my own passivity, my own inability to intervene that had brought us to this?

Years later, I came to believe my diary was a fraud, a fraudulent depiction of what went on between us, and I destroyed it. I think I know now that even the most simple dialogue is too complex in its molecular structure to follow or direct. The dialogue between myself and Julia had begun at school, between children. But even at that simple level dialogue generates its own directions. Julia, certainly, had understood more than I. But even she had not been in control. Even she had never guessed, until the last year, that our dialogue was doomed.

Watching the steady rise and fall of her shoulders now I saw the possibility of the course of events being altered by one crucial wrong decision. Should I have succumbed to the Anarchist analysis and joined Julia when she left Murmansk? Should I have refused to allow her to take Mischa with her, forcing her to remain with me in a Nationalist city? Should I have more persuasively argued the cause of the motherland, Rodina, and the simple values I believe in? A dialogue, I now know, is an infinitely changing gavotte. A shortening of the step here, a lengthening there and the dance would have led us differently.

It would be easy to say, then, that our parting was determined. Easy to say that as people we were so different, that we shared nothing of the most simple ideas of what being alive at the beginning of the twenty-first century was about. But that would absolve me from all responsibility; it would also mean that I must turn away from Julia for ever. Instead I seized the responsibility for what had happened with both hands. That responsibility had been my vital comfort in the days since she had left me. The fault, if fault there was, was mine.

During the night I rose from the chair two or three times to tend the stove. A huge, roughly tiled monster taking a log a half-metre long, it could be stacked to burn until the iron pipe glowed red hot.

Once, returning to my chair, I saw her eyes open. I placed my hand close to hers and she took it, smiling. 'Take no notice of the others, Costya,' she said, very softly. 'I never for a single moment thought you would betray me.'

I found it difficult to breathe, impossible to speak.

'I told them you were here to help me,' she murmured.

'Of course I'll help,' I said, recovering my voice. I had an overwhelming need to persuade her, as if conviction was an integral part of her getting better. 'I'll do whatever I can. Whatever it takes.'

'You promise.'

'I promise.'

Then her eyes closed, though the smile took some seconds to drift from her face and her breathing again became deep and regular.

22

In the big Murder Room at District 13 the atmosphere was charged with activity. Men moved about carrying files or sat at desks, hunched, whispering into phones. As I headed for my office and the wavy outline of Dronsky I could see through the frosted glass of the door, nobody as much as nodded a greeting.

I had half opened the door to my office when the pungent smell hit me. Fish, it seemed. And onions, fried. Dronsky, seated behind my desk, was already looking with alarm at the expression on my face. Standing, he fumbled the top button on his collar and tightened his tie.

'I thought you might need breakfast, Chief,' he muttered guiltily. Arranged on my desk was a styrofoam cup of coffee and, spread on a sheet of newsprint, two greasy buns, the source of the evil smell.

'You thought I wouldn't be in this morning, Dronsky,' I said. 'What are they?'

'One meatburger, one fishburger. I don't have a preference, Chief.'

I looked at V.I. Lenin seated on the filing cabinet. 'You don't,' I said to Dronsky, 'but he does. Is that right?'

'It's a sort of parlour trick,' Dronsky mumbled.

'Show me.'

He lifted the meatburger. V.I. Lenin gave a low hiss.

'Not his breakfast of choice,' I said.

Dronsky pointed to the fishburger and the cat raised his paw.

I shook my head. 'You two get started on your breakfast. I'll find myself a cup of coffee and you can bring me up to date.'

I took my time collecting my coffee from the machine and making my way back. Wandering slowly through the Murder Room I stopped and sipped coffee and strained to overhear some of the muted conversations. 'Fifteen sacks of bananas . . . A quarter-tonne of American frozen peas . . .' It didn't take long to confirm what Dronsky had told me. I strolled on across the room sipping my coffee.

By the time I opened the door Dronsky was licking his fingers. A screwed-up newspaper sat in the empty wastepaper bin and only the layered odours of fish and onion suggested that V.I. Lenin and my deputy had consumed two large burgers in as many minutes.

'We've pulled in a few possibilities while you were away, Chief,' Dronsky said, pulling down the back of his jacket and making the collar sit away from his thick neck. 'Sergeants Bitov and Yakunin have them downstairs.'

I finished my coffee and we went down to the basement where in the corridor outside the cells Sergeants Yakunin and Bitov had a dozen men seated on the benches that stood along the blank wall. A single chain ran through the handcuffs holding each man's hands behind his back. From time to time a man would rise in a surge of anger to shout abuse at the men in the cells across the corridor. The chained men, Dronsky explained, were a mixed bag of prime offenders who had survived the recent fighting. Yakunin and Bitov were now working through them establishing alibis for the Monstrum murders.

Dronsky handed me the batch of files on the men and I stood reading with my back leaning against the door jamb, the men springing up and down like jack-in-the-boxes to shout and reply to insults hurled at them through the bars. It was good solid police work of the sort that often produced results, but I had doubts about this approach to a case when half the background data had been burnt, blown up or deliberately destroyed during the Civil War.

In any case, as an investigating officer I've always preferred a sense of opposing an individual, a single adversary. Someone to think about, to imagine – in the end to second-guess. I looked at the men lined up by his sergeants. Rapists, women beaters, even kitchen murderers who had served twenty to twenty-five years. Probably not more than a tenth of the number of prime offenders living in Presnya and easily accessible surrounding boroughs. It seemed so improbable a stroke of good fortune that we should have him here, the Monstrum, among the dozen scruffily dressed men of all ages, long haired or crop headed, scarred often, preferring to shout at the men behind bars than to answer the sergeants' questions.

I called Bitov over. My back to the men, I asked if any of them looked promising.

'Third from this end,' Bitov said. 'Vladimir Simakov. Served ten years for rape and beating before the war. Said to have developed some nasty habits with women during the war.'

'Said by who?'

'His neighbours.'

'What sort of nasty habits?'

'He's said to boast, when he has a half-litre in him, of village women he enjoyed cutting if they refused their favours.'

'Which side did he fight on?'

'Ours, most of the time, Chief. But he was here in Moscow during the war.'

I grunted and turned towards Simakov. He was about forty, thick-shouldered in a tattered singlet, two scars showing bright pink on his cropped skull. A day or so of beard highlighted his cheekbones and small reddish eyes. He sat forward, his elbows resting on his denim thighs, his fingers interlocked so that the back of one hand sat into the palm of the other. As he lifted a chained hand to scratch his ear, I saw that his fingernails were bitten back so far that each finger seemed to have a small raised pad of flesh at its tip. I turned back to Bitov. 'Blood group?'

'We're checking.'

'Alibis?'

'We're checking them out now. But nothing that's going to worry us, is my guess.' He smiled. '*But* . . .'

I lifted my eyebrows.

'He definitely knew the last girl, Lydia Primalova. Lived in the same block. Two or three staircases further down.'

'I like it,' I said slowly. I looked at Simakov again and this time he was aware of it. There was no doubt that he was a brute. His small red eyes flicked towards me, then down to the worn green linoleum floor and back again to me. I ran my tongue slowly over my upper lip. Was this our man? I saw him slipping through the alleys of Red Presnya, the huge plastic bags on his hands . . . the knife . . .

Suddenly Simakov raised his head. His shoulder muscles swelled and rippled as he barked ferociously at the man in the cell in front of me. 'What you looking at? You Anarchist scumbag. I'll get the keys and be in there at you.'

He smiled, a brief thin grin of triumph at whatever effect he had had on the man behind bars. For a minute or two my eyes rested on him while he pretended to stare down at his scratched army boots. Was this a man who could track a woman through the rubble of the city, leap on her, rape and murder her and then carefully mutilate the corpse? Certainly he comfortably fitted all the prejudices. But did he fit the facts? If we had DNA printing of course, we could have him, if he was our man. Maybe next month . . .

'Do we have fingerprints?'

'The old records are gone, Inspector,' Bitov said. 'But we're fingerprinting the lot of them as soon as we can borrow an ink block from Robbery.'

'Continue work on the others,' I told Bitov. 'But focus on Simakov for the moment and see if you can establish any connection between him and the other murdered girls. Don't release him without my permission.' I looked at Dronsky. 'Without my permission or deputy Dronsky's, of course.'

'Very good, sir.'

Dronsky looked gratified.

'What news of the streetwalker, Valentina?' I asked him.

'No sign of her at her place. No word of her on the Bullfrog. I've done two hours at the rail stations while you've been away. But nobody's admitting knowing her friend Maria. Some of these girls change their names more often than they change their knickers. All we had to ask for was a tallish, mousy-haired woman who's on the game. These days that fits half the women of Moscow. Our only chance is to have Valentina with us to spot Maria as she goes about her business.'

'She has kids.'

'One, Valentina thought.'

'Maybe she spends a few nights with the child, then goes back to work for a couple of nights when money gets short.'

'I'll keep at it.'

'Let's just hope Valentina hasn't taken it into her head to skip the area.'

He nodded. 'One near miss with the Monstrum's enough for any girl. If she's really decided to skip, she may have moved up to one of the hotels. She told me she thought a girl like her should trade up while she was still young. We'll keep after her.'

We walked back to my office and I threw myself into the swivel chair and watched while Dronsky lit a cigarette, inhaling and letting the smoke trickle from his mouth, eyes almost closed.

I remembered when I enjoyed smoking like that. For a moment or two I swung in my chair. Fatigue curtained my brain. I saw the wreaths of Dronsky's cigarette smoke building in shifting layers above my head and I thought of walking back from all-night parties in Murmansk when the dawn spring mists wreathed about the ships in port . . . Walking back with my arm round Julia's shoulder.

Looking across the desk I became aware that Dronsky was watching me expectantly. I blinked my eyes fully open. Was he expecting me to produce some rabbit out of the hat, some brilliant new line that would send them all scuttling off in a new and fruitful direction?

'So what's the next move, Chief?' He made a short almost soundless whistle and V.I. Lenin leapt from nowhere into his arms.

I scowled. Dronsky beamed. I looked at my deputy's face and felt a great surge of generosity towards the man. Dare I promise him we'd have the Monstrum in the cells by the end of the month? No. Absurd. Could I perhaps promise a small nugget this afternoon? I had the impression that it was the sort of thing Dronsky was waiting for. I tightened my grip on the arms of my swivel chair. What in God's name was I thinking of? I had no nuggets to offer just to put Dronsky's mind at rest. My own mind was blank.

The cat in his arms, Dronsky made for the door. There, he stopped and half turned. 'You don't mind me saying, I've a strong idea you've something up your sleeve, Chief.'

I lifted my arms to display empty sleeves.

He almost winked. 'I know the way you like to work. But the moment you feel prepared to discuss it . . .'

I waited until the door closed behind him before I let my shoulders slump. From the wastepaper bin rose the oily fragrance of fishburger.

*

The bronze plaque set into the concrete door pillar of Moscow Forensic announced that it was constructed by a Stakhanovite team in the bitter winter of 1969, that completion had been in forty-five days from foundation stone to topping out and that the labour heroes who had led the team to triumph had been awarded the Medal of Soviet Construction Workers. Above the plaque a large, crudely daubed sign said: *You are entering a dangerous building. This is an official warning of structural weakness. In the event of the sudden appearance of major fissures or explosive cracking sounds, please raise the alarm with the handbells provided on each floor and exit quickly and calmly.*

I stepped through the swing doors. The lobby was long, low and dark. A guard in militia uniform sat behind a desk. In black fur hat, long black overcoat and boots a young woman sat, legs crossed, hands in her lap on a bench seat. Natalya was unmoving.

I walked slowly across the hall and stood before her, breathing the cold air out of my lungs. 'In a completely literal sense,' I said after a moment, 'I don't know how to thank you.'

It was as if she hadn't heard me.

'It's all I can say, Natalya. I won't say sorry, or try to explain myself. But I don't know how to thank you for what you did. You saved Julia's life.'

'It was touch and go.' She stood up.

'I know.'

'I mean my decision. I was balancing my Hippocratic Oath with the benefit to the world at large. I nearly let her go to her Maker. I'm still not sure I did the right thing.'

I stood back in shock. 'You're not serious.'

'Why not? Why shouldn't I be serious. I'm the one who believes crimes should be punished, remember?'

'But to let someone die. A human being . . .'

'Barely.'

I closed my eyes.

Natalya stood up beside me. 'What did she have to say to you about the grenade attack? What did she say when you asked her to justify injury and death to innocent bystanders?'

'She was sedated. She was too weak to answer.'

She touched the side of her black fur hat, straightening it on her brow. 'What did the others say, then? You must have faced Denisova or the Siberian or *one* of the creatures with the facts.'

'No . . .'

'People like that need to know the facts, need to have them thrust down their throats. People like you, too.' She turned and flipped open her briefcase and was pulling out a large photograph. 'Let's see what your squeamishness makes of *that*.'

I was looking down at a photograph, so glossy it seemed slick with blood. I saw a metal table rimmed with a blood gutter, a mortuary table. A bloodied girl of about eight years old lay on her side. It was as if a huge wind had torn off most of her clothes leaving tatters of cloth to disguise her nakedness. She was almost completely bald; a hand was missing, a leg bent the wrong way, forward at the knee.

'One of your ex-wife's victims.' Natalya thrust it at me. 'Keep it,' she said. 'Present it to your Julia instead of a medal. Two other children will be scarred for life. One received a shrapnel ricochet in the eye.'

'She didn't know all this when she threw the grenade.' I despised the faltering note in my voice.

I thought for a moment she was going to slap my face. 'Listen to me, Constantin. Killing the tyrant is something that decent people sometimes decide they have to do. It was right and courageous to try to kill Hitler. But killing a tyrant in a public place, throwing grenades from behind five rows of waving schoolchildren, is terrorism. Every terrorist knows that killing innocent people is part of the game. Get it into that thick block of wood you call a skull – *she doesn't care!* No terrorist could possibly care. Or they wouldn't do it. Or if their conscience drove them to do it because there was absolutely no other way, they'd choose some place, some time, when *they* took the risks. Not the front ranks of cheering schoolchildren.' She leaned her face towards me. 'We can argue all night about principles. But we can't argue with that.' She pointed to the photograph. 'It's child-simple, you oaf.'

I folded the photograph and shoved it into my pocket. Natalya had already turned and was striding towards the stairs. 'You're going to need a pass from the desk,' she said over her shoulder. 'We have to work together. Let's do it.'

I got my pass from the guard and mounted the concrete stairs after Natalya. I caught her up at the first landing. From there we walked side by side in silence past broken windows, their metal frames wrenched out of true by subsidence, stepping over cracks caused by an opening in the concrete block construction of the building. 'They got a medal for this too,' was all she said.

The woman at the laboratory desk was in her early thirties, big, mannish in her movements as she rose to greet us. Her assistant, Andrei, was a small bearded man of the same age. Both clearly had worked with Natalya, and as a consequence, greeted me in a friendly manner until they caught Natalya's own frosty attitude to me, at which point they became more formal.

We spent the first five minutes listening to complaints. Lena Ivanova had been in charge of the laboratory before the siege. She had returned only ten days ago. 'My first thought,' she gestured to the building around us, 'was that a shell had hit it while we were away. But no, my superior tells me, not to worry. No shell came within a half-mile. The building's just sliding down the hill.'

'Death from natural causes,' Natalya said. 'So tell us what you have for us, Lena Ivanova? I could hear by your voice when you called this morning that there's a surprise in store.'

'A shock, even,' Lena's assistant said, with a broad smile.

Lena restrained him with a sharp glance. It was clear she was used to running a laboratory in her own way, at her own slightly lumbering pace. There would be no short-cuts to her revelations. She led us over to the desk where several plastic trays were arranged. 'First, the peripherals,' she said to Natalya, carefully excluding me from her eyeline. 'In the matter of the fourth Monstrum murder, that of Lydia Primalova,' she began.

'First the most important question,' I interjected. 'Did you get any prints likely to come from the killer?'

Lena's face tightened. 'Andrei's in charge of prints,' she said.

I turned to him.

'No prints,' he said. 'I thought perhaps we could lift something off the plastic bags he used as gloves but there's too much sweat and slime inside . . .'

'Slime?'

'Some of her bodily fluids inevitably got onto the inside of the plastic gloves. We're still trying. But I'm not hopeful.'

'What about murders one, two and three?'

He pulled a face. 'The only really promising possibility was some pieces of plastic found near number two. And frankly the dusting was so amateur that I've only got one barely workable thumbprint.'

'We have a possible suspect,' I said. 'Is it worth sending this print over?'

'Save yourself the headache, Inspector. If you've other evidence, the thumbprint just might clinch it. But alone . . .' He shrugged an apology.

Lena inserted herself between Andrei and me. Turning back to Natalya, she smiled. 'Let me show you what we *do* have, Natalya.'

232

She led us to a desk and gestured to Andrei. He lifted the first tray and Lena prodded at the small plastic envelopes with a broad forefinger. 'Evidence bag one contained seventeen hairs, eleven of which certainly came from the victim herself.' She lifted another plastic envelope distinguished by a round green sticker. 'But the remaining six are darker, shorter, have more natural curl. Quite possibly male. It could well be useful once you have a suspect.'

I thought of Simakov and his razored head and scowled. 'The surprise result you mentioned,' I said. 'What is it?'

Lena Ivanova raised her hand without looking in my direction. 'The second evidence bag was quite interesting.' Andrei presented a second tray, much larger than the first. In it were scores of small plastic envelopes. The woman's broad finger flipped through them. 'Most of this is almost certainly rubbish,' Lena said. 'We've got a huge variety of fibres such as you might have if you pressed your way through a crowd for instance. In the midst of all this there might be something significant, but from what you tell me about the stage the investigation has reached, there's no present way of knowing. I'll keep it all on file for as and when you want it. But this—' she took a single envelope, this time marked with a red sticker – 'is of very much more interest.'

She was talking to Natalya, keeping me on her shoulder. 'As you said in your notes, you suspected some of the fluff here might be carpet fibres. I would say very new, very expensive carpet fibres.'

'What chance have we of finding where they come from?'

'It will take time to run a thorough check and even then we might never succeed in tracing them to source.'

'Why not?' I said.

Lena turned slowly on me. 'Because they are not only expensive but Western, Inspector Vadim. And we're still trying to rebuild our Western contacts.'

'You're saying the victim, or perhaps the murderer, has recently been in the West?' Natalya said.

'Or in a house furnished with Western carpets,' I put in.

'It looks like it.'

'That's your surprise for us?' Natalya said.

'No,' Andrei lifted a finger. 'There's more to come.'

This time Lena looked at him indulgently. 'Let's move onto our prize piece.'

'Not yet,' I said. 'Let's stay with the carpet a moment. There's more I'd like to know. What colour is it?'

'A steel grey. A blue-grey you might call it.'

I was conscious that for the first time I had Lena's attention. 'You're suggesting a house carpet.'

'Yes.'

'But could it be an aircraft? A steel grey carpet makes it at least equally likely.'

'I suppose it does,' Lena Ivanova said reluctantly.

'Or a car? A limousine perhaps?'

'An expensive Western car, yes.'

I saw Natalya's head turn towards me. 'A limousine,' she said. 'That's a thought.'

I shrugged. 'OK. Now let's hear the surprise item.'

Lena Ivanova lumbered across to a long desk. It was set under a large window which had a hairline crack from corner to corner sealed with brown paper tape. She took the chair before the microscope and bent forward to peer into it. It was a minor piece of theatre. She nodded confirmation to herself and swung her chair round. 'There's no doubt about it.'

Andrei, the assistant, was moving from foot to foot.

'The Adamov test on the semen scraped from the victim number four's thigh shows her assailant was an A secretor.'

'What does that mean?' I said.

Lena Ivanova glared at me. 'A homicide inspector who's never heard of A secretion?'

'I don't mean I've never heard of it,' I said. 'I just wanted you to explain the particular significance in this case.'

Lena Ivanova was mollified. Natalya allowed herself a hint of a smile.

'*A* secretors are simply a category, of course,' Lena said. 'No special significance in itself.'

'But . . .'

'Think of Modina and Golikova.'

Natalya, I saw, was looking shocked.

'What is it I'm missing?' I said.

'You came late to the murders, I know.' Lena got up from the desk and turned to face us. She was savouring the moment. 'We have four victims . . .'

To tell her there were probably many more would be to sidetrack her. I nodded agreement.

'Tania Chekova, last week's victim, was found in pouring rain. Anything that might have been left on her body, any semen in particular, was washed away long before she was examined.'

Natalya looked sombre.

'That leaves three victims,' Lena said. 'I, of course, did not do the tests on the semen traces left on the bodies of victims one and two, Anastasia Modina and Nina Golikova. But I have read them and reread them. The significance of the killer of the last victim, Lydia Primalova, being an *A* secretor, Inspector Vadim, is that the killer of victims one and two was *not*.'

I stared at her. 'Jesus God. You mean the man who killed victims one and two didn't kill number four?'

'Yes, Inspector,' Lena Ivanova said, with a small smile of triumph. 'Perhaps you already have your first copycat Monstrum.'

It was a crisp day. The night's snow had settled and the sun glittered along rooftops. I was still provincial enough to be impressed by the huge area of Red Square, the swallowtail crenellations of the Kremlin and the gaudy brilliance of St Basil's candy-striped onion domes in the sunlight.

We walked slowly, pacing deliberately. Natalya had her gloved hands hooked by the thumbs in her coat pockets, her head forward, looking towards the ground. 'I suppose,' she said, 'that you think that I have no right to take a position on your relationship with your ex-wife.'

'Your right comes from the fact that I asked your help. And the fact that you gave it.'

She nodded and we paced on silently. 'Oh my God, Constantin,' she suddenly exploded. She brought her head up with such force that her hair rose from her shoulders like a startled flock of birds. 'You're such an impossible innocent! An innocent at large in a city jungle. What am I to do?'

'Could we not be friends?' I suggested uneasily.

She stopped and took my arm. 'I doubt it,' she said. 'All my instincts tell me we are marked for so much more. Lovers or bitter enemies. What's it to be, I wonder, Constantin?'

'I'm a plain man,' I said. 'I don't dabble with the future.'

'Don't be ridiculous. We all dabble with the future. We spend our lives trying to shape it to our will.'

'I don't understand you,' I said. 'I always thought you were at pains to show me that you were completely unpolitical.'

'I am not neutral, Constantin. I hope one day to hear you say you share my views.'

'You sound like Julia.'

'I wouldn't if you took the trouble to listen.'

'Please, Natalya. We have important things to talk about. Either we have two murderers, working together, or we have, as Lena Ivanova suggests, our first copycat Monstrum killing.'

236

She removed her arm from mine. 'Yes, we have work to do. We have no time for other things. So be it.'

We walked in silence for a few minutes.

'So let's forget any murders which may or may not have occurred during the actual fighting . . .'

She side-glanced me and reluctantly nodded agreement. 'We have to. For all practical purposes, we have four murders. And two murderers who work together – or a copycat. Frankly, neither possibility seems likely.'

'Is there any possibility of an error? This *A* secretor test, is it really certain?'

'Lena will not have made a mistake on that,' she said defensively.

'So in your view we definitely have two murderers?'

'I can't really believe that, no.'

'The science points that way,' I said. 'Two men. The murderer of the first two girls. And, quite separately, this last killer, someone inspired by the Monstrum hysteria?'

'The murderer of the first two girls . . .' She looked exasperated. 'Why don't you admit that you haven't even properly read the notes? In there,' she pointed over her shoulder, 'you didn't even recognise the names of Anastasia Modina and Nina Golikova. Our first and second victims, Inspector Vadim. Both eviscerated. Both with various organs removed. Both struck across the back and silenced by biting into the windpipe. All these unpublished details were replicated by the murderer of Lydia Primalova. Did he dream up the details? Of course not.'

'So it's the same man, you're saying. Lena Ivanova has got it wrong.'

'Perhaps,' she said almost sullenly.

'Well?'

'I don't know.'

'She's a fellow professional. You don't like to think it.'

Without asking me, she walked ahead and pushed open the door to a tea-room. I followed her in, catching the door that swung back in my face. The tea-room was small, hot and crowded with couples seated at tiny tables so that, as they bent forward, their foreheads almost touched.

Natalya was already sitting at a windowseat. She had removed her hat and gloves and was brushing back her hair with both hands, hardly bothering to look round to see if I had followed her in.

I sat down opposite her and she avoided meeting my eyes. When the girl came I ordered tea. I wiped steam from the windows and looked out through the smeared glass at the hazy figures moving along the street. Natalya's face was set, not sullen but clearly troubled. When the tea came, I paid and poured some for her from the squat metal teapot.

She lifted her cup, held it under her chin and breathed in the vapours. 'It's only right,' she said carefully, 'that you know that there could be another explanation for all this.'

'Which is?'

'Lena didn't do the two earlier forensic tests. Her lab had not yet reopened.'

'I know that. Who did them?'

'I arranged to have them done. By a friend.'

I waited.

'Professor Kandinsky, my old boss.'

'As a favour?'

'I'm not sure where else I might have gone.'

'Could he have missed the fact that the other semen tests showed the murderer to be an A secretor?'

'I don't believe so,' she said reluctantly. 'In the past his work has been internationally recognised.'

'In the past? What does that mean? Things are different now? He drinks?'

'No. Here in Moscow,' she said slowly, 'people were going through a very difficult time. The Anarchist currency had collapsed. We all needed the new rouble to live. Perhaps I shouldn't have given him the work.'

'You're saying he's unreliable?'

'Only from a Nationalist point of view.'

'He's an Anarchist?'

'No, Constantin,' she said witheringly. 'He's a democrat.'

'A democrat? Our party is the party of National Democracy. What's wrong with being a democrat, for God's sake?'

'You must tell me. But first I'll tell you that Professor Kandinsky is an *outspoken* democrat. He believes in the rule of law, Constantin. From the same background, indeed, an old friend of our President Peter Romanov.'

'A friend of the president? Then if Kandinsky was going through a bad time, surely his friend the president could intervene on the professor's behalf?

'Intervene against Koba? Are you mad?'

I glared at her, reluctant to take the argument down that road. 'So your Professor Kandinsky . . . is he competent or not? That's all I need to know.'

'He is fully competent, but on reflection it's possible that he did not have access to the necessary equipment,' she conceded shortly.

'You mean he might not even have made the test?'

'I'll ask him if he was able to do it . . .'

'And he'll say yes.'

'Not Professor Kandinsky. If he did not make the test, he'll admit it.'

Perhaps my lip curled. 'He needs the test fee. You're probably the only medical examiner supplying him with work. What fool is going to admit that he failed to carry out full tests on body one *and* body two?'

'Give them names, for God's sake. They're women, not things.'

'I've no head for names,' I said.

'You've no head for anything except Julia.' She rapped the table in front of her. 'Why are you so short of time? Where have you been these last three days? On some errand for her? Risking your life as her courier to one of her Anarchist groups?'

I looked round in alarm but there was too much background noise for anyone to overhear. 'No,' I said. 'I was on official business.'

'What business?'

'I can't tell you that.'

She pushed her unfinished tea aside and got up. I followed her out and slithered across the ice to catch up with her.

Even in the cold wind that came across Red Square her face burned with anger. 'I warn you, Constantin,' she said. 'I warn you here and now, I'll turn her in if you were off on her filthy business. I'll denounce her to the Cheka if she involves you.' Her face was flushing angrily. 'I made a great mistake while you were away. Hippocratic Oath or not, I should have left the gorgon to die, fuck your mother.'

'For Christ's sake, Natalya!'

She stopped and turned to face me. 'No,' she said. 'For your sake, Constantin.' Her mouth twisted. 'But are you worth it, I ask myself?' People were stopping on the broad sidewalk as she waved her arms at me. 'Are you worth it, Constantin? Oh my God, I doubt it. I really have to doubt it!' She stared at me furiously for a moment then turned, shouldering aside the bystanders, and stomped off along the boulevard, her boots kicking up white puffs in the fresh snow.

23

I fixed V.I. Lenin with a baleful eye. He turned away with a show of feline indifference I didn't really believe and made a silent leap onto a shelf nearly a metre from the floor. I lifted a hand in acknowledgement.

'I want to know,' I said, turning to Dronsky, 'what colour is our prime suspect's pubic hair.'

'Simakov?' Dronsky slowly took out a cigarette and spun it in his fingers. It was one of his little tricks. 'Shall I check?'

I nodded.

He leaned over and picked up my phone and asked for Bitov in the basement. While they were talking my mind wandered. I had somehow to repair my relationship with Natalya, if only to make sure Julia remained safe. A woman scorned is a woman to be feared. But would she really report Julia? Would she really risk involving herself? She might get away with it if she claimed that she had no idea who Julia was when she treated her. I bit my lip. It was possible. Which meant I had to mend fences with Natalya.

Later I could go and see Julia. But first Natalya.

I reached for the phone. It took me a beat to remember what Dronsky was doing there, phone in hand. As I watched he lifted it to his ear, listened and grunted his thanks.

'A very nasty gingery red,' he said. 'Is that significant?'

'Forensic found short dark curly pubic hair on the last girl. Not hers.'

'Mother of God.' He thought for a moment. 'No fingerprints to pin him down . . .'

'What about his lodgings?'

'More like a bear's cave than a human habitation. But nothing there to connect him with any of the murders. A gun – but who doesn't have a gun in Presnya these days. And a knife that Dr Karlova says is very unlikely to be the murder weapon.'

'You're not hopeful.'

'His alibis are still telling us different stories. But we do know he lived in the same block as victim four, Lydia Primalova.'

'Work on establishing a connection with the other victims. If we can't come up with anything there . . .'

'Then I think we're going to have to face a few facts, Chief. First and foremost that we're probably holding the wrong man.'

I looked at him. 'Do you have children, Dronsky?'

'A boy and a girl. Five and three. I pray God by the time they grow up Russia will be different.'

'And your wife . . . what's her name?'

'Nina . . .'

'A wife, two children and a cat.'

'Two cats,' he said. 'I think the smell of them on my jacket drives V.I. Lenin mad with jealousy. That's why he's taken such a shine to you, Chief. As far as he's concerned you're a home waiting to happen.'

I glared at the cat. 'Enough of that, Dronsky. Go down and run over Simakov's story, then get off home. Give yourself a chance to give the wife a hand with the kids like all good Russian husbands.'

He hesitated by the door, looking awkward. A flash of resentment, even. 'Did you know that Nina was injured in the bombing?'

'No. No, I didn't.'

He opened the door. 'Sorry, Chief,' he said. 'I thought that's what you were getting at. That I wasn't putting in the hours here.'

'Listen, that's not what I meant, Dronsky.'

He had nodded briskly and closed the door behind him before I could say more.

The damn cat looked at me and hissed. I gave it a two-fingered salute. 'Remember,' I said. 'Your days are numbered. Strictly numbered.'

Dronsky had left his cigarettes and matches on my desk. I took out one of the long yellow cigarettes and tried juggling as he had. But that was clearly another trick I was going to have to learn.

I lit the cigarette and called Natalya's office. It took a moment or two to get her to the phone. 'I'm smoking my first deliberately chosen cigarette in months,' I said.

'I'm holding a scalpel with which I am just about to open the chest cavity of a man who has been in the river for a month.'

Down the phone line I heard a thump and a hiss. 'I have just plunged the scalpel in,' she said. 'Small pieces of tissue have been blown out of the incision by the escaping gas.'

'I'll talk to you later,' I said.

'Only if it's about the case.'

'Natalya, you yourself said there was something between us . . .'

'With the scalpel I am now opening the stomach . . .'

'That's enough.'

'I'm glad you agree, Constantin.' She put down the phone.

I dressed in black. In black jeans and a black pea-jacket. There was snow lining the streets and across the wasteground but much of it was so dirtied under the occasional street lamp that it offered not too much of a contrasting background.

I drove the car until I found myself approaching the river, then found a piece of wasteland and drove the car safely off the road. The last half-kilometre I covered on foot, crossing the wasteground, ducking into destroyed buildings to wait for ten or fifteen minutes for any sign of a Cheka tail.

There was none. Nevertheless I continued to cover the ground at a snail's speed, sometimes even doubling back once or even twice before I took a crucial turning. The temperature was down close to freezing but I could feel the prickle of sweat on my collar. I stopped and crouched for a few moments in a doorway, watching the empty street. The sheer excitement of the thought of seeing Julia again was multiplied by the memory of what she had said to me last time about being in New York. The concert with Jimmy Gabriel. *'I missed you, Costya.'*

I would talk to her about other things too. About Leonid Koba. About my own feeling, my conviction about him, that he was the best hope for Russia. Perhaps I would even tell her about my own small role in Russia's future.

The truth was, I was beginning to nurture a hope. Perhaps at this moment, just the first seeds of hope. The hope that Julia, after all that had happened to her, would pull back from the brink. Would turn away from the Anarchists who surrounded her. Would come back into the light.

It was over an hour later that I reached the street with the deserted factory. The wall to the right of the gates was collapsed in two or three places and I slipped into the front yard with ease and crouched, looking towards the darkness where I knew a sentry was located. Taking my torch from my pocket I covered it with my fingers so that only the most shielded light would show and flicked the switch three times.

There was no response although now that my eyes were becoming accustomed to the angles of the factory outbuildings I seemed to make out the shape of a woman leaning against the factory wall.

Then why did she not reply?

I covered the torch and flicked the switch again. Three times . . . and another three.

I thought of the girl with the Kalashnikov and imagined her leaning against the wall, her eyes closed maybe in a few moments' light sleep. A catnap. Sentries did that sort of thing, I knew from my own service days, and could start out of it disorientated, their fingers pressing on the trigger. I put the torch away. Picking up a piece of cement the size of a golf ball, I tossed it out into the middle of the courtyard, crouching low as it rattled towards her.

The shadow of the woman by the wall did not move.

I was very disturbed by now. There was too much moonlight to make it possible to cross the front yard unseen but any thought of creeping round to enter the factory on the riverside would get me shot dead by a Kalashnikov. I was desperate. I flashed the torch another half-dozen times. I threw concrete and bricks. I called softly across the gap between myself and the woman. But she still made no movement.

Was she dead? Cold fingers ran up my back at the thought. But it brought me no closer to Julia.

The soft snow was soaking into the shoulders of my jacket. My face was numb and tight with anxiety and cold. I did it without thought. Without weighing risks I stood up and walked with my hands in the air into the open moonlit space.

I braced myself to hear Roy Rolkin's voice echo cheerfully: *And about time too. Creeping about there like an old woman afraid of the dark!*

But there was no voice, Roy's or anybody else's. Nothing happened. Walking across the space, hearing the crunch of broken glass beneath my feet, I slowly dropped my hands. Three-quarters of the way across I took the torch from my pocket and shone it at the woman leaning against the wall. It was a tall thin gas cylinder resting against the brickwork.

I took a deep breath. Moving into the narrow alley where I had driven the car under the Siberian girl's instructions, I came at last to the side door Natalya and I had been led through that first night. The door was open.

Inside there was no movement, no voice. The corridor I had waited in was empty. On the office table was a guard's unfinished meal. Two chairs lay on their backs. A bottle of mineral water had rolled onto the floor. The room in which Julia had lain was empty, the bed stripped back as if she had been dragged from it. For just the fraction of a second I saw her, in my mind's eye, pushed down onto the cement floor of some basement cell by Roy Rolkin. Roy Rolkin who had always wanted her.

I heard a choking gasp and realised it was my own. In a frenzy I ran through the rooms, banging doors, kicking furniture aside. I was shouting her name, shouting like a lunatic . . .

I pushed past the airforce officer and hammered on Natalya's door. When she opened it I pushed it in her face and walked into the room.

Wordlessly she closed the door and rested her back against it. I saw she was wearing her work clothes. Late back from the laboratory – or from a visit to the Cheka? 'Are you drunk, Constantin?' she said.

I shook my head, my mouth frozen with hatred.

'Then would you like a drink?'

I felt as if I would explode towards her and grasp her by the neck. 'There's nobody at the factory,' I rasped out the words. 'Julia's been arrested.'

For a moment she looked at me without speaking, the most dangerous moment of her life. 'Arrested.' I launched myself towards her.

'Or decided to slip away quietly,' she said.

The words brought me to a stop. I stood hunched in the middle of the room. Seconds, perhaps minutes passed. *Or decided to slip away quietly*.

Natalya stood there, her arms folded across her breast,

her amber eyes holding me in a cool, level glance. 'Why not?' she said, her voice without inflection. 'Julia has no further need of treatment from me,' she said quietly. 'And you are no further use to her. So why not move on? Without a word. That's the terrorist lifestyle, isn't it? Take and move. Take and move on . . .'

At my sides my arms seemed to be whirling free.

'Sit down, Constantin, before you fall down. I've not just come back from the Cheka if that's what you're thinking. Much as I'd have liked to denounce your Julia, I'm aware I would be denouncing you too.' She paused. 'And I couldn't do that,' she added bitterly. 'I couldn't do that to *myself*.'

As she came forward I walked past her and pulled open the door. Outside it was snowing. From time to time a passing car slurped brown slush over me as I made the long walk home.

24

Wheels locked and screamed behind me. Headlights rushed my shadow across the road. I had no idea which way to throw myself. I guessed left and the car brushed my right shoulder, skidding past, tearing metal panels as it bounced off a concrete lamp-post, spinning like a top until it crashed, rear end on against a factory wall.

From my position flat on the pavement I looked up. Twenty yards away a police car sat facing me with its radiator spouting steam, a single working headlight winking raffishly.

The two officers who climbed from the wreck took a few minutes to convert their shock to anger but when they fell on me it was with the fury of very frightened men. While one tried to haul me from the pavement, the other seemed intent on kicking me down again.

'You vodka-sodden wreck,' one of them was shouting. 'You pox-ridden fleabag! You nearly killed us, d'you know that? You nearly killed us!'

Then caution reared its lovely head. 'Turn out his pockets first, Oleg,' I heard the other, marginally calmer voice say as the first man made to resume kicking.

I was rolled onto my back and hands rummaged through my pockets.

I lay with my eyes closed. Unresisting. I seemed to be without sensation of time or place, in my own small pocket of numbness. The silence above me was unbroken but for the heavy breathing of the two officers and the steady hissing of the cracked radiator of their car.

'Inspector Vadim . . . ?' When the officer repeated my name his voice was close. He was kneeling down beside me. I opened my eyes to see that he was checking my face against my ID picture in my warrant card. He looked up and nodded gloomily to his colleague.

I reached up and took the wallet from him and climbed, aching, to my feet.

'You were walking in the middle of the road, Inspector,' the second man said tentatively. 'As I came round the bend I had to step on the brakes and throw over the wheel to miss you.'

There was a long pause while I lifted one shoulder and rubbed at my ribs. 'I blame myself,' I said. 'Are you both all right?'

'Nothing broken,' the first man smiled slowly, relieved. 'Shaken up, that's all. The car's a write-off . . .'

'In the course of duty,' I said.

They both nodded gravely.

'How far are we from your district station?'

'Next street, sir.'

'Let's go.' I massaged my shoulder while the two officers took their belongings from the wrecked car. 'I'll file a duty accident report,' I said when they were ready to move. 'We lost the suspect but fortunately the three officers emerged unharmed. Wasn't that the way it was?'

'That was the way it was,' the officer called Oleg said. 'There's certainly no sign of the suspect, Inspector.'

At the local militia station I signed an accident report and a couple of salary stars for the two officers' action in coming so promptly to my assistance. I added a passing mention of minor damage to the car in the course of our hot pursuit and filed the documents in triplicate with the duty sergeant. When I had finished I asked for the use of an office with a phone and was shown into a box-like room with a metal desk and splay-leg chair.

The accident had acted as catharsis. I was drained but thinking clearly again. I had to find out what had happened to Julia. There were two alternatives. She had simply moved camp as Natalya insisted; or she (and the others) had been arrested by the Cheka. Only Roy Rolkin would know. It took me nearly half an hour to track him down at home.

'Dynamo hockey is wiping the Canadians off the ice,' Roy shouted down the phone. 'Better still they're doing it in Montreal. I'm watching it now.'

'Roy,' I said. 'Listen to me. There's a rumour around that an important Anarchist figure came in on the amnesty deal tonight.'

He grunted.

'One version of the story even claims it was a woman.' I paused. 'It's not Julia, I suppose?'

He exploded. 'If it was Julia, I'd know wouldn't I? She's my case. I'd be the first to hear.'

'I'm sure you would.'

'I was talking to my chief just ten minutes ago and he didn't mention any big Anarchist surrender. Where d'you get your lousy information from?'

'It's just one of the officers at District talking. Amnesty's in the air, you know how it happens. And we've got a terrific piece of American skirt working from our station as one of the amnesty commissioners. So everybody wants to be in on the act. Natural enough.'

'Tell your man if he opens his mouth that wide again, I'll pull all his fucking teeth,' Roy said irritably. 'If we'd got Julia I would know within minutes. And I've heard nothing.' He grunted again. 'Canada's just scored, fuck your mother. Get off the line and come round and watch this game.'

But I decided not to go round to Roy's. A Station 5 vehicle dropped me off where I had left my car and I headed back towards my apartment at Fili. I had read extracts from the Bible. I had heard of the slough of despond. Now I knew what it was, knew what it felt like. Julia had not been betrayed by Natalya and hauled out of the factory by a Cheka specialist action team. She had left of her own volition. A few hours, maybe even less, before I arrived at the factory.

She had left without letting me know. There could be no doubt it was a conscious decision. Natalya was right. I was no more use to her now. So once again, I was being tossed out of her life.

There are times when I can't understand how my own emotional world is shaped. As I drove I imagined the meeting of the sisterhood. I tortured myself with the very words in which Julia announced to her companions the decision to move base. In my mind's eye the Siberian leans forward and asks about me. Was I to be told? Would anyone be left to let Inspector Vadim know what had happened? With total clarity I can see Julia's face. The line of the mouth hardens. She is silent. Then her deputy, Denisova, repeats the question. The four other senior colleagues gathered round the table are motionless. 'With respect,' Denisova says, 'we must have a decision. Will Vadim be informed of our move to a new base camp? Or will he be allowed to draw what conclusions he chooses?'

And Julia's face softens a fraction, before it hardens again. Constantin Vadim, she says, must be left to draw his own conclusions.

And even as I played this comedy for myself I realised what a lie it was. Julia had chosen. Not reluctantly. Deliberately. She had chosen quite deliberately to exclude me from her life. I must hold on to that. I must at all costs avoid excusing her. I thumped my hand against the steering wheel in a gesture of movie rage. But it was despair I felt. Natalya was right. Far from betraying Julia, she was right about her.

So do I feel contrition for having suspected Natalya? Do I go straight back and tell her she was right?

No, brothers. None of those things. None of the things a decent man would do. Instead I drive the Economy past my own apartment and on a dozen blocks into the forecourt of the old Soviet nomenklatura building where Dr Imogen has her apartment and I persuade the armed concierge to call up to her and ask if she will accept a visit from Inspector Constantin Vadim.

And a few moments later she has accepted.

Just believe me, brothers, when I tell you that you can follow what this next hour was like only if you imagine me playing in a thirties Hollywood movie. When she opened the door she was wearing a short black cocktail dress, high heels, and was carrying a highball glass three-quarters full of ice and whisky. You could see her, in the sinuous way she moved, in the long-lashed reflective look, in the glistening perfection of her lips, as a brunette Lauren Bacall. On my side, the rumpled Humphrey Bogart role was irresistibly forced upon me by the torn pocket on my jacket and the dampness I could feel across the shoulders. She nodded towards the bar that occupied one end of the long room. 'Help yourself, Constantin, while I find something to go with the drinks.'

I rounded the bar and stood staring at the array of bottles on the backlit shelves. Vodka would be too crude and obvious. And who ever heard of Humphrey Bogart drinking vodka. I chose Scotch, Glenmorangie. Something that called itself a single malt. I added just a touch of plain water in the hope that that was the right thing to do and walked back round the bar.

I eyed the seating arrangements. To choose one of the overstuffed armchairs would isolate me in it for the rest of the evening. The sofa, too obvious. A Hollywood move would be to begin at the bar, establish a certain intimacy in the conversation. And then move, perhaps directly to the bedroom?

She returned in a few moments with a dish of smoked sturgeon on fingers of brown bread. The sharp tang of lemon juice rose into my nostrils as she placed the dish on the bar.

She nodded towards the Glenmorangie. 'Most Russian men I know would have gone straight for the vodka,' she said.

As she spoke she sat on the high barstool, the way women used to in old Hollywood films, the leg slowly raised until one glistening toecap was taking the weight on the footrail . . . the other leg drawn up slowly to cover the exposed thigh . . . accompanied by a slow smile and just the faintest pursing of the lips in acknowledgement of my thraldom. You know.

'I have a confession to make to you, Constantin,' she said. 'From that very first moment we met in the office of that absurd little man, Brusilov, I laid a wager with myself. Ten days, I said, before we were alone spending the evening together.'

'You've won,' I said. But the truth of the matter is that I thought I had.

She laughed. 'I understand you've been away. Not sampling the delights of a new girlfriend, I trust.'

'No girlfriend, no,' I said.

She was silent a moment. 'That girl who runs the pathology department, Natalya Karlova . . . she has a certain womanliness about her, I won't deny.'

'I barely know her. I'm new to Moscow, remember,' I said.

'Ah . . . So you've had little or no time to . . . make friends?'

'With Dr Karlova? We work together . . .'

'Don't let it go further, Constantin. Trust my instincts about the woman.'

'Now I'm curious.'

'She's trouble. She used to work for me. Nothing but trouble. Not so much rebellious as disloyal.' She paused. 'We're natural rivals, she and I.' With ringed fingers she brushed the subject of Natalya aside. 'So then, my handsome Constantin . . .' Her perfume was hitting me in waves of pure sensuality. 'I must guess why you're here.'

I leaned forward on the bar and swirled the Glenmorangie in my glass. With my free hand I held my torn pocket in place. I raised my eyes to hers.

'You've come for my profile on your Monstrum. Am I right?'

'I'd like to hear more some time,' I said evasively. 'Maybe we could set up a meeting.'

'But why not talk now? The two of us. How can you take me seriously as a woman, Constantin, if you aren't prepared at least to entertain my ideas?'

'But of course I am. Of course I'm interested.'

'OK,' she said slowly. 'I want you to think about this. I see him as someone who has become brutalised by the war. Yes. First and foremost he is a victim of the war.'

'A victim.'

'That's right,' she said. 'Cops tend to take a very narrow, restricted view of victims. Russian cops are as blinkered in this regard as the NYPD.'

'The NYPD?'

'The New York cops.'

'Maybe it's because the NYPD gets to see the real victims,' I said. 'The old ladies beaten up on the pavement. Young girls like the one I saw on the plinth outside the flag factory carved up by some raving lunatic you call a victim.' The more beautiful the woman, the more ready men are to concede to them in intellectual argument. But even Imogen's superb thighs didn't justify extending victim sympathy to the Monstrum.

She pursed her lips, in mild irritation this time. 'Let me go on.' She looked at my glass. 'Help yourself to another drink.'

'For you too?'

She shook her head. 'Where was I?'

I knew where *I* was. At least in imagination I knew.

Now listen, Costya, I told myself. Ask questions but try not to interrupt. This is a lady who likes to have her own way. Massage the situation right and her way will be your way.

I got up and went round the bar to refill my glass. I'd never had whisky with this depth of taste before. I made a note to ask old Polina at the station job shop if she ever got her hands on anything called Glenmorangie. This time I tried it without water.

'OK,' she said. 'Brutalised by war . . . lost and isolated by the peace . . .'

I held up my hand. I could not just keep quiet and let my luck roll. 'We have evidence,' I said, 'that the first attacks took place before the war ended.'

'I wasn't aware of that. How many attacks?'

'We've firm evidence on one only. Anecdotal evidence on maybe a dozen.'

'Anecdotal evidence, Constantin. Really. Homicide investigation is a science. And even if there *were* victims before Anastasia Modina it doesn't really alter my case.'

'Which is?' I thought this time I'd better listen.

She made herself comfortable on her barstool. 'Now, I'm not saying there was not a history to this brutalisation. Probably a family history. Abuse by a father. Even by a mother.'

I sipped the whisky. I knew that Americans were fond of spreading victims about. 'Abused by his mother?'

'Yes . . . it happens every day,' she said. 'The effort of the abused is concentrated on escaping from the grey, frightening world of abuse-memory.'

'But how will I know him when I see him, or interrogate him? You see what I'm asking. How close can a profile get?'

'It can't tell you the shape of his head or his blood type. But a profile can be quite precise.' She leaned forward on the bar. 'Here we'd be talking about an utter obsessive. Maybe even someone who finds half the pleasure in the hunt, in evading the hunt, in taunting the hunter . . . whatever the risk. Certainly someone whose obsession makes it difficult, nearly impossible, to carry on a normal life. Someone who at work will be unable to perform anything but the most routine functions.' She sat frowning, concentrating. 'Repetitive labour enables him to concentrate in the manner he has to, so your man will very often be a daily labourer working on a construction site or maybe, even better, on the roads. Hard physical activity acts as some minor and purely temporary palliative. So you frequently see such subjects voluntarily engaging in harsh physical activities. Pumping iron, for example. Activities which will bring them way above the pain threshold.'

I nodded, my eyes low as she shifted her legs, slipped off the stool, walked round and began to pour herself a drink. I sat mesmerised by the way the backlit shelves gleamed on her hair. By the liquefaction of her dress as she reached up for her drink.

'You should have let me do that,' I said.

She ignored me. She was speaking now in a monotone, almost as if she were looking into the future. 'Such subjects will demonstrate certain obsessive behaviour patterns. One might be collecting. Collecting anything – stones, useless pieces of metal . . . Or it might take the shape of staying up all night and sleeping during the day, or of shouting at dogs. Or walking patterns, constantly covering and re-covering one small patch of ground . . . all or any of these behaviour patterns can precede the crisis.'

'And what might bring that on?'

'Almost any traumatic event in the subject's life.'

'Such as?'

'You can imagine . . .'

'I can't.'

'Don't be deliberately obtuse, Costya,' she said. 'The death of a mother would be an obvious trigger to crisis.'

'The mother who had abused him in childhood?'

'Why not? I've seen a subject launched into crisis by the death of a child he had been systematically abusing for years. You have to understand that these acts of violence against the person are themselves a desperate attempt to give an unbearably grey life some vivacity, some theatre.'

I was silent.

'So?' she said.

'I'm thinking.'

'You must keep an open mind.'

'I am.'

Her eyes narrowed angrily and she threw her hands in the air. 'You're quite ridiculous, Constantin. You're more concerned by the way I cross my legs, by the amount of thigh I show you, than by my ideas on profiling your Monstrum. I find your attitude insulting. I find it disappointingly masculine . . .'

I opened my arms apologetically. 'This is all pretty new to me,' I said. 'But I'm listening. Really. I'm listening.'

She hesitated. 'You really are taking it in?' And when I nodded enthusiastically, she smiled. 'All right,' she said, tentatively. 'If that's so, good.'

'The subject, you said, might be triggered into crisis by the death even of an object of abuse.'

'Yes.'

'One of the men we're holding is Vladimir Simakov. A short while back his younger sister died. Tuberculosis. She was about eight. When they found her, she was badly bruised. Probably bruised over a fairly long period. Simakov claimed she'd been in trouble with some group of beggars a couple of times. The police accepted his story.'

'And?'

'Later that night Anastasia Modina was murdered.'

Her eyebrows shot up. 'Is he a solid suspect?'

'We have lab problems but he could be.'

'And you never made a connection? His younger sister's death . . . then an almost immediate act of violence.'

'Hold it. We've only just picked up Simakov. It's old-fashioned police work, previous history stuff, that's put us onto him now.'

'But once you had picked him up? And started looking into his background? Did you make a connection then?'

'My deputy Dronsky did suggest that maybe his sister's death had tipped him off his rocker.'

'Crudely put but basically what I was suggesting. That the loss, even of the subject's former abuser or abusee, can precipitate crisis. How exactly did you get onto this man?'

'Simakov's name only came up when my team started hunting through lists of men with a record of violent sexual behaviour.'

She suddenly looked immensely animated. 'You have corroborating evidence?'

'I wouldn't put it as strong as that. He knew Lydia Primalova, the fourth victim.'

Her eyes glittered. 'And he's also beginning to fit the profile I was sketching for you.'

'Well, maybe,' I said, reluctantly.

'OK. Number one, death of his sister. Anything else you can see?'

'He works on a building site,' I said reluctantly. 'And he's a crazy enthusiast for pumping iron. But so are a lot of other veks.'

'It's shaping up in a very interesting way. What about obsessive patterns of behaviour?'

'Nothing I know of.'

'It's worth checking.'

'A good set of fingerprints would be worth a hell of a lot more.'

'Perhaps,' she said. 'But if you'd seen these profiles work out in the United States, you'd be impressed.

Very impressed, Constantin.' She paused. 'You did read Professor Benson's book.'

'Not finished yet, but extremely interesting . . . May I keep it a little longer?'

'If you think it might help.'

She slipped off her barstool, letting her skirt ride high. I glimpsed an inch of bare flesh above the silk and beyond that a warm darkness. I experienced a sudden, compulsive need to be steeped in her. She was totally and openly aware of it as she held out her hand. I slid off my stool in acute discomfort. She took my hand.

I'd like to tell you we moved together balletically into a large luxuriously appointed bedroom. The truth is different. The bedroom was as large and luxurious as a man could wish for, but I was so painfully erect that, crouched over to diminish the pain, I saw myself in the huge mirrors hopping and skipping along beside her like some lustful monkey.

25

It is still an hour or so off dawn as I approach Fili. I drive along the Marshal Zhukov Prospekt watching the first touch of lemon yellow lighten the eastern sky and ask myself how I feel. Throughout my whole body I feel a flush, a flush of triumph. That much is clear. My bitter feeling of betrayal by Julia has been pushed to the back of my mind. It will surge again in the next hours or days, I'm sure of that. But for the moment I am close to being at peace. I have slept with my first Western woman, my first American woman. It would be tempting to say it was no different, but sex with Imogen Shepherd *was* different. It's well known that Russian women quite like to take a positive role in lovemaking. Julia certainly had. The theory is that Russian men are bullies in the living room, lambs in the bedroom. I don't know.

But I know that Imogen's extraordinary demand that we verbally share the sexual experience made it quite different from anything I'd known before. The whole experience was completely at her orchestration, but I was far from being reduced to a willing lamb in her bedroom. I had not been allowed the role. She had pleasured me but equally required me to pleasure her. Sometimes these moments had come together, sometimes separately. Prude that I am, I was somewhat alarmed at the vigorous performances of oral sex she required of me throughout the night.

The lights of passing cars streamed past me, lulling my senses. Perhaps, most of all, I knew I would need to absorb what had happened to me. Emotionally I am not quick on my feet. But I knew something *had* happened to me with an importance far beyond a spectacular one-night stand. I was at least sure of that.

With these scrappy reflections on what for me had been an experience of more than ordinary impact, I left my car and approached my apartment building in Semyon Lane. Automatically I glanced up at the windows. Counting the still unfamiliar floors I, at first, thought that Madame Raisa's light was on. Then, with a shock that stopped me, I realised it was my own.

What was I to think about that? There was no question of my having left the light on myself. I stood in the lane and stared up at the old building. It took me half a minute to notice that mine was not the only light on. A very faint glow was coming from one of the rooms of Dimitry, the inspector of water standards.

I ran forward and let myself into the building. Deciding against the lift I ran lightly up the stairs. The recent cleansing of my loins had released all sorts of energies and aggressions in me. That tiny false Dimitry was searching my apartment! One more floor taken at American Superman speed and I would catch him red-handed.

The glass-ball landing light was on as I reached my door. Dimitry's door was partly open. Thus the very faint gleam I had seen from the street below. I turned my handle silently and, bracing myself, hurled the door open.

From the living room Roy's voice shouted. 'Enough of your Wild West tactics, you drunken whoreson. Come in and join us.'

Roy was sitting on the sofa, uniform jacket unbuttoned, the crate of French wine Imogen had given me open on the floor in front of him.

'Not a decent drink in the place,' he complained, tossing aside an empty bottle and taking the corkscrew to another. Inspector of Water Standards Dimitry was standing in the corner of the room, a half-apologetic smirk on his face, drinking Château Margaux from the bottle.

I walked forward into the middle of the room. 'What the devil's going on, Roy?' I said, conscious of my anxiety to let Dimitry know of my acquaintance with a Cheka colonel if he didn't know already. It's by these little signs I know I'm frightened.

'Developments,' Roy said. He looked up. 'You know your neighbour, Sergeant Dimitry . . . whatsisname . . . Cuntstruck, late of the Soviet KGB, now of our own dear Nationalist Cheka.'

I stared at the false inspector of water standards and turned back to Roy. 'What developments?'

'Don't you get shirty with me, Costya. What have you been doing all night while I've been working Dimitry's balls off? Don't tell me, I can smell it on you. Disgusting! What was she like? Not your American piece of skirt by any chance?'

'Developments, you said.'

'Look at him, Dimitry, he's had his share of plunder and he just wants to go to bed and sleep it off. But not yet, Costya, my peach. You could have a long day dawning ahead of you. You're coming with us.'

'Is it Julia?' I said. 'Tell me that at least.'

Roy waggled his head. 'It's about Julia,' he conceded. 'The rest you hear on the way down to the Lubyanka.'

I've said you can't be a Russian without being terrified by the name of the old All-Russian Insurance building. The Cheka headquarters, the scene of God knows how much misery and suffering in nearly a century since the first days the Soviets took it over. I was being taken to the Lubyanka. And what for? Did Roy know I'd been in touch with Julia? My God, did he know that Natalya had been treating her? The extent of my worries at least must have been written clearly on my face. As we left my building and crossed the pavement to where a large unmarked car was drawing up for us, Roy nudged me and winked.

'For God's sake, Roy,' I said, and even I could hear the strain in my voice.

'Tell him, Dimitry,' Roy said amiably. 'Why not?'

The little man paused on the pavement as the driver got out of the car. 'We've got Madame Raisa in a downstairs suite,' Dimitry smirked. 'Me and a couple of the lads have been grunting her all night.'

Grunting is their term, the Cheka's. It's supposed to mean questioning but everybody knows it means beating. It refers to the grunts of pain that come from stunned, near-unconscious victims. The grunts of horror from gagged women when their bodies are abused by the torturers. Roy has often boasted about sessions in his devil may care fashion.

And if Madame Raisa, a totally innocent go-between, was being tortured in the Lubyanka basement, my heart went out to her. But in fear too. Because I knew there was no resisting these men; she would be bound to confess she had delivered messages. And I, when the first electrodes seared my penis, would be bound to admit it was Julia. What harm could it do, now? Julia, you were right not to entrust me with the secret of your new headquarters.

Green and cream corridors are what strike most people about the inside of the Lubyanka. On the first basement floor the cream is scratched and chipped. On the concrete steps leading down to the lower basement floor the cream walls are often stained with patches of a rusty brown.

We passed along the corridor and Roy plucked me by the sleeve to guide me into an interview room opposite the black and silent doors of the cells. Reaching forward he closed the door before Dimitry could follow us in. 'Sit down, Costya,' he said. 'Let me fill you in.'

I sat down on the interview chair and Roy eased his hefty haunches onto the desk.

'It was keen-eyed work by Dimitry Whatsisname that did it,' Roy began, taking a cheroot from his uniform jacket pocket, waggling it at me, flicking it across when I nodded, and taking another.

I got up to get a light from him and drew a hot draught of tobacco smoke into my throat, held it there and blew it out slowly. It takes a lifetime not to be a smoker.

I sat down. He lit his cheroot and nodded approval of the first drag. 'Of course I assigned Dimitry to the apartment next to you as soon as you came to Moscow . . .'

'You didn't think to tell me.'

'Ah . . . you know what a forgetful sod I am, Costya.' Roy winked down at me.

'When it suits you.'

'How many little run-ins between Katya and you have I forgotten,' he mused.

'Run-ins?'

'At parties . . . a few drinks.' He slipped off the desk. 'A few drinks, a bit of music . . .' Hands in the air, cheroot smoke curling towards the ceiling, he started to dance vigorously to his own singing: 'Yeah, twist and grope . . . Come along, baby . . . just twist and grope . . . twist and grope . . .' He stopped and grinned hugely. 'Forgetful, that's me, fuck your mother.'

I felt sick deep in my stomach.

'OK, OK,' he said. 'Dimitry was there to watch over you. Just in case Julia made contact and for some reason I can't begin to guess at, she didn't want me to know.'

'Come off it, Roy . . . You know why Julia would be wary of our side. Even with an amnesty. There have been enough broken promises. We both know that.'

'We do, we do, Costya. Which is why I put little Dimitry onto it. And of course he reported back each day empty handed. Until yesterday.'

'What happened?' I was having great trouble not making it obvious I was shaking with fear. By tensing every muscle I could control the trembling of hands and lips, canalise it into a shudder which I would then pathetically fail to disguise as a sudden movement, a cough or a crossing of the legs.

I don't think any of this escaped Roy. 'Yesterday,'

264

he said, 'Dimitry was in the park. Doing some shopping at the market there apparently. And suddenly he sees his neighbour. Madame Raisa. You've met her, of course.'

'On the stairs.'

'Little Dimitry has confessed to me he has a penchant – isn't that what the old nobility used to call it? – for Madame Raisa's girth. She's big, uh? Bosom like the figurehead carving of an old sailing ship. I like them slimmer myself. But not Dimitry . . .'

'Get on with it, Roy.'

'Just painting you the background. Because none of this would have happened if little Dimitry didn't lust after Madame Raisa. Little men often have a thing about big women, you know.'

'Roy . . .'

'All right. Dimitry in the park. Madame Raisa sixty, seventy metres away. If he hadn't . . . well you know . . . he would have walked on. He'd finished his shopping by that time, herrings I think it was, and was on his way home. Now most of us might not think a string bag of herrings the best accompaniment to a romantic moment of chance. But not so Dimitry.'

I rocked back on my chair.

'I'm coming to it, Costya. Don't be impatient. Dimitry changes direction. You understand he has just passed the old bandstand whilst Madame Raisa was making for the café. Oh yes, she was making for the café when Dimitry changed direction. And before she reaches the café doors, closed against the weather at this time of year, a young woman comes out.'

I held the cheroot in a clenched hand.

'The young woman was of an Asiatic cast of feature. Siberian, perhaps. Beautiful in her way, no doubt, although I'm a confirmed European myself. Under the eye of Dimitry, this girl approaches Madame Raisa on the café steps and they exchange a few words.'

I forced myself to ask, 'This Asiatic, who was she? That must be the significance of your story.'

'It is. Her name is unknown to me. But her *nom de guerre* is Slavina.' His eyes were on my face. 'For the last year of the war, she was a senior member of Julia's divisional staff.'

'Ah . . .' I nodded. 'And what happened then?'

'Dimitry attempted to apprehend her. Between you and me as police officers, Costya, I think he made his move too early. The girl went like the wind.'

I had seen it myself. 'So?' I shrugged out the question. 'You didn't get her.'

'She'd had time to talk to Madame Raisa.' Roy came off the table. 'Dimitry was certain of it. A message was passed.'

'He'd say that anyway to cover for the fact that he'd missed the Siberian girl.'

'Maybe. Maybe not. There's one way to find out.'

'Down here,' I said. 'The poor woman. She's down here?'

'Not the happiest circumstances to be paying us a call,' Roy said. 'But aren't you curious about the message? Aren't you wondering why Madame Raisa was chosen as the recipient?'

There was no point in pretence. 'Why should I be wondering?' I said. 'If one of Julia's staff contacts the woman who lives in the same block of apartments as me, it's because Julia wants to contact me. Stands to reason.'

But the most awful mixture of joy and horror was coursing through me. Joy that Julia had been trying to make contact, to tell me where she had moved to. Horror that an innocent go-between had been dragged off to the Lubyanka. But had the Siberian told Madame Raisa where they were hiding out? Surely Julia would not have allowed such information to be imparted to a third person.

266

'So you've had Madame Raisa down here for hours,' I said. 'You must have got out of her all she has to give by now.'

'Dimitry has, that's for sure. But she's a tough old bird. Would you believe, in sixteen hours of hard grunting, she's said nothing. Claims she doesn't know the Siberian, which I believe, and that no message was passed. According to her the Siberian was offering sexual services – there are a lot of lesbian whores hang around the Park Café for any middle-aged lady with the money and appetite for that sort of thing.'

'Maybe it's the truth. Maybe Dimitry's eyesight's no longer than his legs.'

Roy laughed. 'Evil wretch you are, Costya. But I don't think you believe that. No. What I want you to do is this. I want you to go down the corridor and have a word with Madame Raisa.'

'What sort of word?' I asked in horror.

'I'm not asking you to give her a kicking,' Roy said. 'She knows any message was meant for you. Believe me, at this moment she'll be more than happy to be relieved of the responsibility. In my end of the business, you get a good handle on human nature, I can tell you.'

Roy let me be alone with her. It was some part of his deviousness which I had no time to fathom. I stood in the cell under a single high thick glass light and looked down at the figure in the flowered dress on the bed. She was turned away from me so that I could not see her face. The red hair was matted black just below the crown and damp ringlets rested on the back of her neck. Her strong legs were bare although a stocking hung around one ankle. Not moving from the middle of the room, I said softly: 'Madame Raisa. It's Constantin Vadim.'

She began to turn almost immediately but it was a slow and painful movement. Her face was bloodied and her lips swollen. The dress had been ripped open at the breast and, as she completed the turn, I could see a dark bloodstain on the material between her legs. I think she was aware I was staring at it because she gave something between a sigh and a confirmatory nod. 'They know no bounds, these torturers, Constantin,' she said.

Her voice was weak and she was breathing heavily. 'Uncivilised brutes. Did I not warn you against that false Dimitry?' She tried to smile and it was painful to watch her swollen mouth twist up at the sides.

I felt a totally irrational surge of pride. Who, other than a Russian woman, could hold out for over sixteen hours against ... My sense of pride faltered. Her torturers were of course Russian too. I sat on the bed beside her and took her wrist. Her pulse was beating at some incalculable rate, over two hundred a minute perhaps, in shallow, machine-gun-like bursts. I was sick with fury at what they had done to her. But I knew there was nothing I could do to help her. If Roy decided she was of no more use she would be released. If Roy decided she had more to tell, Dimitry and his man would be allowed at her again.

I tried to put my hand under her head to support her but she winced as it came into contact with her damp hair. As I changed position to support her round the shoulders I saw there was a print of blood on my palm.

I wasn't thinking clearly but I knew Roy was right. I had to take the responsibility from her. 'The Siberian girl,' I said. 'She had a message from Sonya.'

Madame Raisa nodded. Her head hung forward. She was bleeding from the ears. With my free hand I supported her chin. For a second I watched as the blood welled up in the tiny cup which was the lobe of her ear, reached the rim and overran to trickle down the side of her neck. 'She said she would meet you. In two days. At the Park Café.'

'No.' I put my lips so close I touched her bloodied ear.

'At the factory on Vatutin Street. If they come in here again, tell them that,' I whispered urgently.

She was too weak to ask why. She nodded her head. 'Vatutin Street,' she said. 'I'll tell them that.'

'Now rest,' I said. I lowered my arm until she was again lying on the bed.

'Ah, Constantin,' she said. 'You should have seen me dressed to play Massenet's *Manon*. I opened the 1995 season in Smolensk . . .' Her face, though bruised, was also of an alarming greyness. What could I say to her? I felt a terrible sense of shame. As I sat looking down at her, her eyelids fluttered closed. Her breathing and pulse continued their mad race, leaping and stopping at intervals. I could not believe that she would survive much longer. But her eyes opened again and she smiled her swollen smile up at me. 'I told them nothing,' she said.

'I knew you wouldn't.'

'I swore on my life, Constantin,' she said.

Her eyes were closed. I might have tried to take her pulse again, but I saw no point. 'Vatutin Street,' she said, between swollen lips.

26

'No doubt at all they've been hiding here,' Roy said as we stood in the room where Julia had lain in bed just two nights before. He walked forward and looked down at the mattress. 'I'd say one of them lost a lot of blood. What about you, Costya?'

'It looks like it.'

Various members of Roy's special squad, led by Dimitry, were going through the room. 'Shall we print the place, Colonel?' one of the men asked, putting his head round the door.

I held my breath while Roy considered. 'Hardly worth it,' he said. 'This is certainly the address the old opera singer gave before she sang her last aria.' He beamed at me. 'Julia was here. I can near as dammit smell her.'

Why did that phrase, out of all the other insults Roy had offered, bring me closer to hitting him than I had ever been since our days in the playground?

He breathed deeply. 'Good smell on her, too,' he said. We both knew what he was talking about.

He turned away and ignored me while he walked through the other rooms of the factory offices and talked with Dimitry. I wandered about, stood in front of the stove, now dead, that I had tended through that frightening night. Beyond the open gate to the firebox there was a pile of ashes, the ash of burnt paper, grey as the morning light.

'Found anything?' Roy was beside me before I could bend down. He crouched and put his hand carefully into the firebox. 'Every sign of a quick exit,' he said.

'Once they knew you were onto Madame Raisa they'd hardly be likely to stay.'

'Exactly. So we could figure that they cleared up and burnt their vital papers as soon as the Siberian woman, Slavina, got back here. Only a matter of hours ago.'

I nodded.

'Except that,' Roy said, lifting a handful of ash from the stove and letting it pour through his fingers, 'there's not a scrap of warmth left in it.' He pointed an index finger and plunged it deep into the ash in the firebox. 'Not a single degree centigrade of warmth left.'

'What do you conclude from that?'

'You're the policeman,' he said. He saw my look and smiled. 'I'm just the blundering secret policeman. What does the investigating officer conclude?'

'That they left even before Madame Raisa's meeting in the park.'

Roy didn't react either way. Still crouched before the stove, he was thinking. 'It's not possible, I suppose, Costya,' he said slowly, 'that you've been here before?' He hopped round like a frog to look at me, a matter of inches between our eyes.

'No,' I said. I rested my hand flat on the floor. 'It's not possible.'

He stood up. 'Very well,' he said. 'Take your word for it. Anyway it'll all show up in the fingerprinting if you're pulling my pecker.'

'I thought you'd decided against fingerprinting?'

'Changed my mind. Prerogative of women and secret police officers.' He winked. 'She's clever, our Julia, but I'm just one step behind her, Costya.'

A shout from outside caught his attention. Members of the squad checking the factory yard had found a shallow grave in what had once been a flowerbed. I guessed immediately that it was the grave of the other member of Julia's group who had been wounded in the grenade attempt on Koba's life, but for a moment Roy seemed to think it might be Julia herself. His face was grim as he ordered the body to be dug up.

We stood watching as two of the men found shovels and quickly uncovered a woman's body wrapped in a sheet. I turned and walked away because I'm not happy at any time at the idea of examining decomposing remains, but Roy interpreted this as fear on my part that they were about to unwrap the shroud and reveal Julia's face. From a distance I saw him turn. 'It's not her,' he called to me. 'It's one of them, but it's not her.'

I think the incident went some way towards persuading him that I had not been in contact with Julia before. Impossible as I always found it to know how his mind worked, I think his grip on my arm, as we walked back to his car, showed some sort of sympathy for the moment of dreadful anxiety he imagined I had undergone.

27

I was exhausted but I could not go home to my apartment. I told Roy Rolkin's driver to drop me at my office. I shook hands with Roy as I left him and prayed that my loathing didn't show. When his rodent Dimitry waved me adieu from the car behind I felt such a murderous anger surge that I wanted to run over and drag him out onto the pavement. I could only see Madame Raisa's swollen lips and the great red patch on her dress between her legs.

I climbed the steps towards the three round yellow lights that hung over the doorway. The night sergeant was just going off duty. I walked across the great circular reception, my footsteps echoing on the tiles. A few lights shone behind glazed office doors but there were no ringing telephones, no bustling detectives or lines of anxious supplicants. I went through the swing doors and crossed an empty Murder Room. My office door was open. I went in and slumped into my swivel chair. I could feel my lips trembling as they had when I was a child, confused at the violent shouting in my parents' bedroom.

I thought of the false Dimitry and shuddered. I thought of Roy Rolkin. An innocent middle-aged lady had been beaten and abused on the orders of someone I watched football matches with on television. All other aspects of my long night had been obliterated.

The jangling of the phone a few inches from my ear brought my head up with a painful jerk. Burnt-out ends of dreams smoked in my brain. I reached for the phone. 'Moscow District,' I said, smacking my lips to get the saliva flowing. 'Red Presnya. Homicide Inspector Vadim speaking.'

'Constantin?'

Was I dreaming? I stared at the receiver in my hand in disbelief. Looked past it to the darkness of the empty Murder Room beyond my office door. No, I was awake. Fully awake. And this was Julia's voice on my office phone.

'Are you free to speak?' her voice said.

'In God's name, what are you doing? Phoning here of all places . . .'

'Where better?' she said, and I could tell she was smiling. 'I had someone following you from the factory. I had to speak to you quickly, to tell you not to worry.'

'Not to worry . . . !'

I heard her laugh burbling over the phone. 'You must come and see me. Block A, Pasternak Flats. It's out in the New Districts. Babushkin. Can you find it?'

'I can find it. When?'

'Leave it a few days. But as soon as you can after that. I've been without you too long, Costya.'

The risk she took to talk to me!

After she rang off I sat there with my head singing.

28

Dronsky let me sleep at my desk until nearly ten, then woke me with a cup of coffee and the offer of a bite or two from his fishburger.

'You need something in your stomach for the bad news, Chief,' he said.

I eyed him as I sipped my coffee.

'The suspect Simakov is clean,' he said. 'At least as long as we're still working on the basis that there's only one Monstrum.'

'That's the basis we're working on.'

'He's alibied up to the armpits. On the night of the second murder he was on an all-night government project a hundred kilometres from Moscow.'

I nodded. I hadn't held out any high hope, even after Dr Imogen's profiling. 'Have you released him?'

'He goes this morning, Inspector. With your permission. The chief warder was refusing to keep him another night.'

'Was he troublesome?'

'Not in the usual way. He sat on his bunk all night slapping his own face. He started the moment we arrested him. By this morning he was black and blue and screaming with pain every time he struck himself.'

I was suddenly wide awake. What had Imogen said? Repetitive acts? Pattern of self-inflicted pain?

It was eerily close. And yet the real tests had cut Simakov clean out of the frame. 'Dronsky . . . Did Dr Shepherd ever ask any questions about Simakov?'

'No, Chief. What sort of questions?'

'About his background or habits.'

'No, sir. Nothing like that.'

He knelt and began to collect the fax papers scattered across the floor. I yawned. There was no denying she had come close. Curious. But for the moment I had enough to think about. I pushed the thought aside.

I picked up my coffee and walked to the window. Red Presnya was not a sight to inspire even bad poets. I watched a red fox slink along a broken wall. These Moscow foxes had grown sleek and plump on human pickings during the fighting. My mind wandered off to the forest trails of Arctic foxes we used to follow as boys. You could sell the whereabouts of a fresh trail to the hunters for a hundred roubles in those days. Strange how good Roy Rolkin had become at picking up the trails.

I turned back to Dronsky. 'So we've got nothing. Four murders with exactly the same *modus*. But at least *two* murderers if we're to believe some retired old professor Dr Karlova entrusted with the tests.'

'You can trust him,' Natalya's voice said coldly at the open door. 'And if you're not prepared to believe *me* you can meet him yourself any time you choose.' She threw a folder of papers on my desk. 'Request for burial for Lydia Primalova. I've finished with her, the poor thing. Any reason not to turn her over to her sister for burial?'

'No . . .' I looked up at her. 'I'll sign her off to Nellie Christiakova this morning.'

I had things to say to her which I couldn't say before Dronsky – things I didn't want to say now. 'Perhaps we can get together later,' I said. 'We've a number of things to talk about.'

She stood in her white coat, her hair caught up in a chignon, looking down at me. Her expression softened. 'You look as if you've had a long night, Inspector. Even as a doctor I'd recommend a few hours' rest.'

After she had left, Dronsky scratched at his cropped head. '*Even* as a doctor . . . What did that mean, Chief?'

I'm sure he knew.

*

It was Sergeant Bitov who disturbed my midday snooze. He was ushered in by Dronsky, an intimidating thickness of papers under his arm.

'I think you should hear this, Chief,' Dronsky said, stationing himself to one side of the desk.

'Hear what?'

Dronsky gestured to Bitov to begin as I swallowed a yawn and rubbed at my face. The scratch of stubble across the palm of my hand reminded me of what I must look like. 'Can this wait till later?' I tried to keep the pleading out of my tone.

'No, Chief,' Dronsky answered for the sergeant with a firmness I'd not heard before.

'All right, Bitov.' I told them to sit.

He could hardly conceal the satisfaction on his small pug face. 'On re-examining the depositions of the relatives of the victims involved in Case 4320, the so-called Monstrum murders—'

'You've just read through the files again?'

'Yes, sir.'

'Good. And did you find something we all may have missed before? Is that what you're saying?'

'I did, Inspector. Or at least, I think I did. Perhaps you've seen the connection already.'

I shook my head. 'Give me one of your cigarettes, Dronsky, will you?'

I took the cigarette and a light from Dronsky and nodded to Bitov. 'In your own words,' I said. 'Please.'

'In the normal course of duty, I read all the notes of your interview with the sister of the last victim, Lydia Primalova. And I registered that you brought up the question of her being a churchgoer.'

'Gromek, the night-watchman, had said she was. Her sister, Nellie Christiakova, knew nothing about it.'

'Let's hold that thought for a minute, Chief. Church-goer. Right?'

He shuffled through the file on his knees. 'In the case

277

of the first victim, Anastasia Modina . . . Her mother was interviewed by Sergeant Yakunin. Myself taking notes. The mother, Vera Modina, gave a deposition later in the day at this district station—' Another shuffle of papers. 'At 2.30 that afternoon, to be exact—' He leaned over and put the deposition on my desk. 'That is the statement you will have read when you took over the case.'

'Yes.' I looked down at the document for the first time.

'But checking my notes of Sergeant Yakunin's questions I realised that there was one reference present in my notes which had not been included in the deposition.'

I waited.

'If you take page 5 of the deposition, Inspector . . .' He waited while I found the typewritten page '. . . you will observe the sentence reads as follows: "My daughter Anna normally returned from these meetings at a late hour . . ."'

Waves of sleep were assaulting me. I was in danger of passing out in the middle of Bitov's big moment. I turned to Dronsky. 'Vodka, Dronsky,' I said. 'If Bitov really has come up with something . . .'

'I have some in my desk, Chief,' Dronsky said, hurrying out. He was back within moments. A bottle of Borodino and three tumblers were arranged on my desk.

'Pour,' I said.

The first jolt cleared my head wonderfully. I took the bottle and poured again for everyone.

'What meetings were these the daughter attended?' I asked. I knew I had to be careful. The answers were probably all contained in the pages I had still not read.

Bitov cleared his second vodka with a gulp and nodded enthusiastically. 'Exactly the point, Inspector. The meetings were described by the mother as some sort of youth meetings. What made me think again was the time she returned from these meetings. After all, she was murdered on her way home at half-past one in the morning. She was only seventeen. It put me to thinking, Inspector.'

I might have said that it should have put him to thinking a lot earlier but I was in no position to throw stones. Instead I poured more vodka for all of us.

'Last night, sir, the thought came back to me. I got out of bed and lit the lamp and began to rustle through my notes. My wife made her feelings known,' Bitov said, proffering his glass, 'but I found the place and was able to check what the dead girl's mother had said first time myself and Sergeant Yakunin interviewed her. She said, and I quote now from my notes:

"*Vera Modina*: The following night is Sunday.

Yakunin: What does that mean?

Vera: The night she went to the meetings.

Yakunin: You mean she went to the meetings every Sunday?

Vera: That's right, yes."'

That seemed less than earth-shattering. I looked at Bitov, let my eyes slide across to Dronsky then swivelled back to Bitov: 'Is that it? All of it?'

'That's it,' he said triumphantly. 'The *following* night is Sunday.'

Was he mad? Or so stupid a plank couldn't beat sense out of him? 'Bitov,' I said. 'You're going to have to explain.'

'Certainly, Inspector. There's a priest here in Presnya named Father Alexander. Well, not really a priest as I hear it. A sort of unofficial priest, if you can have such a thing.'

I knew him, of course. Hadn't I even awarded him a medal in some dripping stadium in the suburbs? Father Alexander from Red Presnya.

'Father Alexander—' Dronsky began, but I lifted a hand, 'Go on, Bitov.'

'At that very moment I nearly knocked the lamp over with excitement, Inspector. Because the people who believe in the Father, in Father Alexander, are known as his Following. That's what they call themselves, a member of the Following. So when Yakunin in his questioning got into that mix-up with the girl's mother about the following Sunday, it all became clear. When Vera Modina said, "The Following night is Sunday" she meant the meeting of the Following takes place on Sunday.' Bitov's voice rose in triumph. *And* there's mention of Lydia Primalova also joining a church. And why didn't she want her sister to know? Because it wasn't a regular, straightforward church. It was Father Alexander's cult. I'll stake my pay on it.'

I emptied the vodka bottle in a last generous distribution. Was this it? Two out of four victims members of Father Alexander's Following? 'Dronsky,' I said. 'Go with Bitov. Talk to everybody who knew victims two and three. I want anything at all that suggests they might have been attending a church – certainly anything that tells us they knew anybody who was part of Father Alexander's Following.'

Dronsky finished his vodka. They were at the door when I stopped them. 'Just a moment. This church. Where in Presnya is it?'

'It's hard to say for sure,' Dronsky said. 'It's located in the old tunnel complex that Brezhnev had built for the Commissars. There's one entrance to Father Alexander's on the Presnya district boundary at the Belorussian main line station. There's a sign up there.'

I turned to Bitov. 'This is worth half a dozen salary stars, tell your wife.'

'I knew I'd crack this case,' he said, the pug face gleaming with alcohol sweat. 'Simakov was a waste of time, you know that, Inspector, for all that American doctor said.'

Behind him I saw Dronsky stiffen. I motioned him back into the room. 'What *did* the American doctor say, Bitov?'

'She was just chewing the fat about the investigation . . .'

'Asking about Simakov?'

'She was convinced . . .'

'That Simakov had killed the girls?'

'Yes.'

'Whereas we know now he couldn't have.'

'That's right, Chief,' he said uncertainly.

'When was this?'

'The day we picked him up. She came down from her office to look over the suspects. We talked about Simakov.'

'What about him?'

'His background, habits, hobbies . . . bodybuilding . . .'

'Bodybuilding . . .' Pumping iron. I dismissed them both and sat staring into space.

Curious, yes.

29

We were in a small park just off Old Barricade Street.
A thin coating of snow covered what grass there might
have been but the main concrete path had been cleared
by passing feet. I watched the old man in the wheelchair
rolling towards us and hung back while Natalya hurried
forward to meet him. He stopped at the base of the statue
of a young boy and Natalya bent down and kissed him
on both cheeks before moving round the wheelchair to
push it towards me.

Muffled in a heavy overcoat and a hat with earmuffs,
he gave the impression of being a large, probably once
very tall man. Perhaps he was somewhere in his early
seventies, clean shaven, strong jawed, more formidable
than I'd somehow imagined the recipient of Natalya's
charity would be.

He extended his hand as Natalya slewed the wheelchair
to a stop. 'Ivan Kandinsky,' he said. 'Natalya has told me
rather a lot about you.'

'There's not that much to tell, Ivan Sergeivich,' I said
coolly. I think I was making a deliberate effort to shrug
off the charm with which I had already endowed him.
But there was nothing of the old, lovable, absent-minded
professor about him. He came straight and disconcert-
ingly to the point.

'You have concerns, Inspector Vadim, about the quality of the recent work I undertook for Natalya.'

'I needed to ask you to confirm certain things, yes.'

He opened his large hands in a gesture of invitation.

'Do you possess the facilities to establish whether or
not a test specimen is that of an *A* secretor?'

'Yes.'

'And did you do those tests on the specimens Natalya gave you?'

He reached into his pocket. 'Anastasia Modina,' he said, 'and Nina Golikova.' He handed to me a sheaf of notes bound in a brown paper folder. 'The record of the tests undertaken.'

I took it and handed it to Natalya.

'I've already read the copy Professor Kandinsky made for me,' she said. 'If you like, Constantin, I'll check these notes against my copy.'

'If you would.' I turned to Kandinsky. 'You understand the significance of the question, Professor.'

'Very clearly.' He made no attempt to avoid my eye. 'And I can see why you had doubts about my tests.' He grimaced. 'In your position I, equally, would have asked questions. But there's no room for doubt. You have four murders, but apparently more than one Monstrum, Inspector.'

Natalya turned the wheelchair and we walked back towards the statue.

'Do you know this park, Inspector?'

I shook my head. 'I'm new to Moscow.'

'This is *still* called the Pavlik Morozov Park.'

'Should the name have been changed for some reason?'

'That you must decide yourself, Constantin,' he said, slipping easily into the use of my name. 'Everyone must decide for himself.'

'Is it a matter of such importance? The name of a small Moscow park?'

He nodded emphatically. 'Pavlik Morozov was the son of a peasant during Stalin's days. He is honoured by this statue for having denounced his parents for hoarding grain.' At a gesture of his hand, Natalya stopped the wheelchair and turned it so that he faced the statue. 'You will readily see how important it is that we all decide

283

whether the statue should remain. Should we approve of a boy who denounces his parents?'

I stared at the boy in the Pioneer uniform, the same uniform I had worn as a child of the Soviet Union. I was too young to remember the story of Pavlik Morozov, though I had no doubt that I had once known it. 'What happened to the boy's parents?'

'They were deported to a labour camp. History has no more to say about them.'

'And the boy himself?'

'He was killed by other peasants. Thus the statue. He was the youngest Soviet martyr. An example to all. What do you think, Constantin? About renaming the park.'

I stood looking up at the statue. 'I think the park should be renamed,' I said. 'But I think the statue should remain.'

He raised his eyebrows.

'As an example to all.'

He nodded. 'Have you noticed how dead the sculptor has made the eyes?' He smiled and the hardness flowed out of the face. 'Make Natalya bring you to my apartment when you have a spare hour.' He looked towards Natalya. 'I must go, my dear girl.'

'I'll take you back,' she said, 'now that you've satisfied each other.'

I watched them go. I watched her long legs and the way her body moved as she bent forward to exert pressure on the handle of the wheelchair. When they had disappeared through the park gates I sat for a few moments on a bench beneath the statue. I had no doubt that Professor Kandinsky had done the A secretor tests. I had no doubt that they were negative. I could not believe that Moscow's Institute had made a mistake with the other available semen samples. *Ergo*, there were two murderers. At least.

I was aware that my mouth had fallen open. I could feel the cold tingling on my teeth. The idea of a Monstrum had been hard enough to absorb. A monster who would tear women to pieces like a wild animal. But two of them . . . or three?

I stood up. Pavlik Morozov looked down at me. I lifted my head. I was looking full into that small self-confident face. The eyes were dead but there seemed to be a faint smile of derision on the lips.

I walked an hour, then called Natalya's office. She picked up the phone.

'I apologise,' I said.

'For what specifically?'

'For everything. Most immediately for doubting your professor. Is there any possibility that Lena at the laboratory was wrong about the last girl, about Lydia Primalova?' I added hurriedly.

'Finding evidence of A secretion that wasn't there? No.'

'No, of course not.' I began to whistle.

'What are you doing, for God's sake?'

'Whistling through my teeth. I'm trying to accept the fact we have more than one Monstrum. It sends chills down my back, Natalya.'

'Have you released your suspect, Constantin?'

'We have no reason to hold Vladimir Simakov. He may be a monster but his alibis prevent me thinking he's a Monstrum. Will you take a walk with me?'

'Now? This afternoon? While you are so frantically busy with this new development in your investigation?'

I grunted. 'Listen, I am not frantically busy. I should be but my mind is a shameful blank. Will you walk with me while I wait for my sergeant to try and confirm a connection between the last of the murdered girls and a certain priest who holds services in the tunnels below Moscow.'

'Father Alexander?'

'You know him?'

285

'Everybody knows him,' she said. 'He was never ordained of course, but he's carved himself such a patriotic niche that His Holiness, the Metropolitan, wouldn't dare condemn him. He was even decorated for services to the Nationalist State by Koba himself.'

'So he was.'

'You've established a connection for the first girls?'

'The first one. And a possible connection with Lydia.'

She was silent.

'Shall we meet?' I said.

'Somewhere far from all this. Can you find Trinity bridge?'

'I will.'

'At the Kremlin wall. Go through the Kutafaya Arch. I'll be waiting.'

Darkness had fallen as I passed through the stone arch onto Trinity bridge, then onto a deserted embankment. I stood for a moment. Snow fell like a curtain behind the Trinity tower and swirled and floated across the Kremlin wall. When I was a child in Murmansk my mother used to take me to the Monument to the Heroes and we would stand together and listen to the snow falling. Aged six or seven I was easily persuaded. I closed my eyes and listened now.

When I opened my eyes again Natalya was emerging from under the yellow gleams of one of the Art Nouveau glass and metal globes that light the bridge. She wore her fur hat and long black topcoat. Against the steadily falling snow, she looked like one of those girls in a French advertising poster from the *belle époque*. But her fine features were untouched by a welcoming smile.

We came together without touching, more like two swordsmen closing on each other, intensely aware of the other's movements within the intimate yellow circle of light on the snow.

When finally we stood perhaps a metre apart, she lifted

her eyes to my face. 'Tell me, Constantin, what happened last night after you left my apartment? What persuaded you that I am worthy of talking to now?'

On my way there I had debated how much I would tell her about last night. Obviously I would say nothing about my visit to Imogen Shepherd. But I had decided I wanted Natalya to know about Madame Raisa's lonely courage because somebody should know about it.

Perhaps also because I wanted her to know that Julia had not abandoned me, as Natalya had contemptuously accused her of doing, when I was of no more use to her.

'So Madame Raisa never told them where your Julia is now hiding,' she said coolly. 'But did she tell *you*?'

I stood silently, leaning back against the low wall, looking up at the Trinity tower soaring in the snow-flecked sky. There was no one else on the bridge. We were enclosed with the two towers at each end. 'Yes, she told me,' I said.

'So you'll be seeing Julia again very soon?'

I made a gesture with my gloved hand. 'Perhaps we can talk about something else?'

'We can talk about whatever you wish, Constantin,' she said.

'One of the things I came to tell you was that I found myself strangely touched by your professor.'

She seemed unsurprised. 'He has that talent,' she said. 'It's rare. Being with him, most people, unless they are entirely bound up in themselves, know they are in the presence of a significant man. Defining what makes him so significant takes a great deal longer.'

'I simply meant that he struck me as trustworthy. Honest. How long have you known him?'

'Since I first came to Moscow. Two years.'

'And what makes him significant?'

She smiled crookedly. 'I'm not sure you're quite ready for that, Constantin,' she said. 'Or better still, make an opportunity to find out for yourself.'

287

She swept snow from the granite coping and leaned her back against the low wall beside me. Squinting under the edge of her sable hat up into the falling snow flakes, she pointed. 'Do you know this tower?' She was pointing to one of the gate-towers in the Kremlin wall.

'I don't know its name.'

'It's called the Secret Gate. To my mind it stands for all the secret gates throughout Russia. A monument to all the millions of Russians who for five hundred years have been dragged through secret gates to be beaten and kicked and worked to death . . .'

'It belongs to the past, Natalya.'

'You can say that when your friend Madame Raisa was tortured in the very same basement of that very same building where Russians have been tortured for a hundred years. Where is your sense of history, Constantin? Where is your sense of continuity?'

'I don't understand you,' I said shortly. 'Unless you're making some glib comparison between past and present where there's none to be made. Today we're fighting for the soul of Russia. We're not picking over the bones.'

She walked away from me, five, ten paces, then stopped and turned. 'And that justifies what was done to Madame Raisa?'

'Of course not. People like Roy Rolkin will finally be brought to justice.'

'You believe he will be?'

'They always are,' I added recklessly.

'In some other world, perhaps. Not in our world.' She faced me, challenging me to contradict her.

'Not in Leonid Koba's world. Is that what you're saying?'

She nodded barely perceptibly.

'Your Professor Kandinsky agrees?'

Again she made the same small, sharp movement.

'You oppose the government? Even though President Romanov is at the head of it?'

'President Romanov was led into a velvet-lined trap. Koba is in control.'

I inhaled sharply, a draught of cold snow-laden air. 'Is there some sort of organisation?' I pulled myself up. Did I want to know the answer to that question? 'You've no need to answer that,' I said hurriedly. 'In fact don't answer it.'

'You remember how the Nationalists and the Democrats first came together?' She spoke slowly as if the conversation were taking place in her own living room. 'It was seen as a marriage of necessity.'

'All other parties were threatened with being swamped by the new Marxist-Anarchist Popular Front.'

'At the time, there were some Democrats who did not agree that the party should join with Leonid Koba.'

'Professor Kandinsky was one?'

'He broke with his old friend Romanov on this issue.'

'And you're telling me you think he was right to have done so.'

'Romanov is an honest man. But he's full of pride and easily manipulated by someone like Koba. So Koba gives him the trappings of power, the great Kremlin office, the illusion of rule. The Americans are happy because they remember the moving poetry written by our president. Such a poet could not be building a police state.'

'A police state?'

The snow whipped and scattered around us. 'Join us, Constantin. Join the fight to persuade President Romanov to step back from the brink.' She came close, sliding her arms round my waist, leaning back to look into my eyes. 'You are a good man, Constantin. I know that. But your Leonid Koba is another Stalin. He'll plunge Russia back into the Dark Ages.'

'No,' I said. A wave of panic rose through me. I pushed her away.

'We must act, Constantin, while the eyes of the world are on us.'

'Act?'

'We must support President Romanov as the real leader of Russia.'

'How?' I was staring at her through the transparent curtain of falling snow. 'Demonstrations? Marches? Flag-waving in favour of President Romanov?'

'We must *act*,' she said again, hard as ice.

'You talk about action. What action?'

'We must reject this government before the rest of the world formally recognises the new Russia. Before Koba can establish his secret police state.'

'Natalya . . . Slow down.'

'Madame Raisa was not an isolated incident,' she said, looking into my eyes.

'We've just emerged from a civil war, for Christ's sake. Things must get better.'

'It's what Russians have been saying from time immemorial,' she said bitterly.

I stood opposite her, the snow brushing my face.

She shook her head. 'Playing the innocent is just another way of taking the wrong side. Join us – or you'll regret it for ever, Constantin.'

30

I parked my car and walked back to District 13 by way of the Bullfrog, still hoping to see Valentina among the jostling groups of street-corner whores. I had never been in the street as business was picking up for the evening and as a provincial I found myself gasping at the way the girls laid out their wares, streetwalkers descending on lone men like clouds of mosquitoes, frightening and desensualising in their numbers, their high-heeled boots clattering across the cobbles, their great fur-lined, leather-studded greatcoats ripped open to display naked bodies as they drew close, and as quickly snapped shut again. This was no free peep-show. Besides, the night air hovered around zero.

It's true there were some normal-looking women among them, girls who looked like girls, but there was a high percentage of grotesque creatures too, men/women in clown masks with mobile ruberoid lips or with shaved heads and scars, complete with surgery needle marks, painted down their cheeks. Drunks reeled along in the shadows, supporting themselves from doorway to doorway and occasionally charging into groups of girls, whooping and scattering them until they were tripped and kicked where they lay in the snow and slush.

At just above eye level, above the vodka bar entrances, there was another display in progress. Half-naked girls sat in bright windows framed in pink and lime green neon, reading, watching television or talking and laughing among themselves. Some of them displayed seedy tableaux, nineteenth-century execution scenes with girls bent over the block, their skirts thrown up to show their stockinged thighs, or pairs of nuns, in no habit that I had ever seen on the streets of Murmansk, pleasuring each other for the passers-by.

Bitov and Yakunin had checked over all these houses several times and reported an ever-changing population of girls. I suppose any night Valentina might appear there, beckoning to some likely passer-by, but I doubted it. Valentina was a survivor. She knew that this was the time to go and visit some family in the country, go anywhere out of Moscow. That was my guess. Which meant that our tenuous link to anyone who had actually seen the Monstrum was gone. But what use was the Valentina link, if there really was more than one murderer? I shook my head. The very idea of plurality made me angry. I didn't believe it. But then I *did* believe Natalya's professor. And if I believed him I had to believe there was more than one Monstrum.

I pushed my way through a mass of girls, waving my badge at them, and was forced to snatch it away as a hand lunged for it and painted fingernails poked and grabbed at my fly. Ducking and twisting away from their laughter, I turned off the Bullfrog towards the District station. The street ahead of me was rubble on one side and a long low block of what had once been shops and offices on the other. Exploding shells had ripped the front off the ground-floor shops so that each was an empty concrete compartment with hanging fittings. A few lights were visible in some of the rooms which had retained their windows. There were plenty of men about, mostly looking up at the windows so I guessed the business of the Bullfrog had overspilled into some of the side alleys.

I'd had my fill of sights in the Bullfrog itself so that I wasn't really looking up at the windows as I passed although I was aware enough that those on the lower level invariably contained girls. But although my mind was on the Monstrum as I wondered what possible source of satisfaction it could be to carve the innards out of a girl in this way, my eyes were, even so, drawn up to windows that were either brighter or more colourful than others.

It was in this way that I only half registered the tableau in one of them. An eighteenth-century prison whipping was about to take place and half a dozen men were being assembled on the sidewalk below the window by a tout who was collecting a rouble each from them. I think it must have been the reaction of the masked victim which made me stop. She had not yet been stripped and attached to the whipping board, the delights we were promised were in store for us by the tout, and was standing smoking a last cigarette with her tormentor, a dark-haired girl in riding boots and a home-made three-cornered hat. I was standing a few feet from the rest of the clientele, having shown my warrant card to the tout when he approached me for a contribution.

When the masked girl looked down and saw me there something happened. The sort of faint shock that could have been recognition . . . then an almost physical shrug of the shoulders when she remembered she was masked. Running one hand through her blonde hair, she turned away, pulled tighter the blanket which she held around her shoulders, and continued talking to her friend.

I crossed to the concrete stair that led up to the flat. By the time I reached the door one flight up I could hear the whip singing and thwacking. I turned the handle and went in, staying back in the doorway until the short performance was over. A certain amount of the illusionist's art went into the whipping. To the men huddled in the cold below it probably seemed as if the masked victim was suffering outrageously, but whip and girl never came into contact as far as I could see from my angle. Blood running from the 'wounds' was definitely watered ketchup dripping slowly from a tin can suspended out of sight of the viewers above the victim's head.

When the short *guignol* was over and the curtains drawn, Valentina took off the mask and pouted sulky lips. 'I've done all I could to help,' she said. 'Maria's gone. Left the area. She's working some other district. Be fair, Inspector.'

'You really believe that?' I asked her.

'Look, come, have a drink,' she said. She poured me a glass and sat, stripped to the waist while her companion washed the ketchup from her back. 'I'd spend a week trailing around the stations with you if I thought it'd do any good. But it won't. Here's what I think has happened. I think when Maria got home and told someone the story over a half-litre the penny dropped.'

'That's the first time she realised the man she'd seen was the Monstrum?'

'I'm certain of it. She would have made a God-awful fuss otherwise. She wouldn't have just cursed the bastard for trying to make off with my night's earnings and strolled off.'

'All sounds right,' I said.

'Maria's lying low. Probably spending some time with her kid. She doesn't plan to get involved in this.'

'I don't blame her,' I said.

'You're not a real inspector, are you?' she said, waggling her bare breasts as her colleague dried her back.

'I'm as real as they get,' I said.

She laughed. 'When I've finished here tonight I'm going off to stay with my sister. I'll be back in ten days and I'll look you up and we'll go back to your place to compare notes, as the businessmen say.'

I finished my drink. 'Watch yourself, Valentina,' I said. 'And call in at the station as soon as you get back.'

I left and went down to street level. The curtain had already been drawn back. In the window, the tormentor was striding up and down with an amplified cracking of

294

her whip and the tout had assembled another eight or nine customers.

The show must go on.

I sat in my office swinging back and forth on my chair, jumping every time the phone rang, picking it up in the hope and fear that it was Julia. Most times it was a wrong number or no number at all because the phone system was no longer capable of routing calls. Today, whenever there was anybody on the line it was a call for an army barracks in the suburb of Lublino, mostly it seemed a girl offering services to the officers' club. To while away the time I asked some of the callers for their qualifications and enjoyed their efforts at self-description. Sonya Tukinin was small, but a very smart dresser. American underwear. Plump and very shapely. Everybody was jealous of her big tits.

Not everybody perhaps. Not Lydia Semyonova. Lydia was close to two metres tall in her special built-up army boots, guaranteed completely flat chested and with muscles hard as whipcord. Hair cropped to the skull. Mean spirited and wilful. I asked her why she didn't join up.

When the phone rang next time it was Imogen Shepherd.

'Constantin,' she said – no reference to our night together – 'how does my profile fit? Did you check out Simakov's details?'

'He's not our man,' I said slowly. 'Can you rewrite your profile for a priest?'

She was choking with anger. 'I don't appreciate your flippancy,' she said. 'I don't appreciate it one little bit, Constantin.'

'He's just become our prime suspect,' I said. 'The priest.'

She gave an exasperated sigh for which I couldn't entirely blame her. 'Constantin. Will you kindly tell me what you're talking about?'

I rocked back in my chair. Through the window I watched a single light out across the railway line that flickered bravely then died. 'We've got a name,' I said. 'A sort of priest. I'm sorry about Simakov but this one is shaping very well.'

'What are you saying?' Her voice crackled like breaking ice.

'His name's Father Alexander. He might easily be the common link with all the girls.'

'Have you talked to him yet?'

'Not yet.'

'So what makes you think it's him?'

'I don't yet, but I'm speculating. A common link with two of the four girls. Maybe with all of them.'

'Motive?'

'If he's our man, maybe human sacrifice is what does it for him. Maybe he even fits your profile.'

'I find your tone insulting and unprofessional. This is all pure guesswork.'

'Mostly,' I admitted. 'I'm just going to see him now. The only thing I really know about him is that he's a troglodyte . . .'

'For God's sake, Constantin! Be serious. Come over to my apartment straight away.'

'I'm on my way to Belorussian station to see Father Alexander.'

On the line there was a pause. When she spoke again her voice had softened. 'Last night was good, Constantin,' she said softly. 'Very good. You have talents that please me very much.' She paused. 'When you've interviewed your priest, come straight back to my apartment.'

I should have felt a spasm at the very thought. But I didn't. I felt nothing. I suppose I could work something up. I mean, when I got there I'm sure . . .

'Constantin . . . Constantin, did you hear what I said?' Her voice was on the edge of shrill. 'I just asked you to come over and see me later this evening.'

'It'll be late,' I said, 'when I get through with the priest. The false priest, whatever he is . . .'

'I don't care how late. Do you?'

'Let me see how it goes.'

'Are you saying no?' There was disbelief in her voice. 'Are you saying you don't want to come?'

'I'm just saying I'd like to leave it for tonight . . .'

There was an intake of breath on the line. Her voice was cold now: 'Is it possible you were lying to me about another woman? Constantin, I must tell you frankly, I am not prepared to stand in line.'

'There are no others,' I said, irritated at being forced into the assurance.

'Is it the Karlova girl?'

'Natalya's a colleague. A friend.'

'About her, Constantin, there are things I can tell you. She is not at all what she comes on to be.'

'Imogen,' I interrupted her. 'I'm saying it'll be past midnight when I'm through. That's all. And, in any case, after last night . . .' I tried to lighten my voice.

'After last night,' she said harshly, 'I feel betrayed. It's a feeling I don't relish. No woman does.'

She put the phone down on me.

I drove with Dronsky to the Belorussian station, a huge iron-ribbed nineteenth-century building. Somewhere behind it was a wasteland of marshalling yards. From the protected parking lot where we left the car, I could see green and red hand-held lanterns swinging in the darkness and hear whistles and shouts and sometimes even snatches of singing as steam locomotives sniffed and wheezed in the darkness.

While Dronsky was locking the car, I walked slowly ahead, up the broad stone steps. Beggars sitting, lying, standing, smoking, spitting, talking, filled the area covered by the overhang of the portico. An endless stream of people passed me on their way in, few or none of them carrying luggage. Dronsky caught me up as I reached the top of the steps. I could see into the booking hall. In the small spaces between human beings I detected an ornate pattern of floor tiles and on the walls chipped terracotta statuary from the time of the tsars.

'Take a deep breath,' Dronsky said. As he pushed open the glass door a fetid heaviness swirled out, engulfing us as we stepped inside. I grunted, fighting back the nausea. Only the poor smell as sweet. Or perhaps the dead. Dirt and decay are probably biologically close. I looked at Dronsky. His face had a peculiar blue-pink tinge which I had to hope was the neon strip lighting around the canteen door.

There were other feeble lamps on walls and ceiling but the press of people, dark bundled, vaguely human shaped, seemed to absorb light so the whole great hall was steeped in a foggy gloom.

Part of that gloom I saw was fire smoke. I looked in astonishment at the wood stoves burning in three or four places in the middle of the tiled floor of the booking hall.

'The Belorussian Inferno,' Dronsky said, next to me. 'It's filthy, it's dangerous, but it's warm.'

I was beginning to sort out people from people. Men from women. Women from children. Travellers from station dwellers. Most people were here, it seemed to me, on something approaching a permanent basis.

'They come here,' Dronsky said, 'when they've nothing left anybody can steal.'

'How do they live?'

'By stealing themselves, mostly. A little tapping ... begging ... you're better off of course if you've got young girls in the family.'

'How many men does it take to police a place like this?'

He smiled. 'It's more or less self-policing, Chief. The people who run it are the young guys in the biker outfits.

298

Some of their enforcers are young kids. The way it works is you can pay a fee to the Commune, as they like to call themselves, and you're assigned space and protection.'

'What about us?' I said, glancing round. 'How do they feel about plain-clothes?'

'They don't like us a lot,' Dronsky conceded, 'but they tend to leave us alone.'

'Tend to. Is that good enough?'

'It's the only deal in town.'

Take my word, brothers, I can't easily tell you what the next two hours were like. Even during the Civil War, Murmansk was nothing like this. Up there in the far north we were a frozen backwater. Some sort of normal life continued. We were never invaded by wounded ex-soldiers, by waves of drunks and beggars, by twelve- and thirteen-year-olds trying to get started in the business of selling themselves. I wandered with Dronsky, my inarticulate Virgil, through the great mass of deprivation spread out before me. We talked, questioned, offered pathetic bribes to such a range of poverty, a spectrum of misery, that I felt sick at heart long before it was all over. Vladimira was just one of many.

An old lady, not old really, still in her fifties, but looking old, with a dirt-tracked brown face and one leg, the stump of the other badly bandaged, a watery fluid oozing through the outer layer of newspapers . . . She lay in a broken car seat against a far wall of the Belorussian. The lamp above her head cast a feeble light but just adequate to read by. The book resting in her lap was Goethe's *Leiden des Jungen Werthers* – the Sorrows of Young Werther.

Born the daughter of an admiral in Odessa, at a time when the Soviet Union seemed, to the Soviets at least, about to inherit the earth, she had grown up in the embankment house beside the Moscow River, her life sheltered and privileged as it might have been in tsarist days. She had lost her leg to a stray shell when Yeltsin bombarded the parliament building in the early 1990s. Her life had been a downhill slide ever since.

Her privileges now – a broken car seat, no interference from marauding station children, a place under a lamp – were bought for her by the tall, heavily made-up girl in high heels who leaned against the wall behind her. Vladimira's daughter, Claudia, worked the officers' sleeping cars, frequently travelling to Minsk and back. She was saving for some sort of accommodation for her mother.

'We're looking,' I said, 'for an unusually tall girl, probably close to 1 metre 80. Wide shoulders. Short dark hair. Sometimes called Maria . . .' We showed our artist's impression but to my mind it was just a woman's face plucked out of the air.

The girl's clothes were all carefully composed to project what she was, an elegant tart. But there was a bruise across her cheek not entirely covered by her make-up and she'd yawned, politely, her hand over her mouth, at least twice in the last two minutes. 'She works the Belorussian . . . ?' Claudia asked frowning.

'And the Finland and the Yaraslavl . . . Probably most of the big stations,' Dronsky said.

'She's been known to work Red Presnya.'

'Red Presnya.' Claudia shivered. 'You wouldn't find me working the Bullfrog with him about.'

'The Monster, Monstrum, whatever you call him,' her mother said. 'The one you're after. What have things come to, Inspector? When I grew up the law was the law . . .'

The girl looked down at her mother. 'Don't worry, darling,' she said, reaching down to take her hand. 'I'll keep well away from Presnya.'

'Some of those officers are not a lot better, Inspector.' The mother released her daughter's hand and eased herself into a more comfortable position on the car seat. 'When I was a girl, our Soviet officers were *gentlemen*.

Look at the bruise on her face. A colonel did that to her.'

'I walked into a lamp-post, I told you,' the girl said, a half-smile on her lips. She turned back to me. 'What class of girl is your Maria? Foreign businessman, officer class . . . ?'

'I doubt it. She doesn't work the train,' I said. 'She works the forecourt.'

'A bluenose?' the girl said.

Dronsky nodded. 'Yes, a street girl.'

'Then I wouldn't know her.' She stopped to yawn again, smiled and said: 'Sorry, I've been up and down to Minsk for the last three days non-stop. They don't like you sleeping in their time. Not surprising. And I wouldn't put much weight on her name. Almost all girls, officer class or common soldier, use different names every week. It's to confuse the pimps. They're onto us all the time.'

'So we're looking for a tall girl who works the forecourt of the Belorussian *sometimes*?' I said to Dronsky. 'Not hopeful.'

The girl's head turned. 'Lemon!' she called. 'Over here . . . here . . . here . . . here . . .'

I looked round to see that she was guiding with her voice a blind station boy of perhaps twelve or thirteen. When he was close enough she went forward and touched his shoulder. 'This is my friend Blind Lemon,' she said. 'There's not much going on in the Belorussian he doesn't know about. He'll help you if he can.'

'Hallo Lemon,' I said. 'I'm looking for a girl. A woman, really. Her name could be Maria. All I really know about her is that she's very tall. Her voice would be coming from up here where I am.'

'A bluenose,' the girl said.

The boy stood next to Claudia, his head well below her shoulder height, and unselfconsciously put his arm round her thigh and began caressing it. When he brought the other hand up, she gently removed it from her crotch.

'Perhaps if you're a good boy and find out something for me.' She patted his head.

'I'll have to ask Sex-change,' the boy said. 'Or Doc Marten. They might know her.'

'You ask Sex-change,' Claudia said, 'and let Vladimira know if you get anything. Then we'll see.' She gave him a friendly push.

'Doc Marten?' I said. 'Sex-change?'

'These are children who have never known their true names, some of them.' Claudia's mother wriggled about in her chair. 'They pick up names or adopt ones they like. That boy over there's Mick Jagger. The one with him is Burger King. Like the names of the bluenoses, they're always changing.' She smiled and raised her eyebrows. 'A society in flux, you might say, Inspector.'

'If the boy does come back with anything . . .' I said to Vladimira.

'I'll get a message to you,' she promised.

'Sorry we weren't more help.' Claudia looked at her watch. 'I must be going. The Minsk express leaves at 10.15.' She bent down and kissed her mother. As she knelt there whispering to her, I couldn't easily put together this composite of modern Russia: the grimy face of the old woman, the suppurating newspaper-wrapped leg, and the black patent leather high heels of her daughter, her red skirt stretched tight above nyloned knees . . .

We moved through the shifting crowd across the booking hall. There were children everywhere. Children of all ages. Small ones squealing with laughter as they chased each other across the crowded forecourt and older ones, eleven, twelve, thirteen, drawing on cigarettes, leaning against walls, posts, wooden crates, each other, sullen eyed and opportunistic. No doubt with names like Sex-change and Burger King.

But even in a place like this the dictates of youth fashion held sway. Black leather or plastic leather was dominant, decorated with old hammer and sickle regalia from the days of the Soviet Union. Confusingly, both girls and boys favoured cropped hair. A minority wore a lank, longer cut. Or perhaps no cut at all. For footwear, laceless, battered Russian army ammunition boots, several sizes too large, seemed to be in vogue.

'They're as dangerous as they look,' Dronsky said. 'From the age of eleven or twelve, most of them are carrying. Anything from a kitchen knife to a police issue 7.59. If we don't move fast, they're Russia's future. Does anybody care? I don't see them if they do.'

I looked at him. And realised that from our first meeting, every single remark of Dronsky's had been carefully neutral. Filtered for any dangerous comment on the world we live in. Until now.

'Do *you* care, Dronsky?'

'I've got two young kids at home,' he said. 'If I didn't care about them, I wouldn't care about all this . . .'

'But you care about them.'

He nodded, tight-mouthed. 'What about you, Chief,' he said. 'Do you care enough to do anything about it?'

I looked at him sharply.

'Natalya says you're a decent man. That you're open to ideas.'

'Do you talk a lot to Natalya Karlova?'

'Quite a bit.'

This was not the Dronsky I knew. 'Something tells me we should have a few drinks together some time,' I said.

He did Groucho eyebrow movements. 'I'd like that, Chief.'

We had reached the far end of the booking hall now. Thick smoke swirled from some of the open hearths and lay above us in a dense fog through which the roof lights were barely visible. Dronsky pointed. Just ahead of us was an arch from the original 1860s building. A banner was spread across it which read in black on white: THE

CHURCH OF THE CATACOMBS – ALL WELCOME! As we pushed our way through the crowd I could see, let into the arch on bolts ten centimetres thick, double doors of steel, probably installed a century or so later when Moscow acquired its underground nuclear shelter system of which this was an emergency exit.

We were still a few steps from the doors when a group of boys, six or seven, swept in from somewhere on our right and came to a skidding stop between us and the door. They were about twelve or thirteen years old, pinched faced, crop headed, swaggering once they'd regained their balance. They wore a bizarre mixture of clothes: leather, as fashion clearly dictated, but a motley collection of caps and woollen hats. The boy who was obviously the leader wore an old Great Patriotic War German peaked cap with the ear protectors down. 'Where do you boyars think you're going?' he said, his head bobbing from side to side.

Dronsky made a movement forward but I touched his sleeve. 'Who's asking?'

The boy made a short-step circle round me and reappeared to stretch up towards my face. One of the other boys said: 'This is Sex-change. He's Father Alexander's doorman.'

'That right, Sex-change?' I asked him.

He nodded. 'Cost you,' he said.

'It says welcome,' I said, lifting my chin towards the banner.

'Not police.'

'I've come to see Father Alexander. It says *all* welcome.'

A few crop-haired girls of the same age leaned against the wall to watch. Sex-change glanced at them. 'One of you can go down,' he said. 'Not both.'

The girls tittered. I could feel Dronsky was about to move beside me. I turned to him. 'Make it an early night, Ilya,' I said. 'I'll go down and have a word with the Father.'

Dronsky looked uncertainly from me to the crowd

of children and back. 'If you're sure, Chief. My wife'll wonder what the devil I'm doing back at this time. The girlfriend stood you up, she'll say. She's got a sense of humour.'

'Give her my best.'

'Give her the best from me, too,' Sex-change said to a shriek of laughter from the girls.

I thought for a moment Dronsky was going to hit him. But he let his raised hand drop and raised his thick eyebrows at me. 'Goodnight, Chief,' he grunted.

'This way, Chief—' Sex-change pointed to the entrance – 'if you're going to be a paying guest.' He paused. 'Which you are. Right?' His chin was up, challenging.

I nodded.

I was taken down a turning concrete staircase deep into the earth. Three or four of the boys accompanied me at a distance. Sex-change walked beside me. 'Where are you from, Sex-change?' I asked him.

'Fuck knows.'

It was the end of conversation. In the low bare tunnels the lighting was blue in caged overhead lamps spaced out every fifty paces. The ventilation seemed to sweep through, as a gust of warm wind from some distant source, every few minutes. After a few dozen metres more my escort's voice echoed in the tunnel. I turned and he gestured to an opening on my right. 'That'll be ten new roubles,' he said.

I paid and he turned away. The other boys were grinning. I listened for a moment and could hear the scrape of their ammunition boots echoing and re-echoing in what seemed a parallel world. Then I started along the tunnel.

The tunnels. My guide never mentioned that there were turnings off the main tunnel. Several turnings, all leading, bewilderingly, down straight, apparently endless tunnels. Have you noticed that only concrete can be dank and dusty at the same time?

I walked for some time, ten minutes perhaps, through this concrete rabbit warren, my footfalls echoing weirdly behind me as if I were being followed by myself.

I could be lost, brothers. I could quite easily be lost. That was the thought elbowing its way in as I passed down one tunnel, reached another, identical, tried to turn back, then found it impossible to distinguish what I had been thinking of as the main tunnel. From where I stood the overhead, wire-caged blue lights merged into a distant straight line. Every twenty seconds the air sucked or puffed past me. Is this Monstrum country? Is this where the beast lives? Is it through these tunnels that he moves, hunched over his dripping booty?

Of course I'm a coward at heart. I know that. I suppose any honest man knows it. I'm not incapable of showing courage at the moment that courage is needed – but cowardice is my position of rest, so to speak. And the courage is not always there, like foaming lager beer, on tap.

At this moment it certainly wasn't.

But just a moment now. My world was changing. Ahead, several of the overhead lights were not working. An explosion had occurred here. The walls were brown and scarred. Broken light holders and cable hung from the roof. My nerves were raw edged now. I turned at a T-bend and both ways, left and right, the blue lights merged into pale blue lines along the tunnel roof. There were many dark patches now where dead light holders dangled. I hurried on past them towards the not far distant spools of bluish light. My shoulder brushed the rough concrete of the wall. When my foot kicked something I started like a gazelle.

A man lay on the floor in tattered rags. Not a man: a jumble of bones, a skeleton . . .

Yes, it took time for my heart to stop its frantic gallop. I forced myself to look. The scraps of clothing were just recognisable as uniform. The body was a relic of the fighting in the tunnels that took place during the last National attack on Moscow. Insects and vermin had all but picked it dry.

At a crossing point, a low domed area from which six or eight roads radiated, my fear of this tunnel world took on more reasonable proportions. I had assumed too much. Assumed the lights and circulating air meant people used these places, that if I kept on I must meet some members of the priest's Following. But of course the lights meant nothing at all. This whole complex had been lit and ventilated since Brezhnev's day.

I sat on the low circular wall in the centre of the domed roundabout, elbows on my knees, chin on my locked hands, and counted the puffs and sucks of the ventilating system. Since Brezhnev's day.

Leaning forward, I listened. The tinnitus was burbling through my ears. But there was something else too. The sound was there again – but stronger. Music.

Even as I ran forward and stopped, fearful that it had gone, I heard it again. Not just music. Church music. And I knew that if I could look at myself, I'd be smiling: sweating and smiling.

It was a church of great magnificence, if indeed it had ever been designed as a church. More likely the great, cavernous space had been earmarked for Communist Party meetings. The horseshoe-shaped auditorium was furnished with benches in red leather and the area of the altar to which the blaze of candlelight led the eye was rich in carved woodwork and tapestries of cloth of gold.

There were perhaps fifty people crowded before the altar where I could see, over the heads of the kneeling worshippers, two priestly figures moving among them.

I'm not sure if it was the music, the sparkling light of a thousand candles or the sheer relief that I had escaped from the tunnels, but I found myself profoundly moved. For a few minutes I stood in the shadows until I became aware that a woman was standing beside me. Overweight and no longer young, she was dressed in a long grey caftan, heavily splashed with water so that it stuck to her prominences. 'Come forward,' she said, taking me by the arm. 'All are welcome . . . all are welcome in God's house.'

I detached myself from her. 'I haven't come to join the Church, Mother,' I said hastily. 'I am on important business. I must see Father Alexander immediately.'

She shook her head. 'Tonight is the night of monthly baptism,' she said gravely. 'Your business will have to wait on God's business. You're welcome to watch. Even more welcome to join them in the bath.'

I shook my head.

'Commit yourself, brother,' she said. 'You will never regret it.'

Father Alexander was in the bath. But so were perhaps fifty or more others, mostly, it seemed to me, women and girls.

I stood in a lofty room decorated as it might have been in the time of the last tsars, with rich red and gold painted walls and glittering chandeliers above the steaming green waters of the bath.

Around the sides in cubicles and arches girls stood in naked groups or sprawled indecorously on wooden benches exchanging banter with the swimmers. Couples, mostly young but some of them in their forties and fifties, sat holding hands as they might have done in summer in the park.

As I was introducing myself, Father Alexander had waded to the steps and like a Russian Neptune stood in shallow water, his huge beard dripping, his genitalia more plumped up than a priest's should be in the act of baptism. If that's what was going on.

'Come in and join us,' he boomed. 'Baptisms are a communal activity.' A few girls were by now standing in the water round him. 'I can't talk to you like this. Just drop your clothes on the bench there.'

'This is police business,' I said.

His raised arm was thick with muscles. 'Join us my friend, before some of the girls take it into their heads to give you a ducking in the Lord's name.'

I thought of slapping down my badge in front of him. Insisting that a Moscow homicide inspector did not interview suspects naked in a bath. But the anticipatory giggling of the girls persuaded me. As they began to move towards me, I turned away and began to strip off my clothes. Ignoring the cheers and clapping of the girls I leapt into the warm water, submerged myself and came up next to him, water streaming from my shoulders.

'Forgive the girls, Inspector. The exuberance of youth.' He turned to the girls around him, clapping his hands. 'Leave us now, friends. You heard him. The inspector has come to ask me a few questions.'

He turned back to me. We stood with the water just above our knees. 'Now, how can I help you, Inspector Vadim?'

I waded into deeper water and rested my arm along the side rail. I looked away from him. In my first confrontation I had been effortlessly worsted. What was I doing up to my waist in water beside a man who might easily be the sadistic murderer of several girls?

'Magnificent, you're thinking.' He was wringing out his beard. 'Built for the *vlasti* at the time of Brezhnev. Was it ever used? God knows. But the generosity of the past never falters.' He gestured to the steaming water, the chandeliers. 'Who pays for all this, you ask. You do – and millions like you,' he beamed. 'The whole system's connected to the Moscow power supply. Nobody has yet found out how to disconnect it. When they do . . .' he shrugged. 'We shall have to think of moving. I favour the Black Sea coast – is such travel in your experience, Inspector?'

Underwater, girls swam around us, wriggling like minnows. I tried to throw off the familiar magic he was weaving round me. Tried to see him as the sinister satyr he might be.

'Get out of the pool,' I said.

The eyes were dark and perhaps what people sometimes call luminous. That's to say they were eyes that fixed on me, a staring, glaring hypnotic fix, that I knew I had to break. 'You must have an office of some sort,' I said.

'Of course. If you prefer to talk there . . .'

'I'm here to talk to you about the murders in Red Presnya.'

He looked up. '1905 Goda Street runs just above our heads. Are you the police officer in charge of the case?'

'I am.'

'Very soon everybody in Moscow will know your name, Inspector. You will become as famous as Sherlock Holmes, the Scotland Yard detective who solved the Jack the Ripper murders.'

'Some, at least, of the murdered girls were members of your cult.'

He looked at me without speaking.

'Let's go to your office,' I said.

I dressed quickly in one of the narrow arches that cloistered the bath. When the priest rejoined me he was wearing sandals and a long white robe with a cross in gold thread embroidered on his breast. The staff he carried was of curved and polished ebony. In manner or demeanour he had nothing to do with the figure in the bath. 'Let's see, your voice tells me you are a northerner. I've a soft spot for northerners. Petersburg was my home for many years. I loved Petersburg. My passage to Moscow might be put down to fortunes of war . . .'

'Let's start with what goes on here,' I said roughly. I was angry at myself now, at this man who had coaxed or threatened me into the bath and was now trying to lead me meandering through his past. I had to climb back from the absurd position in which he had so effortlessly placed me.

'What goes on here? Much as you see,' he nodded soberly. 'We are an orgiastic creed. Essentially, as orgiasts we believe that a society in which there is total availability of sexual outlet will be less violent, less acquisitive, less ... *anti-social* than societies we have fashioned hitherto.' He plucked at his drying beard, giving it body. Now that it was no longer slicked down with water, it grew in volume before my eyes. 'It seems to be working,' he said modestly.

'You have a large number of young women among your following.'

'Of course,' he agreed readily. 'I watch your eyes, Inspector. I can see you'd be among the last to blame me.'

His office was perhaps constructed more recently than the tunnel network. An anteroom of stained-glass panels formed a wall in which a heavy door gave onto the office proper. Here a wide nineteenth-century desk and high-backed chair occupied the centre of a rich Turkey carpet. Five or six deep sofas were placed in a half-circle round the desk. 'A creed, you said.'

He gestured to me to take one of the sofas and brought a bottle of vodka and two large glasses from a cupboard behind the desk. 'I take it as a given that we all believe in Heaven,' he said, 'even if not in God.'

'Is that your creed? A Godless Heaven?'

'Why not. Of course we would all define it differently, uniquely. Here among the Following, I preach that our object must be not to usurp the fundamental need of individuals to design their own Heaven. Not to impinge on *their* images by imposing images of our own.'

311

'And what do you have left, as preacher, if you don't do that?'

'What you saw in the bathhouse. You see there are no preconditions for our attainment of Heaven. It's not realisable by faith or good works. Attainment depends on your ability to define it. That's all. The simplicity of the idea leaves the theologians aghast. What have they left to talk about?'

I drank a good draught of a smooth, smoky vodka. 'And the orgies?' I asked.

'We are orgiasts. Self-proclaimed. Would you ask us to be orgiasts without orgies? After a long orgy we pray to see the shape of Heaven, praying for a glimpse of the sun on its domes and turrets . . .'

'Pray – who to, if there's no God?'

'We pray to ourselves of course – to each other.'

He was smiling. What was the man talking about? Heavens without gods. Prayer to each other. And a thumping good orgy each weekend. I could see, at least, that he had a formula. 'Four girls murdered in Red Presnya in the last two months,' I said. 'The possibility of many others before that, during the war. How well did you know any of these girls?'

He nodded to himself as if he had long ago decided this moment would come. 'I knew the first girl to be killed, Anastasia Modina, quite well.'

'You'd had sexual relations with her.'

'It's the role of the shepherd to leave no lamb without guidance.'

'You're laughing at me, Father Alexander.'

He shook his head.

'Worse, I think you're laughing at Anastasia Modina.'

'On the contrary.' His face was suddenly blank.

'Why didn't you come forward?'

'And tell the police what? That Anastasia had been a member of the Following. That she had left here that evening probably less than an hour before she was murdered. I knew the police weren't going to find the murderer. In the chaos of the end of the war in places like Red Presnya, there were killings every night. Old scores being settled. Rapes ... What good did it do to tell the parents of a girl like Anastasia that she spent her Sunday evenings in the arms of some complete stranger?'

'And when the other girls were killed?'

'My thoughts were the same when Nina Golikova was killed. By the time Tania was murdered I had issued orders that women should go home in pairs. Or that they should be accompanied by one of the men. Obviously my instructions were not obeyed to the letter.'

'The fourth victim, Lydia Primalova, was a member of your following too.'

'Yes.'

'Contraceptive pills were found in her bag.'

'German make? I encourage all the girls to use them. You've seen the result of unwanted pregnancies upstairs in the Belorussian, Inspector.'

'How often do you hold your orgies?'

'Every weekend.'

'Sunday night. The murder night.'

He nodded slowly.

I found it impossible to know what he was thinking. There seemed to be a wall between him and the consequences of his actions. Was that the reaction of a psychopath? Or simply a committed cultist?

'Lydia Primalova, the last victim, was the only one not killed on a Sunday. Can you suggest anything to account for that?'

He stood for a moment, brushing his beard flat on his chest as if he had spilt wine or breadcrumbs on it. 'New members have to undergo certain formalities,' he said. 'An induction process.'

I smiled. Smirked probably. The priest nodded gravely. 'You're right in what you're thinking. Lydia Primalova was a virgin. I don't allow virgins to become members of the following. There was a ceremonial defloration.'

'By you.'

'Of course. There were others present but defloration is normally carried out by myself.'

'What time did she leave?'

'Close to half-past midnight. She said she was getting a lift home from her sister. Two of the women conducted her to the Maisky Square exit.'

'I'll want to speak to them.'

Where did all this bring me? Close, I knew that, but not quite close enough. I stood looking into those unfathomable eyes, at the cherry-red, fleshy mouth. Surely, I had here all the essential elements of the beast. 'You live down here?' I asked him.

'I spend my life down here.'

'What do you do after one of your sessions on Sunday nights?'

He looked at me, his heavy eyelids half closed. 'I am not to be found up on the street with scalpel and surgical scissors, if that's what you mean.'

'You have witnesses that you were still down here when Lydia Primalova left?'

'A few members are always here. There are twenty or more of us living down here. Yes. I have witnesses.'

'Those who live down here, are they all women?'

'Some, not all.'

'And of the men, are there any—' I thought of the orgies and of Father Alexander himself – 'are there any of . . . unusual tastes?'

He shook his head at my naivety. 'You're talking about a people who have lived through the degradations of the last years of the twentieth century, the insecurity and bloodshed of the first years of this century and you seriously ask me that question. Come and join us, Constantin. You have the innocence we seek. Because our orgies *are* innocent, you see. We're not members of the Following to hurt each other. We're here to enjoy each other. And think and pray a little that the future will be better than the past. Can you fault it?'

He spoke so easily and unhurriedly that I could almost feel the hand on my sleeve, drawing me forward. 'Listen to me.' My voice rose angrily. 'Understand that this is a murder inquiry. You are one of the prime suspects. You and the men who assist you down here. Everybody who knew what time these four girls left, which exits they would be taking and whether or not they were likely to be alone.'

'We're talking of several dozen members of the Following.'

'I'll start with the permanent members of your Following. How many men live down here?'

'All the men who live here permanently were injured in the recent fighting. Most of them seriously injured. I very much doubt if you'll find your Monstrum among them.'

'Nevertheless I want a full list,' I said stubbornly. 'There must be one permanent denizen of this place physically capable of doing what was done to those girls.'

He spread his arms wide. 'I am not your murderer, Constantin. I would not shed blood.'

'You led a National patrol through the tunnels. Koba decorated you for it. There was blood shed then.'

'I led a medical team to the injured men in a surrendered Anarchist command post. If the Nationalist authorities wished to indulge in a little benign misrepresentation and decorate me for my efforts, who am I to refuse? Especially when a free tenancy down here accompanied the medal. But rest assured I shall cooperate in any way I can.' He swallowed his vodka in one gulp. With the back of his hand, he wiped his bright lips and smoothed the wings of his thick brown beard. His eyes never left mine.

In the silence my attention was momentarily distracted.

315

A shadow flicked across the stained-glass panels which divided this office from the anteroom.

'I have a visitor,' he said. 'Excuse me.' He walked to the door and opened it. As he stood in the doorway, talking to the visitor in the anteroom, I got up to use the phone on his desk. Sergeant Bitov answered the office number.

'I'm in the tunnels. Father Alexander's catacomb church. Collect Yakunin and get down here right away. I want names of everyone who was here on the nights of the murders, what time they left and who they left with.'

'How many people are we talking about, Chief?'

'I don't know. Maybe a hundred.'

There was a silence from the other end.

'I know,' I said. 'Bring along anybody you can. Pick up half a dozen uniforms if necessary. This is hot.'

Father Alexander closed the door and came back into the room. A waft of church music and incense came with him.

'How do my men get down here?' I said. 'Don't tell me through the Belorussian.'

'Our entrance is in Grachev Street. There are dozens of entrances to these tunnels. I'm not responsible for the child-extortionists in the Belorussian.'

I repeated the information to Bitov with a warning about the young thugs in the Belorussian. Father Alexander waited with his head bent, his eyes on the carpet at his sandalled feet. I could see behind him that his visitor was still there on the other side of the stained glass.

'The officers are on the way down,' I said. 'You promised me your cooperation.'

He lifted his eyes from the carpet. 'You shall have it,' he said.

I left Father Alexander by a side door in his office and came almost immediately onto a well signposted crossroads. I could take the stairs to the Grachev Street entrance via the tunnel on my right. To the left the tunnel carried a posted warning: *This tunnel leads to exits in the Bullfrog, Belorussian and Maisky Square areas. Friends are warned that some of the walkways are no longer properly lit and are sometimes used by undesirables.*

Let cowardice be my guide. I started for the right-hand tunnel, the direct way up to Grachev Street. But I was stopped by the thought of the list of exits the other way led to.

The Bullfrog, Belorussian station and Maisky Square were all areas within a few hundred metres of where a killing had taken place. A murderer leaving the catacombs could make his way to a point on the surface to lie in wait in the certain knowledge that Anastasia Modina or whoever was his chosen victim for the night would be passing on her way home. If the killer were Father Alexander he would know the girl's time of leaving, roughly when she would arrive at the top – and her route home from there.

The murderer . . . I stood at the bifurcation of the tunnels and shook my head. I had to remind myself that there was no single murderer. Semen traces from different men had been found mixed with the blood on the dead girls' thighs. There had to be more than one Monstrum.

These moments of epiphany strike at odd times, fuck your mother! But strike they do. Even Constantin Vadim. Semen traces from different men? Of course there would be semen traces from different men! *Each of the victims had just left a religious orgy, for God's sake!*

I had already passed the warning notice and was deep into the half-lit tunnel before I thought what I was doing. The semen that streaked the girls' legs was from the male orgiasts. Perhaps even, the Monstrum, when he struck, had not ejaculated. Perhaps he cut pieces from the girls and then ran for the nearest catacomb entrance, carrying his bloody trophies down through these tunnels.

Automatically I looked down, momentarily expecting to see a trail of blood along the tunnel floor. I felt something between triumph and trepidation. I knew what I had done. I had resurrected a single Monstrum. When I looked up again I was staring at a sign that read: TO THE BELORUSSIAN.

31

I did not come to the surface in the station, as I had imagined I would. Instead I emerged from a sort of low concrete pillbox in the marshalling yards behind the station buildings.

It had stopped snowing and clusters of lights at different points of the huge yard showed the sides of long trains of oil cars or darkened passenger carriages. The huff and clatter of shunting steam locos was the only sound in the dead whiteness around me and the whole great goods yard seemed to be empty except for some distant men with flashlights. From that direction too, I now heard the barking of dogs.

I picked my way very carefully among the criss-cross of snow-covered rail lines, heading for the brightest clutch of lights which I supposed were around the main gates to the goods yard. The Belorussian itself lay huge and dimly lighted just beyond.

It was a short but laborious journey, my stride broken every third or fourth pace as I stepped over lines or between sleepers. Every now and again I was confronted by the long dark line of an empty train and was forced to work my way under the coupling between the carriages. My hands soon felt raw from the rough cold ironwork of hooks and buffers; snow had turned the soles of my shoes back to cardboard and my trousers were soaked to the knee.

Emerging from between the carriages of one empty train I was faced with a welcome splash of light. I stood for a moment to watch the Minsk officers' sleeper pull past me. Sliding from the blackness to my left it moved forward with a slow, rhythmic clanking across my front.

From where I stood the brightly lit windows were no more than a few yards away. I saw colonels unhooking their uniform collars, majors smoothing their hair or raising their glasses. There were women in most of the compartments, young women I supposed like Claudia making her second or third trip in twenty-four hours.

As the train gathered speed the detail blurred. I saw train servants carrying folded blue blankets or bent over samovars making tea. I saw officers jacketless in red braces, half-naked girls, each quick image with its own story. And then with a final rattle this bright caravan had disappeared into the night.

It left a bleak snowscape.

I had still two hundred metres to cross to reach the gates and I could see now that I would be forced to walk round or duck under several dark stationary trains.

For ten minutes I crossed deserted loading bays and clambered between carriages or goods cars. I had just negotiated one such, had carefully selected an even patch of snow and jumped down when I heard a hoarse whisper behind me. 'Brother,' a voice said. 'For charity's sake, a cup of snow.'

I looked up. What I had taken for an empty goods wagon was a cattle car with a small window laced with barbed wire. A hand with a tin cup had been slipped through the wire. I saw the wrist twist and the cup fell in the snow at my feet.

I picked it up and stared at the strands of barbed wire. The hand had been withdrawn. I could now make out a face and the flickering whites of a man's eyes. From inside the wagon came a heavy shuffling, like stabled horses. 'Who are you?' I said. 'Where are they taking you?'

'A cup of snow,' the cracked voice said. 'Whoever we are, you will not deny us a cup of snow.'

I bent and packed snow into the cup. Then gripping the heavy padlock on one side of the sliding door I lifted myself and the cup level with the lacing of barbed wire.

The stench from inside shocked me. A hand snatched at the cup and for a moment I heard wet snuffling sounds and further back a low chorus of piteous cries. There were women among them. When the cup reappeared, thrust through the barbed wire, I took it and jumped down. As I was filling it, four or five other cups plopped softly into the snow beside me.

I filled them all, tight-packed, hooked the index finger of one hand through the handles and with my free hand swung myself up to the window.

I thought for a moment I was about to lose my fingers. Hands snatched at the mugs. My knuckles cracked, my hand was twisted this way and that. When the last cup was wrenched from me I jumped down to the snow, massaging my hand. I felt I had been savaged by a toothless but ferocious beast.

I swung myself up, this time with more care. What I took to be the first face I had seen now filled the window behind the criss-cross of barbed wire. 'There are dead in here,' he said. 'We've been three days without water. Nearly a week on a knob of bread.'

'Who are you?'

'Soldiers of the old Anarchist army. Men and women, both.'

'Prisoners? Captured in the battle for Moscow?'

He gave a croaking laugh. 'Prisoners? No. Credulous fools who surrendered under the terms of General Koba's amnesty, my friend.'

I stared speechlessly at the shadowed face.

'And you?' he said. 'What are you? A rail worker?'

'Yes, a rail worker,' I said.

'I'm surprised the Cheka guards let the likes of you near this train. Be careful, friend. They have dogs. And whips.'

I had recovered enough to speak now. 'Tell me,' I said urgently. 'When did you give yourself up?'

'Most of us, less than two weeks ago. We were assembled by night in the warehouses. We were already near collapse from hunger when they loaded us onto this train. That was three, perhaps four days ago now.'

'How many are you?' In my shock, I could think of nothing else to say.

'Sixty to the car . . .' the voice answered. 'We already have eight dead.'

More tin mugs were pushed out to me and I found that I could most quickly fill them by scooping snow from the roof of the cattle car. After perhaps a dozen tin mugs were filled we began talking again.

'Do you know where you're being taken? Have the guards said anything?'

'The guards laugh and say "Magadan" when we ask where they're taking us but we have no means of knowing what they mean. In here some say they have heard of Magadan. That it's a bad place. What does Magadan mean, friend? You're a rail man. Is it a place?'

Magadan. I knew where Magadan was. What Magadan was.

'Tell us, brother,' the voice said urgently.

'I don't know it.' I barely kept my voice from cracking. 'I've never heard of Magadan.'

But Magadan is known to everybody who has read the history of Russia. It is the furthest east of convict settlements. The centre of 160 separate camps in Stalin's days. The subject of a bitter paradox: *The journey to Magadan is the worst journey in the world. Then how can it be better to travel than to arrive?*

Cold, hunger, work and the sadism of Stalin's guards . . . a slave market in the main square. Would it be any different for these men in Magadan tomorrow?

'Railman. Will you post our letters?' a voice from further back asked.

'I'll post your letters,' I whispered through the wire and I could hear and smell the surge of bodies towards the window. Hands came through the wire holding folds of dirty paper, scraps from exercise books, few in envelopes. I collected them and stuffed them into my pockets. As dogs barked further down the train I whispered 'Good luck' to the men behind the wire, though I knew there would be none for them, and I jumped down into the snow.

I dared not look back at the hands thrust through the wire. I clambered under the coupling of the train in front of me, banging the side of my head against the heavy iron hook – but I swear I barely felt it. This train too, I saw, as I emerged on the other side, was another endless line of cattle cars, from which came faint cries and groans and the piteous rattle of tin cups against barbed wire.

I was purged of fear as I walked towards the yard gate. As the bright lights glared down on me and the dogs leapt forward on their chains, I bawled for the Cheka sergeant to come running out of the guard house and hurled my identification at him hard enough to slap him in the side of the face.

Vassikin's little boy was wrong. The good people have not won.

32

We had modern ruins in Murmansk, a few buildings collapsed or half collapsed as the sub-standard concrete crumbled to dust in the one air raid the city suffered in the war, but nothing to compare with Babushkin. Once I had turned off the Mira Prospekt I was quickly surrounded by concrete blocks, sown like dragons' teeth across the suburb. Many were dark-windowed white stumps fringed by the rubble of the collapse of the top five or six storeys. Some looked as if a vast animal had snapped a wall or two away and I could make out the dark rectangles of abandoned apartments. Red Presnya was not the only district of Moscow to see heavy fighting.

A few blocks showed a scatter of lighted windows across their cracking surfaces, but the streets between them were empty of people or cars, barely lit by infrequent street lamps, littered with debris. Through this grey and brooding suburb I drove, following the police map propped up on the dash.

There were few street signs or block numbers and the effort of concentration mercifully kept at bay more than the occasional darting thought about the Anarchists in the cattle cars. About the great slave market at Magadan. About the six, seven, eight million dead that Kolyma's gold and diamond mines had claimed in the last century. And the hundreds of thousands more to follow.

The effort needed to find my way pulled me back from this abyss and made me concentrate. It was not until I had located Block Pasternak A and hidden my car behind streets of corrugated iron that I allowed myself to think about my errand.

I was to confront Julia with the truth. With the truth that she was right all along. That my own perception of the Russia of our past and our future had been childish, addled and utterly wrong-headed. That the lifeline back to the old community of the village had been cut long ago, or if it still existed it pulled towards a quite different shore.

I walked like an automaton, hearing only the crunch of glass and rubble under my feet. When I was challenged I lifted my hands. My sense of surrender was total.

'Shall I say you look as if you've just seen a ghost?' Julia said, when we were alone in the bleak graffiti-covered apartment that was her present headquarters.

'Ghosts,' I told her. 'Tonight, I have seen ghosts from the past.'

She took me by the arm and sat me by the stove. Its pipe disappeared through a hole, stuffed with charred asbestos cloth, in the outer wall. But the fire glowed red enough to warm the room.

I had been conducted here by various lieutenants clambering through a dozen apartments connected by doorways knocked in the concrete walls. The warren of rooms and staircases so created baffled the police and housed hundreds of outlaws, petty thieves, *stoke* dealers, wanted men and politicals like Julia's comrades. The police, she said, never came here. It would need a battalion of infantry to clear the whole of Pasternak A.

We sat either side of the stove. She had poured vodka and set it at my feet. She was pale, a pallor heightened by her black jeans and sweater. But her movements had regained that extraordinary vigour and decisiveness which she'd inherited, or perhaps copied from her mother. She sat opposite me, her legs crossed, her hands folded in her lap, and waited.

I suppose it's shock. At first I couldn't talk, couldn't even reach down for the cracked glass of vodka. I lifted my eyes to her face. My mouth opened and closed but my throat was constricted beyond the power to produce words. It was Julia who came to my rescue, as I suspect she had tried to, many, many times. 'Tell me about Madame Raisa,' she said.

I could do that. Very carefully I told her about what had happened. I told her that even so, even though these things had happened, I was still able to persuade myself that this was an exception.

'That things would improve?'

'Yes, that things *must* improve.' That in times of trouble, banal evil, characterised by someone like Roy Rolkin, rose towards the top. When the soup pot boils ... yes, we all know the proverb. But I had retained my belief that National Democracy was right for Russia. That Leonid Koba was the man to lead us. And that the Amnesty Law was a unique and far-sighted act of reconciliation.

And don't imagine, brothers, that I don't know what you're thinking. Already you're thinking what a poor creature I am. What a gullible fellow this Constantin Vadim must be.

Well, damn you ... To everyone else it was all obvious, you think. You all knew from the beginning that National Democracy was little more than the same again, the Russian past served up with a different ladle – but from the same battered soup pot.

My eyes were on Julia now. On a plain wooden chair against the shattered wall of the room, this room leading to other shattered rooms and others and yet more, she sat in her black jeans and sweater, her face, her eyes, slightly misted as I told her what I had seen at the Belorussian. 'At least three trains,' I said. 'Men, probably women too, packed as they would not pack cattle. Your comrades, Anarchist soldiers who had accepted the amnesty. There will be barely ten men in a wagon who will survive to Magadan. *Magadan*, Julia. The regime that I believed in sends prisoners to Magadan.'

326

She shook her head. 'There's nothing for you to feel ashamed of,' she said. 'You made an honest choice in favour of your vision of Russia. Other men have included Magadan in that vision, men like Roy and Koba. Not you, Constantin. That was never part of the future as you saw it. You remain free to choose again.'

I drank the vodka and she left for a few moments to prepare me a tray of food. For a moment I sat there, the stove's heat on my face. *Free to choose again.* What did she mean by that? The obvious political choice, of course. The choice between the shameful National Democracy which I had embraced and her own views, far more sophisticated than mine but, I'd always thought, intellectually cold.

Free to choose again. Was it possible that Julia meant something else too, by those words? Did she mean that *I* (not she) had chosen our separation? Was she forcing me to take at least my part in the responsibility for her leaving Murmansk with Mischa? And was she therefore saying that I was free now to make that choice again?

I swear the blood rushed through my body so strongly I could feel the pulse beat in my fingertips against the empty vodka glass.

When she returned she was carrying a rolled straw mat under her arm and a tray with bread, cheese and a plate of cold meat. She set the tray on her chair and rolled the mat out on the floor, 'We've no table for eating on,' she smiled. 'Sit here with me, Constantin. We shall make our own *déjeuner sur l'herbe.*'

I looked around this shuttered room. I was moved, as I had so often been moved, at Julia's ability to encourage me to inhabit a world of *her* imagination. *Déjeuner sur l'herbe.* On the concrete floor of this wrecked home we spread the mat, the food and settled ourselves . . .

I wonder now how could I have been so *easily* misled . . . And of course I knew. It was all those useless details. How Koba spoke, how he ate breakfast, how he walked across the room. I had persuaded myself, so easily, that this was real knowledge. 'I thought I knew a thousand things about Koba . . .'

'There is only one thing to know,' she said to me as we lay, resting on our elbows, the food and drink on the straw mat between us. 'Russia has been visited by another Joseph Stalin.'

I wanted to tell her the whole truth: that I worked directly for Koba. That I was his double – but I held back. I was afraid of ridicule. But more afraid of the effect the truth might have upon her. Afraid that on that boundary where love and hate are believed to exist, she might find distaste in a body which could so easily slip into the form of the man she hated. As you can see, brothers, I was already thinking of a future.

'I have information, Constantin,' she said, 'through a network of Anarchist sympathisers, that the camp system of the 1930s, 1940s and early 1950s is being remade. Perhaps these people are right who say that nothing's changed: that a Russian can only escape serfdom by travelling to the West.'

'You're saying we should allow ourselves to be driven out of our native land?'

'I believe we should fight back. But, the hour is late. The Cheka now controls the army and the bureaucracy more completely than it did under Beria. The only traditional institution it seems we Russians will never abandon is our secret police. Through Anarchist sources I already have information of Jews being arrested at night for cosmopolitanism, of Chechens being removed to ghettos on the outskirts of cities.'

I could do nothing but breathe in the facts she gave me. Yesterday I would have summoned my defences to hold facts at bay, but today I had no resources to resist them, no will, no wish to resist. Natalya, whom I respected, had told me that Leonid Koba was another Stalin. Julia, whom I loved, was telling me the same thing. 'Is there no common ground between you and the democratic part of National Democracy?' I asked, hoping desperately.

Julia smiled. 'None. I oppose the structure of democracy as readily as I would tear down a Nationalist government. There is no meeting ground. You are about to make the journey from the Nationalist camp, Constantin. Don't imagine you'll be able to rest overnight at some bland little Democratic wayside inn.'

'There are things I must tell you,' I said. 'You know Roy Rolkin is after you.'

'I know that.'

'He has a special commission from General Koba to hunt you down.'

'I'm flattered.' She collected up the plates and took them from the room. I watched her, dazzled by the sinuousness of every movement. When she came back she was carrying three or four old embroidered cushions which she threw at me, laughing. 'If you're to sleep here tonight, Costya, you'll need something softer than a straw mat.'

She lowered herself down beside me as I placed the cushions for our heads. Lying side by side, she put her arms round me. Her shape moulded mine. Somehow it brought back in seconds all the longing of years. I gently touched the small of her back and could feel the bandaging still there. I put my hand round the back of her thigh and for a moment pressed her towards me. 'You're full of pain, Costya,' she said. 'But now most of it is good pain. Creative pain.'

I never liked this talk. Perhaps I'd been wrong in the past to reject it. But I'm a simple man. Pain is pain. Change may be good. Necessary. But pain is still pain. I let my body roll back a fraction. 'One pain never recedes. I can never stop the pain of Mischa,' I said.

She nodded slowly and kissed me very lightly on the lips.

'I have a great need to know more, Julia,' I said.

'More about his death?' She was stroking my hair. 'You do pointless hurt to yourself, Constantin. I've told you all there is to tell.'

'More about his life. In that last year with you. What sort of boy was he?' I lifted myself on an elbow so that I looked down on her. 'Was he kind, funny . . . give me something. Something I can add to my memories of him.'

The perfect lips parted slightly. 'He was, in that last year,' she said softly, 'even more lively than when we were in Murmansk.'

'Lively?'

'More aware of the world around him, in that sense I mean. He spoke of you until my heart nearly broke. I tried to tell him about making choices between two things you love equally . . .'

'But my choice was the wrong one,' I said. 'I stayed in Murmansk. I chose to separate myself from the woman and child I loved.'

Her hand lay on my neck and her thumb stroked my cheek. 'All that is behind us now,' she said. 'Anarchism, right or wrong, is defeated. More important it's irrelevant.'

'I never thought I'd live to hear you say that.'

She smiled and brought the flat of her hand down my cheek and along my jaw. 'Listen carefully to what I *am* saying, Constantin. Now all argument funnels down to one stark proposition: Leonid Koba is Russia's mortal enemy.'

Perhaps my conversion had been many months in the making, but the conviction that had burst upon me in the Belorussian was total, ready made. I had a great need to speak the words. 'Leonid Koba,' I said, repeating her proposition, 'is Russia's mortal enemy.'

She took my hand. 'You believe this, as I believe.'

'I do.'

Her extraordinary eyes seemed to glow into mine. 'We

will dedicate his death to the memory of our son,' she said. 'What do you say, Constantin? Could there be a more fitting monument?' She leaned forward and put her hands on my shoulders.

'He will die. Be killed, you mean?'

'This time there will be no mistake.'

I thought of Natalya's biting contempt. 'And this time there will be no innocent bystanders?'

She looked at me levelly. 'It may be that some sacrifices have to be made. Our task is to act. The future will not call upon us to account for the sacrifices we have demanded.'

I was silent. I saw and felt, as strongly as she did, the necessity of killing Koba. What tugged at my arm was Natalya's words, that even the tyrannicide would be called to account. 'How will it be done?' I asked.

I could feel the relaxation in her body. 'I shall kill him myself,' she said. 'But I'll need your help. We are desperately short of weapons. Short most of all of explosives. Grenades, Constantin. You must get me grenades. A case is what – twenty?'

I nodded.

'A half-case then should be enough. Ten grenades and a good length of instantaneous fuse. Can you get it?'

My head was spinning. 'Julia, for God's sake! Give me time to think.'

Her arms tightened and she drew me down beside her. 'There's no thinking to be done, Constantin,' she whispered urgently. 'We must act. You and me, we must act together. We must act in Mischa's memory.'

331

33

Long before dawn I was back on the Mira Prospekt, driving south now. Julia's parting words were still with me: 'You were wrong, Constantin, but so was I. Anarchism has failed to rally Russia against Koba.'

'You're ready to abandon something you've believed in for so long, sacrificed so much for?' I found her courage when dealing with herself awesome.

She had given a single, decisive nod of her head. 'Ideology is a decoration. If the defeat of the Popular Front reveals anything it is that we are living in a post-ideological world. What we are witnessing is the death of ideas. The only purity left is that associated with action. Only action is moral.'

I had taken a couple of hours' sleep at most and even that was broken by nightmares. My head ached across each eyebrow and round to the temple. My ears sang relentlessly the one-note song of tinnitus. As I approached the centre of the city, traffic thickened. Passing trucks threw up great waves of brown slush that buffeted the Renault and poured over the windows, for seconds at a time enclosing me completely. In the east there were barely three or four streaks of light.

On the ring road there were fewer trucks. On the Fili road almost no traffic at all. In Semyon Lane I climbed out of the car, closed the garage door and fitted the padlock to the hasp. I was looking for the key when, behind me, headlamps flicked once, throwing my shadow sharp-cut against the garage door.

I turned. I was expecting, dreading, Roy's BMW. But Natalya's white van stood in the turn-off opposite. I raised my hand and walked slowly across the street towards it.

She had wound down her window and as I leaned over, forearm on the roof above her head, I knew she was drunk.

'You keep terrible hours,' she said.

'A policeman's lot . . .'

She grimaced.

'Do you want to come up to the apartment?'

She shook her head. 'No. I thought we might go back to mine. Earlier on I thought that.'

I walked round the front of the van and got in the other side. 'What is it?'

She lifted a half-empty bottle of vodka from down near the gearshift. 'Mainly this,' she said.

'How long have you been here?'

She lifted the bottle again. 'This long. Maybe a little longer when I was just smoking cigarettes.'

I took the bottle from her, unscrewed the cap and tipped the neck to my mouth. I sat back exhausted by its cleanliness and fire. In the villages there are peasant priests who claim that hard spirit washes over you like holiness.

She took the bottle back and held it for a moment without drinking. 'I would not say such things unless I were drunk, of course.' She took a gulp of vodka. 'But, *in vino, audax*.' She fixed me with her large amber eyes. 'Nothing I remember in life,' she said, 'has left me so desperately sad as talking to you about the future.'

I had no answer for her. I took the cigarette she handed me and drew on it as she clicked her lighter. In the flame I saw the marks of tears on her cheeks.

'I understand that there's no point to the exercise, other than the pursuit of immediate pleasure . . . But I'm inviting you to come back with me. To spend what remains of the night with me. Will you, Constantin?'

'No, Natalya.'

'No, Natalya . . . not tonight, Natalya . . .' Suddenly she was furiously rummaging in her bag. 'You're all dreams, Inspector Vadim. All dead dreams.' She shoved something into my top pocket. 'Well, if you won't accept a real woman who loves you – see what a tab of *stoke* will do for you.'

'Natalya, for God's sake—' I tried to pull the tab from my pocket but it had slipped too far down.

'You've just returned from seeing her,' she said in a quieter voice. She crushed out her cigarette, her eyes on me. 'I can see it in your misted eye. Your other-worldly stare . . .'

I held up my hand. 'Don't, Natalya . . .'

I knew something in my face must have brought her up short. Automatically I wiped at the tears on my cheeks.

'What is it, Constantin?'

'Tonight I was at the Belorussian.'

'You went to see the priest?'

'Please. Let me tell you. I emerged from Father Alexander's catacomb into the goods yard behind the station. It was a mistake. The tunnels are labyrinthine. I emerged among trains packed with Anarchist prisoners, men and women packed like animals, desperate for a cup of snow. They had been there three days already. There were dead among them.'

Her face showed all the horror I still felt. 'Oh my God, Constantin,' she said in a whisper. 'Anarchists who have surrendered under the amnesty?'

'Yes. Anarchists who have taken Leonid Koba at his word.'

Her face was drawn with shock. 'These prisoners, where were they being taken?'

'They had heard from the whip-guards talk of Magadan. They had never heard of it. Perhaps they were fortunate.'

She said nothing. There was no need to tell her what Magadan was in our history. She sat breathing deeply.

'It's no surprise to you,' I said.

'No surprise – but no less a shock. What will you do?'

I didn't answer.

'Ah.' She pursed her lips. 'But you've already done it. You went straight from the Belorussian to Julia. Is that not so? To tell her that she had been right all along. That your Leonid Koba was a true son of Russia's soil.'

'Russia has other sons – and daughters.'

'She asked you to join her?'

I turned my head away. A beggar family walked past our front, a straggle of burdened people of diminishing size, adults to tiny straggling children.

'Did she ask you to join them?' she repeated.

'It's better I say nothing.'

She slammed the steering wheel with her gloved hand. 'Better you say *something*. I'm frightened for you, Constantin, and sick with jealousy if you must know. But mostly at this moment, I'm frightened. What did she want of you?'

I took the bottle again and drank.

'What did she want from you?'

'Weapons,' I said. 'Grenades.' Why I said it I have no idea. No excuse. Perhaps to signal to her and to myself the end of Constantin Vadim, the poor deluded fool. The supporter of Koba, the admirer of Koba, the physical double of the repulsive beast. But for whatever reason, I said it. Weapons, grenades, I said. I sometimes fear I will posture my life away.

'Weapons? How could you get weapons?'

'There's the police armoury at District.'

Her breath hissed through her teeth. 'And you said yes. You told her you would do it?'

My courage failed me. 'I said I'd have to think.'

'Get out of the car, Constantin,' she said. 'Get out of the car and walk out of my life.'

I got out of the car and held the door open. There

ought to have been a line from me to have sealed the end of our relationship but I was still working on it when the acceleration snatched the door from my hand. With tyres spinning on ice the white van fishtailed down the road and took the next bend.

34

It was seven o'clock in the morning. I picked up the
phone and dialled Imogen. Whatever uncertainties I had
about her, she was the amnesty commissioner for our
district. She must be told what was happening behind
the Belorussian station – and for all I knew in station
goods yards all over western Russia.

'Constantin,' her voice was languorous. 'Have you just
finished your visit to your sex-priest?'

Sex-priest? When I last spoke to her I hadn't known
the cult was orgiastic. 'Do you know Father Alexander?'
I said. 'The priest at the catacombs?'

'Like half Moscow, by reputation,' she said. Her voice
changed. 'Now, Constantin, you've caught me in the tub
...' She smacked the water for sound effects. 'But no
matter. I'll welcome you back into the fold.'

'Listen,' I said, 'I have to see you.'

'Of course.' Her voice had assumed an extraordinary mellow quality. 'You must come over straight
away.'

'This is serious, Imogen. I have things to tell you.'

'About the Monstrum?'

'No. About the amnesty. Things that as amnesty commissioner you must know.'

'Constantin ...' Suddenly she was theatrically bored.

'The whole fucking thing is a sham!' I shouted down
the phone. 'From beginning to end. The people who
register are being shipped off to Siberia.'

'Really, Constantin ...' She smacked more water. 'I
have visited re-education units outside Moscow. Perfectly
OK conditions – good plain wholesome food. Cabbage

337

soup, porridge. Fish or meat every other day and Western videos at the weekend.'

'I was there, Imogen, at the Belorussian. Long trains of men. In cattle cars. Like the old days. *I was there*.'

She was silent.

'The whole amnesty is a murderous fake. How do you feel about being a commissioner under those conditions?'

'All right, Constantin,' she said slowly. 'You want to supply me with the information to make a formal complaint?'

'I do.'

'These formal complaints take time.'

'Then make it informal – to the US chargé d'affaires.'

'Be patient,' she said smoothly. 'Leave it to me.' I heard her move in the water just before the phone went dead.

Her voice had been dead as the phone in my hand. Whatever Imogen cared about, it wasn't the amnesty.

I sat staring at the phone. I had not said yes to Julia's demand for weapons, not in so many words. Weasel-sharp even with her, I held the idea of the amnesty commissioner like a trump I could play for myself until I resorted to the desperate ends which experience had taught Julia was all there was. And now I'd played my trump. What other way to go was there, but Julia's road?

Natalya's vodka had given me the taste for strong drink. I found a half-finished bottle of vodka and switched on the TV to watch the early morning news. Inevitably there was Leonid Koba (or more likely one of his doubles) visiting the site of an escape of dangerous industrial fluids somewhere. But a few minutes later an item in the Kremlin with Koba talking to the new German woman chargé d'affaires was definitely the real thing. I sat sipping vodka and studying Koba. His moustached smile reminded me of that old Iraqi tyrant of the end of the last century, Saddam Hussein. As he talked to the

German woman he was totally at ease and she smiled and asked about progress on the amnesty and said how important it was to Western opinion that it should be seen to be a success.

The virulence of my hatred shocked me. I got up and snapped off the TV set. I put the vodka aside. I roamed the apartment in a distress that was almost frenzied. I wanted Julia. I wanted my son back again. Or another son. I wanted Julia and me to have another child.

I sat down on the sofa, my fingers reaching into my top pocket. There somewhere was the tab of *stoke* Natalya had contemptuously pushed onto me. It was still before eight in the morning. My fingers dug deeper and found a small square paper envelope. I pulled it out and tore it open. The white powder was salty as I poured it onto my tongue. I crumpled the envelope and dropped it on the coffee table in front of me. Then I lay back with my eyes closed.

My mind, I seemed to be aware, was functioning on two levels. No, my body, I was aware, was in two separate places. No, my mind and my *sensations* were distinct. Was that closer to it? From my mind, I could look as from an upper window, down onto my own world of sensation. Yes . . .

Slowly, like a child on ice skates for the first time I take steps, I slide, I skate . . . I almost fall. But I am moving forward through scenes of my own evocation. I am in the apartment at Murmansk, evoked in every tiny detail; not remembered – *evoked*. The sensation, I am aware, is completely different from the sensation of memory. This is the felt sensation of dreams. Or, as I feel the cool breeze from the open apartment window, it is the felt sensation of *being there*.

Mischa is sitting on the floor, his dark curly head bent in fierce concentration. He is playing with his trains. But where is Julia?

Yes. At a meeting. The University Anarchists. We must

not call it a club or even a group, for both imply an organisation which is anathema to them. Julia laughs at such pedantry. But she is as fierce about her Anarchists as Mischa is about his trains.

There is a click and a triumphant shout from the floor. 'It fits, Papa!' My son's eyes are alight. He pulls the train apart. 'This one—' he waves a carriage – 'fits *this one*.' In his other hand he holds a locomotive. He rams them together. 'There.'

I smile. I feel it in the muscles of my cheek. 'They were made to fit, Mischa,' I tell him.

'No, Papa,' his frown is fierce again. 'You know nothing. *This* is a Cosmos French carriage. And *this*—' he is all didactic emphasis – 'is a Soviet Brezhnev class loco. I changed the coupling myself.'

My mind drifts happily. We play for hours together, my son and I. The patterns on the carpet are organised as rail lines. I try to make trains run to Moscow or Smolensk or away towards the Urals, but all lines run to Petersburg in Mischa's mind.

I stand up to pour myself a beer and shake the aching from my knees.

'Papa ...' His giant head on his small shoulders is turned face up to me. 'Papa, if I ever *had* to leave you, I would be sad.'

I stretch. 'Why should you have to leave, little man?'

'Mama says.' He turns. A large inverted cardboard box is Nevsky station. Petersburg, of course. Skilfully, Mischa reverses a train with three goods wagons under the cardboard arch.

I am all coldness and fear. We have talked constantly, Julia and I, but we have not talked of going separate ways. 'Leave?' I probe casually. 'Why should you want to leave Murmansk?'

'Mama says,' he repeats. He squirms round on the carpet, looking up. 'You'll be sad too if me and Mama have to leave, wouldn't you?'

'I'd be very, very sad.'

'But don't worry Papa, it won't be for a long time yet.'

I lean back against the door jamb. Unasked for, unevoked, I can *feel* its corner in my shoulderblade. 'How long's a long time yet, Mischa?'

He stands and takes my hand and makes me sit on the sofa and sits himself on my knee. 'But can you keep a secret, Papa?' he says.

'I'm a good secret keeper,' I tell him. 'Policemen have to be.'

'You promise not to tell Mama I told you?'

'Told me what, Mischa?'

'Yesterday she showed me the tickets for our journey.'

To Petersburg, of course.

By midday, after a morning's sleep, I was sitting before the desk of the Lubyanka mortuary sergeant. 'I have come for the body of a citizen who died under interrogation early yesterday morning, Madame Raisa Persilov,' I told him.

The sergeant was overweight and near retirement age. He eyed me for a moment and consulted his record book again. 'Madame Raisa Persilov . . . ?'

'She was brought in during Thursday night.'

He shook his head. 'No record of it here.'

'Perhaps not.' I tried to keep my voice flat, neutral. 'But you'll have a body.'

'I don't see how we can have a body without an entry for her arrest,' he said. He flipped through his book and ran his thumbnail down a column of names. 'No. Nobody. No arrest record. And no entry that she was ever signed in here, for any reason whatsoever, citizen.' He stood, fat hands flat on either side of his record book. 'If she's missing, go to your local precinct station and report her as such.' He looked at me and delivered a malevolent wink. 'But if it's just your girlfriend gone for a long walk, they're not going to be pleased at you wasting their time, citizen.'

'She was here,' I said.

'If the book says she was never here, she was never here. Something for you to understand, citizen. Now I'm a busy man . . .'

He stopped because I had taken my ID from my pocket and opened it on the table in front of him.

'She died here during Thursday night,' I said. 'I was with her when she died. There'll be a record. Find it.'

He sat down in shock, his eyes still on the ID in front of him. 'My apologies, Inspector. There's nothing on your application to say who you are.'

'That makes a difference, does it?'

'Of course. Did you want to do your own militia post-mortem on her?'

'No,' I said. 'I'm applying for her body for burial.'

He nodded understandingly: I had been with her when she died under interrogation. Perhaps her family wielded some *blat*, some influence, in Moscow. Naturally I was concerned that a damaged body should be properly disposed of, before the family asked to see it. He smiled unctuously. 'I don't think you need to worry yourself about disposal, Inspector. You can trust us in these matters.' He wiped the palm of his hand across the page of his record book. 'The very fact that the book's clean suggests to me one of your colleagues has already taken care of the details.'

'I'm here as a friend,' I said. 'I'm here to give the body a decent burial.'

He looked at me baffled. 'A friend—?' His manner changed abruptly. 'I understood you to be on official business.'

'I was her neighbour. Go down to the mortuary. She's there somewhere.'

Across his desk, across the open record book which

did not bear Raisa's name, we faced each other. His eyes darted down to the book and up to my face. He stood up. 'Wait here, please.' He turned to leave the room, hesitated, walked back to his desk and picked up his record book and a bunch of numbered keys beside it, and left the room.

Ten minutes later, Dimitry, the soi-disant inspector of water standards, was back in the mortuary sergeant's place.

'Why on earth, Inspector Vadim, tell me that, why on earth should you want to claim the body of Madame Raisa? I just don't understand.'

'It's a gene you were born without,' I said. 'Genetic scientists call it the decency gene. Without it we're born not so much human beings as . . . acquisitive putty.'

He sat with his arms folded tight. His neck had sunk into his shoulders so that his small round head seemed as if it were poised, ready to roll, bouncing, onto the table.

'I want her body released to me. I want to make sure she has a decent burial.'

'You're living dangerously, Inspector,' he said. 'You believe you can talk like that to me here, in the Lubyanka, because of your friendship with Colonel Rolkin. But schoolboy friendships have a way of wearing thin. And when that happens you won't be talking to me like this.' He sniffed. 'Colonel Rolkin has authorised me not to sign over Raisa's body to anyone, Inspector Vadim. To the best of my knowledge she has already been cremated.' He stood up. 'The matter of Raisa Persilova is closed.'

I drove back to the apartment building. In the hall a young man was standing beside a collection of cupboards, rolls of carpet, boxes of books. A woman of about the same age had just come down in the lift. She stood, her foot holding open the grille door, a slightly dazed look on her plain but pleasant face. 'You won't believe this, Kolya,' she said to the young man. 'The place is furnished. Completely. Blankets, bedlinen, cutlery – even discs and a player. A whole set of opera recorded in New York, can you believe?'

I came forward. 'I'm a friend of the last tenant,' I said. 'Were there any personal items . . . clothes, photographs . . . ?'

'All that has been cleared by the caretaker,' she said. 'He's just coming down with the last sackful to burn with the rest in the yard.'

I walked through to the back of the lift to the door that led to the yard.

In the small walled garden the weeds had been trampled by snow. A man in the white cap and the blue uniform overcoat of an airline pilot was crouched beside a small pile of smoking cloth and papers. A well-dressed woman stood beside him.

As I approached, the rising smoke column guttered towards me, filling my nostrils with a sharp bitter smell. The woman saw me first. Her lipsticked mouth moved. I saw her fists tighten in her expensive, foreign gloves. The man turned his head, picked up some photographs which he had rescued from the fire and got to his feet. His expression was wary.

I held out my hand. 'Constantin Vadim,' I said. 'I was a neighbour of Raisa's. And I think a friend.' I spoke quietly to try to dispel their alarm.

He shook my hand. 'Captain Nicolai Persilov. I'm her brother.' He looked at his wife but didn't introduce her. 'The police informed me that she took her life early yesterday morning.'

'Yes,' I said.

'We came to collect her things,' the wife said, 'but they were already out here. Burning in the backyard. It's the brutality I don't understand. Can you explain it?'

Her husband touched her arm to silence her but she

shook off his hand. 'They say her body was seen floating in the river.' There was real anger in her voice. 'The river's been frozen for the last week. How in God's name could she have been floating in a frozen river? How can we believe that?'

'Madame Persilov,' I said. 'They don't even *care* if you believe them.'

The man was alarmed now, unsure of me. He gripped his wife's arm.

'I'm a police officer,' I said. 'Inspector Vadim. I mean what I said. If the facts don't tie up, they don't care.'

'Who are they? The Cheka?'

Her husband visibly tensed. 'Yes,' I said. 'The Cheka.'

'You said you were a friend,' the captain said. 'Were you in some way involved . . . in what happened to Raisa?'

I invited Captain Persilov and his wife upstairs and as we drank coffee I told him the story of Julia trying to contact me through Raisa. It was not as reckless as it seemed because I pared the story down to what Roy already knew.

At the end of my account they sat on the sofa in shock. Their silence they covered by small movements. First one, then the other, in unrecognised rotation, reached forward for their coffee cup, lifted it to their lips and then replaced it with a minute chink against the saucer.

Even the woman, who had been more inclined to press for answers than her husband, was now silent. I watched now as Raisa's brother glanced at her and she nodded. They both rose to go. 'We can't thank you enough,' the woman said.

'It was my problems that involved her with the Cheka,' I said.

'They're the whole country's problems,' she said. 'I was thanking you for telling us what really happened.'

The pilot was at the door, anxious, even at this point

anxious that she didn't say too much. I leaned past her to reach the handle. Her Western perfume rose towards me, musky as incense.

The young couple moving into Raisa's apartment had commandeered the elevator. I accompanied the pilot and his wife down the stairs. Every step of the way as I occupied the space she had just vacated I became more certain. *Musky as incense.* At that time, in Father Alexander's office, it had not even crossed my mind to wonder who his impatient visitor might be. Now I was sure I knew. She was the only other woman I knew who wore expensive Western perfume. And if I was right she knew the sex-priest by more than reputation.

They stood outside on the street, the pilot in his white cap and his wife in her faultless American clothes. He held a pack of charred photographs. She carried a scarf which still reeked of burning.

'If there's anything I can do to thank you,' the pilot said, 'anything I can bring from the West . . . I fly to New York three times a week.'

I shook my head. 'No, nothing I need.'

'Goodbye then, Inspector,' he said. He was about to turn away when a thought struck me. 'Captain . . . there is something perhaps. May I ask how well you speak English?'

'In the air it's the international language,' he said.

'He's trying not to say that his first wife was American,' the woman said with a wry smile.

'I speak it well, Inspector. There's something I can do for you in New York?'

'Yes. A doctor, a woman named Imogen Shepherd . . .' I took my notebook and wrote down the name. 'She qualified at Columbia University, New York.'

'You want me to check her credentials, her qualifications.'

'Anything,' I said. I had no real idea what I was asking. 'Anything at all you can find on her.'

We shook hands. 'I'll be back before the weekend,' he said. 'I'll have something for you when you call.'

35

I was feeling bad about Natalya and our dawn parting, squeezed into the cab of her van. I went back up to my apartment and called her office. A strange voice answered. Dr Karlova, she told me, was away. This was Dr Olga Brodsky, Natalya Karlova's replacement.

'Dr Karlova is away? How long for?'

'I've been instructed that I may be needed for the rest of the week.'

I introduced myself. 'Dr Karlova told me nothing about going away.'

'I understand she had vital research to conduct in Petersburg.'

'What vital research? On the Monstrum case?'

'So I understand, Inspector.'

'And she went without discussing it with me? Jesus Christ!'

'It smacks of unprofessional behaviour, Inspector,' Dr Brodsky said smugly. 'She's a young woman, I understand. Probably with a head full of American popular songs. I feel confident that you'll find my professional abilities equal to the tasks assigned to me in the fight against crime. Perhaps I could illustrate my own way of doing things with a brief anecdote from my last posting . . .'

I held the phone away from my ear as the southern accent droned on. After a moment I broke in. 'Dr Brodsky,' I said. 'Thank you.'

'I'm very much looking forward to discussing the Monstrum case,' she said crisply. 'Can we match diaries?'

'No . . . no . . .' I stumbled but didn't fall. 'Perhaps later. I have no diary with me at the moment. I'll call in as soon as I can.'

'Excellent. I'll spend the rest of the day in the formaldehyde room. I've an interesting theory on the cutting techniques used by the Monstrum which I want to check out.'

'Oh yes,' I said. 'The formaldehyde room.' The thought made my stomach turn over.

'They've specimens there that I would like us to examine more closely. Essentially it's a matter of texture . . . resistance . . . flesh, I mean . . .'

'I look forward to it,' I said. I thanked her and put down the phone. So Natalya had gone – to Petersburg. Why Petersburg? And why not tell me? Was she trying to get a jump ahead of me, was that it? But that was ridiculous. Angry as I felt, as she felt, I knew that crude point scoring just wasn't like Natalya. Or had she come to tell me last night, and abandoned the idea in her fury at Julia's request for weapons.

My hands covered my face. Petersburg. What aspect of the case pointed to Petersburg? Petersburg . . . The priest's background was to be found there. Was that it? Was she checking records for the similar mutilation of young girls in Petersburg? Then why not tell me? Tell someone, other than the ridiculous Dr Brodsky.

I made a conscious effort to put all thought of Natalya aside. I was embarked on a desperate enterprise. I must let nothing stand in my way. What was at stake was the re-creation of Julia's respect for me, even perhaps of her love.

I made another call to District, asked for the Murder Room and got Dronsky. 'I was worried about you, Chief,' he said, 'when you disappeared down that fucking shaft in the Belorussian. I waited an hour, called a team in and lifted the thugs on the door. Made them take us down to look for you, fuck your mother. We were lost for hours. When we reached the priest's place Bitov and Yakunin were down there with a line-up of witnesses.'

Dronsky was upset.

'Ilya . . .' I said. 'I'm in health – OK?'

'You might not have been, Chief.'

'True. How did Bitov and Yakunin get on?'

'It's slow. They've set up a cross-reference chart of fifty witnesses. What time each of our girls left, who with, according to who – you get what I mean.'

I got what he meant. Another forty-eight hours at least. Another forty-eight tons of paperwork – and we still might miss just that one essential remark that could put us on the right lines.

'Listen,' I said. 'You talk to Natalya?'

'Not today,' he said, wary on the phone.

'Did she tell you she was going to Petersburg?'

'Going to Petersburg? No. What for?'

'I don't know what for. Some sort of lead. It's intolerable. The medical examiner has some sort of lead and she takes it on herself to chase after it without informing the senior inspector.'

'Yes, that's bad, Chief,' Dronsky said. 'Very bad.' I could see those thick eyebrows lifting. I don't think he thought it was bad at all.

I was feeling like death. Maybe the after-effects of the *stoke*. I don't know, but I needed a couple of hours' sleep before I resumed my life. 'Dronsky,' I said. 'I need sleep. I'll be in in a couple of hours. Get the priest over there to meet me. There must be something we can think of to ask him.'

I had a small sack with two bottles of Hero City vodka and a burning desire to succeed. But that was all. No real plan. An outline, a shape. But mostly wishful thinking.

I parked the Economy in the station garage and took the stairs to deep basement level. Only the armoury was housed down here.

I'd met the sergeant armourer when I'd first signed for my pistol, but I stood at the scarred counter, swung my sack from my shoulder, dumped it on the floor and flipped my ID.

'Inspector Vadim,' he said. 'Of course. What can I do for you?' There was a fleeting smile on his face but his eyes were everywhere. He looked so furtive that I even considered for a moment that I might go for an outright purchase.

I hesitated, tried to catch his shifty eyes and decided against.

I pulled my pistol from its holster under my jacket and placed it on the table between us. 'I don't want any crap like this,' I said harshly. 'Mother Moscow's too rough a place to haul a gun with a bent firing pin.'

'Inspector . . .' His eyes were on me now. 'I swear when I checked it out . . . let's see . . .' He picked up the pistol, read off the number and took his armourer's book. 'Here we are, Inspector. One hundred. That signifies the weapon's in perfect condition.'

'The firing pin's bent,' I said stubbornly. 'It hits seven on ten. The difference between life and death out on the street.'

He recognised this sort of talk. It fitted his image of himself. 'I'm going to issue you a new model, Inspector—'

'You bet you are.'

'I mean a *brand* new model 38 American handgun, Inspector. I cleaned the factory grease packing off the consignment just this morning. Will that do it?'

I grunted assent.

'The paperwork will take a minute or two.'

'OK. I don't have all day,' I said.

'Right . . . right. The paperwork is in the back office.' He looked at the steel latticework over the counter. 'I'm supposed to lower the grille, Chief,' he said. 'If I'm not at the counter I'm supposed to lock up.'

'I'll watch the shop,' I said. 'You just draw me a new weapon, for Christ's sake.'

'Orders are specific . . .' he said.

I reached down into my sack and pulled out one of the bottles of Hero City vodka. Holding it by the neck I placed it with great deliberation on the counter and with one finger at the base pushed it slowly towards him.

'My brother,' I said, 'has a place just outside Moscow. Nice place. He and his wife do chickens, a few cows . . . Good land too, in the middle of the forest. Originally cleared for a labour camp in the old days.'

He looked up from the vodka bottle and nodded.

'And the house there is great. Old camp commandant's house. Makes a fine dacha . . .'

He tried a smile.

'Only problem with it is the old watchtowers are still standing. He looks out of his goddamned windows each morning and he and his wife feel as if *they're* the ones inside.'

I fixed his eyes with mine. 'Steel scaffolding sunk in concrete. How d'you shift that sort of crap?'

He raised his eyebrows. 'He'd need to find a big diamond-cutter power saw,' he said. 'Even then you could bring the whole lot down on top of you.'

'There's really only one watchtower gives him trouble,' I said. 'The rest are more or less screened by trees. I thought instantaneous fuse might do it.'

He shrugged. But his eyes were wary.

'You've seen that stuff wrapped round the trunk of a pine: a detonator and five feet of fuse and crack! – it's like a clean cut.'

'I've seen that done,' he said.

I pushed the vodka forward. 'Where do you keep your instantaneous in the store?'

His eyes bulged, but he jerked a thumb to the left.

I reached down and took the second bottle of Hero City from my sack. Placing it on the counter, I pushed

352

the two towards him. 'Why don't you just go and do the paperwork on that American handgun,' I said. 'Take your time.'

His eyes flickered one last time, then met mine. 'I'll do that for you, Inspector,' he said. 'No problem.'

Nodding six or seven times at least as he retreated between the gun racks with the bottles of vodka in his hands, he disappeared through the door at the back.

I ran down one set of racks and back up the next. There were guns of all descriptions, of all ages: handguns, Thompsons and Kalashnikovs. But no grenades. I was looking for those green webbing belts, a grenade in each of the dozen or so canvas pockets, that I could remember seeing at Murmansk. But there was nothing.

In the last corridor of shelving, when disappointment and relief were coming at me in equal strength, I saw a pile of boxes. Grenade boxes. I flipped the hasp of the top one and there they were, twenty or thirty grenades in neat line – but submerged in a thick bed of protective grease. It was like looking down at them on the sea bed.

I used my left hand to remove six, each one with a sucking sound as it came away. The spring handles and rings were separate. I grabbed a handful and dropped them into my bag.

For a moment I looked wildly for instantaneous fuse, then my eye caught a row of orange coils sitting on a high shelf. Black for slow burning. Red and yellow for fast. Orange for instantaneous. The rest was easy. Detonators were in a box beside the fuse, against all orders I was sure.

When the back door opened and the armourer came back with the signature book and the brand new 38 Police Special pointing towards the ceiling, I was back behind the counter.

He reversed the gun deftly, spinning it on the trigger guard, and handed it to me. Then with one finger he turned the book on the counter for me to sign. His shoulders were rolling confidently inside his uniform shirt. 'Who wants watchtowers on their property these days,' he said conversationally. 'Your brother ever wants to shift the rest of the bastards, don't you forget to let me know, Inspector.'

In the echoing garage, my footsteps sounded like a challenge to every member of the District to stop me and search my sack. As I dodged between the lines of cars the oily atmosphere seemed to constrict my lungs.

I was wheezing as I reached my car. I'd heard of panic attacks and perhaps this was one. The sack trailing the ground, I leaned against the car and took deep breaths. What I had done was irrevocable. I had stolen six grenades from the armoury. What in God's name had persuaded me that the armourer would not connect the theft to me? Of course I'd seen it all differently. As it was in our Murmansk armoury. I'd thought to see grenades, cleaned of packing grease, hanging in belts from a dozen nails. A grenade missing from one belt or another would never be noticed until the next time they were signed out. And in peacetime that could be months.

But it had not been like that. My hand was trembling against the cold metal of the car. My face had frozen solid. Panic, real panic, flared through my chest.

I could hear the footsteps behind me. The voices. The quickening pace. But it was like that real but distant world of *stoke*. As if I was out there watching my own downfall.

It was Dronsky's hand that fell on my shoulder. I could hear his voice, see the movement of his lips. But nothing I could understand came through. Then with a pop like eardrums clearing as you hit the surface, he came through force five. 'Reported by District 15 in the Riverbend Nagotino area,' he was saying. 'Different but equally dead.'

36

She was swinging by her neck. A big strong dark-haired woman of perhaps forty, although it's difficult to put down an age when the face is purplish and swollen and the eyes and tongue stick out like a cartoon by Yefimov.

You see how easily, brothers, I fall into this insouciant cop-talk, of pretending it isn't human at all, the being hanging up there, in the dark floral dress with its head twisted grotesquely to one side, the whole body revolving half a turn as someone's shoulder in this crowded room brushes against the legs. But she *is* human – or *was*.

Her child is crying in the next room, or next room but one. A sobbing that has started and stopped ever since we arrived. The child is a girl of eight. She found her mother hanging from a skylight when she came back from school. Dronsky tells me a neighbour is doing her best.

The room is a tenement room, three metres by three metres. There's a big brass bed where mother and child sleep whenever the mother is home. There's a hand basin that's too cracked to use and a washbasin and jug and some soap on a marble washstand. The red curtains aren't bad and look quite new. There's a small stove which is out now but has been recently alight and is still warm. The floor is, what? Bare boards, a strip of dark green linoleum and a piece of carpet by the bed.

This isn't the room of a whore who earns two hundred dollars a throw at one of the big hotels.

The District 15 police were quick and efficient. Someone there put two and two together when her unusual height and her preferred work-site at the Belorussian were mentioned. They immediately checked the 'General

Wanted' we'd put out on her and got onto us. She was only found an hour ago.

Theft and street offences take so much less out of you. I looked again at the hanging body in the dark Armenian floral dress. Her back is towards me, her head turned away. Until another passing shoulder causes her to spin slowly and those bulging grey eyes are fixed on me again.

These eyes had glimpsed the Monstrum. These eyes had watched him wield the plank of wood that had brought the streetwalker, Valentina, to her knees. These eyes had come closest to seeing the Monstrum up to his armpits in blood.

For this, under one of her many names, was Dark Maria. Born Madelena Kassarian, in Armenia, some time perhaps in the mid-1970s, the common law wife of a soldier who had fought for the Soviets in Afghanistan, fought for the military *coup d'état* and finally for the Anarchists. He had been killed here in this riverbound suburb defending Mother Moscow against the advance of what I used to call *our* armies.

Madelena Kassarian was a tough, streetwise whore who had sold her body to raise her child. She had not, according to neighbours, spent time at the Belorussian since she had first heard that the police in Red Presnya wanted to speak to her.

On the crowded landing we interviewed a man from the room next door who might or might not have been her pimp or lover. 'Did she ever mention why she was staying away from the Belorussian these days?' Dronsky asked.

'Was she?' His name was Gleb. He stood in shirt sleeves and braces, a dead cigarette under a pencil moustache. With his oiled, brushed-back hair, he looked as if he had just emerged from a film of socialist achievement in the 1930s. Shifting the cigarette deftly with his tongue, he said: 'She moved around from place to place. There was nothing special about the Belorussian for her.'

'Where did she work in the last couple of weeks, then?'

'She's been going to one or two of the bars here along the Proletarian Prospekt.'

I stepped closer so that I wasn't looking past him into the room where they were cutting her down and laying her on a trolley stretcher. 'She knew we wanted to speak to her about what she'd seen that night she was working with Valentina?'

'It wasn't difficult to guess.'

'But she didn't want to get involved.'

He shrugged. 'Hours of questions, identikits that fit nothing. Good time wasted.'

It was a pretty standard view of police work among people like Maria and Gleb. 'Apart from the fact that she stopped going to the Belorussian, has there been anything else different about her in the last week or so?'

'No.'

'No sign of depression? No talk about taking her own life?' Dronsky said.

The shake of the head was barely visible. 'Somebody came up in broad daylight, hit her over the head and strung her up.' He said it in a tone of voice designed to cut off all these irrelevancies.

'You don't think it was suicide?' Dronsky said, writing in his brown leatherette notebook.

The man didn't answer.

I touched his shoulder and he flinched. 'Hit her over the head, you said.'

'An upswinging blow to the base of the skull.' He moved his shoulders like a former boxer. 'The bruising's just under the hairline.'

The police paramedics were rolling the trolley stretcher past us. Dronsky bent over it quickly and lifted the green cover from the dead woman's face. With his free hand he raised the hair from the base of her skull. The bruise had spread out across the back of her neck. 'You should have been a police pathologist,' he said.

Gleb flexed the thin, wiry muscles on his tattooed forearms. He watched the paramedics carry the stretcher to the first bend in the stairwell then he turned his eyes back to us. 'You know a thing or two about death when you've worked in a slaughterhouse for thirty years of your life,' he said to Dronsky.

'We're looking for something like a piece of timber, then. A plank of wood, perhaps . . .'

'Once again,' Dronsky said.

'OK, Gleb.' I lifted my arm and propped myself on the door jamb. 'If Madelena was murdered, why do it that way? A knife's a lot easier surely. Even a few more blows with whatever he hit her with.'

He thought for a moment. Took a brass petrol lighter from his trouser pocket, flicked it until a flame appeared and rolled his cigarette across his mouth to light it. He blew a thin, vicious stream of smoke into my face. 'Your killer wants the local militia to see it as a straight suicide. They're common enough in Moscow these days, right?'

'Common enough,' I agreed.

'And the militia are dumb as oxen like they've always been, so they're not going to connect Madelena Kassarian with the girl from the Belorussian.'

'Except this time they weren't all dumb oxen. Somebody at District 15 put a few of these things together.'

Gleb made a face as if he'd just stumbled across the Eighth Wonder.

'Were you in all day?'

'I sleep late. About ten in the evening I go down to the abattoir to see if there's any work. Everything's casual labour these days.'

'So you were asleep when this happened.'

'You tell me. I sleep heavy. I came round at two, even.'

'Two o'clock you mean.'

'That's what I said.'

'And?'

'I went over and knocked on her door. That's the pattern. Sometimes if she got back really late, she's still sleeping, I leave her. Sometimes we drink tea together and talk about this and that. About life in general.'

'Today you thought she was sleeping.'

'All I knew, she didn't answer. I went back and found yesterday's *Pravda*. Perhaps I fell asleep again for an hour. Next I heard was terrible screams from out here on the landing.'

'Her child.'

He nodded.

'The pathologist puts Madelena's death at about two o'clock.'

He took the stub from his mouth and flicked it into the stairwell. 'I wondered when you were going to start looking at me,' he said. I could read the fury he felt in the muscles of his lean jaw, in those muscles on his tattooed arms. He stood stock still before me but his body was alive with movement.

'District 15 are going to want to ask you some questions about your relationship with Madelena . . .'

'I've got nothing more to say. To you or District 15.' His mouth without the cigarette was tight, almost razor sharp.

'In the course of your conversations with Madelena about life, did she tell you what she had seen that night she was doing business near the cloth factory with Valentina?'

He stood with his small black eyes buttoned on me. 'I know nothing about that,' he said.

'You said she told you about it.'

'Then I was lying. Exaggerating, more like.'

'She must have said something about the man who attacked Valentina.'

'If she did, I don't remember.'

'For Christ's sake, you don't want to leave this monster free to do it again just for the sake of not getting involved.'

He curled his cigarette from one corner of his mouth to the other. 'I've never known the police get it right yet. They'll finger who they want to finger,' he said. 'The more they talk to someone like me, the more they're going to look at me. *That's* life, Inspector. That's the sort of life Madelena and I used to talk about.'

'District 15 are going to take you in for questioning, you know that don't you?'

The muscles rippled in his shoulders and down his jawline. Derisively he snorted smoke through his nostrils.

And I realised I had played this one wrong.

We recovered the weapon that had knocked Madelena Kassarian unconscious, or what I was pretty sure was the weapon, just inside the hall door to the tenement block. It had the right weight and heft to it. A piece split off an old joist, a metre long with the bulk all front-ended. An upswinging blow as the man Gleb had seemed to envisage without difficulty. Like a baseball swing, baseball having rivalled football as the number one sport in Russia over the last few years.

We had also interrogated all the tenants of the old block. A grey-haired woman with a young face and a faint aura of alcohol, whose name I can no longer remember, had been in at about two o'clock. She lived on the same landing as Madelena and kept her door open to chase the kids out who came into the tenement to play or smooch or smoke or drink or whatever kids did to raise hell these days, while Madelena got her rest. It seems Madelena paid her a few kopecks to perform this service for her.

I asked the woman how long Gleb had been living in the building and she told me he had moved there just after the Anarchists were thrown out of Moscow and everybody had taken him for an ex-soldier. Our side, of course. He had befriended Madelena from the beginning and he spent time in her room occasionally, but whether or not he was a paying guest she couldn't say.

'This afternoon you had your door open as usual?'

'I was doing some washing, Inspector, but taking it easy because, in any event, I'm not as young as I look . . .'

'With the door open could you see onto the landing?'

She wagged her head from side to side. 'These dark November afternoons and no light on the landing . . . But my hearing's still good, Your Honour. Nothing much gets past me.'

'And what did you hear?'

'First thing, about one o'clock there were some children came in downstairs. Shouting and screaming, bullying some child, picking on him, you know how children do. I went down to the next landing and told them to clear off or I'd bring my dog down to them.'

'You've got a guard dog?'

'I had one. He died last month.'

'So the children ran off.'

'Then about half-past one, perhaps later, I heard something out there on the landing.'

'You mean a footstep . . .'

'Don't ask me what. It was a noise. Most I could say. Then voices in Madelena's room.'

'But you hadn't heard anybody coming up the stairs?'

'No.'

'So it's possible that someone didn't come up the stairs.'

'You mean that it was Gleb, letting himself out of his room and straight into hers?'

I studied her for a moment. 'Could it have been Gleb?'

'If it was I don't know why he knocked on her door five or ten minutes later.'

'You heard that?'

'Of course. He knocked. Got no answer and went back to his own room.'

'OK,' I said. 'Go back to the other noise, and the voices. How many voices?'

'Just the one. And Madelena.'

'Two people talking.'

'Except the other woman didn't say a lot.'

'The other woman?' My blood tingled. 'The visitor was a *woman*?'

She nodded slowly. 'Spooky, isn't it?' She gathered her shawl around her shoulders and shivered.

'You're sure it was a woman?'

Her young-old face looked severely troubled. 'I suppose I couldn't swear by St Vladimir to it, Inspector, but I told you, when your eyes are going, it's your hearing you have to learn to trust.'

I went back to the District 13, up the wide steps, through the swing doors and into reception, that great circular space below the dome. It was the first time I'd been in since last night at the Belorussian and I was stopped dead by the sight of the long line of men and women shuffling forward to claim their amnesty status, shuffling forward in the first steps of the long journey to Magadan.

I slunk past them and passed through the Murder Room. My office door was open. Father Alexander and my chief, the rotund Commander Brusilov, were making themselves at home. The air was thick with cigar smoke. A bottle of French brandy stood, opened, on my desk. Father Alexander sat in my swivel chair; Brusilov had had a comfortable canvas chair brought in. He sat with his short legs up on a stool in front of him, turning his head and shoulders as I entered. 'Vadim, come in, come in. I'll have you know that Father Alexander has been waiting here upwards of an hour.' His face was flushed. 'It won't do, you know, Vadim. It won't do.'

I looked at the priest, who was a good deal more sober than Brusilov appeared to be. He stood up. 'Take your chair, Inspector.' He swung another from the wall behind him and sat by the side of the desk. 'Commander Brusilov has been entertaining me royally.'

Brusilov had taken his legs from the stool and he now stood up, straightening his grey uniform jacket, running a finger round his high-collared neck. 'Come up to my office when you're finished, Father,' he said. His eyes twinkled with alcohol. 'There's a great deal more about your Following I'd like to hear.'

He half turned as if he were on parade, glared up at me, lost his focus and stalked past, on stiff short legs, out of the room.

I dropped into my chair, took a glass from my desk drawer, poured some of the brandy, and eased back to watch the priest.

'I received your message,' he said. 'I came forthwith.'

I sipped at the brandy, enjoying the smoothness as it ran off the back of my tongue.

'You have some questions to ask me?'

'I have.'

He made an open gesture with his hand.

Now take this carefully, Constantin. Petersburg first. 'You say you come from Petersburg . . . ?'

'I was not in fact born there. Simply that I spent many happy years there before the Civil War.'

'Did you organise a cult there, a Following?'

'I had a Following there, yes. The Village of Love.' He smiled. 'I seem to recall we reached nearly fifty members at the time. Very impressive for such a naturally iconoclastic people as Peterburgers.'

'What happened?'

'I'd not yet learned how to organise and project my beliefs. The police and the church harassed us continuously. We lived in the flood tunnels under the city.' He waggled his beard. 'The accommodations were a good deal less impressive than those I have at my disposal in Moscow.'

'Did any of your girls go missing?'

'Girls drifted in and out of the community.'

'Do you have a list of your membership?'

He lifted his hands, palms towards me. 'I remember a few names if that will help.'

I shook my head. He was altogether too smooth, too relaxed, surely. 'Is Dr Imogen Shepherd a member of your Following, Father?'

He smiled. 'Would that she were.'

'You know her.'

'A dramatic woman.'

'Does she ever come down in the tunnels?'

He was silent.

'I think that Dr Shepherd was your visitor waiting in the anteroom while you showed me out the other door.'

'She comes down from time to time,' he conceded.

'Why is that?'

'She's a student of life, Inspector. Where better to come to see us Russians struggle with our destiny?'

I think I scowled.

Father Alexander smiled. He might even have been enjoying himself.

'I'm investigating a bestial murder case, Father Alexander. Four girls who were members of your Following have already been sexually assaulted, murdered and partially dismembered. Perhaps if you didn't make it quite so obvious that you were enjoying yourself throughout all this, I'd feel more inclined to take you at face value.'

He composed his features. 'I take your point, Inspector. To the police, crime is crime. Four young women dead. But did you by chance examine last month's lists of suicides in the Moskva River? Two hundred and twenty bodies were pulled out. Young women often, with babies strapped to them. Girls of thirteen or fourteen . . . mutilated by shellfire and unable to face a life without a limb.' He drew a breath. 'Nobody welcomes four more young women dead, Inspector. But in the wider, chaotic order of things in Russia today . . .'

I don't like this talk. I don't know how to handle it.

'What was Dr Shepherd really doing down there?' I said roughly.

He sat back, put his hands behind his head. 'We have been old friends for some time, Inspector. I sheltered her during the battle for Moscow. A pretty woman like her . . .' He lifted his eyebrows. 'In the midst of a battle, she would be fair game for either side.'

'So you were able to help her.'

'Just during the critical week or two when the struggle was in the balance. At that time she had a children's clinic on Petrovka, near the old Health Ministry. It had just been destroyed, a direct hit by an incendiary shell. She sheltered with us in the tunnels. There were many thousands of us at that time.'

'And what's your relationship with her now?'

'She renders me some medical services.'

'Tell me.'

He coughed and stroked his beard. 'The practice of an orgiastic cult such as our own should be natural, untrammelled by worries . . . fears.'

I set down my brandy glass. 'You're telling me that Dr Shepherd handles HIV testing for the Following?'

'It's not something I like to talk about, Inspector. You understand.'

'I can see that.'

'I spoke to Dr Imogen today,' he said, after a moment. 'She came down to the catacombs this afternoon.'

'Dr Shepherd was there this afternoon? At what time?'

'Midday, not long after.'

'Can you be more precise?'

He thought. 'She arrived at the latest between half-past midday and just before one o'clock.'

'And left?'

'She had six or seven new girls to test. She was in there, in my office, for about two hours or more. One or two senior women were helping her.'

'You saw her leave?'

'At about half-past three, yes. As did several others.'

So the woman's voice in Maria's room was not Imogen's. It was a thought that had been growing, irrationally perhaps, in my mind in the last two hours. I know I'm not a good analytical detective. I rely on hunches which are, as often as not, misplaced. But ever since the old woman had spoken of hearing another woman's voice in the room where Maria was killed, ideas had been flickering like fireflies through my mind. Most of all I kept thinking of Gromek the night-watchman's evidence and Nellie's and Valentina's about the man in the long overcoat waiting on the corner of the flag factory the night Lydia Primalova was killed. The words came back to me: slender . . . trim . . . cut like an officer's coat . . . Could the waiting man have been a *woman*?

I took a deep breath. I had to learn to shove these conjectures out of my mind. The evidence before me, from Father Alexander and, I've no doubt, when we had a chance to ask them, from the women Imogen had been examining this afternoon, was that the American doctor had not been, could not have been, in Maria's apartment. Whoever killed Maria, it was not Imogen Shepherd.

The priest was looking at me. 'All these timings are clearly of importance,' he said.

I shook my head. 'I thought perhaps they might be. But no . . .' I stood up. 'I'm going to want to do various tests,' I said. I knew the results would be worthless (since we had nothing really to compare them with) but I hoped to intimidate him with the thought. 'You've no objection?'

'None.' His self-confidence was unshakeable. Guilty or innocent, I suspect he would have answered in the same tone of dismissive insouciance. 'Is that all, Inspector?'

'Just one further thing. Do you know a woman named Madelena Kassarian?'

'No . . .' He shook his head. 'It's possible she's passed through the catacombs but if so the name has not stuck. Kassarian – an Armenian girl, presumably?'

366

'She worked the Belorussian. Very tall, heavy build. Maria, she was known as there.'

'We do not accept street girls into the Following, for obvious health reasons. Am I to assume this girl is dead?'

'Yes.'

'And did the death occur this afternoon between one and three o'clock?'

I nodded.

'I see,' he said. He stood up and began to plump out his beard, his head bent as he concentrated. Then his eyes came up to meet mine. 'Not guilty, Inspector,' he said deliberately. 'On this or any other count.'

'And you're quite sure about the time Dr Shepherd attended the six new girls?'

'Within a few minutes either way, yes.'

I opened the door for him and he strode out through the Murder Room. I was far from excluding Father Alexander from the frame, but I had to accept that the woman's voice in Maria's room this afternoon was not Imogen Shepherd's.

And if it wasn't Imogen's, whose was it?

37

Roy's club was smart Moscow. Working among the battered districts of the city as I did, I easily forgot that a different Moscow had survived the ravages of the great siege. Most publicly, this other Moscow existed along National Democracy Prospekt in the stores with armed guards outside and in the many wealthy women to be seen stepping out of their chauffeur-driven cars and into the boutiques stocked with garments from Paris, Berlin and Rome. The great hotels, too, were evident centres of wealth where the excellent security arrangements had persuaded many Russian industrialists to rent huge suites. The scurrilous colour magazines which were a feature of life in post-war Moscow depended on the stories that filtered from the upper-floor suites of the Tsar Nicholas and the Pushkin.

A further layer of Mother Moscow, it was rumoured, existed behind and below the façades of blank official buildings. This was a layer which the masses never saw. Bitov and Yakunin had once talked about restaurants of great luxury staffed solely by transvestites where a ticket to the weekly orgy cost a thousand dollars. If Father Alexander could hold his orgies under Red Presnya why should I doubt the *vlasti* held similar rituals?

But talk of privileged clubs and bacchanalian revels were part of the daily grist of Muscovite rumour, almost a necessity for a people living their own lives in such drab and straitened circumstances. Until Roy Rolkin required my presence at 4335 National Democracy Prospekt, I had been inclined to doubt this other world really existed.

I was wrong. When the palace of one of the most powerful families in old Russia had been demolished during the 1930s, the vast basements had remained undisturbed. Under the Soviet tsars they had served as meeting rooms and furniture stores. Now, entering by an unprepossessing staircase, checked and rechecked against a list held by guards on the door, I was at last allowed into a superb black and white tiled hall, with a barrel-vaulted brick roof. From the curtained archways on my left I could hear music and bursts of male laughter.

Standing here, watching the black jacketed waiters and the uniformed officers moving through the curtained archways, I was conscious that I should have made more of an effort than simply buttoning my collar and straightening my tie.

Roy, of course, would be in uniform, like most of the officers here, with broad red stripes down their grey or green uniform trousers. Many of them had adopted the old tsarist white dress uniform jackets.

The porter who moved into my path was a big fellow dressed as a Russian peasant of the 1880s. I gave him my name and asked for Colonel Rolkin.

'The colonel has a guest with him, Inspector Vadim.'

I was momentarily baffled. 'Did he ask me to wait?'

'No, monsieur.'

Monsieur! I looked the big fellow in the eye. 'I've been invited by Colonel Rolkin. Please tell him I'm here.'

He smiled. I obviously didn't know the ways of the club. 'I meant the colonel has a *lady* guest with him.'

'Ah . . .'

'But I understand she's just leaving.'

'Then let me know when she's gone.' I sat down in a comfortable armchair and reached for the day's newspapers which were piled on the table.

'I'll tell him you're here,' the peasant said.

He walked through a wide, curtained opening to my right. Through a gap that remained in the curtains after he passed I could see into a large room containing perhaps twenty low tables. Officers sat around them, mostly in uniform and occasionally with a young woman companion. Champagne seemed to be the favoured drink. A wooden stand with a silver ice bucket stood next to most of the tables.

I watched the big fellow cross the room. To the right of the fire I could see Roy, in uniform, yes, seated facing my direction. The outline of the woman's head and shoulders, seen with difficulty as people moved back and forth, was chillingly familiar.

I pushed the newspapers aside and stood up. Moving forward, I placed myself at the gap in the curtains. I saw Roy's eyes rise towards me. I saw the smile. I saw his bluff, peremptory signal to me to come across.

I parted the curtains, my heart sinking with fear, my mind racing to begin to guess what answers I might give. Tinnitus came to taunt me in a great buzzing rush of panic. The woman stood, unsmiling. It was Denisova, Julia's valued second in command.

For a moment our eyes met. I detected no expression on her face, no sign of recognition. As something clicked in my head, I looked towards Roy. He was standing next to her, shorter than she was, a hand on her elbow, but he was watching me.

I was perhaps halfway across the room when Roy began to lead her towards a far exit. I reached the table by the fire and the peasant asked me if I would be taking champagne. I suppose I nodded yes. Roy and Denisova had disappeared.

I asked the big fellow when he brought me a champagne glass where the door led and he told me simply that it was an exit out into the rear courtyard. I collapsed into a seat before the fire. There was no doubt in my mind that Roy had wanted me to see Denisova. I tried to force myself to think. I'm not naturally at home in ambiguity, yet some things were clear. If Denisova was in Roy's pay, then he knew where Julia was and had probably known for some time. Certainly Denisova would already have told him that I was in touch with Julia.

In which case, why not arrest me? I sat helpless, not understanding, a fly in a spider's web, waiting for Roy to return.

When he did he was in the best of spirits. He stood before the fire, rubbing his hands and beaming down at me. 'We are definitely making progress, Costya my old friend. Definitely making progress.'

I smiled encouragingly. But I could well imagine it was a sickly smile.

He came and sat down next to me. 'You see all these old fools around you? Celebrated their seventieth birthdays, most of them, before they put on general's shoulder boards.' He flicked his fingers for a waiter to pour more champagne. 'If all goes as it should, I shall put up my first general's star this year.'

I lifted my glass. 'I'll drink to that,' I said.

I knew I had to say something. I swallowed hard. 'Who was the girlfriend?' I asked, with as close to an air of roguishness as I could get, throttled as I was by fear.

He leaned towards me. 'Who would you say she was?'

'At a guess?'

'If you *had* to guess.'

My stomach had turned to water. 'A woman of quality,' I said. 'Somebody from one of the old families, a Yusupov, a Vronsky . . .'

He was smiling. But those cold, wrap-around eyes were focused intensely on me.

'. . . even a Romanov,' I ended lamely. 'Not our president,' I added hurriedly. 'One of the old family of the former tsars. I've seen magazine articles about Romanovs from all over the world. The women are a pretty dramatic-looking lot . . .' I stopped.

Roy smiled slowly. 'A Romanov who fancies a bit of

rough trade from Murmansk? You can do better than that, can't you, Costya?'

A waitress in a short black skirt and white blouse brought us *zakuska* of smoked sturgeon and squares of hot toast. 'Ah, sturgeon,' Roy said. 'Perfect, perfect. And have the waiter bring us another bottle of champagne, will you? I have a feeling my old friend here's going to need it before the evening gets much older.'

The girl left to pass on the order.

'Let's have another try, shall we, Constantin?'

'Another guess?'

He shook his head. He was sitting back, his eyes on me. He had toast and sturgeon in his mouth and he was munching slowly. 'You know who she was.'

'Never seen her before. How long have you known her?'

'I told you, if I ever thought you were holding out on me, Costya—'

'. . . you would feel very sad. Wasn't that the way our conversation went in the basement of the Nunnery?' In my nervousness I had got there too quickly. I had understood what he was driving at long before I should have.

He knew it. 'I'm beginning to get that sad feeling now,' he said.

'That sad feeling,' I said. 'Why is that?'

He indicated the table. 'You're not eating. Now don't tell me they serve smoked sturgeon every day in that police canteen of yours.'

'No, they don't, Roy.' I reached over and forked some sturgeon onto toast. The waiter arrived and opened a further bottle of champagne with a flourish. All the time Roy's Slavic eyes watched me.

When the waiter had gone, he leaned forward, twirling an unlit cigarette between his fingers. 'I saw your face as you crossed the room,' he said. His voice dropped to a whisper.

'My face?'

'As you saw her.' He paused. 'Stricken, fuck your mother, you were *stricken*.' He chuckled.

'Roy,' I said. 'I don't know this woman. I don't know what you're talking about. What's getting to you?'

'You'll be dogmeat if you're lying,' he snapped.

'Stop talking like that, for Christ's sake,' I said. My face blazed red, my eyes watered with panic, my tinnitus sang jeeringly.

'Dogmeat,' he said again.

'I don't have to take this,' I said, although we both knew I had no choice. 'We're old friends, for God's sake, Roy. We go back to Primary 27 together. You can at least tell me what this is all about, can't you?'

'You knew that woman . . .' he said quietly.

'If I reacted it was in embarrassment. The big peasant there told me you had a lady with you. Made it clear I was to wait until she was gone.' I forced a laugh. 'Then you caught me peering through the curtains at her. If I've seen what I shouldn't have, I'm sorry. That's all, Roy. God's truth. Now tell me what you read into *that*.'

He took more toast and forgot the sturgeon as he pushed it in his mouth and munched. He was in doubt. An edge of doubt. Perhaps not much more, but an edge.

'I read into it,' he said, stubbornly but nevertheless uncertainly, I prayed, 'that you've met her before.'

'No, Roy. Never.'

He wagged his head from side to side. 'Dimitry and his boys are dying to get their hands on you. I'm just wondering whether it wouldn't be the best thing . . .' He shrugged. 'On the other hand we could go into the wide-screen room next door, watch the football and be served beers by topless waitresses. What do you think?' A big amiable smile had reappeared on his face.

'I think I've got work to do,' I said, standing and praying my knees would hold me. 'We had another murder this afternoon.'

He walked over and clapped me on the shoulder. 'Come

and take a look at these topless girls first. They come from everywhere. Paris, London, Berlin – even New York. You could write a book about the differences.' He pointed a fat finger and waggled it obscenely.

I got to my car shivering with desperation. Denisova was in the pay of the Cheka. But she had not, for some reason I couldn't begin to understand, told Roy I had been in contact with Julia. Perhaps I just wasn't important enough. I could not think beyond the fact that I must warn Julia immediately.

I drove like a maniac. I took main boulevards and side roads. I changed speed from ninety down to twenty-five kilometres an hour. I turned into blind alleys and I raced along narrow tracks beside rail lines with my lights off. I had taken over an hour for a half-hour's journey but, by the time I arrived, I was sure I would have eluded a night hawk.

I abandoned my car as I had the first time, covering it with weatherbeaten sheets of plywood and rusted roofing iron. Moving among the Pasternak tower blocks, I saw no sign of Cheka listening vans or cars. Most vehicles I passed were burnt out. The few people I saw on foot were moving in family groups, bundles on their backs.

I entered Pasternak A through a hole in a ground-floor apartment and walked through wrecked rooms. At a concrete stairwell I began climbing until I reached the third floor. I was within Julia's domain now, expecting a guard to stop me, hoping it would be one I knew, or one at least who recognised me.

I followed a long empty corridor, using the flashlight I had brought from the car, and turned into the rear-facing flats which led through doorways and holes in the walls to Julia's headquarters. I stopped. I could almost feel the presence of a girl with a Kalashnikov pointing to my chest.

I looked towards the shattered doorway and lifted

my hands. 'Constantin Vadim,' I said. 'I've come to see Julia.'

Glass crunched under a heavy footstep. I suppose I knew the figure filling the doorway would be Roy Rolkin. If I'd paused for a few seconds after the officers' club to give myself time to think, I suppose I would never have come.

Of course, Roy was going to know that if I had recognised Denisova I would rush to warn Julia. If I hadn't known who Denisova was I would have stayed to watch wide-screen football and be served by topless girls from a dozen different countries.

So there you have it, brothers. When Roy punched me in the face I went down among the brick dust and broken glass and twisted window frames and as I half raised my head I saw other pairs of boots come through the doorway.

By the time I got to my feet there were already about ten men in Cheka uniforms around me. Dimitry was holding a sack. He lifted it for Roy to see. 'Six hand grenades and a coil of instantaneous fuse,' he said. 'Hidden in the boot of his car.'

'I'm sad,' Roy whispered. He took the sack and weighed it in his hand, then twisted the neck and swung it round once. 'Hacking,' he said.

He and I were the only ones in the room who knew what he meant. As boys in Primary 27 in Murmansk we would play a game. A coin was spun. The loser stood perfectly still while the other boy had an uninterrupted chance to kick where he wished. In Murmansk winter temperatures, the pain could be excruciating. When the roles were reversed the first boy would remember the pain of the first kick and decide whether he wanted to go on. But this game of hacking was going to be entirely one sided.

The sack swung. I stood still. The weight of six grenades clubbed me across the side of the head and I went down like a stone. I struggled to my feet and the sack swung again. Perhaps I made it a third time . . .

I was aware of being dragged into another room. But the voices around me spoke sentences I could not assemble into meanings. I smelt cordite strongly, in the nostrils – I smelt blood. I was sure there had been much blood spilt here.

I opened my eyes. It was a small room, a bedroom. The wallpaper was blue dots on a yellow background. At waist height three cut-out teddy bears danced across it. Beneath them six or seven real women were sprawled, their backs supported by the wall, their heads lolling forward. In the police floodlight, the quantities of blood between them gleamed black.

The clubbing by the grenade sack had dulled all sensation. I registered that they were the women of Julia's group. The Siberian, her black silky hair matted with blood. The girl with the Kalashnikov, her head leaning on another, an almost self-satisfied smile on her face. And sprawled in the corner, her leaking mouth open, was Denisova. She still wore the grey suit she was wearing at Roy's club, but it was drenched with blood.

Roy was standing over me.

'Julia,' I said. 'Where is she?'

He laughed. 'She's where she should have been a long time ago.'

'Oh Jesus . . .'

'Listen, she's alive,' he said, helping me up. 'I've always had a soft spot for Julia, you know that. The girl's alive.'

'You promise me,' I said, fatuously, given the circumstances. I pointed at Denisova. I'm not sure what I wanted to say, but I was, in any case, incapable of speech.

'You're one of the little cogs, Costya, you hear me? You're one of the millions of little cogs. Never, never think that people like you will ever succeed in turning the big wheels. Now go home and do your policeman's job and keep yourself out of trouble.'

He gave me a friendly punch on the shoulder. 'You hear me?'

I nodded my head and I thought it would split like a grenade.

'Good lad.' Roy ruffled my hair. 'We've got some clearing up to do here.' He looked with distaste towards the bodies against the wall. 'Who'd ever think women had so much blood in them?'

Huge waves of nausea flowed over me. I was retching silently, my head hanging forward.

'Remember what I said, uh?' He lifted my head, one hand cupped under my chin. 'You're a little cog. Stick to what you know.' He laughed. 'Just run along home now, Costya, and play the policeman with your Monstrum inquiry.'

38

It was the longest few days of my life. I waited outside Roy's apartment every evening to beg him to let me see her. I don't think he was taunting me. I don't think he really enjoyed it. He told me she was all right. He would say no more. I asked him where she was being held and he refused to answer. I asked him if she had been tortured and he said nothing. I asked him if that pervert Dimitry was in charge of her and he still said nothing.

I begged him to let me speak to her and he refused. I knew I was sailing close to the edge but I kept at him. When, in exasperation, he invited me up for a drink and a look at a new Italian porn film he'd acquired, I turned away.

But I came back the next night.

To have someone you love in the Lubyanka or the Lefortovo, or any other of the Cheka prisons, infects every second of the day with indescribable panic. It's a panic that surges back and forth through you like wave water. Eating is impossible. Thinking is charged with fear and imagination. Only drinking vodka is some sort of tranquilliser.

Images haunted me. That mark made by the nails of some tortured victim in the plaster wall of the Nunnery basement in Murmansk. The sound of sobbing in the night. The stain between the legs on Madame Raisa's dress.

Perhaps worst for me was what I knew of Julia's character. She would never surrender. She would never sign the atrocity confession or whatever it was that they were demanding of her. Yet it was impossible to win. By holding out on the inevitable, she would simply suffer more. I saw, with a dreadful clarity, that her strength of mind would destroy her body.

I made no attempt to contact Dronsky. The ifs and maybes of the Monstrum investigation were totally beyond my capacity to think. Worst of all, there was no Natalya. No one I could share my burden with. My burden, because I had become convinced that Roy had first made contact with Denisova by trailing me.

Then on the fourth morning of this purgatory, the phone rang.

It was my minder. If he'd ground out the usual instructions to be ready at such and such a time and place I would have put the phone down on him. But this time the voice was different, distinctly upbeat. 'Constantin,' he said. 'You've made the big time' – he used the English words – 'You're attending a reception for the US chargé d'affaires' staff. By next week these same people will be the US embassy itself. It's a big step up for you. Tonight. I'll pick you up this afternoon at two.'

I sat back in the chair. A reception for the US chargé d'affaires' staff. My first thought was that I should get up and go out and get so impossibly drunk that nothing could sober me in time. But as I sat staring at the phone another idea intervened. The American chargé d'affaires' staff. Obviously, since I had been chosen to go, the chargé d'affaires himself would not be present. But the staff were senior Americans, people who were negotiating the imminent change to embassy status. There might well be some opening. The chance perhaps to put in a word about what was happening at the Belorussian, a plea for Julia. She was an internationally known figure. The amnesty was Koba's diplomatic public relations exercise. If I could show somehow that he had outrageously flouted it . . .

I thought of all those men and women even now on their way to Magadan. I thought of Julia sentenced to a living death in the precious metal mines of the north-east. I stood up and walked back and forth across the room. The fates had given me a chance to speak for Julia. A chance perhaps to speak for all of those Russian brothers who had been betrayed by Koba's amnesty. A chance I had to take.

My status had quite definitely improved. I could tell this by the fact that my minder offered me the front seat next to him in the huge car he was driving. Furthermore he took my bag and put it into the boot. This was not how he was when I first met him. But I still didn't know his name.

I got into the car with a sense that I was unlikely to see this apartment again. I was not really sorry. I would hardly be leaving a circle of dear friends. I would name Madame Raisa among my Moscow friends, though I had barely known her. Natalya, of course, was a friend I could talk to more than anybody in Moscow. But she wasn't in Moscow.

So Ilya Dronsky was the only friend I had to think about as we drove through the city. I knew that I thought about him much too infrequently. I smiled now as we sped up Red Presnya Street, past the classical portico of the District station, smiled to think of Dronsky, his brush-cut head bent over the cross-indexed columns of witnesses from Father Alexander's catacombs, a fishburger bun in one hand, a cup of acorn coffee in the other. And the damned cat mewling round his legs, inflamed by the reek of fishburger. There were millions of Russians like Ilya, good men and women in desperate need of a favourable wind to set the ship in motion. In desperate need of a direction in which to sail.

We drove for half an hour. It was mid-afternoon with a low sun on the horizon when I saw Archangelskoye for the first time. Even in my bitterness it made my heart leap. From a mile the pale gleam of sunlight caught a clutch of silver aspen onion domes which seemed to

380

dance above the snowscape. I watched as the domes seemed to float unattached, until the light shifted with our angle of approach and we came close enough to see the white-painted church that supported them.

Before us now was a magnificent yellow ochre wooden palace. The drive from the main gate had been cleared of snow and my minder brought the car to a halt between painted colonnades.

An attendant in a green striped waistcoat and white gloves seized my bag and hurried me through the great hall, up staircases and along corridors to a blue bedroom overlooking the gardens.

There was a small group to greet me. The mute make-up woman and the two professors who had coached me in the run-down dacha on the other side of Moscow stood together before the long window.

'Professor Ruslov,' my minder indicated the shorter, fatter of the two, 'and Professor Deriabin . . . will support you throughout the evening. They will act as interpreters and will elaborate your answers to any questions about Archangelskoye you may be asked.'

'I'm to be asked questions?'

'Americans are known to be the most inquisitive people on earth,' my minder said. 'We have arrived early so that the professors can prepare you.'

It was the sort of reception that magazines before the Civil War called glittering. My first impression as I was discreetly guided into the oval hall was of the magnificence of the room and the colour of the women's dresses. On my tour with the professors we had looked down from the minstrel gallery to where Tiepolos and Van Dycks had recently been hung and the emptiness of the space was all that counted. I moved forward now into the room, alive with the sense of so many people looking directly at me.

I had not yet decided how I should do it. Perhaps it would be an announcement to a group of the most senior people here. Or perhaps I would stop now and make a statement about the amnesty that would be sent straight back to Washington and from there to every corner of the globe.

I felt an intense excitement. Momentarily lost as the adrenalin surged through me. I was being introduced to a long line of Americans. To each I gave a smile, a bow from the neck ... To some I asked simple questions, usually about how long they had been in Moscow ... where in the United States they came from ... I was absorbed, not so much in what I was doing as by the persona of Koba. I smiled, I nodded, I moved among crowds who craned their necks to see me. I had strict instructions from my minder. I was to ask the questions, perhaps make one brief rejoinder if the response seemed to require it – and move on.

There must have been almost two hundred people in the room so it is not surprising that I did not see Imogen until I had been there perhaps ten minutes. Someone I had just met, a grey-haired, senior American from the embassy, was bringing her forward.

'May I present, sir,' he said, 'Amnesty Commissioner Dr Imogen Shepherd.'

She wore a long electric blue dress, her dark hair brushed back from the magnificent diamond earrings that accentuated the length of her neck. I took a deep breath and reached out to shake her hand. Her perfume came to me in a familiar heady wave.

'It's an honour to meet you, General,' she said. Her hand held mine. 'As indeed it has been to serve as amnesty commissioner.'

I tried to disengage my hand but she prolonged the moment before finally letting her palm slide away from mine. 'Tell me, Doctor,' I said. 'As an impartial observer, how is the amnesty progressing? Will you feel able to make a favourable report to the United States government when the time comes?'

'What I've seen so far, General, illustrates how ready people are to come together in reconciliation. Even those who opposed your party in the field.'

'You find that?' I asked. I was experiencing an awesome sense of power. 'You find that trust has been established.'

'I do.'

'And the reaction, you'd say, is proving positive.'

'Extraordinarily so.'

'There must be *some* adverse reaction . . .'

'None that I've encountered. Your former enemies, sir, are enthusiastically accepting the government's assurances. I would go further. I suspect that in many, many cases your old enemies are enemies no more.'

I could make this woman say anything. Her eyes were sparkling with enthusiasm. There was no question of her recognising me. She was mesmerised and determined to mesmerise in her turn.

I was aware my minder was uncomfortable. 'It's been a great pleasure meeting you, Doctor,' I said.

'My pleasure, sir. I can't say how much I would welcome the opportunity to discuss the amnesty further,' she answered boldly.

'I shall see what can be done.'

'Brazen,' my minder muttered as we moved on to the next group. 'She did everything but offer herself, there on the carpet. But you handled that extremely well.'

The grey-haired American official was crossing the floor with another woman, older this time. Beside me I felt my minder tense. 'Fuck your mother, she wasn't supposed to be here,' he hissed in horror.

'Who is it?' I muttered urgently.

'The American chargé d'affaires, you fool,' he said. He started speaking fast, out of the corner of his mouth. 'Diana Hilton, widow, two daughters with her in Moscow, good Russian speaker . . . arrived week before last . . . You've met once, last Tuesday – dinner given by President Romanov , . .'

The American official stood by as the chargé d'affaires and I shook hands. She was a tall, handsome woman in her fifties. 'General Koba,' she said with an easy grin. 'I'm afraid I'm here as a mother rather than in my official capacity. My daughters are in the choir which will be entertaining you later. Maternal pride was just too much for me. I hope you'll forgive me. I'm not sure my staff ever will.'

'A great pleasure, Mrs Hilton,' I said. 'I hope I shall be able to meet your daughters after the concert.'

'They're most anxious to meet you.'

I smiled.

'General . . .' she glanced at my minder and took a step away, which I was bound to follow. My pulse was racing. This was surely the perfect opportunity. No less a personage than the American chargé d'affaires was taking me aside.

'Something I'm bound to say,' she said. 'Even though this is not an official occasion. Maybe especially since it's not an official occasion . . .'

'Please speak frankly,' I said.

'It concerns the amnesty . . .'

My minder started forward and I made a gesture that stopped him. I saw his anxious glance around. I placed my back to him and nodded sombrely to Diana Hilton. 'The amnesty . . . ?' How was I to tell her about the Belorussian station? Was she about to give me an opening?

'I have just this moment read your note . . .' I must have looked nonplussed. She smiled. 'It was delivered a few moments before I left this evening. It provided, frankly, an additional reason for my coming.'

'Some information has reached you? From the commissioners, perhaps? You have some complaint to make about the way the amnesty is operating?'

She laughed. 'On the contrary, General. I think what you intend to do is quite magnificent.'

384

'You approve?' I locked my hands behind my back and looked at her, my darkened eyebrows raised.

'Entirely. No – more than that. Enthusiastically. The appointment of a former Anarchist as Minister for Reconciliation in charge of the amnesty is a master stroke.'

A former Anarchist.

'I can say that it is something the people of the United States will respond to more than to a hundred amnesty commissioners.'

'You think so.' I was already fighting for breath.

'I know so. I pride myself that I know something about the American people. You can send all your amnesty commissioners home – and you'll still have the United States a hundred per cent behind you.'

She shook my hand vigorously. 'It's quite brilliant. Not only an ex-Anarchist, but for Americans at least, the most famous of your former enemies. As a woman and a general she's obviously attracted a great deal of media attention in the US over the years.'

I had to know. One thing I had to be quite sure of. It was a crude and desperate ploy but I had to know that she had done this voluntarily. 'There is,' I said, 'the matter of her acceptance.'

She frowned. 'But your note said that she had already accepted. There would be a short delay before the announcement but she has already accepted.'

'Nothing but the most trivial details remain to be agreed,' I said with a dreadful sickness clutching at my heart.

'Excellent.'

I inclined my head. 'Yes . . . as I said in the note, Julia Petrovna has already accepted.'

39

Of course I'm not sane. Not even remotely sane. I went through the remainder of the reception as though there were glue in my veins. I was taken away early by the professors, who judged it wiser I should miss the concert and the brief vote of thanks to the American singers I was scheduled to make. My minder was distinctly less friendly when he drove me back to Fili.

At home again, in my apartment, I moved restlessly from room to room, a vodka glass in my hand, thinking that perhaps either movement or alcohol would again get the blood flowing.

Above all I knew I had to speak to Julia.

It was past midnight when I arrived at Roy's apartment block. I could see a woman in the background as he opened the door. He was wearing pyjama trousers but no top. His chest was thickly covered by coppery tinted hair and there were tufts of hair on his shoulders and on the outer side of his biceps. He wasn't pleased to see me. 'I've got to see her,' I said. 'I've got to see Julia.'

'For Christ's sake,' he exploded. 'The answer's no. You know the answer's no. She's OK. Unharmed. Good enough for you?'

I barged forward and he reached out and grabbed me by the lapels, pulling me into the apartment. The girl stood almost naked, staring at him in alarm.

He released me and jerked a thumb at her. 'Wait in the bedroom,' he said. 'This'll take five minutes.'

I straightened out my jacket. Buttons had flown from my shirt. I was a lot bigger than Roy Rolkin but nobody strikes an officer of the Cheka. Not if they want to live to fight another day.

'You're off your head,' he said. 'If you thought for five minutes you'd realise it. Now listen. I'm telling you.' He slapped my face lightly, fondly. 'You can't see her. But she's alive. And she's safe. Even comfortable. Nobody's grunting her in a basement somewhere. That's a promise. You believe me?' He looked up at me, reading something from my expression. He stepped back. 'What is this?' he said.

'I know about Julia's appointment,' I told him.

His arms folded across his chest, his bare toes silently clawed the carpet. 'What appointment?'

'I *know*, Roy,' I said.

He turned away and began pouring himself whisky. 'Want one?' He lifted the bottle and shook it until the whisky splashed out of the neck.

I nodded.

'How?' he asked. 'She told you? No, not possible. How?'

'I was at a reception at Archangelskoye this evening.'

'The American kids' concert.'

'The American chargé d'affaires turned up. We talked. No more games, Roy. Julia has joined the enemy.'

'She's joined *us*, fuck your mother!' he said. He handed me a half-full tumbler of Scotch. 'Drink to it.'

I shook my head.

'You think she should have stuck to her principles, do you?'

'I want to know how it happened.'

'You assume too much, Costya,' he said. 'Nothing says you have any right to know.'

'Did Denisova betray her? Was there a shoot-out at Pasternak?'

He drank his whisky, frowning. 'What are you babbling about?'

'You offered Julia her life if she joined you.'

387

He laughed. 'What sort of fairyland do you live in? You think these things happen overnight?'

'You tell me how they happen.'

He swallowed, waved his glass around and looked hard at me, his wrap-around eyes narrowing slowly. 'Back in Murmansk,' he said, 'General Koba selected me to find Julia. Word had got to him that I'd known Julia in the past. That we'd been at school together. So I was chosen – nothing special about that. But the task he gave me *was* special. My mission was to bring her over *to our side*.' He took a deep breath. 'But I had to find her first.'

I felt myself go rigid. 'Did you find her through me? You had my picture put in the Presnya *Pravda*. Is that what it was for, so that Julia would know I was in Moscow? So that she could contact me and you could put a tail on me.'

He shrugged. 'Don't let it worry you, Costya. All's well that ends well.'

'Tell me how it was.'

He rubbed his chest, glanced towards the bedroom door and finished his whisky. 'You did well, Costya. We missed all your early contacts with her. But I had other feelers out. I made real contact with her about a week ago through one of my Anarchist informers. Not before time. General Koba was breathing down my neck. But even this contact was touch and go. Julia's a clever woman. We were in touch but not touching, if you understand me . . .'

'You didn't know where she was hiding.'

'Not at that point. But I was able to open negotiations. Finally I asked for an emissary. More than that, a plenipotentiary.'

'And Julia sent Denisova.'

'Very competent lady. Troubled, very troubled about the deal, but devoted. Through her I made my proposal, General Koba's proposal to Julia.'

'And Julia accepted.'

'Broad terms. And after some discussion, yes. But the

final details were taking too long. General Koba was pressing me. But I still wasn't talking face to face with Julia. Officially, I still didn't know where she was.'

'Officially?'

'I'd had Denisova followed, of course, but that was completely against Julia's terms of the deal. If she found out, I knew the deal would be blown.'

'So that's why you made sure I saw Denisova at the officers' club? Because you knew I'd think she was betraying Julia.'

'And you'd go straight to her. And I could claim to Julia that it was you, not Denisova, who had led me there.' He laughed. 'Once the chips were down, the final details between Julia and myself were sewn up in a matter of minutes. As I knew they would be. But you can say we all needed you, my bratkin, to clinch the deal.'

I felt sick at the way I had allowed myself to be manipulated. I had one more thing to ask. The picture was growing clearer but it was still hazy at the edges. 'If Julia was prepared to accept the offer, Roy, why did the rest of them, comrades who had been loyal to her for years, why did they resist?'

'Resist?' He smiled smugly.

Something screamed in my head. 'You shot them down!'

He raised his hands, laughing. 'Oh, enough, Costya! Enough. I'm busy.' He jerked his head towards the bedroom door. 'You see how busy I am. And yet I still find time to set an old friend's mind at rest. But not all fucking night, OK?'

'I have to see Julia, Roy. I must see her *now*.'

He looked at me, lips pursed.

'Roy . . .'

He turned and walked towards the bedroom door. 'You're a fucking terrier, you know that. More than that, you're a fucking ungrateful terrier. All right. Present yourself at the Lubyanka,' he said over his shoulder. 'I'll have Dimitry meet you and take you to where she is. Nobody's supposed to know where. You get that? You'll have to submit to a blindfold.'

I nodded agreement.

He stopped at the door and belched silently. 'Hey Costya,' he said, shaking his head. 'What I won't do for an old friend!'

Hers was a commanding presence. She sat behind an Alexandrine desk in a room with a high, richly decorated ceiling, stucco on wood. Subdued lamps glowed above bronze horses rearing in battle. A painting of the English Queen Victoria hung above the wooden fireplace. A broad silk carpet separated us.

She was wearing a severe, well-cut black dress, with a gold chain round her neck that dangled between her breasts. She smiled at me as I closed the double doors behind me. 'Constantin . . .' She stood and extended her arms. 'I have so much to thank you for . . . Only you would have helped me when I so badly needed it. Your loyalty, Constantin, has been a beacon . . .'

I stood a pace or two into the room, my overcoat open, my hands thrust into the pockets. She walked out from behind her desk, dropping her arms to her side. She stopped before me. 'Ah . . . that look on your face. I know it so well. You don't understand, is that it?' Her smile of welcome was fading. 'Let me get you something. Coffee?'

I shook my head

'Something stronger?'

She reached back and touched a bell on her desk. 'It might have been better if you'd left it until morning,' she said. 'But Roy said you insisted on coming.'

'That's what I did.' My voice was a croak. I cleared my throat. 'That's what I did. I insisted.'

A white-jacketed waiter appeared and she ordered coffee. When the man had gone she looked at me, a different smile, slow and wry, building on her lips. 'Come and sit down, Constantin,' she said briskly. 'You stand there, a solid Russian lump of pained resentment. My dear, you look just a little *ridiculous*.'

The echoes of all our quarrels five years ago were suddenly sharper, shriller than the tinnitus in my ears. The twists, the turns, my desperate fumblings to catch her soaring comet . . .

'You're right,' I said. 'I am ridiculous. You're also right that I don't understand. I could have asked Roy of course. But I think I need to hear it from you.'

She shrugged. 'You're asking how could I possibly . . . ?'

'No.' I shook my head. I could feel it building in me. 'No,' I said, my voice rising. 'I'm ridiculous. You said so yourself. I'm ridiculous so I'm asking the ridiculous question.'

'Don't shout, for God's sake, Constantin. Control yourself.'

'I'm asking if it's true. I just want to be absolutely sure. I'm asking if it's true that you've accepted Koba's offer.'

The light from one of the great bronze lamps caught her fine cheekbones. 'I've accepted, yes,' she said coldly.

'Of your own free will? You've accepted this filthy offer of your own free will? After what I told you about the amnesty? After what I told you about the trains at the Belorussian packed with the loyal comrades you're now deserting?'

'Constantin . . .' She walked back behind her desk and sat down. The bronze lamp beside her dramatically etched her features. 'Constantin, there's so much you just don't understand.'

I swept the lamp from the desk and it crashed to the floor. In the sudden silence I heard the bulb pop. 'I understand you accepted this offer even when it meant the casual murder of the women who had given you their loyalty.' I leaned across the desk. 'I would have told anybody – anybody, Roy, Koba himself, that you were a woman who lived for principles. A woman whose whole life was based on principle. A woman who took no decision of any note without checking the strength and the rightness of the principle behind it. That's what I would have told *the world*!' My voice seemed to come back under some sort of control. 'My God,' I said. 'I never knew you.'

She watched me without flinching. 'I allow you liberties I allow to no one else,' she said. 'And you know why. Because we once shared something that was infinitely precious to both of us. Now listen . . . I am to be Minister for Reconciliation. And what is a great deal more, Deputy Minister of the Interior before the New Year.'

I felt my jaws slacken. 'Koba's deputy?'

'I won't have you giving me this glassy-eyed, puppy look, Constantin.' She got up, walked to the fireplace, swung round and faced me again. 'We are living with one reality and one reality only – the acquisition of power. The last six months have taught me that differences of ideology are simply ways of clothing the naked struggle for power.' She clenched her fists. 'I've already told you. This is a post-ideological world. My choice was between remaining on the fringe – or taking a place in the very centre. What would you have done in the circumstances?'

I leaned on the desk, shaking my head. 'You had beliefs . . . even if wrong, they had become part of you. Principles . . .'

She shook her head irritably. 'I told you, Constantin. Ideology is dead. Rational principles cannot be honestly maintained. The English philosopher Oakeshott used to quote John Donne: "He who will live by precept will be without the habit of honesty."'

'Did he?' I said. 'And didn't your mother also say that England was a land infested by poets? That you can *always* find an English poet to support your thesis.'

'I repeat – what would *you* have done in the circumstances?'

I was facing her now. 'I hope I would have stood by my comrades. Instead of walking away while Roy's Chekists shot them down.'

'You have to learn, Constantin. These people were little cogs. You understand what I mean.'

'Roy did his best to explain.'

The waiter returned with a coffee tray and set it on a low table in front of Queen Victoria. Before he left he looked down at the lamp and set it back on the table. Then he looked at me and across at Julia, waiting for instructions to throw me out. She shook her head and waited until the door closed after him.

'Little cogs, you were saying.' I could *feel* the snarl in my voice. 'Your comrades were little cogs.'

She made a gesture of exasperation. 'You are absurdly *naif*, Constantin. Denisova and the others all knew I had been involved in the grenade attempt on Koba's life. They even knew that I had planned a second attempt. As Roy rightly pointed out, this information could not be allowed to slip out.' Her eyes widened. With amusement. I swear it was amusement. 'The foreign press would have a field day: "General Koba's deputy accused of attempt on his life."'

'No,' I shook my head. 'You couldn't have that. Not possibly.'

She looked at me quizzically, lifting the coffee pot in invitation. 'You're sure?' she asked.

'I'm sure.'

'So that was your problem, was it?' She looked up from the coffee pot. 'That's why you insisted on racing out here to talk to me. You feared I was ratting on my principles, on all those Anarchist friends and colleagues that you, in any case, couldn't stand to be in the same room with. Costya my love, I find I can't take your objections too seriously. I would have thought you'd be congratulating yourself. I have, after all, come over to your side.'

The heat in the room was stifling. Tinnitus clashed like

cymbals in my ears. 'All right, Julia,' I said slowly. 'I won't confront you with principles. You may be right when you say they do no more than disguise the lust for power. But one objection you do have to take seriously . . .'

'And that is?'

'That if all the arguments, all the differences of principle we suffered in Murmansk were trivial because all principles are pointless – then your decision to take Mischa away from me was based on nothing so much as your own wish to go.'

'The cause is dead, Constantin, don't blame me for that.'

'Mischa's dead too,' I said.

She took a half-step forward. Her eyes flared angrily. 'We both loved him. I will not accept the blame for his death.' She shuddered where she stood. Then she came forward and took my hand. 'Be careful, Costya. Whatever you feel about my decision, keep it to yourself. Denisova and the others died because they knew about the grenade attempts on Koba. So do you.' She made to kiss me as she reached for the bell to ring for the orderly. But I turned my head away in time.

I left the room and was led down a flight of back stairs to where Dimitry was waiting. At the side of the house, Dimitry stood among the snow-laden pine trees, drawing on a cigarette, a near-empty vodka bottle hanging from his other hand. I walked down the wooden steps and got into the car as he opened the door on the other side. Seated in the back of a Cheka limo beside the hated Dimitry, I allowed him to tie the blindfold round my eyes. As it was tightened, I closed my eyes in the hope of closing out so much more than the road back to Moscow.

40

Stoke and vodka don't mix. They were never meant to mix. They cancel out each other's more acceptable benefits, leaving not peace but psychosis. I sat in the jazz club in the Bullfrog, listening to the black band play the music I love, my eyes on Dimitry, opposite me, slumped forward, his chin resting on arms splayed on the table. His tongue hung out like a dog's, his thick eyelids barely clearing his dark pupils. I fantasised about murdering him.

Oblivious, he watched mesmerised as the black girl sang 'Georgia'. Maybe because she was in a Russian club she danced a few steps and swung it about a bit.

'D'you ever see . . .' Dimitry began several times. 'Did you ever see such a wild ass on a girl?'

I signalled the waiter and ordered a full litre. I wondered how much more Dimitry could take before he succumbed to alcohol poisoning.

'You and me, Costya,' he said, 'could be very, very good friends. A Cheka man can often have need of a trustworthy friend in the militia . . .' He wagged his finger. 'And vice versa.'

I tried to sit upright. Amidst all this light and noise and drink and people, words like that, from a cur like that, can make you feel the loneliest man in the world.

'I personally,' Dimitry said, 'think Julia's going to be running this country in five years. She's a big woman, Costya—' he thrust his pelvis at the table – 'in more ways than one.'

Where was Natalya, as I sat here with Dimitry for company? How far, I began to calculate, would it be to walk to Petersburg if I started now? I drank and dozed as I tried to work it out. At thirty kilometres a day, maybe twenty days.

The tab of *stoke* I had taken as we entered the club was working now and my mind slid effortlessly across the snow. I could hear the pony's thudding hooves and the swishing of the steel runners as I came down towards the village. There was a coach with lamps throwing yellow lights across the street. There was an inn and the great gold onion domes of Suzdal or Vladimir or somewhere rose into the moonlight. And Natalya standing in the doorway swaddled in furs.

Then my eyes opened and the rat face of Dimitry was not a foot from mine and he was saying: 'God, I love big women. In her heels, you know, Madame Raisa stood head and shoulders over me . . . Just take a look at those two.'

I moved my head with difficulty. Or was I just moving my eyes? Two women sat at a table next to the exit. One blonde, one dark. Their heavily mascaraed eyes were flicking all the time towards our table. When they got up to dance with each other, Dimitry was entranced. In sparkling gowns that squeezed their cleavages to the maximum they tangoed across the floor.

In the alley the noise seemed unbearable. Dustbins crashed and rolled across the cobbles. Dimitry's head thudded against a door, his outflung hand splintered a window. The two big transvestites dragged him from the cobbles and beat him unmercifully.

The bodies flew across the air space above me, the two transvestites shrieking fury. My vision was filled with pink heels and frou-frou petticoats. Moments it took, even minutes for me to understand how I was seeing it all. A worm's eye view: my head lay against the front wheel of a parked car.

Dimitry's pale face filled my vision as he lay across

the bonnet of the car, blood dripping from his nose, splashing into my eyes. Then blue lights were flashing in the alley and there were running footsteps and a voice that sounded like Ilya Dronsky's as someone helped me to stand up.

I stumbled down the alley with my arm round his shoulders. 'What's happening, for God's sake?' I said, probably more than once.

'One of the patrolmen saw you being taken to the club earlier on by that rat-faced tout. Thought I ought to know.'

'There was a fight.'

'The TVs claim the little fellow stole from one to pay the other. Not a friend of yours, is he, Chief?'

I shook my head.

'Good,' he said. 'We left the *girls* to it. They seemed to be doing a pretty thorough job.'

I woke up looking into a pair of large dark eyes at the level of my own and an inch or two away, so that I took a moment to focus.

The face was round and plump. But it didn't look at all like Dimitry's. 'My name,' the child said, 'is Lydia.'

I struggled onto an elbow.

'And my name,' said a second child, standing next to his sister, 'is Georgi.'

'And my name,' a fully grown, pink-faced woman said smilingly as she entered the room, 'is Nina Andreyevna . . .'

I forced myself into a sitting position on the sofa. Taking the mug of coffee she handed me, I thanked her tentatively. My eye travelled to the plastic foot beneath the right trouser leg.

'Dronsky,' she said. 'Nina Andreyevna *Dronsky* . . . Ilya's wife.'

I half rose to shake her hand and fell back on the sofa. Mercifully all was accomplished without spilling the coffee.

'Ilya asked that you excuse him, Inspector. He went on ahead to the office.'

I eyed the pendulum clock on the wall. It was still before 7.30.

I must remember to look straight ahead. Even the swivel of the eyes involved in looking at the clock caused the pain to rise dramatically from the base of my skull.

I sat back, trying to smile. The room was small, rectangular. I assumed I was in a high-rise block because through the standard metal window I could see only a lowering grey sky. Past Nina Andreyevna I could see into a second room, a neatly laid out kitchen. Nothing would ever cure the sickness in my stomach but there was a warm homeliness about the apartment that began to relax me. I moved onto the edge of the sofa and felt the aches in my shoulders. I suppose I must have winced.

'Perhaps the children are bothering you,' Nina Andreyevna said.

'Not at all. I must thank you for taking me in last night.'

The little girl moved over to stand beside her mother while Georgi nudged up to my knee. I put my hand out and touched his dark curly hair.

'Do you have children of your own, Inspector?'

'No,' I said. 'No.' My hand on the boy's furrowed neck, I felt absurdly close to tears. I took a pull at the coffee.

'To have children today in Moscow is a great responsibility,' she said.

I looked up at her. 'I'm sure it must be,' I said. But I had the feeling she was not talking about the availability of porn channels on television.

'Ilya worries so much. Is he right to, I wonder?'

'I think he might be.'

'He says we can't be too careful into whose hands we entrust the future of our children. If you had children, Inspector, would you be confident that their future's in safe hands?'

Through the warm moist blanket of my hangover I was aware that I was being quizzed. 'Have you ever met Ilya's colleague, Dr Karlova?' I asked her.

She glanced down at her foot. 'It was Natalya who operated on me. But for her I would have lost the whole leg. I was trapped by a concrete block, I don't know, three, four tonnes of it. Immovable without equipment. I had been trapped for eight hours when Ilya found her and begged her to come. Her decision was to amputate the foot. It saved my leg. Probably my life.' She nodded confirmation.

I thought about that for a moment.

'Natalya is the most positive woman I know,' she said.

'And what does *she* think about those to whose hands we have entrusted the future?'

She smiled. A warm smile. The sort you use between friends. 'I think you're playing games with me, Inspector,' she said. 'I'm sure you already know the answer to that question.'

I stood up, keeping my hand on Georgi's shoulders. 'You said Ilya left me a message.'

'He asked me to apologise – he has a few things to do at the station first.'

I tickled Georgi's neck and he laughed. 'First? Before what?'

'He said he will meet you at the cemetery.'

Georgi looked at me with his large dark eyes. Nina Dronsky knew I had no idea what she meant.

'Madelena Kassarian's funeral,' she said.

I patted Georgi's head and stood up. 'Thank you. I won't try to pretend. Where is it to be held?'

'Vagankov cemetery,' she said smiling. 'At nine o'clock this morning.'

The phone rang and Nina Dronsky crossed the room to answer it. She was a handsome woman but the limp made all her movements clumsy for so young a body. She turned back to me. 'It's someone claims to be speaking from a jet plane,' she said. 'Ilya gave him this number. He wants to know if you can meet him at the airport right away.'

I watched from the pilots' lounge as the big jet taxied in and stopped on the apron. There were half a dozen other jets in different international liveries lined up for refuelling or minor maintenance. Airports never cease to please me: the busyness, the sense of a function to be carried out. I waited while the steps were rolled up to the cockpit of the Russian Airways Ilyushin and only turned away from the window when a big British Airways Airbus rolled into position and obscured my sight of the figures in the cockpit. In the Russian Airways pilots' lounge several men and women in uniform sat at a table eating breakfast. Two or three more in comfortable club chairs were reading newspapers. I found it reassuring, though not in the way I might have two days ago, to see that some parts of the capital were already functioning normally.

An attendant came over and asked me if I would like coffee or a drink while I waited and I had already taken the risk and ordered a glass of Georgian champagne when Madame Raisa's brother, Captain Nicolai Persilov, entered the room.

We shook hands and he placed his briefcase on a coffee table and ordered vodka from the attendant. He had dark half-moons under the eyes and a patchy shave that suggested a quick pass-over with an electric razor. His jacket, which had no doubt been hanging up throughout the flight from New York, was immaculate; his trousers were as creased as if he'd slept in them. He gestured to an armchair and dropped into the one next to it, stretching his legs, before sitting upright.

'Your message said it was important,' I said, taking the club chair beside him.

He looked at me, a quizzical look I thought. 'I hope I haven't got you out here on a fool's errand, but I understood you to say that Dr Shepherd was a friend of yours.'

'An acquaintance . . . a colleague, let's say. She's serving on the Amnesty Commission here in Moscow.'

Again that quizzical look. The attendant arrived with my champagne and his vodka and we saluted each other with our glasses. 'All this is part of your investigation into the Monstrum murders.'

The word was spreading. I nodded. 'You checked Dr Imogen Shepherd on the list of medical practitioners?'

'Yes,' he opened his briefcase and took out a printed page. 'Doctor Imogen Shepherd,' he read. 'Born Lincoln, Nebraska, 5 July 1965 . . .'

I lifted my head in surprise. She was older than she looked. Wait a minute. She was *much* older than she looked.

'Graduated from Loxton College, Loxton, Nebraska,' Captain Persilov continued. 'Attended medical school, Columbia University, New York and thereafter got several degrees and lectureships . . .'

I was very impressed. I saw Imogen as a high flyer but perhaps not this high.

'Lectured 1995–96 University College Hospital, London, England. From 1998 to 2000 at the Centre Médical at Toulouse, France – Shall I go on?'

My head swam as I tried to shake it. 'No . . . What was her last appointment?'

'Let's see – there were so many. The last was in Boston. That's where the accident occurred.'

I sat forward in my chair. 'Accident?' I *knew* what he was going to say next.

He nodded. 'The road accident. Boston. That's where she died.'

41

The desk sergeants at reception were changing shift so I caught the two at once. 'Dr Shepherd,' I said. 'Is she in the building?'

One said he didn't know. The other said she just came in. I ran through reception, up the stairs and along the corridor to her office. She was at the door, keys in hand.

'Constantin,' she turned. 'Where have you been these last days? Not in your office—'

I pushed her into the room and closed the door. She looked amused, then wary. 'What is it?' she said. 'I don't like the look on your face.'

'Forget my face,' I said. 'It's yours I'm thinking about.'

She pulled off her fur hat and tossed it onto a chair. Then walked carefully across the room and, still in her sable coat, sat at her desk. 'You're thinking about my face. Should I be flattered?'

I watched her without speaking.

'No,' she said. 'No reason to be flattered, obviously. So why were you thinking about my face?'

'I'm wondering whose face is it? All I know is that it's not Dr Imogen Shepherd's face. Dr Shepherd is dead.'

'That's true,' she said smoothly. She held me with an even, unruffled look.

I gaped at her. I had expected an entirely different reaction.

'Mmm,' she mused to herself. 'You've been doing a little detective work.'

'As you see.'

She was calm. 'I'm sorry you didn't take it further, Constantin.'

I stood there.

'If you'd checked the United States deed poll database, you would see that Dr Imogen Harrow changed her name to Shepherd in Boston, USA on October 14th, 2012.'

'That's you. Imogen Harrow?'

'*Dr* Imogen Harrow. That *was* me. Correct.'

'And now you're Imogen Shepherd. Oh no, not that easy. The birth dates don't work out.'

'Of course they don't, Constantin,' she said. 'Imogen Shepherd, the first Imogen, was *much* older than me. Born in 1965.'

'You're saying you changed your name to another woman's?' I asked, tentatively now. 'Why?'

She turned her head to look out of the window, then back at me. 'I first met Imogen Shepherd over ten years ago. We met at a medical conference in Atlanta.' She looked down at her desk briefly then up again at me. 'One of those stupid moments when, in a crowded room, somebody called out "Imogen!" and we both looked up, realised we had the same not very common first name, laughed . . . started talking . . . and became friends from there. Very close friends.' She breathed in deeply. 'Closer on Imogen's side than mine, if you understand me.' She tossed her hair back, her eyes on me. 'She was an older woman, very masculine . . . well I'm sure you do understand. She fell in love. We remained friends, but for her it was a tragedy.'

I didn't quite know what to say, so I said nothing.

'I'll cut a long story short, Constantin. She was my mentor, my friend. I was devastated when she was killed in an automobile accident on the Massachusetts turnpike.' Her eyes shadowed at the memory. 'It's three years ago now. Imogen left a will. She recorded in it that she considered me her partner. That if such relationships were condoned by law, she would by now have asked me to marry her and she had every hope that I would by now have adopted her name. We all have our dreams, Constantin.' She paused.

'In the will she left everything – her research notes, her considerable fortune, to me if . . .'

'If you changed your name to hers.'

She nodded. She got up slowly, picked up her hat and smiled down at me. 'I admired her greatly. She was a very remarkable woman. I was not unwilling to make the change. If you want to talk more, I'll be back before lunch. I have an appointment at 9.30 with the Minister of Justice.' She bent over and kissed me on the side of the cheek.

I sat there as the door closed quietly behind her. I heard her steps receding slowly down the corridor. I was surrounded, immersed in that familiar warmth and scent. Did I believe her? I shook my head until it span from the effects of last night. Believe her? Of course I didn't believe her, fuck your mother! I leapt to my feet and rushed for the door. Grabbing the handle, I nearly snapped my wrist.

I was locked in.

I was sick with hangover and shame as I stood outside Imogen's flat, or the apartment of the woman who wanted to be known as Imogen, while Dronsky hammered on the door. It didn't make things better that it was Commander Brusilov himself who had had to rescue me from Imogen's office. It didn't make it any better at all.

I looked at Dronsky, who was still finding it difficult to suppress a smile as his fist thudded a tattoo on the door. 'For Christ's sake,' I said. 'When I was deputy inspector at Murmansk Section 7, I always kept a selection of pass-keys in case my inspector ever felt the need to call on them.'

'You only had to ask, Chief,' he said, fishing a heavy bunch of keys from inside his jacket.

It took longer than either of us expected, and the last lock was only breached by a skilful piece of picking on Dronsky's part. When the door finally swung open, he whistled.

'I didn't know we still had apartments like this in Moscow,' he said. He walked in shaking his head at the size of the living room, at the plush furniture, at the leather-topped bar, the thick white carpet . . . and mixed with the modernity, the purely Russian items, the iron-bound chest under one of the windows, the painted wooden panels of saints and religious inscriptions. One fine aged oak panel carried the prayer: *O, Mother Russia, your role is sacrifice. No land like ours has been called upon by history. No land like ours has the deep will to respond.*

Barely more than a week ago, my whole body would have thrilled to the thought. I could imagine myself as the emotion surged through me, thinking, fists clenched, that yes, this is my Russia. But a new, an ugly reality had begun to intrude. That role of sacrifice, I was beginning to see, was assigned just to *some* in Russia. Seldom to the leaders, the politicians. No. It was the ordinary Russian who had been duped for centuries into believing in the high mission of sacrifice. Natalya, I was sure, would say that the time had come to sacrifice no more.

I looked at Dronsky and thought about his wife and children at home in their tower block apartment. Standing there in the middle of the room, hunched in his big parka, his hands deep in his trouser pockets, his round cropped head moving from side to side, why should he look so totally out of place?

In the hallway stood two leather suitcases. Inside were several furs, all of them high quality. In Murmansk we pride ourselves on knowing a little about furs.

'Did she decide to leave without them? Or could she be coming back to pick them up, I wonder?' Dronsky said. He thought for a moment. 'Leave without them.'

We walked through the rooms, Dronsky whistling and wagging his head as he stopped in front of glass shelves with collections of Russian miniatures, of china shoes, of silver handbells . . . He had never seen so much Russian antiquity outside a museum. But I think it was the Western glitz that appealed to him more.

I told him to look around while I went into Imogen's office and looked up her address book. The American Legation was on the first page. Buttoning the number I tried hard to remember the unfamiliar names of members of the embassy staff I had met as Leonid Koba. There was a Mr McMillan ... a Mrs Singleton ... I asked for Mrs Singleton and said I was a member of Leonid Koba's staff. Ms Singleton was out. I was more successful with McMillan. 'Mr McMillan,' I said, when he came to the phone, 'we met at the reception for General Koba.' He didn't know me from Mikhail Gorbachev but it didn't matter. Within minutes he was off to look up the legation's *Who Was Who* database.

Three minutes later I followed Dronsky as he opened door after door: bedrooms, a library, even a small, well-equipped exercise room. 'I just checked out Imogen Shepherd, the dead Imogen Shepherd,' I said. 'What I should have done an hour ago.'

'Don't blame yourself, Chief.' He stopped. 'How close did our Dr Imogen stay to the truth? What was the old lady's speciality? Paediatrics?'

'No,' I said coolly, but I could feel the hair at the back of my neck tingle. 'Dr Shepherd occupied one of the leading positions in Western medicine in the field of transplant surgery.'

'Jesus ... Transplant surgery.'

'Women's transplant surgery,' I said. 'Transplantation of the womb, the uterus. The real Dr Shepherd specialised in *that*.'

Dronsky was breathing deeply, his Groucho eyebrows moving up and down.

'What do you think?' I asked him as we walked into the main bedroom.

'I think there's not a grey carpet in the place,' he said.

I nodded. What else was there to say? 'You're thinking of the carpet fibres on the first two bodies?'

He ran his hand over his razored head. 'Let's see. She's here under a false name,' he said, 'The name of a woman who specialised in legal gynaecological transplant surgery. Forget her story of the two Imogens. Either she learned from the real Dr Shepherd about the market for replacement organs in the United States. Or she already knew and needed a suitable medical background. In war-torn Moscow nobody was going to be checking her credentials. And there was a never-ending supply of suitable organs. How do you like it?'

I said nothing.

'We have four murders, Chief. Perhaps many, many earlier ones, in which organs were removed. What we didn't pick up was that while the precise organs varied from victim to victim, the uterus was taken on every occasion.'

He was right, of course. And however crudely the other organs had been cut from the body, the chances now seemed high that the target organ had been removed with care. 'What else do you think we have?' I asked him.

He stared at the window. 'We have Dr Imogen, or whoever she is, in a position, as doctor at Father Alexander's church, examining – and maybe even evaluating – the girls. Healthy girls only. Free of disease. We have everything from the first selection process to the moment of murder.'

He was a better detective than me. But then so were a lot of people. 'You don't think she dressed in plastic and stalked the girls as they came back from Father Alexander's, do you?'

'I don't know yet, Chief. I keep thinking of that limousine and the story you told me of Comrade Beria driving the streets with his chauffeur. Maybe she has a chauffeur.'

'Who wields the knife for her? It's beginning to look

like it.' I told him of my theory, now revived, that what Gromek had seen the night of Lydia's murder was a *woman* pacing. A tall woman in a well-cut coat and fur hat.

'I like it,' Dronsky said. 'But we still can't crack her alibi for Maria's murder. If it was a woman's voice the old lady heard, it wasn't hers.' He looked at me. 'Is it possible we're looking for a *woman* accomplice?'

'No, I don't like it,' I said. But I think he had shaken me for a moment. I stood in the middle of the bedroom as he opened drawers and tumbled black and peach silk underwear, then shook my head clear. 'Listen,' I said. 'We have to do this systematically. We don't even know what we're looking for. We'll divide up the rooms between us.'

He walked towards the door and stopped at a video screen facing the bed. I couldn't remember it from the night I had been here but I wasn't surprised. A stack of video cassettes sat beside the player. Dronsky bent over. He scattered the stack and was pushing it around with his forefinger. 'She videotapes her fucks,' he said.

'Ah . . .'

'Have you been here before, Chief?' He jerked a thumb towards the bed.

'One night only.'

He straightened up, grinning. 'Then perhaps you'd like to take a look.' He moved towards the door and turned to watch me.

I poked at the pile of neatly labelled cassettes. *Volodya, apartment. 23 June. – Major-General V.I. Ruskin, Majestic Hotel, Petersburg, 3 October – Borya, apartment, 26 July.*

As Dronsky turned away I picked up one of the tapes and slipped it into my pocket.

We found little, perhaps nothing in the other room. But the conviction was growing in me that this apartment had something to give. A woman who videotapes her most

408

intimate moments doesn't, I would think, stop short there. She would be a record keeper of some sort. A diarist, even. The thought made me shudder.

We continued the search. The desk in the main living room was full of papers but they all seemed to relate to her work as amnesty commissioner. Behind bookcases, under carpets, we rummaged and poked in the hope of finding something. But we came up with nothing.

I was in one of the spare bedrooms, sitting on the side of the bed, staring at the mirrors on her dressing table when my eyes seemed to come into focus of their own accord. Or maybe it was just my brain that came into focus.

In any event I *saw* for the first time the reflection I had been staring at for the last minute. It was an overhead lamp. A large circular frosted glass globe. It was attached to the ceiling by a length of electrical conduit.

But the conduit had curled around it a heavy gilded chain. Dronsky was standing in the doorway watching the strange angle my head must have taken as I examined the image in the mirrored table top. I looked up. 'What do you think?'

He scratched the back of his neck and examined the overhead light. 'We could find out easily enough,' he said.

I stood aside while he upended a nineteenth-century silver candlestick and, reaching up, shattered the globe. As the glass fell away, the small steel safe, no bigger than a heavy book, was revealed, held in place above the bulb. Dronsky detached it from the wire basket that held it and lowered it until it hung at waist height on its thick gilded chain.

I left him to deal with the gleaming steel box and continued searching the apartment.

I was in the hallway when Dronsky walked through with the box opened. He had sawn through the gilded chain with his old Soviet army knife and picked the safe lock. A leather book fitted inside so closely I had the impression the safe was made for it. I lifted it out with care.

It was a photograph album. Page after page showed the faces of young girls, pretty some of them, others plain. There were perhaps thirty or forty of them altogether, all named and dated and with an additional descriptive note. *Pretty chestnut hair . . . Big, gorgeous blue eyes . . . A lovely smile . . .* The last four girls were names I knew: Anastasia Modina – Nina Golikova – Tania Chekova – Lydia Primalova.

Dronsky was nodding to himself. 'I think,' he said, 'we've found our Monstrum.'

I placed the album back into the safe. 'I doubt it,' I said. 'But I think we've found our Monstrum's keeper.'

We were in a hurry to leave now. Neither of us thought the apartment could yield more, but Dronsky insisted I looked at some English writing he'd seen in the kitchen earlier.

It was a chalk scrawl on a memo board. The sort families write their reminders on – dentist Monday – take books back to library . . . that sort of thing. There was only one message on Imogen's board. In English, it read: *HCHO box from dacha.*

'She has a dacha we don't know about,' I said. 'She's going to collect a box from it.'

'HCHO . . . ?' Dronsky read it as if it were Cyrillic: *NSNO?*

'Read it in Roman,' I said. 'HCHO. What is it? Short for something?'

'Formaldehyde,' Dronsky said. 'It's the chemical formula for formaldehyde.'

'Christ!' My eyes passed around the immaculate kitchen with its hanging copper saucepans and its perfect set of Sabatier knives. 'Pull Bitov and Yakunin off whatever they're doing at the moment. We need to know where this dacha is.'

He nodded, dragging his mobile from his pocket. 'Maybe she hasn't left for New York, Chief. If that note's recent,' he said, nodding towards the kitchen board, 'she could be still at the dacha.'

'If that note's recent,' I said, 'she's gone there to collect a new storage box. A new formaldehyde box.'

'Why would she need that?' He glanced up at me as he dialled. 'What are you thinking, Chief?'

'I'm thinking about the Monstrum profile she gave us. "Half the pleasure is in the hunt, in evading the hunt, in taunting the hunter . . . whatever the risk."'

He looked at me, puzzled.

'Collecting was a big part of the profile . . . there's plenty of evidence of that here. And she wasn't pumping iron but there's a mini-gym here . . .'

'You mean what she gave you was a profile of *herself*?'

'I mean she could just be planning one last murder before she leaves.'

He formed his lips into a whistle. 'But this one's personal?'

'Look at the pictures in her safe. Look at the little notes she kept. I think all the killings are personal.'

'Then who would she sign off with?'

It came to us both at the same time.

It took half an hour to persuade Commander Brusilov that we needed a general alert out on Imogen Shepherd. Even showing him the photographs of the murdered girls failed to convince him. 'A purely professional interest, perhaps, Vadim . . . Who knows?' He spluttered into silence before Dronsky's cold contempt. Finally, with warnings that a mistake would be fatal, he gave permission.

I waited in my office exchanging greetings with V.I. Lenin while Dronsky finished talking to the various Moscow airports. Through his contacts at Sheremetyevo International he was assured the net would be drawn tight in less than an hour. 'For the internal trade airports, Chief, we're going to have to keep our fingers crossed,' he said. 'Unless, of course, she's already slipped through them.'

He went out to check with Records to see if they could produce anything on a dacha or clinic that Imogen Shepherd might have bought or rented. I had poured myself a lunchtime drink and was rocking back heavy-eyed in my chair, sipping it slowly, when the phone rang and the operator said that Dr Karlova was on the line.

It was like a long-distance call from fifty years ago. The line burbled and sang. Then suddenly, among distant, hollow clicks, and requests to hold from anonymous operators, I heard her voice.

'Natalya,' I said it all in a jumbled rush: 'Where are you, for God's sake? Are you in Petersburg?'

'Not far from it,' she said.

'Then you must stay there. You must stay away from Moscow.'

'That's something I'll decide about,' she said coolly.

Other voices were talking on the line. I had the panicky sense that we were about to be cut off. 'Listen,' I said. 'I mean I want you to come back. But not yet. Stay away from Moscow for the moment. And then come back. Natalya, I desperately want you to come back.'

The line was crackling badly, the sound breaking up as she spoke. 'Constantin, as ever, I understand about half of what you say.'

'Stay in Petersburg,' I said at the top of my voice. 'Stay away from Moscow.'

'I've been doing some research,' she said. 'I think I might be onto something.'

'Natasha, forget the research. The case is solved. Everything's changed.'

'You've never called me Natasha before.'

'No.'

She was silent for a long while, perhaps waiting for me to say more. But what could I tell her about Julia?

At this moment, on this impossibly crackling line, what could I say?

'How have things changed, Constantin?' she asked at last. 'Has anything changed for instance, between you and your former wife? Tell me that.'

'Just believe me, Natalya, that in the widest sense things have changed.'

The line popped and went clear. 'Constantin, I have believed you in too many things. Not that you lie to me, no. You have the even more dangerous habit of lying to yourself.' Her voice was brisk now. 'I hope all is well for you in Moscow. Please give my affectionate best wishes to Ilya Dronsky . . .'

'Stop,' I said. 'Don't ring off. I have things to tell you. Things to ask you.'

'I'll listen to any questions about the case. But only about the case.'

'All right. First of all a question. Do you know of a dacha Dr Shepherd might own or rent maybe not far from Moscow?'

'When I worked for her she used to rent a dacha out in the hills. But that burnt down. Maybe she took another place after that but I don't know it. Why do you ask?'

'We have to find her, Natalya.'

'Are the scales rolling from your eyes, Constantin? As far as Dr Shepherd is concerned at least?'

'Dr Imogen Shepherd is dead,' I said.

I heard the intake of breath. 'When?'

'She died three years ago. In Boston, America. She was a gynaecologist. A transplant specialist.'

Her voice was hushed. 'Constantin. Are you sure of this?'

'Certain of it. Who our woman really is I can't tell you. But she is not Dr Imogen Shepherd.'

'Transplants . . .' she said slowly.

'Transplants,' I said.

'Am I following you, Constantin? You don't mean it's her?' I could hear the rasp of shock in her voice.

'Yes, it's her. But there's an accomplice ... Some psychotic whose will she has control of ... Her interest is in the market for transplant organs. New wombs for old.'

'Oh God ... is she still in Moscow?'

'I don't know. We have a general alert out for her and we're watching the airports but for the moment she's disappeared.' I hesitated. 'Ilya and I broke into her apartment this morning.'

'Did you find anything that would tell you who she really is?'

'We found evidence. All we need. But for a fully furnished, well lived-in apartment it was unusually bare of clues about where she is now. Just a message on the kitchen board which mentions a dacha.'

'Nothing else that told you more about her?'

I took a deep breath. 'I know now that she's a collector.'

'A collector?'

'She kept a videotaped record of her one-night stands.'

'What are you saying, Constantin?'

'I'm saying I'm there on video. I fucked her.'

There was a long pause. 'So did I,' she said.

'I know.' I swigged down my vodka. 'There's a video of that too.' I turned the video over on my desk. *Natalya Karlova*, the label read. *Room 701, International Hotel, St Valentine's Night, 2014.*

'An experiment, Constantin. A failed experiment. I told her so.'

'Is that why she fired you?'

'Yes.' She gave a short embarrassed laugh. 'It took less than five minutes for my enthusiasm to evaporate. I got up, got dressed and she'd fired me before I made it to the door. She never forgave me.'

'She's not the forgiving type.'

She hesitated. 'Have you watched it?'

'Not yet.'

She laughed a strained laugh. 'Perhaps we should watch it together when I get back.'

I didn't take her up on that. 'Natalya,' I said, carefully, 'there's something else. Imogen Shepherd may be looking for . . . a last victim.'

'That's not likely, is it? Especially if she knows you're onto her?'

'I think she has a personal interest in all this that runs parallel to, or even deeper than her business interest.'

'A personal interest in a last victim? Are you talking about me?'

'I'm not sure, but I think I am. I don't want you to come back to Moscow right now.'

She was silent. 'She's not a woman who takes it well when someone stands in her way,' she said after a moment or two.

'That's exactly what I mean. I think she sees you like that. As someone who has stood in her way.'

'Or you. Keep looking over your shoulder, Constantin.'

'Is it important to you that I do?'

'Of course, idiot.'

'This research you've been doing . . . ?'

'It will take a little while longer. I'll be back in Moscow as soon as it's finished.'

'What will it tell us about Imogen Shepherd that we don't know already? What is this research?'

'It will tell us nothing about Imogen Shepherd. It's research for another life, Constantin my love,' she said. Then very quietly she murmured something that I couldn't quite catch and put down the phone. I think she said: *A life together*.

42

I stood with Dronsky just inside the gates of the cemetery
as the funeral procession formed up out on Malaya
Dekabrskaya Street. I was looking without really seeing,
my mind on Julia, roaming back and forth over our times
together – setting all this experience in the new framework
of what I now knew about her.

Standing there, I was aware for the first time that I
had been dreaming about her last night. An erotic dream
in which we had been out in the woods with a salmon
fishing party at the university, Roy and Katya among a
group of perhaps six or seven others. We were planning
to stay that night camped by the River Kol and had built
big fires in a half-circle on the riverbank. September
temperatures on the Kola peninsula, as I have said, can
be very low indeed. Food and dancing swirled through
the dream. And, informing everything, that peculiar sense
of excitement that comes from the imminence of a night
spent with the girl you love.

Building the fires high we had, each couple, retired to
our own tent and sliding naked into the thickly padded
sleeping bags we had begun to make love. And it was only
after moments of what have to be called bliss that in the
firelight's flicker I saw that it was not Julia lying beneath
me – but Katya giggling and chuckling. *Costya, Costya*,
she was saying, *didn't I tell you I'd have you some time?*
Of course dreams don't have sequence. I was suddenly
standing beside the open flap of another tent, the firelight
umbering the faces of Roy and Julia as they bucked and
squirmed in their lovemaking.

Even standing here, in the Vagankov cemetery I could

still feel the force of that rejection, feel it merge with what I knew was no dream, and drag me down with it.

'You all right, Chief?' Dronsky said. 'You're shaking.'

'Effects of last night. Not much left in the way of body heat.'

He turned his attention back to the procession of mourners coming through the gates. With effort I did the same. What struck me first, as the priests and coffin went by us, was the lonely figure of Maria's boyfriend walking behind it. What struck me next was that the twenty or thirty others were almost all young women.

Ilya glanced at me. 'It always happens,' he said. 'When one of the sisterhood gets done in the line of business, anybody who ever knew her turns out.'

'The way they're dressed,' I said, 'it looks as if they're straight off to work afterwards.'

He nodded. His eyes were scanning each girl. It had snowed in the night though the day was relatively fine for early in December. But the wind was brisk and the girls' short skirts fluttered like flags in each chilly blast. On the gravel pathways there was much stamping of feet and clapping together of gloved hands.

Twice his mobile phone jangled as the procession passed us. First Bitov, then Yakunin. Neither had any information on a villa owned or rented by Imogen Shepherd.

I told them to keep trying but there was something swirling like a newspaper headline in a corner of my mind. I could get no closer than half reading the headline, but close enough to know that it was somewhere, sometime, a reference to Imogen's dacha.

We walked to the side as the service began and stood well apart from the burial under a stand of pine trees. Every so often the wind shifted and snow slid from the upper branches and scattered across our shoulders.

Dronsky was smoking, a quick furtive draw before the cigarette disappeared behind his back, the smoke released expertly as no more than a thickening of his breath in the cold air. There was something unmissable about the style. 'Where was it necessary to hide a cigarette like that?' I asked him.

He pinched the glowing head behind him and moved his heel back an inch to crush the ember. 'It's not on my station record,' he said.

'I don't read records, Ilya.'

'I did five years in a labour camp,' he said. 'Up on the Kola peninsula. Your part of the world.'

'Which government was that under?'

He smiled. 'Does it make any difference? It was just before the Civil War.'

'The military government?'

He nodded. 'I was nineteen, just married. I took an extra night for my honeymoon. The generals were just trying to show they could reassert the discipline of the old Sovietschina. They were making examples. I was one of them.'

'You managed to bury the record?'

'I paid five hundred roubles, in those days that was a year's salary, to have someone wipe it off the screen.'

I was touched. He had just handed me his future. 'Why did you tell me?'

He shrugged. 'You asked.'

'Does that mean you don't believe any longer that I'm an officer of the Cheka?'

'Natalya says it doesn't matter what you are.'

'I'm not sure how to take that.'

He looked at me with a friendly grimace. 'Coming from her, take it as best. She says, at heart, you're one of us.'

'And what does that mean, Ilya? Who are *us*?'

'Just people . . .'

'With some sort of common purpose?'

He looked away. 'You could say that.'

'And Natalya thinks I share that purpose?'

'Of course she does. She wouldn't be in love with you otherwise.'

I felt an extraordinary surge of warmth. 'In love with me? She told you that?'

'Don't tell me it's news to you, Chief.'

'At the moment everything's news to me.'

'You look like you're pleased.'

'Of course I'm pleased, you dunghead.'

'I don't know why, but she seems to think she's got no chance with you.' He scratched his cheek and glanced at me. 'Maybe she thinks there's another woman?'

I stayed quiet.

Dronsky made a great show of musing over the problem. 'This other woman that was upsetting Natalya couldn't have been Dr Shepherd, could she, even though you did have a tumble or two with her?'

'One,' I said. 'One tumble when we first met.'

'It couldn't have been her,' he said decisively.

'Why not?' I wasn't prepared to tell him about Julia just yet.

'Why not? Because whenever Dr Shepherd came into the office *she* was always scratching about for titbits about your women herself.'

'My women! I've been in Moscow less than a month and you talk as if I've got a harem here. What the devil is this?' I said. 'You spend your days rerunning my sex life?'

He glanced at me and grinned. 'Just curious to complete the circle,' he said. 'American Dr Shepherd was pissed because she thinks you've got your eye on Natalya. Natalya's cast down because you've got your eye on someone else. So who *have* you got your eye on, Chief?'

'You, Ilya,' I said. 'Watch out. I find you fucking irresistible.'

The burial was over and the circle round the mound of snow-speckled, light brown earth was breaking up. 'Ask Gleb to come over,' I said. 'He's got something more to tell us. This time we have to know.'

Maria's man wore a black anorak and a fur-lined

leather hat with flaps like a pilot's helmet. He wasn't pleased to see me.

'How did you get on at District 15?' I said.

He spoke through the side of his tense, thin mouth. 'I thought you told me all militiamen weren't dumb as oxen?'

'What happened?'

'They tried to beat a confession out of me, of course.'

I looked at his thin hard face. It would take a lot of beating to make this one confess to something, whether he'd done it or not.

'Your man Dronsky saved me from the worst of it.'

I lifted an eyebrow towards Dronsky.

'I was over at 15 yesterday,' Dronsky shrugged. 'I told them they were wasting their time.'

'I wouldn't be over here talking to you now if he hadn't,' Gleb grunted.

'You would, Gleb,' I said. 'We think it's very possible there's going to be another murder tonight.'

The colour drained from his berry-brown face. 'Christ. Where?'

'It's nothing more than a strong guess. But you wouldn't like to think you hadn't done all you could to help.'

'What does it matter to me,' he said, 'if another whore gets it?'

I looked towards the scar in the earth that was Maria's grave. His eyes followed mine. Still looking at the grave, he sucked in cold air and slowly let it billow mistily from his mouth. 'What is it you want to know?' he asked.

'The night she was working round by the flag factory,' I said. 'What did she tell you about that?'

We walked along the gravel path towards the gate. 'Believe it or not, most nights she never told me a lot about anything. That night I remember she said someone tried to mug the girl she'd been working with.'

'Valentina.'

He nodded.

'You must have got some idea of what he was like.'

He laughed shortly. 'For a girl who's on the game men's faces are like plates with eyes, nose and mouth painted on them. They'll maybe talk among themselves about some of the queerer goings on, but they don't talk to anybody else.'

'You weren't just anybody else.'

'Same difference,' he said.

We left the cemetery and I motioned Gleb to get into the back of Dronsky's car.

'Are you going to finish off the job they started at District 15?' he asked.

'There won't be anything like that,' Dronsky said. He handed out cigarettes and I half turned in the front passenger seat to face Gleb as he leaned forward to take a light. 'She must have said something, for Christ's sake,' I said. 'She must have.'

Still leaning forward for the light, Gleb raised his eyes to my face. 'She said she thought maybe he was from the Belorussian,' he said.

One more step. We needed just one more step. I stayed quiet, nodding to Dronsky.

'The Belorussian?' Dronsky said. 'You mean Father Alexander?'

'The priest? No, she didn't say that.'

A totally horrifying thought was seeping into my brain. I felt a need to make sure there was no room for error. 'You know that Valentina's assailant that night was almost certainly the Monstrum?'

'Of course I do.'

I turned round as far as possible to face him. His gimlet eyes met mine. I felt my heart beating faster. I glanced at Ilya. His tongue was poked into the corner of his cheek. I think he was holding his breath.

'Did she describe him?'

He blew smoke across the car in a thin stream from the corner of his closed mouth.

421

'Gleb . . .'

'She said he had plastic bags pulled over his boots. And over his hands. And like . . . a plastic apron . . . She still thought it was a mugger. You know how they dress up these days to frighten the life out of the girls.'

Plastic bags over his hands. A plastic apron. Jesus Christ. There was no doubt now. It was him. Imogen's collaborator. The beast itself. 'And his face?' I said slowly. 'Did she see his face?'

'She wasn't sure she saw enough of it.'

'Whatever she saw . . .'

'He was wearing a woollen cap with a leather peak and earmuffs.'

'But did she recognise him?'

He looked exasperated. 'It's why she didn't go to the police, fuck your mother. She was scared and she wasn't *sure*.'

My blood was pulsing. 'But she *thought* she recognised him?'

He blew cigarette smoke into my face. 'If she did – your Monstrum is a thirteen-year-old kid named *Sex-change*.'

43

The sky seemed to darken as we approached the Belo-russian, although it was still only mid-afternoon. I dreaded another visit to the place. The pervasive smell, the sadness of the bewildered travellers, the wash of humanity across its tiled concourse all had their effect. Perhaps this city of appearances, of contrasts, is getting too much for me.

I got out of the police car and made my way with Dronsky through the cars and vans parked outside the station. Three other unmarked cars had drawn up behind us and Bitov and Yakunin led a half-dozen plainclothes men across the square, to different entrances.

Through the swing doors the stench again assailed me. In daylight it looked, if anything, worse. The lamps and deep shadows which, at night, gave it its Dickensian atmosphere were replaced by a cold greyness. Unnumbered people were gathered in small groups standing, seated, lying, sleeping . . . A path had been cleared down the middle of the concourse and a heavily laden company of infantry filed towards the door. For a moment I watched their faces. Country boys from the Volga or the Urals, seeing Moscow for the first time in all its grimy confusion. I could share their bewilderment. We are one of the richest countries in the world: we have oil, gas, gold, metals; we have led the race to the stars; our artists and writers and musicians have adorned Europe's culture; but politically we vacillate between the whip-guard and the serf. In politics we have still to reach the forefront of the *nineteenth* century.

Within the great hall there was no sign of Sex-change at the doors leading down to the catacombs. Dronsky signalled to other officers to cover the exits and we headed for the corner where the mother of Claudia, the girl who worked the officers' train, had her bed space.

Old Vladimira was, I think, pleased to see us. Claudia, she told us, had just got back from the Estonian border. She was in the canteen buying food. 'Lemon,' she said to the blind boy next to her, 'go and tell Claudia Mr Vadim and his friend are here.'

The boy scrambled to his feet and, hands extended before him like a boxer, danced rapidly across the concourse.

Both Dronsky and I crouched down low beside Vladimira. 'We're looking for one of the station boys,' I said. 'Sex-change, do you know him?'

'Everybody knows Sex-change, Inspector.'

'Why is that, Vladimira?' Dronsky gave her a cigarette. 'A station character, is he?'

She shrugged. 'He can be vicious with the other boys. But they all dote on him as far as I can see. Perhaps it's because he seems to be the one who's always got a tab of *stoke* to hand around. Poor Lemon adores him.'

'Where is he now?'

She frowned. 'He's usually about in the evenings. A bit glassy-eyed on *stoke* by this time. But he's usually to be found. Why is it you want him, Inspector?'

'The usual police questions,' I said. I got to my feet. Claudia and the blind boy were threading their way through the milling people, the family groups standing protectively around their luggage, the long lines at the ticket counters snaking back through the crowds.

She smiled when she saw us and handed out hamburgers to her mother and the blind boy. 'I'm sorry I didn't buy one for you, Inspector. Still looking for Maria?'

'No,' I said. 'I'm not looking for Maria any more.'

She picked up my tone immediately. 'You found her?'

I told her briefly what had happened. She nodded slowly. 'And who are you looking for today?'

'Sex-change,' I said, 'have you seen him?' As Claudia shook her head I saw the blind boy, who had slid his back down the wall until he was in a sitting position, move his head sharply towards me.

'How is it that Sex-change always seems to be the one with the *stoke*?' I was asking Claudia but watching the blind boy.

She grimaced. 'I think a few honest citizens making their way home from the bus stop could probably answer that for you, Mr Vadim.'

Lemon gave a quick glare of disapproval in Claudia's direction.

I moved over and crouched beside him. 'You're a great friend of his, Lemon,' I said. 'Can you tell me where I can find him?'

'You're the police,' the boy said.

'I need to talk to him, Lemon,' I said. 'Where is he?'

'Gone.'

'Just gone? Where to?'

'All the boys have gone. Burger King, Doc Marten, Macdo, Sparkplug ... there's none of them left here now.'

'Have they moved stations?'

'They're riding the rails.'

I looked up at Claudia. 'He means riding the boxcars. Every train has kids like them travelling the country. If they know you want them for something, you'll never find them, Inspector. They'll be scattered like a flock of pigeons. They could all be all over the country by now.'

I stood up, my knees cracking. The blind boy took a vast bite from his hamburger.

'I think Sex-change has been doing some very bad things.' I was still talking to Lemon.

He chewed vigorously, pretending not to realise I was talking to him.

'Lemon,' I said. 'Did you know about these bad things?'

He turned his head away.

Dronsky knelt down beside him and took the hamburger from his hand. 'When the inspector asks you, Lemon, you answer, understand me?'

Dronsky's Moscow accent made the boy's sightless eyes open wider.

'Did you know about these bad things?' I asked him again.

'It's good you tell them, Lemon. You know that,' Claudia said.

He looked down. He was mumbling. 'Sex-change does work for Father Alex's American doctor. I don't know what. He doesn't tell. Blood work, the other boys call it.'

'Blood work?'

The boy extended a hand and grasped wildly at the air until Dronsky caught his wrist and closed his thumb and fingers round the hamburger.

Claudia, I noticed, was looking white-faced. 'This blood work, Lemon,' she said in a half-whisper, 'does Sex-change do it himself?'

The boy nodded briefly. 'At night. Sometimes the others help.'

'Holy Mother!' Claudia said. 'Holy Mother of God!'

Lemon stared fixedly at the hamburger in his hand. With a quick, ducking movement of his head he tore a large bite from the hamburger, overfilling his mouth, champing and chewing like a famished animal.

We stood on the edge of the bath and watched the line of naked men and women singing as they descended the steps and waded forward to where Father Alexander stood up to his thighs in water. His broad back was half towards us but we could see the band of cloth of gold round his shoulders and ropes of crucifixes round his neck. As each naked applicant approached him he laid his hand on their head and recited words we could not hear, then pressed forward until the recipient of his baptism into the

426

Following was ducked beneath the water. Church music swelled and cries of elation from the baptised echoed through the vaulted chamber. When the girl we had sent spoke to Father Alexander, he lifted his head towards us and nodded.

We were waiting just off the main bath, in a richly tiled bathhouse, steam swirling around us. It was hard to see how big it was but, from the main chamber, tunnels and cubicles seemed to turn off in every direction. Girls with towels wrapped round their waists or casually draped over their shoulders floated through the thick mist of steam pouring from the vents of ornate enamelled stoves. Tinkling bells rang and Russian church music played. Dronsky's finger was hooked in his shirt collar. His face was salmon pink. 'I can't stand much more of this, Chief,' he said. 'I don't know if it's the heat or the girls . . .'

I could make out a small group of people approaching. The girls were quite decorously swathed and there were, unusually, some men among them. Then, as they got closer, the knot of people parted and Father Alexander came forward. He was wearing a long white bathrobe. His beard was tangled with steam and sweat, even his Mephistophelean eyebrows were plastered down. 'I've been trying to contact you, Inspector,' he said. 'But nobody at your station would tell me where you were.'

I introduced Dronsky and the priest led us through a series of tunnels which brought us to his office. Once there, he poured vodka. I could see he was a changed man. He said nothing as he carried the vodka to us, simply handing the glasses, first to me then to Dronsky, his eyes cast down toward the carpet, before turning to walk back behind his desk.

'I don't suppose for a moment I know everything,' he said.

Like the policemen we were, we remained silent.

He looked awkwardly from me to Dronsky. 'You're looking for Dr Shepherd, is that right?'

'She's not at her apartment. Is there anywhere else she's likely to be?'

He shook his head.

'What do you know about a dacha she has?'

'There's a place she *calls* the dacha. It's an American joke, perhaps. It's down in Nikulino, an industrial suburb of the city. It's an old ruined church she part converted. But she's not there. She's left Moscow.'

'You've got a lot to tell us, Sasha,' Dronsky said. Sasha is used as the diminutive for Alexander. Normally it's friendly but there was nothing friendly when Dronsky used it. 'We don't have time to prise it out of you. What makes you think she's left Moscow?'

'Dr Shepherd has left the country,' he said flatly. 'She left today.' He hesitated behind his desk, uncertain whether to sit down.

I walked to the corner of the room and sat on the arm of one of the giant sofas. Dronsky stayed where he was, centre stage. Father Alexander remained standing uncomfortably just behind his desk. 'I suppose I've known that Imogen Shepherd had her own reasons for running the medical centre for me down here,' he said. 'The truth is that I've ascribed all sorts of mildly deviant sexual motives to her in the last year – lesbianism, a passion for teenage boys . . . But I never for a moment realised what she was doing.'

'And what was that?'

'She was carrying out the examinations for the Following . . . I explained that to the Inspector . . .'

Dronsky nodded.

'But her real purpose was different, I see that now. It was first to establish those girls who were totally free from infectious sexual disease, AIDS obviously, and all the lesser conditions, and to identify those girls who would be genetically suitable for her purposes. I think she took

DNA material from each of the girls she tested. Once she was satisfied, that girl would be on her list.' He paused. 'For killing.'

'You know a great deal, Sasha,' Dronsky said. 'What was her purpose in coming down here?'

'Her other purpose, I'm sure now, was to meet the station boys on safe ground. I've chased off these station kids ever since I've been here. My communion attracts teenage boys like flies . . . naked girls bathing together, it's not surprising . . .'

Dronsky nodded tight-lipped.

'You don't approve, Deputy Inspector Dronsky, but it's quite without harm. I'm a believer, you see. I actually believe in the power of sex to bring relief to our minds, Deputy Inspector Dronsky—'

'Go on, Sasha, before I throw up. The station boys . . .'

'They often make their way down here. Imogen asked me to bring some of them here into the office so that she could talk to them. Her story was she wanted to study them. You know her interest in forensic psychiatry that she talked so much about . . .'

'Down here, in this very room, you laid out a selection of the most disturbed kids for her.' I watched Dronsky's anger mount but I decided to hold back for the moment.

'At that time I really thought she was a highly qualified American doctor with a Hippocratic interest in these boys.'

'When did you change your mind?' I asked him from my place at the back of the room.

He turned to me with some relief. 'Very slowly,' he said. I began to realise that she was in no way helping the boys, that the group she had selected – Sex-change, Macdo, Sparkplug and the others – were if anything worse. And then I discovered that she was passing them *stoke*.'

'That's how she paid them?'

'I'm sure it is. As a doctor, she had access to any amount. I said I would not have *stoke* down here. She tried to persuade me she was using it on the boys for scientific purposes. She could be very persuasive . . .'

Dronsky grunted.

'Then, early this morning she came down to collect her papers from the safe. The results of her examination of the girls. I came in to find her burning them in the ventilator shaft. It was then she told me she was leaving Moscow straight away.'

'And you didn't think to call the police,' Dronsky said. 'You thought just let her fly away and this cloud hanging over your bogus community will float away with her.'

He looked at me. 'I thought something like that, yes. I admit it.'

'You didn't think about the girls who'd been murdered.'

'I still had no clear idea what was happening. Not until I talked to Sex-change.'

I got up from the sofa. 'You talked to Sex-change today?'

'He came down looking for her. One of the boys had seen her upstairs in the Belorussian.'

'What did you tell him?'

'I told him Imogen was leaving Moscow. That she'd already left.'

I was watching the priest's face. 'Go on.'

'He broke down and sobbed his heart out. Suddenly he became a child again.'

Dronsky bared his teeth at him in disgust. 'He'd ripped open four girls, maybe dozens more . . .'

'Save it, Ilya,' I said. I turned to the priest. 'What happened then?'

'He told me everything. He sat on one of the benches in the tunnel out there and told me exactly what had happened. How she'd looked after him and given him food . . .' He hesitated. 'I think there was some sex involved too. And finally the *stoke* of course. She completely subjugated him. Some women, you know, Inspector,' the

430

priest said. 'Some women . . . they're obsessed with teen-age boys. The totality of their control and command—'

'So did he confess to you or what?' Dronsky cut across brutally.

'He confessed,' the priest said heavily. 'He told me everything. At first, slowly. He began by telling me about the prostitute, Maria somebody, who was hanged.'

'By Sex-change?'

'And two or three of the others . . .'

I looked at the priest's slumped shoulders. It was suddenly clear. The woman's voice that the old lady had heard in Maria's room was not a woman's voice at all. It was the not quite broken voice of Sex-change or one of his helpers as they struggled to suspend her heavy body by the cord. I reached out and touched the priest on the shoulder. 'Go on,' I said. 'He confessed to other things too?'

Alexander nodded. When he spoke his voice was cracked. 'In a haze of drugs,' he said, 'she taught them what to do. God knows they are violent children. They roamed Russia during the war, fighting for their young lives. None, I would guess, was a stranger to killing. In her private operating theatre the American doctor taught him what she wanted from him. Sex-change told me it was not difficult.'

'Did he tell you how it was done?' I asked him. 'I mean, how a killing was planned?'

'He told me that she would name the girl, and take him to a place she had chosen among the ruins. She would wait, near, in her car, for it to be done.'

I thought of the testimony of Gromek, the night-watchman at the flag factory, and of Nellie, his accomplice. They had seen a tall, slim figure, a *man* they thought, in a well-cut coat, pacing impatiently. Imogen's preference was obviously to be at the scene of the killing, near enough to watch the hunt, the last moments of the pursuit, the bringing down of the victim . . . Father Alexander was pale-faced as he looked up at me. 'She carried a surgical

431

box. An ice-box. Afterwards, it was made to look as though . . . the girl had been attacked in a blind fury.'

'And when he told you this, you still didn't call the police, fuck your mother!' Dronsky shouted at him.

'I tried to keep him here. But he ran. I swear I couldn't find him. He knows these tunnels better than anybody. He's gone. Sex-change will disappear with his name.'

'And if we hadn't come down here now, you would have let the whole thing slide away?'

'It was over. There would be no more victims. I thought perhaps there was no point in involving the Following, in destroying everything I'd built here.'

'And Father Sasha would continue to maintain his excuse for taking his pick of the young girls of Red Presnya,' Dronsky said.

'You're right, of course.' He leaned forward, his hands splayed on his desk, his head bent. 'But I'm not alone in the world, Deputy Inspector Dronsky, in confusing what I believe with what I would like to *think* I believe.'

44

I left Dronsky to supervise arrangements at the airports
and drove straight down to Nikulino. It was an area
of sodium lights and huge high-rise tower blocks on
the outskirts of Moscow where the countryside, though
engulfed by the growth of the city, is still visible in a
sudden clump of pine trees or a barn and a patch of land
squashed beside factory buildings.

With Father Alexander's instructions the church was
not hard to find. It was down a dirt track from the
main road, a ramshackle wooden structure of three small
green onion domes perched over a listing nave. A fourth
dome was missing with only its carved collar still silhou-
etted incongruously in place. The abandoned churchyard,
where empty graves showed up as holes like eye sock-
ets, was used as a dump with several dozen rusting
earthmovers and farm tractors embedded in mud and
light snow. Some sort of lean-to farm buildings, maybe
abandoned, maybe not, grew like tree mushrooms from
the base of the nave. The light was yellow sodium, thrown
by a single concrete lamp-stand in the tractor dump. It was
a grim, unwelcoming place.

I left the car, unbuttoning my holster and loosening the
pistol as I approached the arched front door. One minute's
examination of the oak, iron-studded double door told me
I wasn't going in that way.

I stood listening for a moment and heard nothing but
the traffic on the main road then I moved round the side of
the white-painted wall. Another similar but smaller door
halfway down the nave looked no more promising. But a
small deep-set window with a thin chicken wire mesh at

about three metres above ground level did. I pulled over a couple of wooden crates, balanced them precariously, scrambled up to where I could pull the wire aside, heaved myself into the window embrasure – and felt my gun slide from my holster and drop to the ground.

I could, of course, have climbed down to get it but I had already scraped one knee badly pulling myself up to where I was now crouching. And I could see through the window down into the converted nave where there was silence and deep shadow and, I was sure, no one.

I checked I still had my pocket flashlight, then broke the window with my elbow . . . waited a moment while the glass pattered on the stone floor below, and hit it again to make a big enough hole to crawl through onto a ledge on the other side of the window. Gradually becoming accustomed to the darkness now, I could see that the small nave had most recently been used for cattle. Where a shaft of sodium light came through a hole in the roof I could see rough timber cattle stalls along one side of the nave wall.

It was a long way from what I'd expected. I used the flashlight to check that there were no obstacles below and dropped down onto the stone floor. I landed well and steadied myself. For a moment I stood, controlling my breathing . . . absorbing an atmosphere heavy with damp and cattle, but, with the light slanting in through cracks and holes, still somehow redolent of chanting voices and incense. This church had been old when Peter the Great built St Petersburg, when Tsar Nicholas built Murmansk . . . Old when the 1917 revolution had turned out its priests and given it over to cattle stalls.

Then I pulled myself up with a start. I had to remind myself I no longer had a right to these romantic notions. The new Russia of Leonid Koba was reviving other Russian traditions. Powerful traditions I had preferred to close my eyes to. I shook my head. Why was it always a struggle for me to live in the present? Why did the past always seem to beckon so seductively? Was it because all of us, innocent and guilty, were locked into this preference for a bloodstained past? Were we condemned to be ruled for ever by illusionists? Was it this that made Russia the land of Potemkin villages and Stalin constitutions?

I moved out into the middle of the nave, letting the torchlight play over the worn wooden cattle stalls. I was in the wrong place. That was obvious enough now. Had Father Alexander deliberately sent me off on a wild goose chase? Or had there been some purpose in getting me here?

And then something. A sound? An animal in a stall? No.

But if I listen I hear something behind me. Not cattle, no. A shuffling footstep. It comes forward and stops, comes forward and stops, moving from one carved pillar to another. And then a distinct sharp clink. Of knife blade on stone, is what shrieks in my mind.

Constantin, you dunghead. You think of your pistol on the ground just a metre away but on the far side of that oak wall. But you stand in the shadow of a reeking cattle stall, frozen with fear. Colder than you've ever been. Numb, nevertheless, with terror.

Ahead was a timber screen. Someone had long ago prised the carvings off it and broken parts of it away, panels large enough to throw myself through. I made four paces before the shotgun exploded, loosening tile and brick-dust and even the bats among the roof timbers. As I rolled across the floor of the nave a whole shower of tiny particles seemed to be falling around me.

Lying paralysed on my back, I could see the flit and swoop of a dozen or more bats.

I could also see an old lady, a village babushka in a long skirt and headscarf and baseball cap pointing a double-barrelled shotgun down at me.

I wasn't hurt. That's to say I had no warm wet patches or stains spreading on the stone floor beneath me. 'Little

Mother,' I said, my arms extended to her like a baby in a cradle, 'I'm not here to steal your cow. I'm a police inspector . . .'

The dark, seamed face surveyed me. Her finger, I saw, was firmly hooked on the second trigger.

I licked my lips. Fear like this, ordinary fear, I can deal with much better. 'I would like to get up,' I said. 'I'd like to get to my feet.'

'Don't even think about it,' she said. I wondered if it helped me to know she was a devotee of dubbed American cop shows.

'I'm a police officer,' I said, still on my back. 'A police inspector. Moscow District 13. Red Presnya. We are engaged in a homicide inquiry.'

She stepped back a pace, gesturing me up with the barrel of the gun.

Very cautiously I got to my feet.

'How did you get in?' she said.

I looked towards the broken window.

'A police inspector?'

'I was given the wrong information,' I said. 'If I'd known the old church was being used by an honest woman to keep a cow or two in . . .'

'A cow or two? There have been no cows here since the American doctor bought the place.'

The words gave me a thump in the chest like a shot-gun blast. The priest hadn't sent me on a wild goose chase at all. 'Watch me very carefully,' I said to the old lady. 'I'm going to take my police warrant from my pocket and hold it up for you to see I'm who I say I am.'

'Two fingers,' she said.

'What?'

'Use two fingers and move slow.'

I did what I was expected to do, as seen on TV. A cautious movement, my eyes on the twin black openings at the end of the shotgun barrel. Very slowly I held the warrant at arm's length in a shaft of light and hoped she could read.

'It looks like you,' she said. She nodded to herself. 'Yes, it's a good likeness.'

'Are you going to put up that gun?'

'It's still got one good shot in it. I want to know what you're doing here first.'

I knew I had to be right first time with my answer. 'Dr Shepherd,' I said slowly, 'has left the country.'

The babushka's face took on a look of pain and confusion. 'She can't have,' she said. 'Left the country . . . ? How could that be? She was here this very afternoon.'

'She won't be coming back, Mother,' I said. 'When did she leave?'

'An hour or two? She collected some things and was gone.' Her face was screwed up with bewilderment. 'You mean she won't be back?'

'Ever,' I said. 'From here she drove to the airport to catch a plane to America.'

'America . . .' she said. 'All that way.'

I paused a moment, watching her face. 'She's wanted by the police, Mother.'

She nodded slowly. She asked no questions. With a peasant fatalism she accepted the change of authority. The American doctor was gone: the police were here. So be it. Slowly she broke open the shotgun and took out the one remaining unspent cartridge. 'You'll want to look at the farm.' She gestured with a movement of the head.

'I will,' I said.

She held the shotgun in the crook of her arm and shuffled in her felt boots across the nave and through the wide gap in the tumbledown wooden screen in front of us. Taking a bunch of keys from under her shawl, she opened a small side door and I felt a blast of colder air sweep into the nave.

We stood in a small courtyard where snow flurries etched out the black cobbles. In front of me was an old single-storey farmhouse with a barn attached. There were signs of recent repairs to chimney stacks and guttering. But no lights, no curtains in the windows. Indeed the windows threw back our wavering reflections, the babushka's and mine, as we crossed the cobbled yard and I had the impression that they might well be painted or boarded from the inside.

She let me into a small windowless hall. Closing the door, she turned on concealed overhead lighting to reveal blank white-painted walls, straight and trim enough to be pressed metal.

No trace of the interior of the old farm building remained. The floor was polished wooden strip and the door facing us even more obviously steel than the walls. Beside it, a red light glowed at shoulder height in a metal box of numbered push-buttons.

'You know the code?' I asked the babushka as we approached the door.

'I have it in my head,' she said proudly. She stood the shotgun against the wall and positioned herself in front of the door.

I was about to speak but she put her finger to her lips. 'Listen,' she said. 'The death year of the great Comrade Stalin . . . 1–9–5–3 . . . Will I ever forget it? Thirteen years of age I was and suddenly the earth stopped spinning. I couldn't imagine how we'd live without his presence here to guide us. My own mother couldn't stop crying for a week. Of course we knew it was a Western plot but by then the evil had been done.'

'The code,' I said, as I saw the tears rising in her eyes.

'Then that fool Khruschev took over and disgraced us in the eyes of the world . . . banging his shoe like that at the United Nations. Behaving like a Russian peasant. For that we could never forgive him . . . Not fit to wipe the lord Stalin's boots.'

'The code,' I said.

'The last great year in our history: 1–9–5–3 . . .' She punched in the numbers.

'Identification,' the device said in English. She leaned forward and placed her lips close to the circular grille below the red light. 'It's old Anna Fyodorovna,' she whispered conspiratorially. 'It's Anna and a police inspector.'

The glowing light faded and a lock clicked.

'When was all this building work done?' I asked the old woman.

She pursed her lips. 'Three years ago or more,' she said. 'Just after the Anarchists took Moscow. The doctor set it up as a young women's clinic. Only the very worst cases were brought here. For most of them, there was nothing she could do. They're buried in the churchyard there.' She sighed. 'During the siege we were busy all the time.'

I opened the door and entered. Lights came on automatically. Immediately I knew what sort of place I was in. The low humming and the ambient temperature gave it away. My stomach lurched in alarm as I looked at the bank of small medical refrigerators along the wall. There were perhaps two dozen or more handles. The babushka, I noticed, had stayed outside in the hallway.

I pulled one of the handles. The tray slid towards me. There was more of it than I had steeled myself for. Something quite long and red-black in a frosted plastic bag. It looked like something V. I. Lenin would have given his eye teeth for. I slammed it closed and pulled other trays. Some were empty. Some contained similar horrors. In my revulsion it had taken me a drawer or two to realise that each bag was neatly named and numbered. I wiped away the frosting with a single sweep of my index finger. I was looking at the uterus of Valentina Matsky. She had not gone to stay with country cousins after all.

I closed the last tray and looked towards the babushka but she seemed indifferent to my discoveries. I was prepared to believe she was unaware, in any real sense, of what the frozen bags contained. I indicated the far door. 'Where does that lead to?' I asked her.

'It's the doctor's laboratory, Comrade Inspector,' she said. 'And of course, the garage on the other side. It's not locked if you want to go through.'

'You go on ahead of me,' I said. I had no wish to find myself locked in this morgue alone.

She shuffled obediently across the room. I followed behind her. We entered a small laboratory with a huge theatre light above a compact operating table and stainless steel sinks with elbow-activated taps.

I thought at first that, like the first room, it was barely functional, then turning I found myself looking into the eyes of a photographic portrait on the wall. It was of a handsome woman of about fifty-five. And for some reason, I felt sure it was an American woman. A rather long, strong, kindly face, short, almost bobbed hair and a warm smile. There was no caption but I felt no doubt, was convinced in fact, that I was looking into the eyes of the *true* Dr Imogen Shepherd. And equally convinced that she had been the young, *false* Imogen's lover.

I turned to the babushka. 'Did Dr Shepherd come in here this morning?'

'Just long enough to pick up a specimen box.' She gestured.

'A specimen box?'

She shuffled across the room and through the far door. I stopped in the doorway. It was a small garage with a large Mercedes gleaming blue-black under the lights. I stepped forward and opened the driver's door. The seats were black leather; the flooring, the pale grey of our carpet specimens. I leaned in. The interior had been converted. There was no back seat. The carpet had been stripped out and replaced by shiny red rubber matting.

'These are the specimen boxes.' The old woman pointed to a rack of half a dozen metal boxes where the back seat would have been. I took one out by its handle and opened the metal clip. About the size of a lunchbox, it was divided between a glass compartment and a compact battery-powered refrigeration unit.

It was a business. A highly organised business. But I knew it was not going to be the clinical, metallic refrigeration boxes that would stay with me in memory. The image that would haunt me would be quite different – the image of that green plastic tent over the Stalin plinth, and the plundered body and white, dead face of the eighteen-year-old victim.

45

I got back to an empty office. V.I. Lenin was seated on the fax machine, busy scavenging the fish from the bun of one of Dronsky's abandoned breakfast fishburgers. Too busy to hiss or raise a paw in greeting. 'Since you're asking,' I said, 'things are definitely hotting up in the homicide business.'

Lenin kept his head down over the fishburger.

I sat at my desk. I was exhausted, my eyelids heavy and burning. I took a cigarette from the drawer and lit it. What was the point in trying to pretend I didn't smoke? Trying to pretend in front of a cat. I put an elbow on the desk and cupped my chin on one hand. Waves of weariness passed over me. Weariness and desperation. The pace of the last few hours had not pushed Julia from my mind, but had somehow blunted the enormity of what she was doing. It came back now in an image of bent men and women dressed in 'devil skins', the coarse cloth of striped prison clothes, stumbling into their intolerable sleeping huts, parched or frozen, depending on the Siberian season, but all of them cut off irrevocably from their families and loved ones – as Julia's own actions had cut me off.

I was, I realised, paying for my innocence. As hundreds of thousands had done under Communism. And as hundreds of thousands of others would now. They would pay for their loyalty to Julia and their innocence of her ruthlessness, accepting her reassurances as Minister for the Amnesty. They would surrender themselves in their thousands as soon as the announcement was made. And the United States and Europe would return thousands more who had fled there and claimed asylum.

I was shaken out of my reverie by a piercing yowl from V.I. Lenin as the fax started to bleep and buzz under him. He leapt off the machine and was out through the open door even before I could laugh at him. I would have let the sheet join the scatter of useless new government edicts on the floor if I had not seen the Russia Airways logo at the head of the page. I got up and retrieved the page before it fell. It was an unsigned message but I had no doubt that it was from Madame Raisa's brother. It read:

Information just received from a contact in NYPD.
Jean Lucy Harrow. Born, Cleveland, Ohio, 1983.
Mayapple Correctional School, Cleveland . . . 1995
Committed for serious assault, Hodge-Dower Psychi-
atric Hospital, 1996. Released 1997.
Change of name to Mary Roan: 31 convictions for
prostitution, 9 convictions for assault in 5 separate
states by 2001.
Under several names – McKenzie, Parton, Salvatore,
Nyquist – convicted of conspiracy to illegally import
human tissue, 2005.
2008 reverted to own name, Jean Lucy Harrow.
Resident London. 5 convictions for the illegal import
of human tissue.
2012 makes claim in Mass. Superior Court to inherit
the $2 million estate of Dr Imogen Shepherd on
grounds of being her legal partner in common law.

Raisa's brother had contacts. I screwed the paper up and threw it in the bin. Jean Lucy Harrow had disappeared into the mist. In conditions of chaos or civil war some-where in the world she would no doubt set up shop again. If I closed my eyes I could almost smell the perfume, see her sliding onto her barstool. A woman

I would never begin to understand, a beautiful, *soignée*, well-dressed *ghoul*.

A woman, who, for some incomprehensible reason, had taken a taxi all the way down to Nikulino in order to collect an *empty* specimen box. My mouth sagged open. It was fatigue that was misting my brain. The box was designed to do one thing only – to contain one of Imogen's, or Jean Lucy Harrow's, specimens.

But she was fleeing the country. Sex-change was riding the rails a hundred miles from Moscow. Whatever Gothic ideas of vengeance had sent her back to the laboratory at Nikulino could not be put into practice now.

When the phone rang it was Dronsky from the airport.

'No luck here, Chief,' he said.

'You've established which flight she took?'

'Not yet, Chief. It's one big fucking bazaar here. They're expecting some VIP visit. Troops and police milling all over the place. Nobody to answer simple questions about flight lists and the like.'

'Do your best, Ilya. But don't get hung up on New York schedules. My guess is she might have taken a shorter flight: Warsaw, Berlin, Paris even. So that she's landed and away before we can radio ahead to hold her.'

'Maybe.' He paused. 'Constantin . . .' It was the first time he had called me by name. 'I just want to say I'm really pleased about the news,' he said.

'News?'

'About Mischa. It's fantastic. Really is fantastic.'

I sat up in real shock. 'What are you talking about, Ilya?' I'd never even talked to Dronsky about my son. 'What about Mischa?' But the hope was bursting through me.

'You don't know? You don't listen to your messages, for Christ's sake?'

I rang off and thumped my finger on the *Play* button.

Natalya's voice was sombrely excited. 'The most marvellous possibility, Constantin. But it's only a possibility, as yet. Please remember that. I've been to Pavlovsk cemetery, just outside Petersburg. It was something Julia said under anaesthetic, Constantin. Just a hint – but I wanted to follow it up. There is no grave at the cemetery as Julia described. Better than that, there are rumours of a column of abandoned children taken charge of by local monks. There's some slight reason to hope, Constantin. I'll catch the next plane back. I love you. And *only* love you.'

I was mad with hope. And as mad with fear. Mad with fear for a six-year-old child, struggling through snow blizzards in a column of abandoned children. Images terrified me as they came flowing through my mind, of the older boys with their lanterns on long sticks at the head of the column, of Mischa's flagging strength . . . of him trailing farther and farther behind until he stumbles to a halt in the snow.

Talk to me, someone. Before I scream. I got up from my desk and burst through the door into the Murder Room. Heads lifted and bent again over their phones. No one here to tell that my child just might still be alive.

I went back into my office and played Natalya's message over again, analysing each phrase, each intonation to each phrase, trying to wrench more from it than was there . . .

When the message ended I got up, shaking, to pour myself another vodka. A new time/date announcement was followed first by a check-in, no-news reports by Bitov and Yakunin from the smaller airports. I had poured the vodka and was about to snap off the machine when another time/date announcement preceded the unmistakable voice of Dr Brodsky, Natalya's replacement as chief pathologist. Her tone was harrying: 'Inspector Vadim, I am warning you, as senior homicide officer, that I am

445

about to lodge a complaint to Commander Brusilov. It is impossible for me to carry out my assigned role in the circumstances . . .' I was looking for cigarettes. 'I insist, categorically insist, that, as acting senior pathologist I should attend this callout . . .'

'Attend what you like, my darling,' I said, sticking a cigarette in the side of my mouth.

'If it is indeed a Monstrum killing,' the voice grated on, 'as appears the case, then my experiments of the last two days—'

I passed through the Murder Room at a run, careless of papers and phones knocked from desks. Crossing reception I entered the corridor to where that dreadful odour hung in the air and the sign over the door read: FORENSIC PATHOLOGY.

I pushed the swing door and tried not to see some of the things that were going on on the cutting tables ranged round the room. A girl in a green overall stained with old blood approached me, her gauze mask sagging below her nose, her eyebrows pushing at her hairline.

'I'm Inspector Vadim,' I said. 'From Homicide.'

Her manner became marginally more welcoming.

'I want to see Dr Brodsky. Is she in her office?'

The girl's eyebrows raised even further. She pulled the mask down. 'God, no. She was furious. She's lodged a complaint with the commander.'

'There's been a callout. Is that right? Another Monstrum callout?'

'Half an hour ago.'

I plucked at her sleeve and regretted it when I saw the smear of blood on my fingers. 'Where? Where was it?'

She offered me a clean part on her other sleeve to wipe off my hand.

'The airport. Sheremetyevo. The pathologist is there now.'

'Who called her out?' I said. 'Deputy Dronsky?'

'No. I took the call, myself. It was the airport police, I suppose.'

'You suppose? How did they identify themselves?'

She shrugged. 'Just a voice. A woman operator—'

The kernel of an idea was forming. 'Accent,' I said. 'Did she have an accent?'

'Everybody in Moscow has an accent these days.'

I turned away and grabbed a phone from the nearest desk. 'Give me Sheremetyevo,' I said to the operator. 'Airport police.'

It rang and somebody picked up at the far end. 'Inspector Vadim. District 13, Red Presnya. You've had a murder reported in your area.'

'We've had hundreds,' a cheerful voice said.

'I'm in no mood for anything but straight answers. Was there a murder reported this afternoon or evening?'

'No, Inspector.'

'You're sure?'

'I'm looking at the incident board in front of me now.'

'And you've no record of the District 13 pathologist being called over to you.'

'Hold on.' He half covered the phone as he shouted round the office. 'None,' he said. 'Nobody knows anything about a call to 13.'

'Jesus.' I put the phone down.

The girl was looking at me in alarm now. 'Did I do something wrong?'

I found I couldn't think fast enough, but a terrifying thought was driving me now. I held the girl by the arms, oblivious of the blood on her overalls. 'What was Dr Brodsky's problem? Why was she complaining to Brusilov? If there was a call for a District 13 pathologist, why shouldn't she go?'

The girl looked at me as if I was mad. 'Because it wasn't any longer her job to go,' she said.

447

'Why not?'

'Dr Brodsky was only the temporary pathologist. And I'd hardly put the phone down when Natalya Karlova herself walked back in from Petersburg.'

46

'We have a difficult situation here, Inspector,' the airport sergeant's voice said over my mobile. 'We're expecting the arrival of a senior Arab diplomat – and the way things are between Russia and the Islamics at the moment—'

'Get on with it,' I shouted at him. I was steering the Renault with one hand, my foot down hard on the accelerator, blue light flashing and siren whooping ahead of me up the long road to the airport. 'What difference does an Arab diplomat's visit make, for God's sake?'

'The difference of about fifty men. The whole of the rapid reaction team have been allocated to guarding the concourse and the VIP area. It's orders from the top. I can't spare you a single extra man, Inspector Vadim.'

I swerved hard enough to almost leave the road. I knew it was no use shouting at the duty sergeant. I bit on my lip. 'Is Deputy Inspector Dronsky with you in the control room?'

'I'll pass him over,' the sergeant said with relief.

I heard voices and footsteps, then the familiar, reassuring voice: 'Chief, it's me. Dronsky.'

'Ilya. Fill me in, for God's sake.'

'OK. Nothing to be done about the Arab visit. Accept it. That leaves fifty men I've rounded up to search the airport.'

'Fifty men to search 150 hectares—!'

'Stick to driving the car, Chief,' he said, as if he were sitting beside me. 'They're doing a good, methodical job of the search ... I'm running it by video camera from up here in the control room. Communications are good.

We can talk to them and get feedback. How long will it take you to get here?'

I swerved past parked cars under the huge red neon *Sheremetyevo* sign. 'I'm pulling into the forecourt now.'

He gave me instructions on how to reach the control room and I braked in the VIP section and ran from the car leaving the door wide open behind me, the light flashing, the siren screaming.

I pushed through the swing doors and heard it as I ran, across the concourse, Dronsky's calm voice repeating: 'Message for Natalya Karlova. This is Ilya Dronsky. Your medical callout was a fake. You are in danger. Personal danger, Natalya. Stay with other people and find a uniformed officer as soon as possible.'

I could have added to his message warnings about Imogen Shepherd, but he was probably right to keep it short.

This part of the concourse seemed to be full of armed police. I had slowed to a quick walk but not in time to avoid being noticed by two uniformed men with Kalashnikovs.

'What's the hurry, Grandad?' A blond twenty-year-old boy stood in front of me, his Kalashnikov pressed against my chest. Boiling inside with frustration, I showed my warrant card, waited while the boy took it, examined it with a ponderous air, handed it to his companion before finally passing it back to me. 'Sorry, Inspector,' he said, with a brief salute. 'But you can't be too careful . . .'

I nodded agreement and moved on past him to the unnumbered staircase Dronsky had described on the phone.

I could see the bank of television monitors even before I pushed the glazed door. Dronsky was on his feet the moment he saw me and pointed to a large light-display map of the airport area, roadways, maintenance hangars and passenger buildings above the bank of monitors. The system was simple. To search an area on the map you hit the number on the keyboard. The precise cone of vision covered by your chosen surveillance camera was shown on the light display sweeping back and forth across the map.

At the same time the large central monitor was activated to your camera choice. All other monitors rotated through the surveillance cameras, changing picture every five seconds.

'You've got two additions to what you see,' Dronsky said. He pointed to a small control box on the desk in front of him. 'Every camera carries a low-power searchlight activated by this button. And this dial will give you zoom-in or wide angle, as you choose.'

'But we still have just fifty men to cover 150 hectares of airport.'

He lit a cigarette and handed it to me. Then lit one for himself. 'I've split the fifty men into ten squads, each under direct radio control from here. I've positioned them so that one of the squads can get to any part of the airport in a matter of minutes.'

I ran my eyes over the rotating pictures on the smaller screens. They showed open hangar doors with lights and men working on Tupolevs or Boeings; they showed dark, out-of-the-way corners with not a soul in sight. They showed the busy entrance to a flight attendants' canteen and would rotate again to show long bleak alleys between concrete warehouse buildings. Occasionally we would pick up a group of militia but they seemed pitifully few to cover the huge and mostly bleak area of the airport.

'I've got a request in to the colonel in charge of the diplomatic protection squad to pass on any information about passengers found in parts of the airport they shouldn't be,' Dronsky said. I knew he was just filling time for me. 'Nothing so far,' he added.

I looked down onto the concourse. People streamed from the arrival gates pushing trolleys loaded with purchases from abroad. In one single glance I saw up to fifty armed police. I would have rushed down with a bribe for every single one of them if I thought it would have diverted them to *our* search.

On the light display, Dronsky was working his way across the airport from west to east. 'Fill me in, Chief. When would Natalya have arrived?'

'Up to twenty minutes before me, maybe,' I said. 'The call from Imogen was taken by one of Natalya's assistants. It said she would be met at Information on the main concourse.'

He was thinking quicker than I was. He had buttoned a number and was talking to the information desk before I realised what he was doing.

Bent over his microphone, he said urgently. 'Militia control. I'm talking about an American woman about thirty-five years old, with dark hair. We're not sure what name she might be using. Did any such woman leave a message for a Dr Natalya Karlova in the last half-hour?'

He flipped the amplifier and I heard the girl say: 'I remember the American woman. Mrs Jean Lucy Harrow?'

'That's her,' I said.

'Very agitated. I asked her what flight she was on but she didn't answer.'

'Did you see the other woman arrive?'

'Dr Karlova, tall, blonde hair pulled back in a clip. Carrying a green canvas medical bag.'

'What was the message?'

'Recorded here,' the girl said. 'Here it is: "Lufthansa maintenance area". That's all.'

'How long ago?'

'Ten, fifteen minutes at the most.'

While Dronsky directed a unit of airport militia to the Lufthansa area, the girl was checking her records. 'Exactly thirteen minutes ago,' she said. 'But she was stopped on the concourse by a pair of troopers and asked for her papers. Always happens on a security exercise. The troopers know there's no real emergency so they pick on any good-looking women on the concourse and give them a good going over. You know what I mean?'

'No emergency?' I said, and I could hardly speak for fury. 'You mean there's no goddamned Arab diplomat arriving?'

'Just an exercise. No need to say I mentioned it.'

'Wait a minute,' Dronsky put a hand on my arm. 'It works for us. If she was stopped and questioned it means we're only minutes behind.' He swung round towards the big central screen.

As Dronsky worked methodically on the central screen, my eyes flicked across the slowly rotating pictures on the smaller screens that surrounded it. Every five-second change seemed to take an hour. My stomach was churning in panic. I scanned shadows and saw something in almost every one of them. I was willing Natalya to appear on one of the monitors and terrified of the shape with a knife which I would see behind her.

Then, beside me, I heard Dronsky grunt. 'Number twelve,' he said. We were in long shot down an alley between brick warehouses. On the small screen I could just make out the figure of a woman. Then, shockingly, the image transferred to the central screen. Natalya, carrying her medical bag, hurried towards us, hatless, her blonde hair lifting in the wind.

Dronsky was issuing orders to the nearest militia team. I shouted to her. I jumped from my seat. Dronsky pulled me roughly back again. 'Watch the screen, for Christ's sake,' he said.

I think I have never felt so helpless in my life. I watched Natalya turn a corner, check the direction boards on the brick wall and start across an open apron of concrete and for a second I experienced a wild start of hope as a tractor-loader trundled across in front of her. In my ear I could hear the crackle of Dronsky's line to the militia unit. 'They're just south of runway six. Three minutes,' he said to me. 'They're not more than three minutes away.'

The camera was roaming widely now, scanning ahead of where Natalya was walking. 'To the right,' Dronsky said. 'To the right, fuck your mother!' Panic swamped me. My eyes glazed and refocused. I was looking deep into shadow. But this time the shadow moved. It was Imogen. And as she moved the light caught the square metallic box she carried in her right hand.

In close-up on the central screen, no detail was missing. She wore the collar of her black cloth coat turned up and a dark plaid headscarf knotted under her chin. Her white face without make-up gave her a frightening, thin-lipped appearance. I could even see the rate of her breathing from the clouds of thin mist that billowed from her mouth. Then her head turned sharply in response to something she had seen or heard. For a moment I was staring her full in the face. It was a face drained of colour, but tense with expectation, the lips turned downwards, the eyes narrowed, the breath coming faster in short exhalations. I thought of her own words from the profile. Perhaps it was the first time I had looked into the face of someone completely insane.

The central screen changed. Natalya was passing the first of the Lufthansa maintenance hangars. Her manner was puzzled, wary now. I could read her thoughts. *There should be people's voices, the crackle of radios, flashing blue lights. What's going on here?* But she kept on walking, her steps slowing as she looked from side to side. 'Turn back,' I whispered. 'Turn back for God's sake and run for your life. *Turn back!*' I wasn't whispering now. I was shouting, shouting into the screen. Thoughts were flashing through my mind. Intolerable thoughts. That on the day I regained my son, I might lose the woman I loved.

'She's OK,' Dronsky said beside me. His hands were

pressing down on my shoulders. 'Two jeeps have crossed the runway . . . It's minutes now.'

A wide-angled shot now filled the central screen. From the shadow on the right we saw Imogen move forward. Perhaps she called out, because Natalya stopped dead and began to take a step backwards. A light curtain of snow was falling between them. They seemed to be talking across the sixty metres which separated them but Imogen was moving inexorably forward and Natalya was moving cautiously back.

Then I heard a gasp from Dronsky beside me. He touched a button and the picture on the central screen dissolved. For a moment I saw only snow piled against warehouse walls. 'Bottom left,' Dronsky said. 'Oh my good God.'

I raked my eyes down the screen. A shadow broke and re-formed. It was Sex-change.

On screen, the boy rose from the shadows and disappeared round the corner of the building. I looked at the display. Dronsky called up the section and the big screen flipped image and Sex-change was running, hugging the wall, along the side of a warehouse. As he turned again, Dronsky changed image, caught up with him again and zoomed in on him as he stopped, crouching in the shadows. He was clearly visible now, in anorak and woollen hat. Across his knee rested a thick timber baton.

I was on my feet. I took one last look at the light display panel. To reach the hangar Natalya would have to pass the corner where Sex-change was waiting.

I couldn't turn away. Couldn't move. I saw Imogen pull back into the shadow and, from another angle, Sex-change rise to his feet and move towards the corner of the hangar. 'The searchlight,' I gasped at Dronsky.

He hit the button and the screen whitened with light. I saw the boy's face as he turned, and Dronsky zoomed in on him. For a second his lips were pulled back, bared

455

. . . then he turned away, holding the heavy baton ready, and scuttled soundlessly round the corner.

Natalya was running. For her life. At that distance it was hopeless. I screamed as I watched the rise and fall of the baton as Sex-change caught her across the shoulders.

Imogen Shepherd on the edge of the shot looked as though she were laughing.

Three steps at a time down the back stairs from the control room, I reached Dronsky's Jeep. I found myself behind the wheel and Dronsky in the seat beside me as we took off, tyres spurting snow, and accelerated between the office blocks and hangars.

Perhaps it took three minutes, spinning round corners, sliding into piled snowbanks, with Dronsky shouting directions in my ear before we reached Lufthansa maintenance.

I recognised the corner of the warehouse. The searchlight was still on, pointing down to where Sex-change had crouched. I brought the Jeep to a halt and leapt out.

The lights of three airport militia Jeeps were seconds behind me. I yelled to the lieutenant to fan his men out and search behind the buildings. There were lights everywhere: headlights, rearlights, flashlights, overhead lights. My head span. Time telescoped.

Perhaps I had moved a dozen times, or perhaps I was still standing in the same spot when I saw a young soldier with a flashlight in his hand recoil from something behind a pile of empty crates.

My breath whistled like hot steam from my mouth as he dropped the flashlight and vomited against the side of the warehouse. He turned to me with a totally white face and pointed. 'There's a woman down there,' he said. And vomited again.

I couldn't go forward. Couldn't move. I looked at the

young militiaman and at the spray of vomit down the front of his greatcoat and our eyes locked. 'Like a wild animal, fuck your mother,' he screamed at me, from less than five metres away. 'Both of them. He's killed both of them!'

I heard Dronsky's voice beside me and we began to move forward together. A stack of empty crates higher than a man's head stood against the wall of the hangar. Imogen's body was sprawled on her back on the snow. A wall light glared down on the bloody mess scattered around her.

Natalya's body was face down. There was blood on her hands and the back of her head.

I knelt and lifted her. There was a look of intense horror on her face – but it was not a dead woman's face. Her mouth was moving as if she were weakly gasping for breath.

'Move her as little as possible, Chief,' Dronsky's calm voice said from behind me. 'We've got an ambulance on the way.'

By the time it arrived Natalya had smiled once and fainted twice. I had sat her up so that her back rested against the packing crates and covered her with a militia greatcoat. These few movements had spread blood and flesh from Imogen's body over both of us.

The ambulance crew were quick and efficient. Natalya was lifted and strapped lightly onto a stretcher while I held her hand.

As they carried her towards the ambulance my mobile was ringing. I took it from my pocket. It was the airport police control room. 'We've picked up somebody on 41–C, Inspector,' a woman's voice said. 'But it seems to be a young boy. Twelve or thirteen.'

'What's he doing?'

'He's just leaning against the wall there. Hold it, I'm going into close-up. Yes I thought so. He's crying. He's covered with something, blood perhaps? And he's crying his heart out.'

I could see into the lighted back of the ambulance. A doctor was giving Natalya an injection. The doors closed and the ambulance pulled away.

Dronsky's arm was round my shoulders. For some reason I couldn't fathom I was on my knees. 'She's all right, Chief,' he was shouting at me.

Why was he shouting? Why was my body shaking under the slow hammer blow of sobs? Natalya was saved. I swept Dronsky aside. While he struggled to regain his balance on the ice-covered apron, I ran for the Jeep.

47

The headlights of the Jeep sought out the shadows as
I drove fast down the long, dark alleys between warehouses and hangars. My line was open to the control
room and the woman's voice was calm and unexcited.
'We've picked him up in 51–B, Inspector. That's two
roads over to your right from where you are now.'

'What's he doing?' I screamed at her. 'Tell me what
he's doing.'

'He's on the move. Running or jogging you'd say,
down towards 51–C junction.'

'So do I reverse?'

'Reverse and run parallel with him. Take the service
road to your left and you'll reach the corner just about
as he does.'

I reversed the Jeep. The snow here was thick in these
narrow canyons but the wheels gripped. I killed the lights
and moved forward slowly.

Ten feet from the corner I braked and skidded across
the snow-covered cement. I got down, leaving the engine
running. Taking the gun from its holster, I removed the
ten-round clip and threw it down onto the snow piled
against the hangar wall.

I already knew what I was about to see. My mind had
stopped functioning when the ambulance doors closed on
Natalya. When I knew she was safe.

I was not thinking as a police officer about to effect
an arrest. How could I be, treading softly through the
snow towards him? But it was with some terrible sense
of disorienting shock that I heard the sobbing from round
the corner of the next building, ten or fifteen paces away.

I stepped forward. My shadow fell on the boy, his back to the hangar wall, bare-headed now, his face tiny, drawn white, except for the streaks of frozen blood.

I cried out. I think he recognised me. He *must* have recognised me. For my part I could never forget those round dark eyes. I ran forward. 'Mischa . . .' I cried. *'Mischa!'*

He looked at me and rubbed at the blood and tears on his cheek. 'My name's Sex-change,' he snarled.

I shook my head. 'You're Mischa again now,' I said, as I slipped and stumbled towards him.

He leaned forward stretching as high as he could – and spat in my face.

Then, as I flinched away, he turned and ran.

I followed tracks through the snow. There was no art required in these virgin canyons. I switched off my contact with the control room and walked, unloaded gun in my pocket, after my son.

At the end of the hangar a wider space opened out. The snow here was oil-stained in ugly patches. A track led straight across it to the darkness beyond.

I ran forward across the concrete apron and stopped abruptly. He was there in front of me, sitting on a waist-high wall, his legs dangling, his feet not quite touching the ground.

I stopped about three metres from him.

'OK,' he said. 'Come on.' His hand was extended, waving me towards him. 'Come and take me, come on, come on . . .'

'We're not on TV,' I said. 'You'll be able to cry all you want to in a few hours from now.'

I walked forward. I could see, I could *feel* the depth of suffering in those brown eyes – but the face was tight, bold, sneering . . .

'Mischa,' I said.

And he laughed.

460

'Mischa,' I said again.

He cocked his head, listening . . . seemed satisfied at what he heard. And with a sudden movement threw up his feet and rolled backwards over the wall.

I had not heard the Rapid Transit train approaching as he kicked his feet in the air. When I climbed down to the level of the track, there were five or six militiamen with me and I made no effort to touch the shattered body that they were rolling roughly into a Velcro waterproof bag.

48

She woke four or five times during the night and held herself close to me. Sometimes I could see her amber eyes open, staring into mine. She would lie like that, unblinking, and then her lids would slowly close and the deep rhythm of her breathing would begin again.

I don't think I slept a lot. Perhaps twenty minutes here and there. I lay tight against her naked body but I thought of Mischa, of walking out to the monument at Murmansk, the British Hurricane fighter plane that he so much liked, and trying to explain to a five-year-old that America and Britain had sent these aircraft and trucks and Jeeps and food to help Russia once, long ago.

'What sort of food?' he would ask each time we came to this point in the story, and I would tell him what my grandfather had told me about American ration boxes with tins of jam and bars and bars of chocolate. And he would dance and skip around the base of the Hurricane and I would think how mean and reluctant a monument this was to all the British and American seamen who had lost their lives bringing aid up to our Arctic Murmansk.

At about seven, a little before dawn, Natalya awoke and this time she eased herself away from me and sat up in bed with the sheet drawn up to her neck. Under the hairline I could see the flowing colours of the bruise to the base of the skull. But the X-rays had been clear. A bad headache, the doctor had said, and a back that would ache for a day or two.

I sat up too. 'Why did you pull away?' I asked her.

She smiled wanly. 'I have things to tell you,' she said.

Things about Mischa. I nodded. 'I'll make some coffee and then you tell me.'

I got up and pulled on my shirt and trousers and went into the kitchen to make the coffee. When I came back she was sitting up in bed, but wearing a dressing gown and brushing her hair.

I sat beside her on the bed and gave her her coffee. Through the window I could see the dawn rising on the towers and domes of the Kremlin no more than a mile or so distant. Some of what I imagined were the office windows were already alight. For a while I sat there, hunched forward, sipping coffee, wondering if Julia had yet moved in.

'When I went north,' Natalya said, 'it was in desperation. A few words Julia had repeated again and again that night I removed the grenade pieces from her back. Words that probably meant nothing. But they were enough to take me to Pavlovsk.'

I turned my head towards her. I had said nothing yet about Mischa. Neither to her, or to anyone. I had no words, or phrases to encapsulate the idea.

'I borrowed a Jeep,' she said, 'and drove out there. If my hopes collapsed I would at least see the headstone. I would at least stand before the grave of someone who meant so much to you.'

I think she was lying, but it was a sweet lie. I think she went out to Pavlovsk because only this would make me see Julia for what she really was. But it hardly mattered now.

'I went to the graveyard,' Natalya said. 'I went to the yew tree that stands in the farthest corner and I looked . . .' She paused. 'There was no stone. No sign of a grave.'

She reached out and touched my cheek. I swallowed hard and tried to tell her, but there were no words, no phrases . . .

'I asked the priest there and he said there never had

been a stone of the sort I was describing.' Her arms slid around me. 'Constantin,' she said, 'I wanted to call you straight away. But I thought how cruel it would be if I raised your hopes only to discover Mischa had not survived the war.'

I nodded dumbly.

'Listen, my beloved,' she said. 'I immediately went to the orphanage at Pavlovsk. There was nothing. But orphanages circulate lists of names and descriptions. There were fifteen lists there from all over the country . . .'

I gripped her hand, desperate to tell her. 'It's no good,' I said. 'You won't find him.'

'I found something. The name of an orphanage just outside Moscow at Borisovo, near the airfield there. On the Borisovo orphanage list until a year ago was a boy named Vadim: *Mikhail Constantinovich Vadim.*'

'But he'd left . . .'

'He'd run away last year. He was twelve. He and a group of other boys were traced as far as the main rail line.' She stopped. 'There's a woman there who brought Mischa from Pavlovsk . . .'

Borisovo orphanage was a converted labour camp. An area of long forbidding huts enclosed by wire and unmanned watchtowers.

We arrived at about four o'clock in the afternoon when the children were being paraded for supper. We drove in with the orphanage director, who stopped his car to allow us to watch the parade.

The children were aged from about five to twelve or thirteen, all dressed in blue anoraks and over-large fur caps. Each child carried a polished mess tin held across his breast, and a spoon and tin mug in the other hand. It was impossible to know whether there were both girls and boys.

We got out of the car as roll call proceeded. Names were called and answered. Mess tins were inspected for cleanliness. Plumes of breath rose into the air. The staff walked about and batted their gloved hands together and stamped their feet while the children stood strictly at attention.

Perhaps the whole parade lasted less than a quarter of an hour before they were marched off in columns towards the canteen hut. It seemed to me, watching the posturing and self-satisfaction of the staff, to go on for ever. Beside me Natalya slipped her gloved hand into mine and squeezed hard.

The director, Oleg Sinkovsky, nodded his own satisfaction with the conduct of the proceedings and led us to his office. When he had checked the stove and answered a phone call from his wife, he summoned Nadia Rybin and left us alone.

She was a tall thin woman of about forty and wore the grey dress of a staff member of the Borisovo orphanage. She had a long, mournful face but a friendly, rather shy smile as she glanced into the outer room and closed the door behind her.

Natalya crossed the room towards her and shook hands. When I was introduced she bobbed awkwardly.

'Why don't we all just sit comfortably,' I said. 'Natalya tells me that you've been kind enough to agree to answer a few questions about my son, Mischa.' I managed these sentences, brothers, although God knows how, as if I really were a parent trying to fill the gaps in his knowledge of his long-lost son. But the truth was completely different. I hated every moment I was here. There was no relief in this place for me. I had seen him as he was sitting on the coping above the railway track. I *knew* him as he had once been playing on the carpet in the apartment at Murmansk. The very last thing I wanted in this world was to know in detail, incident by incident, month by month, how he had been worn down, honed by circumstance, to the psychopathic thirteen-year-old who had taunted me at Sheremetyevo.

Nadia Rybin sat on the edge of a chair and placed a plastic file cover on her lap. Natalya took the sofa and I sat on the edge of the director's desk. I waited while the woman dropped her head and searched through her file. 'Perhaps you'd first of all like to look at these, Inspector.' She handed me three or four photographs.

I looked down at the first. It was a Mischa I had no problem recognising, a six-year-old with dark curly hair and bright eyes. It had been taken not more than six or seven months after Julia had left to join the Popular Front forces.

The next two were of a similar Mischa, a year or so older, but with a thin pinched face now as if he were living in permanent cold and hunger. I studied them, though the pain was almost intolerable. It was like taking a last look at the boy I had lost.

Then I looked at the final photograph. A fuzzy blow-up of a camp group photograph. A head and shoulders of a boy with close-cropped dark hair, his mouth pressed by experience into that thin vicious quality of stamped tin. Much as I wanted to stand and scream denials, it was, of course, undeniably Mischa.

I handed the photographs back to her. I was beyond speech. I got up and walked around the director's desk. Natalya glanced at me but I turned my eyes away from her. 'Natalya tells me,' I said, and I could hear the thickness in my voice, 'that you were once with Julia Petrovna's Anarchist Women's Division in the Army of the Popular Front . . .'

She zipped back the photographs into the red folder and nodded. 'I was a junior officer, a company commander. A captain. I have declared my earlier misplaced allegiances, Inspector. I changed sides during the war. I was formally pardoned as a matter of record.'

I held my hand up to stop her. 'I promise you I am not interested in establishing fault,' I said. Although if that were entirely true, what was I doing here at all? But the fault, I was establishing, was entirely my own.

She nodded again, that nervous bobbing of the head. 'Thank you,' she said. 'I hope what I have to say will be helpful. Helpful in tracing your son.'

I looked at Natalya's composed, alabaster features. I was frantic to tell her. In a day or two, perhaps. In a week. 'Go on, Nadia Ivanova,' I said. To help her, or maybe to help myself, I fixed my eyes on the intricate floral patterns of the director's carpet.

The stove glowed heat into the small wooden room. A wooden pendulum clock, a cheap, over-shiny, made-in-China model, ticked insistently. 'We had retreated before the main Nationalist drive on St Petersburg,' Nadia Ivanova said slowly, 'and were trying to regroup and establish our front. As far as we were concerned, that meant holding the rail interchange at Pavlovsk.'

'When you say *we* you mean the Women's Division?' Natalya said.

'The *Petrovna*, as we used to call it. We were full strength at about 15,000 women, two motorised infantry and an armoured brigade.'

She saw my head come up and smiled, a distant pride. 'Are you surprised, Inspector? Did you think of the *Petrovna* as a token women's unit?'

'I've no doubt Julia made sure you were much more than that.'

'She did. We were well trained and well supplied. We knew she would refuse to allow the generals to throw us into the line in hopeless holding actions to preserve the men's divisions or to preserve their vanity.'

'You had faith in her. In Julia.'

The woman's face half crumpled with the memory. 'You can't imagine,' she turned to Natalya, 'what it's like to be commanded by women, to fight alongside women, to gain the comradeship of women. She gave us all that. We weren't fighting for the Popular Front, Inspector,' she

467

said, turning back to me. 'We were fighting for ourselves, for Julia Petrovna.'

'And yet . . .' Natalya interjected drily.

'Yes. And yet I left the division.'

'Why was that?' I asked her.

'Our division was less effective than some in one way only. It was a way, as women, we all accepted. We were less mobile.'

'Because you had children with you.'

'Yes.'

'What happened?'

'One day we were moving into position. This was at Pavlovsk, when I realised something was wrong. As signals officer I was in a position to hear that *all* units were moving up to the front.'

'What was unusual about that?'

'Up to that time, one battalion had always been delegated to take charge of the children. There were three, four hundred children of all ages.'

'So you knew that day something was different,' Natalya said.

'I had two boys the same age as Mischa. They were all quite good friends in fact . . .' For a moment she struggled to control herself, then ground tears from the corner of her eyes with her knuckles and looked up at me. 'The order had been given . . . Julia Petrovna had given the order . . . She was like that. She knew that all those women could not be consulted, could not be *asked* if they were prepared to give up their children. So she acted.'

'What did she do?'

'She had already done it. She had issued to every child three days' rations.'

I felt as if my mouth had fallen open. 'Then she turned them loose—?'

'The children had been pointed in the direction of the nearest Nationalist stronghold – Novgorod, I think it was – and told to march in columns.'

'In January?' I said. 'In the snow?'

She took a deep breath. 'It took me three days to find them. By then thirty or forty other women had deserted like me and some had already caught up with them. Of course the children were in a pitiful state. The young ones had eaten or lost all their rations. Many were suffering from frostbite or hypothermia. Some, very young ones, had fallen by the roadside.'

'What did you do?'

'We found a monastery. In the middle of a blizzard as we struggled down the road with our column of children, we saw lights through the snow. A monastery where the monks came out and took us in. It was too late for some,' she said. 'For both my boys.'

We sat in silence in the small hot room and waited for Nadia Ivanova to continue.

'But Mischa survived,' she said, with pathetic brightness. 'And most of the children.'

'Did you stay at the monastery?'

'For a week or so. But it was in a war zone. The monks took advantage of a break in the weather to move us to another of their monasteries in the Demiansk hills. And after that they moved us again and again. To avoid the fighting. We were outside Yaraslavl when the Nationalists took over and made us an *official* orphanage.'

I had come this far. Why not know some things? 'What sort of boy was Mischa by then?'

She shrugged. 'You will think I am a sentimental woman.'

'Why should I think that?'

'I'm embarrassed to tell you, but I came to think of him as my own. I tried to make him my own. But Julia was too strong for me. The memory of her was too strong.'

'What are you saying?'

'Mischa did not need another mother. Even then, as a child, he showed qualities the other children admired.'

She shrugged. 'I suppose that Mischa is a leader, as his mother is a leader.'

It was as if I had never fathered him.

'He became . . . what shall I say, aware of his strength. Aware that he could lead other children. He became harder. In the circumstances we lived in, we all became harder. One dreadful night there was a murder in the camp. One of the girls was killed. Mischa was suspected.'

'Wrongly suspected?'

'The girl was thirteen. Mischa was eleven, but she was his girlfriend. Such relationships are strictly forbidden but the truth is that they are common here. There are new pregnancies among the children aborted every week. Mischa was questioned . . . denied any involvement. Unwisely, he denied even knowing the girl, which we all knew to be an untruth. The case was due to come before the director when roll call showed that four boys had escaped. Led, I've no doubt, by Mischa.'

I stood up. I had no wish to hear any more. 'Thank you, Nadia Ivanova. Thank you for telling me all this.'

We collected our coats, thanked the director and walked towards the car waiting just inside the wire gate. Children were streaming back from the cookhouse, accompanied by meaningless shouts from the staff.

'On the surface at least,' I said, 'it doesn't look much like an orphanage.'

'The director believes only a military organisation will control the children. Teach them values.'

'And does it?'

'It browbeats them. It means that they talk and dream of nothing but escape. I must warn you, Inspector, that when you find your son, you'll find him greatly changed. These boys are something much like hungry young animals today. But there's still good in them, I believe.'

We stood beside the car.

'Did Julia ever make enquiries that you know of? Did she attempt to find out what had happened to Mischa?' Natalya asked her.

'I never heard of an enquiry about Mischa from her.'

'But then, presumably, she would not have known where he was,' I said. Was I still excusing her?

'Before the war ended, I sent word to the division,' the woman said. 'To Julia herself.'

'Do you know she got the message?'

'I sent a list of the children to the divisional head-quarters. Many of the other women, mothers of children here, wrote to them or sent them photographs or small gifts. One or two of them even deserted and made their way here to claim their children.' She reached out and shook my hand. 'But of course, these other women weren't carrying the weight of leadership.'

I looked towards Natalya but she seemed to have no questions. She had looked away.

'Do you blame Julia Petrovna for what happened?' I asked Nadia Ivanova.

She was silent. 'Julia Petrovna was a leader,' she said at length. 'A leader is not a leader unless she's prepared to make hard decisions. How can I blame Julia Petrovna?'

I sat beside Natalya in the car. A column of boys was being marched back from some work site. They carried shovels on their shoulders and trudged, head down, faces in the collars of their anoraks. On the command of the warrant officer marching at the head of the column their heads came up and they broke into a weary rendition of our national song, 'Rodina'.

I sat with my gloved hands on the wheel. Nadia was leaving the director's office. She stopped for a moment as the boys marched past, her eyes seeming to scan each one. Then she turned and made her way back to the staff hut.

471

'She's an honest woman, Nadia Ivanova,' Natalya said. 'Like all of us she's still struggling with her past. She still can't bring herself to blame Julia.'

'Nobody ever has,' I said.

49

I lived the next days in a state of shock so deep that I have only stark, unrelated memories, like the shutter snap of a camera. Dronsky handing me coffee; Natalya's face in lip-biting concern; the cat, V.I. Lenin, staring silent indifference. Most real to me were the hours when, having persuaded Natalya to give me *stoke*, I scuttled away with two tabs to my apartment and drank and dreamed of Mischa playing trains . . .

'Mischa,' I say, 'what did you think of us, your mother and your father? What were your six-year-old's thoughts as you marched away through the blizzard in that column of children?'

And his head lifts from the French-made trains he is playing with and his pouting child's lips slowly thin and lengthen, until Sex-change sits upon the low wall and the murmur of a real train fills the darkness round me.

Of course I thought of suicide, but most of all I thought of guilt. Was it I or Julia who had taken that first fatal step from Murmansk – was it really me and not her who had divided us? Even at this late, late stage I had to know.

It was a thought I pondered as I trawled pointlessly through the Belorussian station. Or sat down and drank cans of White Flag with Claudia's limbless mother.

I don't know why I chose Vladimira. She was a neutral listener, I suppose. For whatever reason I explained it all to her, most of it. 'Vladimira,' I said. 'It's something I must know. Was it me or Julia?'

'She left you, Constantin,' she said. 'Of course she did. Only a Russian would see it some other way. Only a

Russian – or a madman.' And she patted my hand and opened another White Flag and wondered if Claudia's train from Minsk would be on time or not tonight.

Most days I sat in my office watching V.I. Lenin move from table to filing cabinet to shelf. Ilya Dronsky, I knew, was keeping away from me. Perhaps Natalya told him it was better. Mostly he stayed in his own office-alcove off the Murder Room and handled the intricate administration involved in closing a homicide file in Moscow. He gave me the final report for signature and I read only the last page. He had estimated the numbers from the shipments from the Nikulino laboratory at forty-seven murders, numbers I had no reason to question. Culpable persons were described as Jean Lucy Harrow, a.k.a. Dr Imogen Shepherd, US citizen, and a thirteen-year-old minor, Russian nationality, known as Sex-change, real name unknown.

I took my pen and signed my name on the bottom of the page.

Winter was fully with us now. Snow every day and sometimes all day. And temperatures I was more familiar with. On the evening of the party, I went to Natalya's apartment. I had not seen her for several days now and when I had she had looked me over thoughtfully and if we were alone, kissed me on the cheek, wistfully, like yesterday's lover.

Tonight she opened the door and for a second her old brilliant smile flashed before slowly fading . . . Without speaking she opened the door and gestured me in, walked across the room and poured me a glass of wine. 'No more *stoke*, Constantin.'

I shook my head.

'That must be what you've come for.'

'No.'

She wore blue jeans and a white roll-neck sweater. Hands on hips, she looked at me uncertainly. 'Really?'

'No. I'm finished with *stoke*,' I said. 'It's not dreams it gives you, it's nightmares. Tell me how you are, Natalya. Even Dronsky says you are hardly here in spirit these days.'

'I've been extremely busy,' she said cautiously. 'Organisational work at the lab.'

'Dronsky says you haven't been into the lab for days.'

'I don't have to account to you for my movements, Constantin.'

'No.' I paused. 'You're not preparing to leave Moscow again?'

'Would you mind if I were?'

I lifted my eyebrows, found as much as a nod or shake of the head far too complicated to envisage, and raised my glass and drank. 'Have you seen Professor Kandinsky since you got back?' I asked.

'Yes.' She paused. 'You've no political allegiance now, Constantin. No figure to be loyal to. Do you want me to arrange a meeting with the professor?'

I shook my head. Events had stripped me bare. I could not just take up the comforting mantle of political commitment. Especially one that believed in law, in an even-handed justice. I saw Natalya's look and I was on the edge of leaving when she took my arm. 'Why did you come here tonight, Constantin?'

'You'll laugh, it seems so inconsequential. A friend of mine is giving a party.'

She did laugh. A short, unamused laugh. 'I think if I had been given a hundred guesses about why you're here tonight, I should still never have suggested you had come to ask me to a party. Is that really why you came?'

'Yes.' My face seemed to be burning. 'A party. Believe me, Natalya.'

'What sort of party?'

'A party to celebrate my friend's promotion to general.'

Her eyes narrowed. 'A general, no less.'

'And to welcome his wife's arrival in Moscow.'

'There must be more to this. You're hardly in a party-going frame of mind. What more is there, Constantin, my lost love?'

'Don't say that. Don't say it yet. I may still find my way,' I said. 'But put your red dress on and the blue-stoned necklace I once saw you wear, and come with me tonight, Natasha. Will you do that?'

'Your friend won't mind?'

'Roy will be enchanted that he has so beautiful a woman to flaunt his new general's shoulder boards in front of. His wife, Katya, to be honest, will not be pleased at all. Will you come?'

'With not more than the ghost of a foreboding.' Tongue in cheek, she smiled. Then reached up and kissed me. 'Yes, I'll come.'

In the car Natalya was speaking. 'I've traced a group,' she said. 'They operate from Vladimir and claim to have the fullest database on missing children in the whole country. It's commercial of course. They charge three hundred dollars for a first run-through.'

'A waste of money,' I said.

Her head jerked round. I concentrated on the mass of white lights reflected off the snow. 'A waste of money . . . Constantin? What do you mean, a waste of money? It's a chance to find Mischa.'

It was time to tell her. I span words in my head. I balanced a phrase here and a phrase there. Then finally: 'Mischa and Sex-change were the same boy,' I said brutally.

I could feel her whole body recoil. 'What are you saying, Constantin?' I could see only the streaming head-lights, the speckled red tail-lights, in front of me. But I could hear the distress in her voice. 'You can't believe that? It's madness, Constantin. Wickedness, even.'

'I have to face it,' I said. 'I, who have faced so little

in my life. My son and Sex-change were the same boy.'

We were pulled into the forecourt of the restaurant where Roy's party was to be held.

She reached out and turned my face towards her. 'Can you possibly believe that?' she said, in a voice barely above a whisper.

'I spoke to him,' I said. 'Before he fell under the train. You forget. I spoke to him.'

'You hadn't seen your son for five years, Constantin. Faces change. My God, you're suffering a nightmarish illusion.'

My head was splitting. 'I have to learn to face reality, you said so yourself,' I said harshly. 'There's no room for gullible innocence like mine.'

'I also said it was the first thing that made me fall in love with you.' She reached out and put an arm round my neck. 'Now look at me. You're scourging yourself. You cannot really believe this?'

'I do.' I got out of the car.

She got out and slammed the passenger door closed. 'But you saw Sex-change at the Belorussian, Constantin. If it was Mischa why didn't you recognise him that first night?'

'He was wearing an old German prisoner's cap, pulled down low. His face was obscured.'

'You would have recognised your son.'

I shook my head.

'This is masochism,' she said passionately. 'A delusion you willed upon yourself. You understand, Constantin. You are punishing yourself for your belief in Julia.'

'Mischa and Sex-change. They were the same child,' I said stubbornly.

'No,' she said firmly. 'I saw surveillance videos with Sex-change in them at the Belorussian. I saw photographs at the orphanage. That was *not* Mischa. I am a pathologist with much greater experience of facial structures than you. *It was not Mischa.* You must believe that, Constantin.' We faced each other in the snow. 'You'll drive yourself mad. It's a guilt fantasy you're suffering. Don't you understand that it's guilt that creates this awful belief in your mind?'

But I was sure she was wrong.

Roy had chosen Maxim's as the finest restaurant in Moscow and the glowing mahogany and brass and red plush as a suitable setting in which to celebrate his elevation.

He met us in the entrance, surrounded by waiters in tail coats and his own uniformed aide-de-camp. 'Costya, Costya . . .' He stood back to look at me. 'You look, what shall I say . . . pale. Worse. Like a sick girl.' He slapped his hand against my cheek. 'Come and get some drink down you, bring the colour back into those cheeks.'

'So you made it, Roy,' I said. 'A general's shoulder boards before you start to lose your hair.'

'Congratulations, General,' Natalya said when I introduced her.

Roy bent over to kiss her hand. 'I think it's *Costya* who should be congratulated myself,' he said, his eyes moving over her as her coat was taken. 'Not only does he arrive with a mystery woman who will make all our own military wives look positively dowdy – but he's caught his Monstrum . . .' He took Natalya's arm and slipped the other hand round her waist. 'He's deep, our Costya. He's one of these difficult fellows.'

'I think you exaggerate, General.'

He stopped and looked up into her face. 'I'd ask you to call me Roy,' he said. 'But not quite yet. Not until I've got used to beautiful women calling me *General*. I don't mind admitting it, you know. I like it.'

'And so you should.'

He glanced over his shoulder at me. 'She's wonderful. Your mystery woman's wonderful.' He turned back to

Natalya. 'I've known Costya since we were so high. Women are all over him. But for my money—' he shook his head theatrically – 'he's ninety-nine per cent predictable.'

'Which makes that rare one per cent so stimulating,' Natalya said easily.

'You should know!' Roy shouted his delight. 'Now you go and find Katya,' he said, turning back to me. 'And I'll introduce Natalya to the delights of really good French champagne.'

The big restaurant room was arranged with a long, high table running the length of one wall and eight or ten round tables set in front of it. Each was covered with a pink-hued cloth and cutlery and glasses sparkled in the light from chandeliers. In the main space before the tables and on the steps leading down to it were perhaps a hundred people, many in uniform, many men in dinner jackets and every woman I could see from where I stood, bedecked with expensive jewellery.

I had no wish to exchange banter with Katya. I chose my place against a wall and leaned back, watching the frenetic energy expended all around me. There were, as I looked more closely, faces that I recognised from newspapers and television. The Minister of Rail Transport. A Deputy Minister of Waterways. The Minister of Siberian Metallurgic Exploitation. The Foreign Minister himself. A woman with her brown hair piled high and roped with pearls was a distinguished Moscow theatre actress. A man, more casually dressed than most, a performance artist known even in Murmansk. One or two of the generals had achieved media fame in the recent Civil War . . .

All for Roy Rolkin. All gathered at Moscow's premier restaurant to celebrate his elevation to general. I didn't believe it. But then if I'd believed it as he told it, I wouldn't be here.

'There's nothing so tragic,' a small, round pretty woman

murmured to me, 'as an existentialist roaming the world for a definitive act that nobody recognises he has committed.'

'It's one long silent scream,' I agreed affably. 'But there it is. We can't quarrel with it. That's life.'

She glanced up at me again, smiled briefly and moved on. Katya, I saw, was on the other side of the room. She had spotted me and was giving unmissable signals.

What harm could come to me now? Those few remaining aspects of humiliation and pain, I suppose, that the last week had failed to produce. I could walk across the room and take Katya by the arm and remove her from the senior officers she was talking to and bundle her onto a table in the middle of this glittering room and tear at her clothing and lift her, hands under her thighs . . . and roar and bellow like a rutting orang-outang.

I took a glass of champagne from a passing waiter. Yes, I could do that. But you'll be relieved, brothers, to know that self-immolation is far from my purpose in being here tonight.

Why then am I here? Why am I really here? Not to congratulate my old friend Roy. Not even for the excellent champagne he was bound to have on offer. You see, brothers, I have suspicions about the real purpose of tonight. I think we might be having *visitors*.

I inserted myself in a small group, my back to Katya. 'The incompetence of the first announcements about the Monstrum affair really surpasses understanding,' a woman in an ugly flowered dress was saying. 'At the All-Russia News Agency we are trying to pick up the pieces, but I promise you it isn't easy.'

'What pieces are they?' I asked.

'If we'd set out to provide a bloodied trail for the mongrels of the Western press we couldn't have done a better job.'

'I don't follow you,' I said.

'The West is not interested in Russians, murderers or victims. The West is interested in Westerners. So we provide a young, beautiful and highly mysterious American woman as both murderer and victim. We accuse her of trafficking in transplant organs, prowling the streets in her limousine seeking victims. Immediately the Western press claims it smells a cover-up . . .'

'Why should anybody think there's a cover-up?' I asked.

'Because it makes a better story.'

'What sort of cover-up?'

'If they don't have an answer they look for one that fits. Obviously Lavrenti Beria, when he was head of the Cheka, springs to their minds. Prowling the streets in *his* limousine. So they're running stories on Beria every day in the Western tabloids. And do we have any response? No, of course not.'

'What sort of answer?' I asked her. 'The two murderers are dead.'

'How convenient, the Western press says. How very convenient! And back they go to their stories about a latter-day Beria, a general or a minister even, prowling the streets. Every day their gutter press carries the most appalling insinuations.'

I looked blank.

'That the American woman doctor is a cover-up for a government minister.' She made way for me to enter the circle. 'Have you an interest in this affair?'

I nodded. 'As the senior inspector in charge of the investigation,' I said.

'Are you really?' The woman smoothed back her grey hair. 'At the risk of being offensive, young man,' she said, 'I would suggest you lose no time in gaining some instruction in handling the Western press.'

For half an hour I drifted. Natalya, I saw, was surrounded always by a half-dozen men. Katya, happily, had disappeared for the moment and was no doubt energetically tonguing some young waiter or aide-de-camp across a tumble of uniform coats and braided caps.

I managed to stop Roy in mid-movement between generals. 'What is it, old friend,' he said. 'Has someone made off with that gorgeous creature you came with?'

'Roy, I need to speak with Julia. I *must* speak with Julia.'

He lifted his hands in a gesture of hopelessness.

'Don't play games with me Roy, or I'll make sure your promotion party has a very embarrassing ending.'

He froze. 'Listen, Costya,' he said. 'The world spins faster than you can keep up with, right? So the problem's yours, not Julia's. Certainly not mine.'

'Where is she staying? Here in Moscow?'

'Don't be a fool. Stay away from her.'

'I want to know where she's staying.'

He looked at my face. What did he see? The wrath of a weak, angry man. I know because he laughed. 'Jesus Christ, Roy, tell me. Where is she staying?'

He lifted my hand off his arm. 'I've been good to you, Costya.' He tapped my chest with his index finger. 'But don't think for a moment that things can't change. You understand me?'

'I understand but I still need to know where she's staying.'

'You and the world will know that tomorrow night, my friend.' Superfluously he consulted his watch. 'At six o'clock Moscow time the public announcement will be made by General Koba and Julia together. From six o'clock tomorrow, she joins the government. Official. Until then enjoy the party. Take your lovely lady home and do your worst with her. I wish I had your kind of luck.'

'What kind of luck?' My fingers were twitching like a lunatic's, anxious to grip his fat throat already bulging under the constriction of his general's collar.

'Don't you ever stand still long enough to look around, Costya? Your ex-wife and your new tumble are two of the best-looking women in Moscow.' He was already turning away. 'Your luck, little brother, is to get to screw one while you bask in the reflected glory of the other.'

Two or three more glasses of champagne. A few deft movements to take me out of Katya's line of sight, and we are bidden, all of us, to table.

I am at one of the round, flanking tables with Natalya, thank God, on my right and the short philosopher of sympathy on my left. As immensely efficient waiters served smoked sturgeon and *blini*, I felt Natalya's hand clasp mine beneath the pink tablecloth. I followed her glance and saw that white-gloved officers of the Cheka were quietly ushering the regular waiters out of the room.

Natalya leaned her head towards mine. 'What's going on?'

'Have you not guessed what this evening really is?'

She touched my forehead with her own. 'Perhaps,' she said.

I released her hand and turned my attention to the top table. Roy and Katya were taking their places. The round-faced woman next to me was saying: 'There's a darkness in the Russian personality which you can't pretend doesn't exist.'

With that I could agree.

'I like to think of it as Russian Gothic. We're gifted, astonishingly talented but still on one level, like a primitive people, we have not yet succeeded in coming to terms with chance. Is it perhaps, I wonder, the great distances of Russia that make coincidence play such an important part in the Russian novel?'

Roy was rapping on the table with a large silver spoon. Gradually the voices around me fell away to silence.

'Dear friends,' Roy said. 'I have a confession to make. You have all kindly agreed to come tonight to celebrate my promotion to general. But I have brought you here under false pretences.' He laughed jovially. 'Not that the shoulder boards aren't real,' he said, tapping his new badges of rank. 'But celebration of a minor event in the scheme of things is not the purpose of my asking you here tonight. Much more important is that tonight you will have the opportunity, before the explosion of press conferences and television interviews, to meet with a new member of the government.'

Beside me I felt Natalya stiffen. She took my hand again under the table and held it tight.

'. . . one in whose recruitment to our cause,' Roy continued, 'I am proud to claim that I was able to play a small part.'

I looked at the faces at the small round tables. They were baffled, frowning. They knew nothing of the announcement to come. The generals and ministers at the top table seemed equally puzzled. Though Merkovsky, the Foreign Minister, I saw, kept a small smile playing on his lips.

'But first . . .' Roy glanced towards the wings, a dark open doorway to his right. 'It is with enormous pleasure that I welcome my chief, the man responsible for so much of the good fortune that has befallen Russia in the last months, General Leonid Koba himself.'

The whole room stood in a storm of applause.

Koba had materialised in the small dark doorway. He wore, unusually, the uniform of a general of the Cheka. He came two or three paces forward, smiling broadly. I could anticipate every gesture: now he would touch the side of his moustache, now he would nod and purse his lips.

He played with them, knowing that while he stood there the applause would not die away. Then he turned and stretched his hand towards the doorway – and Julia in a shoulderless, floor-length black gown walked into the light to a second's silence followed by a gasp of astonishment as the guests recognised her.

The applause became more frenetic, as if to make up for the *faux pas* of silence that had greeted the general's choice.

'Constantin . . . Constantin . . .' Natalya was whispering in my ear. 'I want you to come with me to Professor Kandinsky.' Her voice was almost inaudible but bitingly urgent. 'What we see here tonight is an alliance of the forces of darkness. The good people must act. Act or go mad.'

I pushed her hand away and concentrated every micron of my attention on Julia.

There she sat, at the top table, Leonid Koba by her side, smiling, toasting each other. Then on Koba's prompting, Julia got to her feet.

'I don't want to stay for this,' Natalya hissed in my ear. 'I think we should go, Constantin. Just get up and go.'

I shook my head. My eyes were on Julia. She was clapping her hands to a slow and stately rhythm, her faultless shoulders turning as she included first one group of guests then another in the applause. Then she lifted both hands in the air, high in the air, and let the applause slowly die away.

Koba, I could see, was smiling broadly, behind her. Automatically my hand reached for my right ear just seconds before he did so himself.

Julia's voice was clear and bell-like. 'I realise,' she said, 'that there is no need to introduce myself. Government wanted posters up and down the country have done that most effectively.'

The guests laughed, tentatively at first, then taking their cue from Koba, they hammered the tables with the flat of their hands in appreciation.

When the room quieted, Julia went on to speak of the troubled past and the hopeful future. She praised the foresight of Koba and the breadth and depth of his vision for Russia. And she ended with a touching peroration. 'Tonight,' she said, her bare shoulders glistening under

485

the chandeliers, 'I stood in my room and looked out along an avenue of bare chestnut trees to a statue of a Russian family. A man, woman and child carved in the old style of Soviet realism. Not, the artists and critics among us might think, a very good statue. But buried in the stone of that monument there was, I felt, a monumental truth. And that is the truth, which after many false starts, finally brought me here tonight. That truth is one that Leonid Koba has never flinched from repeating to Russians and the world: Marxists, Anarchists and Nationalists, we are all part of Russia's future as we have been part of Russia's past.'

In the ringing applause which greeted Julia, Natalya leaned close to me. The candlelight caught yellow points in her eyes. 'Can you bring yourself to blame her?' she said. 'At last?'

I made no answer. But, in my head, I had already travelled far past blame.

50

At Nikulino I turned off the main road and onto the track. Snow and sodium lights are a bilious combination: the three listing onion domes of the church rose sickeningly against an orange-yellow background.

I could barely hear the crunch of snow under the tyres. Many vehicles had passed up and down the track in the last few days and the snow was packed hard under a loose coating so that it felt as if the Economy was moving over ice.

I drove slowly with the window down. Since nightfall it had dropped to zero temperatures and my cheek was gently flayed by the cold air. But I come from Murmansk. This is the world I know.

I drove without lights. The yellow reflections of the sodium-gleam off the snow were just sufficient for me to see ahead. If I leaned from the window I could see tyre marks beside the track where police cars had parked in the last few days.

Closer to the church, the local police had tied incident tapes (whose red star edging suggested a leftover from distant Soviet times) across the track, but there was no sign of anybody having been left to guard the place.

Getting out of the Renault, I untied the tape, rolled it up and dropped it by the side of the track. I was climbing into the car when I saw a swinging lantern up ahead of me.

I drove forward and stopped by the side of the babushka.

'Ha, Inspector,' she greeted me like an old friend, one hand holding the lantern pole, the other shaking my arm with a surprisingly strong grip. 'You can't imagine what a time I've had. Police, police, police. Crawling over everything.'

'She was a very wicked woman, Doctor Shepherd,' I said.

She nodded reflectively. 'Wicked,' she agreed. There was no way of knowing how much she had known, how much her condemnation of Imogen was merely siding with the new authority. Russians are acutely aware of a change of government. Where the wind sits, we say in the north.

'What can I do for you, Inspector,' she said, 'at this late hour? Can I get you a plate of something to keep out the cold?'

I flinched at the thought. 'I've come to take the car away, Grandma,' I said.

'Ah,' she said, pulling at her chin with her woollen gloved hand. 'Ah . . .'

'There's no need for you to worry about it,' I said. 'No need even to mention it to anyone. I'll be bringing it back before morning.'

'But the doctor's car won't move,' she said. 'The police have been all over it. Dusting it and even cleaning the inside with a vacuum cleaner, but they still can't get it to move. They tried to get it going again today but they say it's missing a vital part.'

In my pocket my hand closed round the rotor arm of the Mercedes. It's normal procedure for the investigating officer to remove the rotor arm from a car needed for forensic examination or evidence of any sort. But when the local militia called to ask if I'd taken it, I'd told them no. Why had I done that?

Did I already have, forming in the back of my mind, some plan? Did I already know, subconsciously, what I later decided, on a conscious level, I was going to do?

Is that how the mind works, brothers? Or is that just how the *sick* mind works? Is a rational act no different from an act of rationalisation? What is true is that I am driven. I am driven by the overwhelming desire to see Julia again.

And now I know how to find her.

I found a place where the church wall provided some shelter and I left the Renault there. Getting out of the car I walked with the babushka to the lean-to attached to the wall where Imogen garaged the Mercedes.

The old woman let me in and watched with a blank face while I replaced the rotor arm, started the engine and backed out of the garage. 'Leave the door unlocked,' I said, 'and go back home. As an officer of the Cheka, I don't want my visit to go any further. You understand me, Grandma.'

She said nothing but she had understood. She left me, mumbling, trudging through the snow with her lantern on a pole.

I had never driven a car like this. It purred through Moscow and out onto the Yaroslavl road. Only once, when I was forced to stop at a level crossing, did anybody recognise me. Then an old couple, peering at the dinner-jacketed driver of this superb limousine, recoiled in astonishment as they made out the features of Leonid Koba.

As the barriers lifted, the old couple stared open-mouthed as I pulled away. I glanced in the rear mirror to see the woman raise a gloved hand like a greeting from V.I. Lenin.

I was, I thought, remarkably calm as the buildings fell away behind me and a long straight road cut through pine forests on either side.

It was a road I knew well. At the wooden mill house I turned across the bridge and saw the first lights of the dacha. Ahead, there were parked cars everywhere, coaches that had brought the press out from Moscow and television vans with crews fitting up camera equipment in the snow-lined road to the main entrance.

They were as surprised as the gate guards to see me and reacted in the same confusion. Perhaps one or two of the photographers got off a few shots of me before the guards hurriedly released the gate and I drove through and stopped before the green-painted front of the dacha. If there were photographs it hardly mattered now.

I left the Mercedes in the front drive and walked up the steps. The door was opened to me by a man in old Russian costume, voluminous trousers tucked into boots, a white collarless shirt buttoned at the throat. The downstairs rooms, I could see, had been redecorated for the television cameras. The panelled walls of the hall were painted in dark green, and gold and white banners hanging from the ceiling carried the double-headed eagle of Russia.

There were six or seven attendants in the hall, standing alertly to attention, among them the housekeeper Olga with whom, after a day being taught here by the professors, I had restored my sanity each night making love to her wearing my Koba moustache and eyebrows.

I had not recognised the house on my last visit to Julia. Blindfolded by Dimitry as a condition of being brought to see her, I had been released into this completely transformed interior. Now I strolled forward through to the terrace room where the professors had inflicted so much suffering upon me and stood looking out onto the garden drive with the leafless chestnut trees and the statue of the Soviet family, honest, enduring, independent and free, standing on the plinth with a light snow filtering down upon them. The Soviet family Julia had dwelt on in her speech at Roy's party. But for her speech I would have never found out where she was staying.

I knew now that Julia's room must be the one above where I now stood. It was indeed the very room I had occupied here. The room where I had enjoyed my bouts of mustachioed passion with Olga.

For a few moments I stood, staring out onto this

agreeable snow-covered garden. Security lights glittering in the fir trees beyond the statue created a fairyland effect. I felt remarkably calm now that I was here. I felt no fear that the real Leonid Koba might arrive early. I needed, after all, so little time.

A steward came forward and asked if I would like some refreshment and I dismissed the idea with a Koba wave of the hand. For a moment a great weariness descended on me as if I were thinking back to days long, long ago. Days when I wore Koba's devil skin with pride. It was no more than a brief moment of weakness. A very Russian weakness, wishing for that world we cannot have, that world which in truth never existed.

But nostalgia dissolves like morning mist before the great mad energy of hate.

I turned back and walked through the hall and up the main staircase. None of the retainers dared do anything but stand at silent attention as I passed.

I walked along the gallery and felt the new deep pile of the thick carpet beneath my feet. In less than an hour the hall below me would be full of jostling, jabbering cameramen and TV crews, waiting for the moment when Julia would come down the staircase.

I knocked briefly on the door and went in.

Sumptuously decorated as befitted the new position she was about to assume, the room had greatly changed from the bare room I had known. Julia sat at the dressing table, half-turned towards me. She laid aside the brush she had been using and stood up.

She looked spectacularly beautiful. She wore a dark blue business suit with a skirt to a little above the knee, a white silk shirt open at the neck without jewellery. I think it was the make-up that unnerved me. It was restrained, barely visible in fact, but I had not seen her so since the day of our wedding.

I closed the door behind me and leaned against it.

'You're early, Leonid,' she said. 'You might have caught me . . . not quite ready to receive you.'

The tone was bantering, flirtatious, confirming, in a few words, some inevitable but as yet unspoken development between them yet to come.

'I've come to tell you,' I said, 'about Mischa.' I made no attempt to maintain Koba's accent. But she seemed not to notice.

She moved her legs so that she was now fully turned, facing me. 'My son, Mischa? I don't understand, Leonid,' she said carefully. 'What have you come to tell me? Mischa died during the war. One of the hundreds of thousands of child casualties on both sides.'

'Mischa is dead,' I said. 'But he did not die in the war.'

She rose to her feet now. For probably the first time in her life I saw her seriously unsettled. She knew there was something desperately wrong. Not just from the talk about Mischa. But from the voice.

'Mischa?' she said, shaking her head rapidly. 'Mischa, my son . . . ?'

Without fully admitting it to herself, without being able to admit it to herself, she had recognised my voice.

'Leonid . . .' she said, forcing bewilderment from her, overriding it as I had seen her do so often in our lives. 'Leonid, I buried my son myself. It was beyond all doubt the saddest moment of my life.'

'You buried Mischa yourself, did you?' My voice was breaking. 'The saddest moment in your life, was it?'

I could see the speed of her thinking, the control she was exercising. That triangle at her throat where the shirt opened had darkened a shade of pink. She spoke rapidly. 'If you are hoping to bring me good news about the discovery of a boy in this or that orphanage in Petersburg or wherever, then I can only, sadly, say no.' She made an almost angry gesture with her hand. 'Mischa lies buried somewhere outside the town of Pavlovsk.'

'Mischa lies unburied: his broken body occupies tray 26 in the morgue at Marisilov.'

In her face I could see the struggle going on. But her control was still complete. 'Why do you say that?' She was no longer sure who she was addressing.

'After Mischa escaped from the Moscow orphanage,' I said slowly, 'he became one of the station boys, one of the *bezprisorny* prowling the rail stations for what he could snatch or grab.'

The make-up did nothing for her now. She had leaned back on the dressing table, frowning at me, within a tantalising fraction of an inch from full recognition.

'He called himself Sex-change, Julia. *Our* Mischa . . .'

The intake of breath was a short, uncontrollable hiss. 'Constantin,' she said, 'Constantin . . .' Her voice reached a pitch it had never reached before. And I knew at that moment that she had been touched where no man had touched before.

The release was fear. Beyond the remnant of disbelief, of shock, the release in Julia was fear.

I crossed the room and she remained statue-still. This close, almost touching her, I could see shivering, orgasmic spasms of fear. And the clouding of the eyes and the sweat on the upper lip . . . But whether that was after I drove the first thrust of the knife into her I could not be expected to know, brothers. By then I was shouting, howling, trampling on her and the blood had splashed the dressing-table mirror and the cream coverlet of the bed and had burst across the walls in a scatter of red reaching up to the high ceiling.

51

I walked out of the room, along the gallery, down the stairs into the hall hung with the white banners, past the roaring log fire to the front door.

Two attendants came running towards me but I threw my arms about me and waved them away. They stepped back. I passed their shocked faces and opened the door into a rush of cold air.

One man had the courage to come out after me. His white shirt, where my knuckles had flayed him, was stained with blood.

'General Koba . . .'

I turned slowly to him and he stopped talking. I made a gesture of the all-powerful. It meant I don't want you in my sight.

The man recognised it immediately and with a half-bow slid back inside.

I went down the steps. Where the fresh snow lay my shoes sprayed drops of blood. The Mercedes stood where I had left it. I climbed inside, started the engine and drove away.

The press corps were barely better prepared. I passed at speed aware of a few flashbulbs only, but then I was beyond the outer perimeter of the estate and driving at mad speed down the narrow road between the pine trees.

What songs sang in my head? Songs of triumph or lament? Dirges, plaints, none of these. Instead my mind played back to me the English Beatles song, 'The Fool on the Hill'.

I suppose I was crying because the dried blood on the

back of my hands was wet again and 'The Fool on the Hill' was filling my head to the exclusion of any other road sounds. I was crying and the road ahead was fading in and out, blurring and sharpening as I increased the weight on the accelerator.

So mad or sane, or mad and just desperate to escape into deeper madness, I flew in this incredible machine between the snow-laden pines. Flew so fast I barely made the bend in the track. Flew so fast it was at the last second rather than the last minute that I saw the red barricade lights in front of me.

Flew so fast and yet still the incredible machine shuddered and bucked but never deviated from the straight as I sat braced, pedalling the brake with all the strength I had.

Between tears and blood and tears of blood I saw red lights flashing. I saw two, three figures running forward, saw masked faces and the glint of weapons in the powerful headlights.

If I'd been thinking, if I were more capable, I would have sat for whatever awaited me.

But we think so very little in our time here. I was out of the car and up the bank stumbling and flailing through the pines, running, as I heard the ugly crack of bullets passing me, running for my worthless life.

When the grenade exploded I was almost expecting it. Not the thunderous crack somewhere beside me but the singing of shrapnel pieces about me and the burning spatter of splinters in my back.

Air, of course, is what you lack in an explosion. You gasp, you swallow, you scream a silent scream in panic, because for that moment the air has been blown and sucked from the world. At least, your world.

And when the clean cool *stuff* came flooding back into my lungs I was on the ground, kneeling on all fours, my hands over my face from which the blast had torn my Koba moustache and eyebrows, and I could hear, just there behind me, the crash of single footsteps.

I turned my head. A torch beam from the right hit my face. A masked figure stood five feet from me, a machine-pistol raised until I could see the faint scoring around the black tip of the barrel.

I had turned towards my executioner. On one knee. I wasn't pleading for life or death but I'd spread my arms out . . . somehow it seemed the thing to do. Except that I was laughing.

And before me, the barrel wavered and slowly fell. And I heard a gasp of more surprise than I thought possible to put into that strange animal sound. And a voice, *her* voice, said: 'Constantin . . . Constantin.' And a hand came up and peeled the mask from her face, and Natalya stared down at me as if I had just arisen from the dead.

52

Which, in a sense, I had.

I was not present at the climactic moment of that night when the ambush was rearranged to receive the limousine of the real General Leonid Koba approaching from the Moscow road. When my gentle Natalya herself took him to the side of the track and put a pistol to his head and suffered the gore to fly all over her before he slumped and rolled among the pines.

I had returned the Mercedes to its garage and removed the rotary arm and driven back to Natalya's flat where I had let myself in and lain in the darkness on her bed and felt more at peace than I could ever have believed I might be.

I had committed tyrannicide. Tyrannicide, no more or less certainly than Natalya was doing now.

Of course you'll only believe me, brothers, if you're ready to accept that there is seldom just one single motive for our acts. Just as an argument, however strongly put, will seldom persuade us all. Natalya says it's what gives the lie to those who tell us that democracy is not founded deep in human nature.

At some time during the night I heard Natalya let herself in. She knew I was there. Without putting on the light, she came and sat by me on the side of the bed. Her hand held mine, mixing the blood of others. Tomorrow, perhaps we would talk about what we had done. For now, it was enough to listen to each other's breathing. Then Natalya got up and took her shower and a few minutes later I did the same.

I had thrown logs on the fire and the warmth was

seeping back into the room. Standing by the window, wrapped in the duvet snatched from the bed, we listened to the sounds of Moscow shaking itself and rising up for a new day.

EPILOGUE

For the photographers gathered at the Zagorsk dacha it was a night gorged with photo opportunities. They had no sooner swarmed past the guards into the murder room and trampled the blood of Julia Petrovna into the carpets and filmed and photographed the gore on the walls, and done their pieces to camera on the blood glut of Zagorsk, than they were called to another scene of death.

There, in the pine forest not five miles from the dacha, lay the body of President Leonid Koba, shorter by half a head, where all the indications were that he had lifted a Walther pistol to his temple and blown much of his skull away.

President Romanov had reacted with speed. At midnight he made his television address to the Russian people calling, above all, for the light of *glasnost* to be shed on the murder in the dacha and the suicide of General Koba.

Most Russians who watched the broadcast – and that was indeed most Russians – noted in the first few minutes how much more authoritative, more confident the old president seemed to be: 'However the confused kaleidoscope of last night's events is rearranged,' he said, from his office in the Kremlin, 'it suggests only the most sinister interpretation as far as General Leonid Koba is concerned. He was seen entering the dacha near the town of Zagorsk and leaving, distraught and, many witnesses claim, bloodstained, a few minutes later. During that time span the Anarchist leader Julia Petrovna was horribly murdered in a manner that strongly suggests the recent Monstrum murders in Moscow's Red Presnya district.

Then, within less than an hour, the general's body was found by the roadside where he himself apparently put a bullet in his own head.

'What makes the story even more difficult to piece together, brothers and sisters, is that there were, throughout the period of the murders in Red Presnya, persistent rumours of a large limousine seen trailing the unfortunate victims. It is this fact that has led to demands for a further investigation to be made into a possible connection between the government limousine and the murders committed in Red Presnya. The solution to the murders, which has been offered by Senior Inspector Vadim, has not been accepted as a full account by the government. Inspector Vadim has been returned to his former duties in the north and replaced by his deputy, Senior Homicide Inspector Dronsky. Until further investigations are complete no definitive statement can be made either on the death of the Anarchist leader, Julia Petrovna, or on the suicide of General Koba.'

As a postscript the Russian president revealed that the purpose of the press gathering at Zagorsk had been to announce to the world the appointment of Julia Petrovna to the post of Minister in charge of the Amnesty. The distinguished professor of jurisprudence Ivan Kandinsky had now been asked to fill the post left vacant by the tragic death of Julia Petrovna.

We sat in my office, or rather Dronsky's office as it now was, Ilya, Natalya and myself. And V.I. Lenin, the cat.

I poured vodka for the three of us, a generous dribble into the cat's milk bowl, and lifted my glass to Dronsky. 'A toast,' I said, 'to the better man. You've earned the top job here, Ilya. Best of luck in your new assignment.'

Dronsky looked at me – and then at Natalya. 'A good police officer in the Russian tradition,' he said, 'knows exactly what the investigation will produce before the first witness is questioned. Would you like to hear how this one is going to work out?'

'I think we would,' Natalya said.

Dronsky eased himself back in his chair. 'First I think we're going to establish that General Koba had been conducting a sexual relationship with Julia Petrovna for the last several months. Second we're going to discover photographs and details of the murdered girls supplied to Koba by the missing former Chekist Roy Rolkin, which suggests that Koba took an unhealthy interest in the details of the Monstrum murders.'

I nodded encouragement.

'Finally, and most surprisingly, we're going to discover witnesses to a liaison between Julia Petrovna and Roy Rolkin. This liaison came to the knowledge of Leonid Koba last night and led directly to the awful glut at the dacha at Zagorsk.' He lifted his glass. 'More than that, I can't say.'

He stood up. Natalya kissed him and I shook his hand.

'You forgot something,' Dronsky said.

'I did?'

'When you cleared your desk, you didn't take everything.' He jerked a thumb towards the cat.

'As a newly converted democrat, I gave him the choice,' I said. 'Stay with you here and be nourished on fishburgers. Or inhabit a tin cat-kennel in the yard in Arctic Murmansk. He indicated he'd stay.'

'Something you'll have to learn to live with,' Dronsky said.

With my arm round Natalya, I looked back at the cat. Would he lift a paw in salute, a final, graceful *Ave atque vale* to see me on my way. Our eyes locked as I willed him to respond . . .

From his now undisputed place on the filing cabinet, V.I. Lenin issued a sibilant hiss.

I could have spent the rest of my life searching for Mischa. It was, of course, Julia's death that released me from the delusion that had haunted me. The image of Mischa's face which my sickness had placed on the thin shivering body of Sex-change.

I know now that it was not Mischa who died under a train that night. I know that he is alive, serving a term in a children's labour camp perhaps or riding the rails from Yaroslavl to Orel, from Orel to Perm, from Perm east to God knows where . . . I could have spent the rest of my life looking. And I did spend every second of the month's leave I was given before I was transferred back to Murmansk. But I knew in my heart that, even if I found him now, he would be as dead to me as if Julia had really buried him in that country cemetery outside Pavlovsk.

So we live in Murmansk, Natalya and I, in one of the older apartments off Unity Square. She is an extraordinary woman, my Natalya, the strongest woman I have ever known. I recognise now that what I have always thought of as strength (in men as well as in women) is no more than a willingness to sacrifice others on the altar of their own belief or gain. Natalya's strength is different. She *donates* it, to her neighbours, to her patients and, most of all, to me.

Of course I know that, like me, she believes Mischa is lost for ever, but she continues to search databases and to visit distant youth labour camps and training schemes, even though she is now pregnant. Perhaps *because* she's now pregnant.

You wonder what happened to Roy Rolkin? So did I until a few days ago when, I admit, he set my pulse into a fast gallop with a letter postmarked Hungary. Roy Nekrassov, he calls himself now. He had, he told me, moved to Budapest for his health, although, he hinted, he still kept some contacts in Russia. The letter was an invitation to Natalya and myself to come and watch his

502

football team, Janus Athletic, which he had bought with his savings, which of course, as a senior Cheka officer, had been considerable. The team, he said, was dedicated to me. Janus, the Roman god with two faces.

You get the point I'm sure. Roy *knows*. But he will keep discreetly quiet in Budapest as long as I remain equally discreet about his new persona. In times of strife, he says, it's remarkably difficult to manage on only one identity.

And Mother Russia? Pour me another glass of that vodka and I'll tell you in few words. Our country is stumbling out of the darkness – although deep patches of shadow remain, as perhaps they always will remain in Russia. But against the worst, we can still place the best: our extraordinary resilience as a people and our abiding belief in ourselves.

Of course, our new democracy is deeply unpopular. As yet, it offers neither bread nor circuses. It is flayed in the press and jeered at by the omniscient young. Many people see it as a foreign import designed to let the worm into the Russian bud.

Democracy, I am beginning to understand, cannot be taken for granted. But for a nation to whom illegality is so sweet, the miracle is that we are working our way towards a basic rule of law.

From the window I see Natalya walking down the street towards the entrance to our apartment block. She wears a light spring coat, unbuttoned, and her hair bounces as she walks. When she passes people in the street she smiles, or waves. She is a Russian who radiates hope. And next week Ilya Dronsky and his family will come to spend a few days with us. Simple pleasures.

Believe me, brothers, those of you who are fortunate enough to live under the rule of law should take notice of what happened here.